The Eagle's Claw

I0641405

THE EAGLE'S CLAW
By Donald T. Morgan

Published by Creative Texts Publishers, LLC
PO Box 50
Barto, PA 19504
www.creativetexts.com

ISBN: 978-1-64738-129-5

ACKNOWLEDGEMENTS

My heartfelt thanks to the following:

To my late wife Betty and my two sons Clai and Grant for allowing me to steal many, many hours of quality time for the writing of this novel.

To the many members of my Wordwrights Writing Class who endured readings from the manuscript countless times.

To my friends and members of my critique group: Melody Groves, Judith Avila, Kathy Wagoner, Dennis Kastendiek, Phil Jackson, and Su-Ellen Lierz.

And finally, to Daniel Edwards, Christopher Lane, and the other folks at Creative Texts.

I owe a debt of gratitude to you all.

Table of Contents

Prologue

Sleep brought a restless dream stitched together from tattered tales heard over the years of a tall *Indah* man with brown hair and sad, gray eyes and a small, tawny woman with long, black tresses and a pretty smile. The *izdan*, well past school age, yearned to be able to read and write. The man, a teacher at the Indian school, helped her learn. They talked and laughed and grew toward one another.

Married in the white man's way, they left the reservation. The woman often returned to her mother's wickiup, but the schoolteacher never came. That was good because a man gazing upon his mother-in-law risked blindness. The young wife blossomed with health and happiness and child. Strength and pride replaced the longing in the white man's eyes.

One day, a rodeo came to the reservation. The *Tinneh* loved a rodeo. What fun watching pale, gaunt men flop around on bucking horses. Some of the People rode too. The crowd cheered whenever a cowboy rolled in the dust, be he white or tribesman.

A hush fell over the stands. A magnificent roan pranced into the arena. A devil horse with fire-eyes and a black mane writhing like a nest of serpents. Its great hooves struck sparks from the earth. No one could ride him. No one ever had. No one ever would. They offered the bribe of money to any who succeeded. The men stirred restlessly, but advised by *diyi*—the shamans among them—they refused the challenge even though the prize was hefty.

The white man with gray eyes stepped forward. A schoolteacher was always needy, and he had a family on the way. He would claim the reward.

Death stalked the arena. Evil corrupted the air. The roan danced in savage glee. The smell of sweat and manure and hot dogs and dust hung heavy over the crowd. Invisible owls screeched. Whippoorwills cried, and coyotes barked.

From the uneasy safety of his dream, the boy watched the man mount the haughty horse. The chute opened. The roan shot out, bucking and whirling in a frenzy. The *Indah* rode him! He rode the wicked beast.

Enraged, the roan flung himself against the fence. The man was hurt. The animal twisted savagely, and the rider fell. The demon horse wheeled.

The woman with the pretty smile ran into the arena to turn the frothy beast aside. The horse charged on, driven insane by talons of monster owls buried in his withers.

The man was dead. The dreamer thought the woman was too, but she

moved. Her body strained in birth even as she died.
And he knew he had seen himself born.

Chapter 1

June 1946, Edge of Mountain Apache Reservation, Southern New Mexico
After foraging for an hour, Román Otero came up with six empties: three strawberry, two Grapette, and a Coke. Old man Fish, who owned the store in the little reservation settlement of White Pine, traded him a full bottle of strawberry for his empties.

Mounting his pinto, Román glanced at the elementary school where a game of gypsy softball splashed noise against his eardrums. He urged the mare eastward along a powdered dust road past the Indian Agency building, a stone church, and family camps of small plank houses, brush shelters, and canvas tipis. Upon arriving at Dead Scout Canyon, he slid to the ground and put his mare to graze while he nursed his drink. The strawberry was no longer cold, but warm soda pop made him burp, and he liked to burp. The bubbly water filled an empty belly better than anything. A man would *never* go hungry if he could buy four bottles a day.

Román belched loudly, once in each cardinal direction, beginning in the east as all things begin and proceeding as the hands of a white man's clock move. The ritual complete, he drained the bottle and dropped it on a rock.

The noise flushed a woolly spider from beneath the flat stone. Román nudged the creature with his toe. The little beast scooted sideways on eight hairy legs and froze. Cane-Woman claimed if you killed a spider, Grandfather Spider would try to kill *you.* And his grandmother knew about such things. He hesitated, his foot suspended above the tiny animal. Abruptly, he dropped his heel, glanced skyward, and spoke aloud.

"The white man at the Agency did it. The one with fuzzy hair that's falling out on top." That oughta fool the spiders. They weren't very smart.

When he moved again, he sensed he was not alone in the canyon but decided to stay, even though the image of a Grandfather Spider bent on revenge raised the hair on his neck.

After tying the mare to a piñon, he headed for an outcrop of rock to hide. Could the presence he sensed be supernatural, like Eagle? Cane-Woman served Eagle, and that gave her power, although Román wasn't sure how that worked. Was this world the same as when the Old Way prevailed?

The mare whinnied. Whatever shared the canyon was near. Tired of cowering behind rocks, he poked his head over the boulder. Below him, he saw his "presence."

No supernatural shared the canyon with him. Clarence Wolf, his mortal enemy, crept toward Román's pony. A year older and almost twice his size, Clare-Ass wasn't just a dumbo. He was a bully, to boot.

Román scooped up a handful of stones and ran down the hill raining missiles upon his foe. They settled down to throwing rocks at one another with only sporadic accuracy until the morning failed and his stomach growled, reminding him he was hungry. Román reclaimed the mare and wandered off, leaving his enemy to hurl curses at his back.

He ranged from the Capuchas onto the desert hardpan as his gut complained louder. Chewing a wad of sap from a wounded piñon provided little relief. He reined in. Was that a voice, or was his head playing tricks? His head must be hungry too.

Then from far away, so faint the wind must have whispered in his ear, he heard a cry. He scouted and found nothing. Perhaps the Clown, one of the *ga'an*—his grandmother's Mountain Gods—toyed with him. Or maybe the One-Great-God-Who-Was-Three at the settlement church. Three was a strange number. He preferred four. Four was the ritual number of his people.

There it was again. Closer now. A cry for help. He skirted a clump of juniper and cut the trail of a horse. Curiosity set him to following the tracks. The hoof prints made straight for Blind Man's Arroyo, an enormous ditch snaking down the foothills to carry spring runoff to the distant river. He dismounted, stepped to the brink, and peered over the edge.

Chapter 2

La Ciudad de Terreon sprawled across its tight little valley like age rings on a pine stump. Rows of project homes pressed into older residential neighborhoods crammed with ill-fitting commercial zones that leaked down into the narrow old-world streets of the original settlement.

Jim Chandler's Army surplus Jeep motored past the adobe church on the plaza and turned north on NM35. Once across the Rio Chacon—a tenuous trickle known to the indigenous people as Wandering Water—he left the town behind and breeched Snowflake Pass where the Chacon Range met the Capucha Spur.

Almost immediately, the highway entered the Edge of Mountain Apache Reservation and dropped rapidly toward the desert where the rush of air turned hot.

Once across Deep Water culvert, which allowed the steep arroyo to pass beneath the road, Jim bore right at a curve two miles short of his J-Bar-C Ranch, forsaking pavement for the sandy hardpan. His spinning tires played tag with thick columns of dust as the Jeep bounced over treacherous dunes to short-cut the road by half a mile. Regaining the asphalt, he raced north until a red-tiled, white-brick, two-storied house hove into view. A lawn shaded by cottonwoods laid a discordant splash of green across the brown plain.

He turned east onto a long, gravel drive and eased in beside a black Lincoln. Tall and in his mid-thirties, Jim hauled his two-ten carcass out of the Jeep and eyed the balding tires on the sedan. Damned things were still hard to come by since the war.

"What took so long?" his wife asked as she stepped from the wide veranda.

"Stopped at the Cattleman's Club. Why?"

"It's Paul. I'm going to dust his britches until he can't sit saddle for a week. He promised to be back by three to mow the lawn."

Jim glanced at his watch. Almost seven. That didn't seem such a catastrophe, but Judith was no alarmist. He swept off his hat and ran fingers through thick, dark hair.

"Is he on Pedro?" At her nod, he added, "The horse would make straight for the corral if anything went wrong. Let's face it, mowing's not our son's favorite pastime."

Giving in to his wife's sense of urgency, Jim headed for the bunkhouse and told his foreman to saddle up. Chuck Griggs didn't waste time asking questions.

As Jim entered the house for supplies, an unusually restrained Teresa met him at the door. He lifted his daughter and planted a kiss on her tanned cheek.

"Where's Paul, Daddy?" Her eight-year-old voice lacked its customary fire.

"Goofing off somewhere. What say we give him a tanning when he comes in?"

That brought a half-hearted giggle.

Jim rummaged the hall closet for his sheepskin and a jacket for Paul when he heard Judith call. As he walked onto the veranda, the house was in deep shadow, although an invisible sun still provided ambient light. The earth cooled beneath an evening breeze.

He stared into the fading day at a horseman plodding up the gravel driveway. It wasn't Paul. This pony was a paint; Pedro was black. Eventually, the horse shuddered to a halt beside the veranda. Rider and mount made a scraggly pair. It was difficult to tell which was scrawnier, the flop-eared mare or the youngster on her bare back. The boy stared mutely, a lot of white showing around his dark pupils. The mare lowered her head and cropped grass.

Jim cleared his throat. "What can I do for you, son?"

The boy's gaze fixed squarely on Jim's boots. "A yellow-haired kid live here?"

"My son has blond hair. Why?"

"Pony fell down Blind Man's Arroyo." He pointed with his chin. "Not far."

Judith gasped. "Is my son hurt?"

The lad's eyes flicked to her and quickly dropped away. "Leg busted, maybe."

"Can we get to him by truck or Jeep?" Jim asked.

The boy shook his head. "Horses."

As Chuck rode up leading his stallion, Jim muttered reassuring words to Judith and a wide-eyed Teresa before swinging into Chigger's saddle. He led the way southeast past the corral toward a distant gate between the ranch and the reservation that saved them an hour and a half of riding. The remaining daylight evaporated before they reached it. Once they passed onto the Edge of Mountain Reservation, Jim's heartbeat synchronized with the rhythm of Chigger's hooves until the strange calm that had settled over him wore thin. More to break the silence than anything else, he asked the youngster's name.

"Román Otero."

Jim repeated the name silently—ro-*MAHN*...o-*TAIR*-o.

The boy had said it wasn't far, but that meant little. The ponies plodded onward. Just before the night wind swept away the last of Jim's patience,

Román's thin voice startled him. He pulled up to see the boy pointing into a deep arroyo. A sliver of moon topped the horizon and cast faint gray images. The black depths of the gully swallowed Jim's flashlight beam.

His voice rolled across the night. "Paul! Hold on, son. We're coming."

While Chuck broke out a lantern, Jim dismounted and followed Román afoot over the edge of the abyss, half-climbing, half-falling down the wall of the ravine. He stood swaying at the bottom until his eyes adjusted to the deeper darkness. His torch's beam searched out Paul lying nearby. He knelt at his son's side. "How are you making it?"

The boy seemed to wake from a stupor. "Dad! Leg... busted. Tried to jump. Pedro fell."

"Okay, take it easy. We'll have you fixed up in short order."

Paul smacked dry lips. "Water?"

"Román, canteen's on my saddle horn."

The boy raced up the side of the arroyo as Chuck cursed his way down, carrying a portable ring of light from a gas lantern. A low whinny pulled Jim's attention down the wash. He motioned for the foreman to check the pony. When the canteen arrived, Paul upended the container.

Jim took the water from Paul as Chuck returned and shook his head. "You know what has to be done for the pony," he said to his son. When the boy nodded, he addressed his foreman. "Take care of it, Chuck."

Jim slit the denim of Paul's right pant leg from cuff to thigh. The break was a simple fracture, no external bleeding. He fashioned a splint from boards he'd brought.

A rifle shot shattered the silence, dying in fading echoes down the length of the long ditch. Jim glanced at his son, grateful the boy was half out of it.

Chuck walked up with Paul's gear. "Can't get no horse down here, Jim."

"I know a way," Román said and scrambled up the side of the ditch.

Jim could have chewed nails as he waited. Had the little scamp taken their mounts and run away? He had his mouth open to tell Chuck to go find the boy when Román rode up the gully leading their horses.

Jim handed his flashlight to Román and scooped his son out of the dirt, but it took both men to get the boy aboard Chigger. Jim mounted behind Paul.

Once Román led them out of the gully, Jim reined in and peered through the moonlight at the boy on the pinto mare. Obviously from the reservation. Not a blood though. About Paul's age. Little younger. Ten or eleven.

"If you hadn't found my son, it might have been bad. We'll take it from here, but you come back to the ranch house tomorrow afternoon, okay?"

The youngster studied his mount's neck. Sensing revolt, Jim leaned over. "You come tomorrow afternoon, or I'll send someone to get you."

5

Chapter 3

The moon, a mammoth pearl suspended above the rounded breast of the dark mountains, washed the desert a delicate silver. A breeze sharpened the night air. The mare plodded along the trail home. Busy reliving the last few hours, Román was oblivious to the high desert chill and his rumbling belly.

When he'd found the *Indah* boy in the arroyo, he'd looked and listened and left without making a sound. A white stranger wasn't any of his business. Shouldn't even have been on the reservation. Yet Román had led the paint north to the white house with a red top and faced the rancher like a man, despite the thunderous pounding of his heart and a dry, raspy throat.

The huge house looked as gloomy as a cavern, but he'd liked the cars and fine horses. The yellow-haired woman was pretty, even if she was as pale as a mountain aspen. The little girl had been dark-haired like the tall rancher man.

The old mare entered a clearing in the evergreen forest well beyond other encampments and halted beside a shapeless *gowa*, what some called a wickiup.

Román discovered the white man's forgotten flashlight looped around his wrist by a leather strap as he hobbled the mare. He was delivering a stern warning against wandering too far when the mournful cry of a whippoorwill sent ripples up his back. Evil birds, whippoorwills. Fooled around in the night too much. His backside puckered when an owl hooted from the tree above him. Remembering there'd been a death in the village two days ago, he swallowed his lecture and scampered through the flap of the wickiup.

His grandmother sat on a blanket beside the fire pit, her black, knobby cane in her lap. "Better get in here, Roan Orphan. He-Who-Left-Us is fighting hard to come back. Real hard."

He noted she'd used the personal name she gave him at birth and grunted. A grunt was a useful thing. A listener made one thing of it while sometimes the grunter meant another. Román removed a small cottontail leg from a chest and settled on the blanket. His grandmother eyed the flashlight hanging from his wrist but said nothing.

She had another name, a Spanish one… Tonia Otero. But no one on the reservation called her anything but Cane-Woman. He tried to calculate how old she was. The People had been penned up with their Mescalero cousins and Navajo enemies at the Round Grove years and years and years ago. The old woman had been born on the banks of the Rio Pecos during that bad time. Or that's what she claimed.

She might look like a parchment-covered mummy with thinning white hair and a mouthful of gums, but he wasn't fooled. She could still raise a dust devil when she wanted to. Acrid smoke from coals in the fire pit made his nose itch.

Her rheumy eyes, almost hidden by a web of deep wrinkles, rested on him as she steadied the stem of a corncob pipe. "You go hunting today? We gonna eat tomorrow?"

She stared at him so hard he considered going back outside to face the owls and whippoorwills. "I *was* hunting. But I heard someone yelling for help." He was soon lost in the telling of his adventure while the old woman listened without moving, except to pull on her pipe. When she finally spoke, it was in her own tongue.

"The *Indah* rancher scooped out your brains and stole what little sense you had. Tell me where that white boy's pony fell down. We'll go fetch it tomorrow. Then you go to that rancher's house, 'cause he'll pay you for what you done."

"Don't wanna go back." That sounded suspiciously like rebellion. He shivered. He knew better than to fool around with Cane-Woman, but sometimes he forgot and did it anyway.

"He steal your ears like he done your brains? Do like I say. Go get paid."

He laid the flashlight on the blanket and claimed he'd already been paid. She made a wet noise with her lips. "That ain't nothing. He'll pay you better'n that. Money, most likely. That's the way they pay for everything."

"The paper kind?" He'd had coins before, but never bills. Worth a lot of coins.

"What you done was big enough for paper money. Big enough for more'n that, but the white man won't know no better."

"Wish he'd give me a rifle. Then I could really hunt." His mind made other connections. "My father was white, wasn't he?" Ignoring her sharp look, he persisted. "Tell me about him and my mother. Tell me about the rodeo...." His voice died as the old woman hissed.

"Don't talk about them that's forgot. Not tonight. Not after the owls."

He snorted even as his resolve melted away.

Cane-Woman's flesh darkened. Veins bulged in her forehead. "Don't make rude noises, boy. I know things you ain't gonna learn at that school where you go waste your time."

He wasn't afraid of her physically. It was the other thing that put the fear-smell on him. The witch thing. Big Tom Bearclaw claimed those with the Power paid for it with human sacrifice. She had no life to give except her own—or his. He, alone, Cane-Woman called kin, and Big Tom said she'd give him to Eagle one day. Most of the time Román didn't think about such things, but at moments like this... he wasn't so sure.

7

But if Eagle gave her power, why did they go hungry and live in a camp of outcasts? Big Tom in the tipi across the clearing was a peyote shaman who'd stolen the power from another medicine man. Even though the People had avoided him like the pox for years, Tom always knew what was going on in the settlement. Was that witchcraft too?

A crippled-up old man and his wife lived in the little house south of the tipi. Some said the old goat was a bad witch whose medicine arrows got shot back at him. That's why he was twisted and his woman messed up in the head.

Cane-Woman's voice startled him. "She-Who-Was-My-Daughter's gone away. Taken by a devil horse. That's all you gotta know." She always avoided speaking directly of her dead offspring. "Go see the rancher man tomorrow. Then don't go there no more. He-Who-Was-Your-Pa didn't find no happiness here. And you ain't gonna find none in the white man's house."

He blinked. "I don't even know the rancher man's name."

"Chandler. Name's Chandler."

She snatched up the flashlight and made him show her how to turn it on. Waving it in front of her, she spread fresh ashes around the edges of the wickiup and laid sage across the doorway to strengthen protection against *ashee*… ghosts.

Relieved the storm had passed so easily, Román finished the rabbit leg, flipped the bone into the fire, and carefully wiped greasy hands on his trousers before stretching out on his blankets. Slipping away into sleep, he barely heard her shaky voice.

"This here's a right fine light. Expect I'll keep it."

Then he descended into a restless, unsettling dream.

Chapter 4

Blood and gore from the Chandler boy's dead horse gunked Román's arms all the way to the elbows. His grandmother had roused him early to beat the sun to Blind Man's Arroyo, hoping to reach Pedro before predators did. Once the horse was butchered, they hauled heavy chunks of meat on a travois back to the *gowa* where they jerked what they couldn't eat right away.

The sun was at its high point before his grandmother got around to cooking a meal. As soon as they finished eating, she told him to wash up and go to the white man's ranch.

He bolted outside, claiming he had to go for his run. She couldn't object to that. She was the one who insisted he "train" every morning. Nobody else did, but then no one else had a grandmother who lived in the past.

At the base of the yellow-hued bluff that gave Rising Rock its name, he went into a loose-limbed trot to warm his muscles before breaking into a run. In his mind's eye, others raced alongside him on this steep path where he imagined the Ancients had ascended from the underworld. They'd fought the *Indah* in these mountains. *Indah*—the outsider, the enemy. Once, that was anybody who wasn't one of the People. Now it meant the white man.

The trail reached a hogback and dropped into a shallow canyon before looping back to the south. Pride demanded his ragged, rubber-soled sneakers beat the same steady rhythm at the end of his race with the sun as at the beginning. Upon re-entering the glade, he paused to peek through the door of the wickiup. His grandmother was gone.

Still huffing slightly, Román considered hiding out instead of going to the ranch house. He could claim the man hadn't given him anything. That was no good. He had a strong hide-behind-face, but she could see through it every time. Surrendering, he rinsed away sweat and blood with water from a pot and walked down the rutted wagon road to the small meadow where he'd hobbled the mare last night.

Great piles of eiderdown clouds mushroomed high over the Chacons, an uncertain promise of a break in the weather, as the paint slipped into her easiest gait. Román placed a hand over his flat belly, exploring the hard knot that grew with each step. Yesterday there'd been a need. Today he could think of a hundred reasons not to go to the white man's house.

Once he turned off the highway onto the gravel road, the ranch headquarters loomed before him. He reined in and stared. The big, white building must be like living in the Reformed Church down in the settlement. He tried to match the house to the man he'd seen yesterday. That hadn't been a hiding man. Must be the woman who wanted to live in a fortress.

If the rancher didn't give him a trinket, he'd have to swipe something for Cane-Woman. And if the man wanted his flashlight back, he'd have to steal it from his grandmother. They were turning him into a thief. He made his lips a firm, straight line and set his expression. Ready now, he kicked the paint into a walk.

A clock chimed from somewhere inside the house as he dismounted and dusted his jeans. A sly glance at the big, black car in the drive revealed the skinny, dark-haired girl he'd noticed yesterday perched on one sleek fender watching him intently.

"I saw you yesterday. You're Román aren't you? My name's Teresa. Why did you just sit there on your horse? Took you forever to come down the drive. Doesn't your horse know how to trot? Princess does. Princess is my pony. She's a buckskin."

Didn't the girl ever take a breath?

"You don't talk much. You talk American?"

Her monologue left him flustered, but he wasn't about to let her see. She was an addle-brain who didn't know any better than to chatter at strangers.

"I've been waiting for you for simply hours. Daddy said to bring you inside when you showed up, so come on."

"Inside?" His gut churned like a mare in foal.

"Course. You don't expect them to come out here, do you?" She dashed away, banging the screen behind her. Román staggered up the steps but ran out of steam at the door. She reappeared, an impatient look on her angular face. "Come *on*! What's the matter with you?"

The room was big and airy, not dark and dank like he'd figured. Pictures hung on the walls. The rug, as thick and soft as a buffalo robe, would make a good place to sleep. He stayed on the girl's heels until she skipped through an open door and announced he was here.

Rigor mortis attacked his muscles; stupefaction, his brain. The impulse to run came too late. Mr. Chandler loomed before him.

"Hello, Román. We're glad you came by."

He doesn't talk, Daddy." She turned to her yellow-haired mother. "Really, Mommy."

"Hush, child." The woman sat in what must have been the biggest chair in the world with an open book on her lap. She was awful old to be studying like some school kid.

The girl stared at him rudely. "You act like a foreigner."

"You'll have to excuse her," the rancher said. "She's forgotten her manners."

He already knew that. Román was glad he didn't have a candy-stick sister like this one. She yammered like a cross squirrel as they followed her parents upstairs.

The white boy sprawled on a huge bed in a room bigger than Cane-Woman's wickiup. The injured boy had thrown the covers back to reveal trousers that looked so soft and flimsy they'd rip if he tried to sit saddle. The right pant leg had been hacked off to accommodate a big cast. Román nearly giggled at the sight of five pink toes poking out of white plaster.

"This is the rascal who caused all the commotion last night," Mr. Chandler said. "Román, meet Paul."

The boy on the bed grinned despite pain lines framing his broad mouth. "Thanks for coming to the rescue." Paul shot a hooded glance at his father. "Wasn't supposed to be over there, so they wouldn't have found me till buzzards started circling." The white boy gave him a look. "How come you didn't say anything when I saw you up on the bank of the arroyo?"

"He still doesn't," Teresa said.

Her brother ignored her. "Why didn't you let me know you were going for help?"

When Román answered with a shrug, the little girl simpered. "See, what did I tell you?"

Mr. Chandler cut in. "Well, everything came out all right. Paul, don't you have something…?"

Paul burrowed under his pillow and pulled out a small box. "Here, this is for you."

The reward he had come for. But he was struck dumb. He couldn't move. Teresa shoved his arm. "Go on, open it. It's real neat. Wish I had one."

Román lifted the lid on the box holding a gleaming band of silver inlaid with sky blue turquoise, faultless except for a delicate copper webbing.

"It's a friendship ring." Paul lifted a silver chain hanging around his neck. "There's only two of them just alike. And see, I've got the other one. Means we're friends."

The blonde woman spoke up. "There's a chain in the box so you can wear it around your neck until it fits."

Teresa went into a pout. "How come I can't have one? Can't I be friends too, Daddy?"

"We'll see, honey."

Román turned his new treasure over in his hand. For sure, Cane-Woman would take it long before the ring fit his finger. Mrs. Chandler looped the gleaming circlet through the chain. Her fingernails—red as wild strawberries—tickled his neck as she fastened the clasp.

11

"It sure is pretty." He knew from teachers at school the whites liked you to take on over their things.

"Aw, it's nothing," Paul said. "Sit down and talk to me. I get bored doing nothing all day."

"I come play with you," Teresa said.

"Big deal. Paper dolls yet. Come on, sit down."

All Román wanted was escape, but he collapsed on the nearest chair when Mr. Chandler applied pressure to his shoulder. As the others drifted out of the room, Paul settled back on his pillows and indicated a plate on a bedside table.

"Have a cookie." He made a face. "Mom makes good ones, but she still has trouble getting sugar, so they're not as sweet as I like them."

Román took one and thought it tasted great. Then he sat woodenly, his eyes darting around to inspect model cars and airplanes lining shelves on the walls and hanging from the ceiling... until the questions started. Whites always asked questions. Where did he live? Did he have brothers? The white boy was as rude as his sister. Soon Paul knew he was orphaned and lived with his grandmother in a *gowa*. Román glanced at the radio beside the bed when somebody started crooning about a prisoner of love.

"You dig Perry Como?"

"Who?" Did the kid know he wiggled his toes when he talked?

"Perry Como. The guy singing. Teresa says she's gonna marry him someday."

Then the *Indah* boy started in on his name, pronouncing it a couple of times and asking if it was Spanish. "It's a killer-diller name, but I'm gonna call you Ro, okay?"

"Guess so." Could one person steal another's soul by changing his name? What would the kid think if he knew Román was really Roan Orphan, a name no white man would ever hear.

The brown machine on the table started in on "I Love You for Sentimental Reasons." He knew that one. Somebody called Nat King Cole sang it on a portable radio at the schoolyard.

Paul must've got tired of trying to steal his mind and decided to play a game. He hauled out a checkerboard and started teaching Román something called chess. He had no idea what the kid was babbling about, but he wasn't about to sit through it again. When it was clear he was lost, Paul backed up and went over the rules once more.

Román grasped the mechanics of the game but didn't make much sense of it until he looked upon the little gadgets as warriors. Even then, the *Indah* boy ended up winning. Like in real life.

Finally, Mr. Chandler came to the doorway. "Can I borrow your guest a minute?"

Román jumped up; Paul made a face. "Okay, but come right back."

He trailed the rancher down the stairs and out to the corral where Mr. Chandler nodded to two ponies. "Aren't they beauties? Fine stock, good build, recently broke. The black's to replace the pony we had to shoot."

What would the white man think if he knew most of Pedro ended up in their wickiup?

"And the chestnut is yours."

His hide-behind-face cracked. "Mine?"

Mr. Chandler indicated leather hanging over the corral fence. "And there's a new bridle and saddle. You can take them with you when you leave."

This would take some thinking. Cane-Woman would trade the horse before the next sunset. He stalled, claiming he'd have to fix a place for the pony. The rancher told him to leave the horse in the corral until he was ready to take him home.

Román glanced to the west and was surprised to see the sun about to drop over the horizon. His grandmother would be fretting over the reward. Besides, he had some planning to do. The ring was one thing, but he'd put up a fight for the horse.

"I gotta go." He almost forgot his manners. "Thank you, sir."

"You're welcome, son. Why don't you say goodbye to Paul before you go."

The white boy wasn't willing to let things end that easily. "Come back tomorrow, okay?" Román shook his head. Paul worried his lower lip between his teeth. "Well, how about the next day?" When Román stood mute, he frowned. "Well, *sometime* this week. I'm gonna be stuck here forever."

A bubble building in Román's chest burst in a flurry of words. "Can't come back. She won't let me." He was doing this wrong. Why wouldn't they let him work it out for himself?

"But the gelding, son," Mr. Chandler said. "What about him?"

His heart stuttered in his chest. He'd been stupid and lost the big horse.

"Well, let's see what tomorrow brings," the rancher added. "We'll work something out."

The room closed around him. The air thickened. He bolted. Fleeing down the stairs in a headlong rush, he shot through the front door. Only when he was on the paint did Román glance back. The rancher and the little girl watched from the porch.

The sun abandoned the sky, and a single blue-white diamond popped out overhead. The paint pranced homeward, inspired to a faster pace by the cool air and a second helping of grass from the white man's yard. Román fingered the silver and turquoise ring suspended around his neck on a thin chain.

13

The clearing in the pine grove was sweet with the smell of cooking when Román finished his run the next morning. The thick stew of wild potatoes, datil leaves, and chunks of Pedro made his mouth water. Horsemeat wasn't as good as beef or mutton but better than nothing.

He sat cross-legged on a blanket inside the *gowa* and scooped stew into his bowl with pancake bread made from screw-bean flour. Cane-Woman sat on the other side of the fire pit, chewing energetically despite a serious scarcity of teeth.

They ate without speaking until the pot was empty. He couldn't remember ever eating so much. He lay back on the blanket, his stomach distended beneath a thin shirt. Sweat from his exercise dried, leaving him chilled.

"You suppose the Indah man knows how good his stock is?" Cane-Woman cackled at her own joke. She poked the fire with a stick and made a noise with her lips. "The white skins give you a Zuni ring for what you done. That's all their son's worth? But the big prize, they left for the vultures. There's a lesson in that."

For the life of him, he couldn't see what it was.

"The *Indah* don't know everything," she explained.

His grunt seemed to satisfy her. He turned on his bloated stomach to hide his face while thinking about the gift he hadn't yet confessed. Did he still have the big chestnut after running away? If he did, how would he keep the horse out of Cane-Woman's clutches?

From behind closed eyelids, he heard the old woman struggle to her feet and go for her jar of *tulapai*. Even though the sun hadn't reached its high point, he was bordering on sleep by the time the corn liquor transformed her into a storyteller. She usually reserved her tales for winter nights when the Powers weren't around to hear her talk about them, but she seldom obeyed old taboos except when it suited her.

The familiar fable of Child-of-Water slaying Eye-Killer, a monster with a lethal stare, drummed against his ears. Tales like this were how he learned a bear made a bear noise and a bear track and did bear things while the coyote and the deer and the serpent each went its own way. From her stories he knew the blood of the Mimbreno and Mescalero flowed with that of the *Tinneh* in his veins. There was white blood too, but she never mentioned that.

He fell asleep during the telling and woke when the sun penetrated the smoke hole of the brush shelter and burned his eyes. Cane-Woman snored beside her earthen jug. Roused, Román rounded up the mare and rode to the settlement. When he went for a drink from the water tap behind the store, he dismounted within earshot of three young men passing around a bottle hidden in a paper bag.

They'd just come back from fighting the white man's war and were talking about jobs. Two of them, Charles Beaver and Tomas Wingfield, complained they hadn't been able to find anything. The third, a tall, wiry man, admitted he was starting on a road construction crew come Monday morning.

Strong Walker, or Walks as he was known on the rez, had lied about his age and joined the Marines, heading off to war when he was no more than five or six years older than Román was right now. Jose Peyote, the outside name he'd enlisted under, had come back a full-grown Lance Corporal. Román figured Walks was about the best-looking fellow he'd ever seen and hoped to grow up to be like him someday. This was somebody to look up to. Talk was he drank some, but that was part of being a man.

Beaver, a great big fellow everybody said was in the Army's jailhouse when the war ended, accepted the bottle from Jose and took a swig. Wingfield was the odd-man-out. Short and stringy, he had a splotchy complexion.

"What kinda job you got with the road crew, Walks?" Beaver tipped the bottle again.

Jose hesitated long enough so Román got the feeling he didn't like that name anymore. "Grunt work. They'll treat me like a recruit till I earn a chevron or two."

Román shoved his head under the water tap and drowned out their voices. He wiped his dripping head with the tail of his shirt and led the mare over to a noisy game of softball at the schoolyard. He joined the extras waiting for a player to drop out. To his disgust, Clare-Ass Wolf was there and started picking on him within minutes.

"You're last. You come after me," Clarence said.

"If I'm last and come right after you, then you ain't no better off than me."

"You're last, and that's the way it is. And being next to last ain't the same as being last, butthole." Clarence never got too deep into his arguments.

"Don't call me your family name, you fat buzzard."

"Who's a fat buzzard?"

"Don't see no fat on me," Román said.

"All I see's a skinny ass that's gonna get whupped if you don't haul it outta here on that bone-bag jackass. You'n that old mare make a good pair. Looks like she ain't got but one more mile left in her. Bet I can outrun her on foot."

"Hell, so can I, but I run pretty good." Maybe he could get out of this without a beating. After some more name calling, Clarence took the bait. Román looked at the other boy's long legs and added another layer to his trap. "You probably can't run too far."

"Longer'n you can… any time. What say we race to the Agency building and back?"

"I was thinking more on touching the cross on the church door. I got a

15

dime says I can beat you there and back." He stretched the truth by ten cents.

"Ain't got a dime," Clarence complained.

"I do," someone else said. "Come on, cousin, we'll split his dime."

"I got a pocketknife too." Román got into the spirit of the thing and soon had every article on his person committed. If he lost, he'd go home stark naked and with a black eye at the very least over the non-existent dime. One of the other boys rode the mare to the church to make certain both racers touched the cross.

Clarence got the jump on him by half-a count and showed surprising speed. Román ignored the spectators' catcalls and settled into the pace he adopted each morning. Clarence had him by a hundred paces at the church.

Just as Román reached for the door, it opened. He wasted precious seconds darting past a startled black robe to touch the wooden cross.

Crap! The priest gave Clare-Ass an advantage. Now Román had to turn his feet loose. His enemy's distant back broadened; the gap closed. The bigger boy's long legs faltered. Román heard his painful gasps. At the edge of the schoolyard he passed his opponent in a burst of speed. Beaten, Clarence refused to quit until he staggered across the finish line.

Román collected ten cents, a knife, one melted chocolate bar, a dime store ring, and a small piece of real turquoise, losing everything but the turquoise shooting dice behind the schoolhouse. After that, he went off to find the mare.

Everyone had been pulling for Clarence, and that rankled. Nobody was kin, and friendships followed blood and clans. Plus, they were all afraid of Cane-Woman, who acknowledged no clan, which—he guessed—meant he didn't either. Still, he got along okay with most of the kids at school. Wasn't that enough?

He killed the remainder of the day looking for firewood. He had enough for three days stacked beside the wickiup by the time the old woman materialized at nightfall.

She prepared a meal, and after his bowl was empty, he went to relieve himself. When he returned from the woods, he sat down and poked at the fire.

"Grandmother, what did you do with the white man's ring?"

Chapter 5

Román watched from the tree line as a black car like the one from the rancher's house halted at a washed-out place on the wagon track running from the settlement to Standing Rock. He grunted when the driver emerged. It wasn't the big rancher. His woman, dressed up in clothes as fancy as powwow regalia, crossed the washout on foot, her high heels wobbling on the uneven terrain. Two jays chattered noisily over her head. Had Cane-Woman sent them as spies?

He shadowed Mrs. Chandler down the dirt road to the pines sheltering the outcast camp. She stopped and looked around before starting for the small frame house, almost walking past the brushy wickiup where Cane-Woman squatted over a blackened pot. The environment turned hostile as the two women regarded one another. The jays following the white woman now hawked a traitorous alarm. Román slipped behind the wickiup so he could watch and hear without being seen.

"Excuse me, I'm looking for Román Otero's grandmother."

"I'm Tonia Otero, Missus Chandler. I been waiting for you."

A sudden wind raked the clearing. Paul's mother blinked. "You were expecting me?"

Cane-Woman harrumphed like a frog. "Dropped a fork in the dirt. Meant a woman was coming."

"I see. The boy said you'd forbidden him from visiting us again. I've come to ask you to reconsider."

The woman looked uncomfortable standing beside the *gowa*. He grinned. Cane-Woman was playing with the *Indah*. Then his eyes went wide when Mrs. Chandler smoothed her skirt behind her knees and sank to the ground.

Cane-Woman hawked and spat. "His mama went outside, and his papa come here. They didn't fit neither place. The boy is *Tinneh*. I raised him that way. Nobody remembers his white daddy no more. His place is here."

"A visit from time to time might allow him to learn things he's not exposed to here."

"He already gets that kinda learning. The white man's school teaches them things."

"Perhaps, but it's a different world out there. One he must learn to cope with. You said his mother had to try. So will he. Our ranch is just outside the reservation."

Mrs. Chandler placed a hand to the ground and rose, teetering on her high heels a moment before finding her balance. "And then there's the matter of the gelding. It's a fine horse. Very valuable. It's Román's any time he wants it. Good afternoon, Mrs. Otero."

He faded into the forest when she started back to the car. Why'd she have to mention the big red? He'd be in for it now. He headed straight for his hobbled mare.

****

Román hadn't come up with a plan for the red pony by the time darkness and an empty belly drove him back to the wickiup. With his heart in his sneakers, he ducked through the entrance.

Cane-Woman sat silently before the fire pit, and he could see she was mad. Bad mad. His skin puckered like he had a screech owl on his back. He stuck his finger in the pot beside the fire. Still warm. His stomach was complaining, but he wasn't sure food would stay down. Even so, he ate a little before laying the rest aside. Why didn't she say something? A cussing out would be better than this.

When she started mumbling to herself, he thought she was casting a spell. Then she jabbed him with her cane. "Had me a visitor today. I knowed the white eyes was gonna come for you someday, and now they done it."

He sat with his mouth glued shut.

Cane-Woman smacked her lips like she was trying to get rid of a sour taste. "But you already know who come. You was here. I felt you. That painted, round-eyed bitch with her stupid moccasins-on-stilts ain't got enough sense to sit quiet so we could size one another up. No respect."

The old woman whacked the blanket with her cane. "She come to teach me something. All white people do that. It's a wonder the Old Ones managed to get along without the *Indah* around to tell them what to do all the time."

He held his breath. So far, it wasn't too bad. Then he ducked as she swung her stick. "How come you didn't tell me about the horse? Go git 'im tomorrow."

Román swallowed hard and screwed up his courage. "Uh-uh. I need him. The mare's not much good anymore. I need him to get around. You can have the mare. We'll eat her."

"She's like me, too old and stringy. You bring that horse home. We ain't gonna eat him, but he'll fetch us a good price."

"Let me keep him. I need a better ride. I can win races. Win some money. The rancher gave me a saddle. A brand new one. We can sell that. It'll feed us for a long time."

"You bring 'em both home, and we'll see."

18

"Can't. Nowhere to keep the pony. Somebody'll steal him for sure if he runs loose. He's worth a lot of money." He sucked in his breath. Crap! His mouth got in front of his brain.

"Humph."

Was that it? Had he won? He didn't know, but he'd leave the horse at the ranch for a while longer. He might have to go get the saddle, but he'd leave the big red in the corral.

****

Román woke to find Cane-Woman sitting like a stone pillar on the other side of the fire pit. She watched him silently while thinking big things. Maybe something to do with Mrs. Chandler's visit yesterday. The puffy, sagging planes of her face arranged themselves into a curious pattern when she saw he was awake.

"Listen to me, child. Everything you see from up on top of the sacred White Mountain was ours ever since the Old Ones come up outta the underworld. We kept our enemies away 'til the white eyes come along. Their medicine was powerful enough to claim it all. I seen this, myself."

He fidgeted, but she would make her point when she was ready.

"You know about all the lies and treachery and sickness they brung. Them things caused lotsa misery, but taking our Way from us was worse. A free man moves with the seasons, and that's healthy. But the *Indah* says we can't cross his wire fences to places that was ours forever. Because he says so, they belong to him now. So we ain't free no more. A chained man can't do nothing but wait for death. You can't see chains hanging offa us, but they's there."

Ro frowned. Every day he mounted the mare and rode as far as he wanted without seeing a white man, except for people at the government agency or teachers at school.

Cane-Woman leaned forward and poked a bony finger at him. "The time'll come when the white man'll tell you how your life's gonna go. There'll be a fork in the road, and there he'll be. Standing in your way. Then you think about what I'm telling you."

Bitterness twisted her expression. "But think on *this* now. They was a big war, and lotsa our men did the fighting. It's over now, but did our men stay with the whites? No, they all come home except for them that died. They come back because the whites was finished with them and just thrown them away.

"Don't think that because you'n me don't live in the settlement that we ain't *Tinneh*. I live apart for my own reasons, and them reasons don't matter to you. But what happens to the *Tinneh* matters. Without the People to stand between us, the *Indah* will swarm these mountains like ants. White-Painted-Woman will turn her face away, and Child-of-Water will hide in the deep canyons. Think on that and remember it."

The old woman squirmed on her blanket. "As a boy gets to be a man, he hears different voices. The call of a man for a woman rears up. And there's a call for change. Be careful of that one. Like most things, it's both *di yi* and *en ti*. It ain't good and it ain't bad, but it can be either one of them things just by the way a man uses it.

"More times than I can count, I seen a boy become a man and claim the Old Way is bad and new ways is good. *It ain't so!* The Way is the Way. This hunting for change takes our young people outside. And after they get a belly full, they come home. Then they gotta fight to be *Tinneh* again."

Cane-Woman paused to pack her cob pipe. He sensed the point was about to be made. "Since you got the blood of an outsider, that yearning's gonna be stronger. I worked hard to see the People don't think about the foreign blood in you. But if you try to live as a white man, this home will be closed to you forever. These mountains will turn you away. You hear me, boy?"

He gave the expected answer like he did at school. "Yes, ma'am."

"But maybe you oughta learn how the wind blows while you're young and I'm here to help you. So I decided on something. Today, you go back to the white man's ranch."

Ro stared into the fire pit. He can't *ever* go? Now he *has* to go?

"Go and learn the white man's way ain't your way. Learn a hard lesson but a good one. *The eagle's claw don't make the track of a dove.* Learn you are *Tinneh* at heart and this is your home and these are your people. And," she added, "bring the horse back."

He swallowed. "Can't. Promised to cut the grass at the government building."

"If you promised, a man's gotta own his words. So cut the grass and then go." When he avoided her gaze, she cupped his chin in a withered hand. "Do like I tell you."

He broke free and left, pledging nothing. He hadn't even finished thinking things over before the little lawn was cut and the agency man paid him twenty-five cents. He was free now to head for the ranch, but he wanted no part of it. The world was upside down. Somewhere a deer mouse was chasing a fox

He got the mare and drifted by the schoolyard where he joined a softball game. His mood made enemies. Within minutes, he was in a heated argument. Tired of swapping dirty names, he went to the grocery store to spend part of his earnings and wolfed a strawberry too fast to enjoy the flavor. In the midst of a belch, he decided to ride to Big Rock Canyon.

Once there, Román tracked a small coyote up the arroyo. If he could catch it, that would be a sign he was a man, and he'd be free to smoke—or so it used to be. Now, everybody smoked any time he wanted. He lost track of the wily beast within two minutes.

When he returned home, Cane-Woman met him outside. One look, and her face turned dark. "Who are you to forget what I say?"

"Don't wanna go!" That came out louder than he intended.

"Fools ain't give their wants. Go after your run tomorrow." His chin went stubborn. Her voice hardly reached his ears. "Don't think you're stronger'n me. Not yet, child. When I speak, Eagle hears me, and so will you."

She stood with the black mass of the wickiup at her back, and in that instant darkness fell. Her magic had stolen the light in a single moment. Witches drew power from the night. She was almost invisible, but she was very much present.

"Listen, Orphan!" Cane-Woman whispered. "Listen to the night sounds. They's different from day sounds. That's when lost souls come looking for loved ones. That's when witches' arrows fly. Listen, hear that?"

He heard nothing, but the hair on the nape of his neck rose.

"Maybe it's the Wild Ones, them cannibals who eat little boys that ain't got no home." She whirled and entered the wickiup. "Anybody sharing my *gowa* does like I say. Are you ready to stay outside tonight?"

He scooted in behind her. "N-no."

"Then go see the *Indah* man tomorrow." She faced him across the fire pit. In the flickering light of the flames, she was frightening. "You will go."

****

He didn't return to the wickiup after his run the next morning. Instead, he and the paint hid out until almost nightfall. When he came back to the clearing, Big Tom Bearclaw stood in front of his tipi, a clutch of odds and ends in his arms. The man beckoned.

"Is it over? You'n the old woman get it settled?" At the shake of his head, Tom clucked. "Are you crazy, Roan Orphan? You got her muttering to herself. Bad medicine to get that one mad. You straighten up. She ain't one to play games with."

Tom using his birth name shook him a little. "Not playing games."

"Ain't sure what you're doing, but she owes Eagle, and she might pay him back tonight. She's crazy mad. Me'n my old woman's clearing out till this settles down."

"She's not mad at you."

Big Tom shook his head. "I ain't gonna be around if she goes to slinging them witches' arrows. Half the reservation's scared to leave home 'cause she's all sweated up. You give her what she wants. You don't, I might just yank off your thing. You don't wanna go around giggling like a girl, you do what she wants." He stalked back to his tipi.

21

Two owls hooted incessantly by the time Cane-Woman appeared at the wickiup. Román, wrapped in his blankets, pretended to sleep. She saw right through him and poked his back with her cane. But he lay like he was dead until she gave up.

****

The following morning, he sneaked off again, and there was no sign of life around Big Tom's tipi when he returned later. The man had cleared out for a healthier climate. When Román straightened up after slipping through the doorway of the *gowa,* he learned he hadn't won the battle of wills. Cane-Woman blocked his way. She appeared small and frail, but she was as big as a mountain and as strong as a thunderbolt. She spun him around and planted a moccasin in his backside. He shot out the door and rolled in the dust. His blankets landed in the dirt beside him.

"Come back when you figger to mind me."

He lay where he fell for several minutes before getting up and making for the *gowa.* Her bony fist raised a welt under his eye. He cursed and pled, but she turned deaf. He imagined setting fire to the wickiup so she would run screaming into his arms. But he didn't have a match.

He spread his blankets and carefully surrounded them with ashes from the outside fire pit. For good measure, he traced a cross on his forehead and clutched his black-handled pocketknife in his hand before wrapping himself in his blankets. Even so, he spent a miserable night.

****

Román woke at first light and did his five-mile run. Upon his return, he found a bowl of food in the dirt beside his bedroll. He ate silently. Cane-Woman came outside and sat across from him. A morning breeze played with her thinning white hair as she gummed her food.

He bridged the gap shyly. "Why do I have to go?"

She flopped a scrap of tortilla into her mouth. "Go get a belly full of the whites."

"Already did."

"You don't know nothing. Go see how they slave for money and cars and things. Go learn what *Indah* means. It ain't nothing but a word to you, but it's lots more'n that. It's truth." She snorted. "A big man, you. In my day, you'd a been a warrior, a hunter, a seer. Not no more. They stole that from you, and you don't even know it. They'll make you act like a white man, but they ain't gonna let you *be* a white man."

"Then what'll I be?"

"Oh, the white eyes will teach you that. The yellow-haired woman will teach you good." Cane-Woman paused. "You gonna go?"

His chest puffed up, and he got tickly inside. She'd *asked* him. He answered in the deepest voice he could manage. "I'll go."

****

Two hours later, he sat on the paint bitterly regretting his words. The magic had gone, evaporated. He didn't feel grown up anymore. The mare stood patiently on the shoulder of NM35 while he stared down the long driveway leading to the house. A vehicle approached from the rear, but he paid no attention until it halted beside him.

Mr. Chandler smiled from an open Jeep. "Coming for a visit?" Román's tongue got all knotted up. He nodded. "Tie the paint on back and ride with me. I'll go slow."

He slid from the pony, secured her reins, and took a seat beside the rancher, clutching the edge of the windshield. He'd ridden in a school bus on field trips before, but he'd never been in front where he could watch the driver make the vehicle go. They claimed a machine like this had a hundred horses under the hood, but it wasn't as smart as one pony. His mare wouldn't fall off the trail if he watched a hawk overhead, but this thing only did what man told it to do. His heart pounded as the vehicle moved. The paint clopped along behind.

"Glad your grandmother changed her mind."

That didn't call for an answer, so he just hung on tight.

"Paul will be glad to see you. He's still rotting away, according to him."

A minute later they turned down a side road, went through a gate, and pulled up beside a windmill with the biggest stock tank he'd ever seen.

"Thought the mare might want a drink," the man said.

She did. She inhaled so much of the white man's water, Román was embarrassed by her greed. "Sorry, Mr. Chandler. I'll fill it back up."

"No need. There's a valve like the one on the toilet tank in your bathroom. Uh, our bathroom. It fills up automatically. And why don't you call me Jim like everyone else?"

That didn't sound right, but he couldn't say it out loud. So, he didn't say anything.

They both leaned against the vehicle while Mr. Chandler shook a cigarette from a pack and lit the end with a Zippo like a lot of the *Tinneh* soldiers brought back from the war. As he smoked, Mr. Chandler spoke of things that interested him: the grass, the cattle, the depth of the well beside the tank.

He told of starting college in the midst of something called the Great Depression and having to quit school to earn a living when he made his wife pregnant. He talked about fighting Germans over in Europe. He spoke of deep things, like when somebody gave him a job on a ranch called the Double Z

23

before he got his own place.

Román drank it in. This must be how it felt when a blood uncle or a real father spoke of important things to his son. What could be better than this? Mr. Chandler extinguished his cigarette, shredding it until there was nothing left.

Román cleared his throat to get his mouth moist enough to speak. "I got your flashlight. I didn't mean to take it, but it was on my wrist."

"Flashlight? Oh, you mean the one I had in the arroyo the other night. You keep it. I have more. Comes in handy sometimes." Mr. Chandler took off his hat and swiped his forehead. "Hot day, isn't it? A man loses a lot of moisture on a day like this. Hard on the skin."

Ro said nothing, but he allowed his gaze to steal over the man's features. Would he look strong like Mr. Chandler one day?

"Know what I use to help?" The rancher put his hat on the seat and rummaged around in a little pouch, coming up with a small bar in a gray wrapping. "This is the best soap I've ever found. Benchley's it's called. Makes a man's skin feel good after he's been out in the sun all day. Think I'll try it now."

Román gawked as the man emptied his pockets and stripped off his shirt and boots. Then Mr. Chandler jumped into the tank—pants and all. The man's arms and head were deeply tanned, but flesh hidden from the sun was the color of white river rock. After his heavy chest was covered with suds, he held out the soap. "Come on, give it a try."

He hesitated. *His* torso was all one color. Would that look funny? But when the soap was offered again, he accepted. Shyly stripping off his shirt, he went to work. When he saw the suds got him as white as the rancher, he giggled. Mr. Chandler laughed aloud, a good, strong sound. They were having fun together.

He got up the nerve to kick out of his sneakers and climb into the tank with the big man. They laughed and splashed, and Mr. Chandler let him jump off his shoulders into the water. The rancher even threw him up into the air a couple of times so he could belly flop. That was more fun than lathering. But there were more crazy things to come. Mr. Chandler threw their shirts and socks into the tank with them, and they took turns scrubbing them with Benchley's.

He could have kept it up forever, but when Mr. Chandler climbed out of the tank he tagged along. What moisture they couldn't wipe away with wrung-out shirts, quickly evaporated under the bright sun. His damp pants were uncomfortable, but the rancher didn't seem to mind, so he put up with it too. Mr. Chandler combed his hair and handed the comb to Román to tackle his matted mop.

Long before Román wanted to go, the man squinted at the sky and said they had better head for the house. Before starting the motor, Mr. Chandler held out the bar of soap. "Here, you keep it and have some more fun."

When they arrived, the bratty little girl led him upstairs. A fat grin split Paul's face when Román entered. The white boy sat at a table beside his bed, putting together a model airplane. The room smelled of glue and banana oil. "Ro! Thought you took a powder on me."

Neither of them spoke much during the next hour. Paul worked steadily on the plane, now and then asking Ro's help with some small job. At length, he held the model up and examined it critically. Ro's eyes roved the sleek brown wings. The plane was beautiful.

"P-51 Mustang. It saved the air war in Europe," Paul said. "First fighter with the range to escort our bombers clear to Germany. We got jets now, but it'll still be our best fighter when we go to war with the Commies."

"Who?"

"Those Russian Communists who're enslaving Europe. The ones putting up that Iron Curtain. Question is… will this baby fly? We oughta let the glue dry some more, but what the heck. Let's give it a try."

Ro carried the Mustang while Paul clomped down the stairs on crutches. Ro wound the propeller and tossed the craft into the air. After an initial sharp dip, the plane went into a long, graceful climb. When the rubber band played out, it banked to the right and fell to the ground.

"Right wing's too heavy," Paul said.

While they were inspecting the balsa wood and paper toy for damage, a chestnut gelding with a white blaze on his broad chest walked out of the stable into the corral and stood with his head held high. Ro almost went giddy. *His* pony.

"He's a beaut," Paul said. "Go on, ride him. The only exercise he gets is when Teresa gives him a workout."

Ro slipped through the fence. The horse stood his ground, snorting softly as he drew near, flinching only slightly when Ro stroked his nose so the animal would know his scent.

He mounted from the top rung of the fence. The pony shied nervously, but he kept his seat, tangling his right hand in the thick mane. "Okay, boy, let's go." A poke with his heels sent the horse around the corral.

"What're you gonna name him?" Paul asked as the pony drifted to a halt. "I call mine Pedro." A shadow crossed Paul's features, and Ro liked him better for it. "You know, after the other one. Teresa halfway named yours Colorado 'cause he's red. But he's yours to name."

"Colorado. That sounds good." He nodded. The matter was settled.

Ro spied the yellow-haired woman watching from the porch. Suddenly nervous, he glanced to the west. The day had gotten away from him again. "I

25

gotta go."

"Aw, stay and eat with us?"

His stomach lurched at the idea. "Can't."

After strapping his new saddle to the mare, he said goodbye. Gingerly holding the model P-51 Paul had insisted he take, Ro turned the paint toward home. At the end of the long gravel drive, he glanced over his shoulder at the big white house and stuck out his bottom lip. Maybe it wasn't so gloomy after all. And maybe being "Ro" wasn't so bad either.

Chapter 6

Smoke belched from a bevy of heavy machines and spread an acrid blanket over scores of men and tons of equipment laboring through a shimmering haze of heat to replace a two-lane stretch of the crumbling highway north of Terreon.

Jose Peyote swiped sweat from his eyes and bent to his work. He put down on his application paper he'd operated a dozer in the Corps. The crew foreman, a broad, hairy brute called Pulkowski, would probably put him on a machine soon. Right now, he was breaking his back on a shovel. No matter, the twenty dollars a week he earned paid bills and bought groceries.

When Pulkowski disappeared, the college kid beside him leaned on the handle of his shovel and shook a butt out of a wrinkled cigarette pack. "You gonna get this road built all in one day?"

"Just pulling my weight," Jose said. They'd taught him that in the Corps.

The college boy muttered something and dropped his smoldering cigarette at Jose's feet. They were busily plying their shovels when Pulkowski stepped up. "Hey, kid! Report to Mullins up at the crusher. The Indian can finish up here."

The jock dropped his shovel and scrambled out of the hole. "Atta boy, Kilroy! That job pays a nickel an hour more."

The kid's fallen shovel galled Jose. This was the third man moved to a higher paying job in the two weeks he'd been on crew. Heat burned through his shirt. He felt the crosscurrents of his body, the sun sapping his energy while the labor corded his biceps. One kind of strength ebbed, another flowed.

Pulkowski stayed close, so Jose finished the day without another rest break. Today was Friday… payday. That made things bearable. Tomorrow he'd be getting overtime.

When the shift whistle shrieked, he joined the crowd around the jobsite office, a trailer manned by a bunch of clerks. Chairborne rangers, Marine grunts had called them. Acted like chevrons on their arms were silver stars. Someone said they kept the beans, bullets, and bandages moving, but they never did none of the fighting or dying.

A man strutted out of the field office and began bawling names. When Jose heard his, he worked his way through the crowd to claim a dun-colored piece of paper that told how much money he was getting. Whatever it turned out to be, it was more'n he had now. He hadn't been paid for the first week he'd worked. "Hold back," they called it.

Jose's confusion deepened as workers left after getting their little scraps of paper. The only wages he'd ever received had been in the Marines where they counted his money right out in front of him. What was he supposed to do with this paper? As he hesitated, the clerk called Pulkowski's name.

The foreman waved his check aloft. "Hot damn! The eagle done shit."

The big man and a contingent of cronies headed for their trucks and cars. Jose crawled in his battered, black, '32 Ford pickup and followed along behind. The procession moved a few hundred yards down the road to the outskirts of Terreon, halting in the parking lot beside a puke-green adobe building. The neon sign atop the dump proclaimed it Harry's Bar. Pulkowski and company crowded inside the building.

Jose dry-washed his face. The "No Dogs or Indians Allowed" sign on the door stopped him cold. It was the law, someone told him, but during his military service he'd had plenty of drinks in beer gardens overseas—places behind the front lines set aside for alcohol and tobacco.

He peeked through a dirty window. The place was crowded with construction workers yelling orders at two waitresses. Pulkowski and his train formed a line at one end of the counter where a balding man with a white apron shrouding his paunch exchanged their pieces of paper for real money.

The trading post at White Pine would be closed, and Jose needed groceries. He drew a breath, put on a blank expression, and plunged through the door before his nerve failed. No one took notice of him until he stood before the check cashing man.

The barkeep scowled. "What you doing here, boy?"

"Need to get me some money."

"What do I look like, a bank? Get outta here. Can't have no Indians in here. They catch you in my bar, they'll take it outta my hide. Now git!"

Jose backed away, waving his check. "But I got one of these."

"Hold on there," the man called. "What's this, Pulkowski, new blood?"

"Yeah, Harry. The skin works on my crew."

"Okay, Chief. I'll cash your check, but then you scoot on outta here. You endorse it, and I'll give you your money less my half-buck ...uh, dollar handling fee." The barman flipped the paper over and pointed. "Sign your name. You can write, can't you?"

"Sure. I was in the Marine Corps."

"So was my wife's brother, but he sure as shit can't write." Harry snatched the check and handed over some bills. "You come on back next week, and I'll help you out again. Have a beer on the house, but you gotta drink it out back. And don't let nobody see you."

Jose sat on a small boulder behind the bar and looked around. Hell, this wasn't bad. Lotsa Leatherneck beer gardens'd been rougher'n this. He counted his money while working on the beer. The feel of the bills sent his spirits soaring until he thought about how much they had to cover. He was stuffing the greenbacks in his wallet when Pulkowski lumbered around the corner holding two bottles.

"Thought you mighta worked up a thirst today."

"Thanks, Mr. Pulkowski."

"Ski. Call me Ski. Don't seem right, not letting you guys drink like everbody else."

"No, sir. It don't, Mr. Pul...er, Mr. Ski."

The big man laughed. "Mr. Ski! That'll do the job, I guess." He tugged on his drink. "Heard you tell Harry you was in the Marines."

"Yes, sir. I wore the Eagle, Globe, and Anchor. Four years in the Corps. Went in a slick-sleeve and come out a Lance Corporal."

"Oorah, huh? Four years. How old are you, kid?"

"Be twenty in December."

"Man, you musta lied your ass off to get in that young. See any action?"

Images of a rocky Pacific island flashed across Jose's mind. The stink of rotting corpses filled his nostrils. His stomach turned. He swallowed hard and tried to sound casual. "Some. Guadalcanal. Peleliu."

"You fought the little yella bastards, huh? Me, I went the other direction. You're okay, Chief. Most of the guys, they like to buy a round now and then."

"Oh, sure. I'll do my bit. How much?"

"Coupla bucks oughta cover it."

He peeled off two bills, and Pulkowski waddled back inside the bar. Jose finished off the second beer and tossed aside the bottle. As he made ready to go home, a Pulkowski crony came around the building and handed him another beer. By the time he finished that drink, someone came out and suggested Jose might want to spring for another round. Two more dollars disappeared inside.

Hours later, Jose staggered out from behind the bar and found his pickup. As he pulled out of the parking lot, his fender scraped the rear end of another truck. He heard a lot of yelling but kept on going down the highway. Halfway to Snowflake Pass, he remembered he needed groceries and pulled an unsteady one-eighty back toward Terreon.

Good to be home living on the rez and working on a construction crew. Being a working man making money and buying drinks for the fellows brought him closer to his Corps days. Better, even. Because he had a wife and a pretty little girl—the product of a short leave home after he got back from overseas. Yes, sir. He belonged.

One of those all-night stores on Maple was the only thing open at this late hour. He ground to a halt in front of the place.

"Hey, you can't park crossways like that!" the clerk yelled as he entered. Jose headed for the milk cooler. "Only need a coupla things."

"You're taking up all my parking spaces," the man complained. "Park that jalopy right or get outta here."

His goodwill evaporating rapidly, Jose stalked toward the man. His muscles quivered. He was a Marine. Nobody talked to him like that, especially a pissant clerk. "Told you, I'll be through in a minute."

The clerk brought out a short club. "You been drinking, Indian? You get outta here."

Jose felt his face flush. Muscles tense, he leaned over the counter, well within reach of the other man's weapon. "That's right, white man. I been drinking. And when I drink, I get mean. And when I get mean, I like to beat on weak-eyed, broke-dick box-kickers till I get tired. And it takes me a long time to get tired. You put that stick down, or I'm gonna ram it up your fat ass."

The man blinked and dropped the club.

As he walked back to the dairy case, Jose noticed a car pull up out front. This was a clip joint. *Sixty cents* for a gallon of sweet milk. He could get it cheaper on the rez. As he reached for a bottle, the bell over the front door tinkled. He was picking out a ten-cent loaf of bread when someone spoke.

"All right, boy. Turn around... slow."

Jose swiveled to face a scowling cop. "Ain't looking for trouble, Officer."

"Frank here says you threatened him."

"Not till he pulled a club on me. Then I told him what I was gonna do with it."

"That your truck outside? Parked kinda crazy, ain't it?"

"Told the shithead I was just coming in for a minute."

"Don't smart mouth me, boy. You been drinking?"

"Hell, no! Injuns can't buy liquor. You know that."

"You lip off one more time, you're gonna sleep it off in the jailhouse." The officer shifted. His features puckered uncertainly. "You can't pay for them groceries, I'll have to figure you was planning on robbing this place."

"I got money." A buzzing in his head made it hard to concentrate.

"All right. Go pay for your groceries and clear out."

"Ain't finished yet."

"Yes, you are." The officer rested a hand on the butt of his pistol. "Now let's go. Real quiet-like."

Jose thought about taking the man down, but he turned his rage inward and pushed past the cop. The shitty clerk's self-satisfied smirk almost unhinged him. He paid and burned rubber pulling out of the parking lot with the patrol car on his tail. At the city limits, he stomped on the gas, but the old pickup didn't have the guts to build up much speed. By the time he pulled up before a small two-room cinderblock house outside of White Pine, the night had gone sour.

He oughta have re-upped. Be over in Japan screwing their women and drinking their saké if he had. Better'n this. The night was quiet except for the booze buzz in his head. Cool mountain air seeped into the cab, sending him inside the house. The baby started crying as soon as he came through the door. Consuela said nothing, but her look brought a cloud to his eyes.

"Me'n soma the men went out for a drink."

She stood against the wall rocking the fussy baby in her arms while he ate stew she set out for him. Jose pushed the empty bowl away and leaned back. Tonight had been good. It was almost like back in the Corps when he was one was of the guys. A man being a man with other men... not Mexicans or Indians or Anglos. Just Marines.

He'd felt like that again at Harry's. Woulda been better to be inside with the others, but hell, the guys didn't make the rules. His face turned hot. Everything woulda been good if it hadn't been for that weasel-eyed store clerk.

He lurched to his feet, head swimming. He smiled at Consuela and reached for the baby.

She clutched the infant to her chest. "Walks, be careful."

"Don't call me that. Name's Jose. Told you that already. Don't worry. I won't drop her." He settled the child in his arms and chucked her tiny chin. "Wouldn't hurt my little angel."

As if she understood, the infant ceased whimpering. In a moment, she was gurgling and staring at him through coal black eyes. His heart swelled. His little Mary Sue. He gave Consuela a peck on the tip of her nose and went to put the baby in her crib.

Jose stripped and washed sweat from his body with water from a basin. Consuela examined him as he cleaned himself.

"You're so handsome. Pretty soon I won't be so sore, and we can do it again."

"Can't hardly wait." He turned away to hide his reaction.

****

Cold crawling through Jose's bones the next morning brought him awake. He barely had time to realize he'd fallen asleep in a chair before rushing out the door. Bile poured from his mouth and nostrils. When he could finally breathe, he urinated and went back inside to mumble a greeting to Consuela, who was heating coffee. The baby fussed in her crib as he splashed water over his face and gargled to get the sour taste out of his mouth.

"What's the matter with Mary Sue?" he asked.

Consuela handed him a cup of coffee before picking up the child. "She's

31

sick. Hot."

"I gotta go get overtime. Ride into town with me, and we'll take her to a doctor."

"That'll cost money. I'll take her to the free clinic in White Pine if she don't get better. Sometimes you gotta sit and wait, but they take good care of us."

"Seems to me like the government just sends the ones learning to be doctors."

"Honey." Consuela averted her eyes. "There's not nothing in the house to eat except the milk and bread you brought last night."

He pulled bills from his wallet and laid them on the table. His gut rolled when he saw how few remained. He found two more singles in his pants pocket. As she reached for the money, he rescued a bill. "Gotta get some cigarettes."

"A man needs his tobacco," she agreed. The rest of the money disappeared into her skirt pocket.

He glanced at the wind-up clock over the stove. "Gotta go." He pulled her close and reached down to touch the baby in her crib. "She's pretty. Like her mama."

****

Jose's belly complained about yesterday's load of beer all the way to town. Saturday work meant more money—that overtime stuff. So he had to put in the time even if his head felt like it had a witch's arrow in it.

"Hey, Indian!" someone called as he pushed a card with his name on it into the clock that told the clerks how much money he earned. A redheaded man with a face so white not even his sunburn could hide it walked up. "You owe me five bucks for busting my taillight."

"You crazy, man. Go 'way."

"Stay off the booze if you can't handle it. Pulkowski was there. He seen it."

The foreman came over to act as judge and jury. He claimed Stephens—that was the red-headed eight-ball's name—was right. When Jose had no more than a dollar on him, Pulkowski promised to collect next payday.

This wasn't about five dollars. They'd stopped being men together. They were Indian and Anglo again. If he needed proof, he got it when Pulkowski pulled another white college boy out of the trench and sent him to work running messages and supplies up and down the line. All of a sudden, his shovel seemed heavy. Long time till payday.

****

32

That evening, Jose lay in the darkness listening to the baby's labored breathing. The tinny tick of the clock was the only sound audible above the child's rattle. Consuela warmed the bed beside him. Was she awake? He rolled his hips and set the springs to quivering, but she didn't stir.

He turned his thoughts to little Mary Sue. He liked that name. It was a name for this time and this world. Someday people would point her out. "That's Mary Sue, Jose's Peyote's oldest girl." He pictured her with hair cut like women he'd seen in Long Beach. Her lips tinted ruby.

The baby burst into a fit of coughing. The strangling gasps threw a chill over him. The spasm passed; his fear remained. He'd heard coughing like that before. It was the last sound his two brothers ever made. That was a long time ago, back when he was little, but the memory haunted him still. Dawn came, sleep did not. He rose quietly and made coffee, something he rarely did. Cooking was Consuela's job. His was to make a living for the family. He drew on trousers and was about to stretch a shirt across his shoulders when Consuela woke.

"Did I sleep too late?" Worry tinged her voice.

"No, it's early. I couldn't sleep. Anyhow, gotta go to work."

"Didn't know they worked you on Sunday."

"Yeah, they're behind schedule. And on Sunday, I get even more of that overtime pay. Better ride in with me and take Mary Sue to the doctor. She don't sound good."

"She was better last night. Better'n she's been in a week." She fixed her gaze on his left shoulder and spoke in *Tinneh*. "Jose. I was talking to my mother about the baby. She says I oughta take her to Cane-Woman. The old woman's good with this kinda sickness."

His skin crawled. "That witch? She went bad a long time ago. Nobody uses her for curing no more, just midwifing… or the dark stuff."

"They say she's real good with the cough. We don't have to be afraid of her if we pay her and don't get on her bad side. She can help, Jose. I know she can. She calls on Eagle, and Eagle's strong."

"You sound like an old blanket head." He switched to the white man's language. "Wake up and look around you. When's the last time you seen a ghost? What does Eagle do besides fly around and hunt for food and shit on everything down below?"

She covered her ears. "Jose, be careful!"

The fright in her voice angered him. "What happens when somebody who don't have the power calls on it?"

She moaned. "Oh, you wouldn't. You wouldn't dare."

"Wouldn't I? You believe in him so much, I'll call him down right now."

Consuela snatched up the infant and fled through the door. Jose plopped down at the table and sipped cold coffee turned bitter. Why'd he gone Asiatic like that? Scaring Consuela wouldn't make the baby any better. But ignorant superstition infuriated him. Somehow, he had to drag her into the Twentieth Century. She needed to get off the reservation. Get her eyes opened. Then they'd rear his children in the right way.

If his little girl was sick, they'd go to doctors who could listen to her insides with their machines and reach in and pull out what was ailing her. He wanted the kind of medicine man who cured terrible war wounds. Healing a sick baby would be easy for a power like that.

Jose was late getting to the construction site. The job didn't go well. He lost another workmate to an opening somewhere along the line while he remained on the shovel. When he asked about it, Pulkowski told him not to get uppity.

****

Consuela didn't return that night. If he hauled her home after the scare he'd given her, she'd just run away again as soon as he left for work. But one thing was for sure. Because of his bone-headed boast about calling down Eagle, Consuela was too terrified to go anywhere near Cane-Woman.

Jose sat on the front steps and chewed on a piece of bread and a boiled potato from the cooler as the night settled around him. All his life he'd been taught to fear the night and things that moved in darkness. Night duty in the Pacific had been sheer terror for him at first. There were things to fear all right, but they walked on two legs and carried guns and grenades and jabbered in a strange tongue.

The first time he'd stood night fire-watch—guard duty—his stomach twisted up. He hid in the shadows, unable to move a muscle. His top came looking for him and called him every name in the book, demanding to know why Jose hadn't challenged him properly. He'd said he wanted to make damned sure who was looking for him before he volunteered to be a target.

That earned him a reputation as one cool Devil Dog. They called him Big Chief and always wanted him to take the point on patrol. They thought his boots made no noise and left no trail and his eyes read tracks no one else could see. The fuckers believed their own stupid wild west picture shows. Still, he gloried in their back-handed admiration. Sure, he'd been the tip of the spear going downrange more often than not, but he came home alive while many didn't.

After finishing the potato, Jose drove into White Pine in hopes of sharing a beer or two with Beaver or Tomas, but it didn't take long to figure out nobody had any money for the bootlegger. Not only that, but Beaver seemed nettled Jose was working while he wasn't.

The big man looked him right in the eye—like he'd probably learned to do in the Army—and smiled. "Hell, you the one working, Cousin. You oughta be good for a beer or two."

He shrugged and lifted his hands. "Consuela took it all, you know for groceries."

"Where's Consuela at? Ain't seen her lately."

Jose's stomach rolled. His mother-in-law had probably told the whole reservation about him disrespecting Eagle. Had Cane-Woman heard? He broke out in a sweat. His voice was as hollow as an empty jerry can. "She's visiting her mama."

Beaver and Tomas proved thorny company, so he returned to the lonely house.

****

Jose lived each day by not thinking about the next one. His goal was to endure until noon. Then until the final whistle. Consuela hadn't come back even while he was at work. The house got messy. He tried to ignore the dust and clutter, but his Corps training kicked in, and he took a field day... he tidied his berth.

Stephens nagged him at work about his broken taillight. Loneliness weighed him down at home. He missed the baby more than his wife. Beaver grated on him. Tomas wasn't so bad, but he was weak, letting Beaver lead him around by the bottom lip.

The moment Jose had his paycheck in hand, the world turned right side up. He headed straight for Harry's and worked his way to the front of the line. He accepted his money and a beer and claimed a boulder behind the building where he spent the rest of the night drinking and buying beer for his buddies. A floating crap game drifted out back of the bar, and by the light of a pickup's headlamps the ivory cubes flew. The dice spoke against him more often than for him, but that wasn't important. He was with buddies, and that's what counted. Before long, he had trouble seeing and almost tipped over when he reached for the dice.

"Hey! Indian!" Jose saw Stephens through a gray haze. The man's voice was a wound in the side of the night. "Where's my five dollars?"

"In your pocket, I guess," He grinned, but the white man was too stupid to see the joke.

"Pulkowski!" Stephens bellowed. "Somebody get Ski 'fore I tear this redskin's head off."

The big foreman stalked through the yellow glow of headlights. "Now, boys, ain't no need to get bad blood up. Jose, last payday you broke this man's taillight, and if you was too beered up to remember, we'll all swear to it. Only

35

fair you pay for it."

They wanted his money. His money was his manhood, and they wanted to take it away. "Taillight don't cost no five dollars."

"Stephens, you got a receipt?" the foreman asked.

"You calling me a liar, Ski?"

The big man's eyebrows shot up. "Hell, no. But the Indian's got a point."

"I say it's a fiver, and that's what it is. You get it from him, or I'll take it for myself. And I won't be none too gentle about it, neither."

Time to leave. This man with the loud voice and sour face had ruined it all. Jose scooped up what was left of his money and started for his truck. Just as he reached for the door handle, rough hands jerked him around.

"You dirty, weaseling, red-bellied bastard!" Stephens yelled. "I'm gonna take five dollars outta your hide, and then I'm gonna take it outta your wallet."

Right in the middle of his backswing, Pulkowski grabbed the angry man. Anticipating the blow, Jose reeled backwards, lost his footing, and went to the deck. He came up and pivoted in a loose-limbed pirouette. His knuckles thudded against Stephen's temple. The man dropped without a sound.

"Christ!" Pulkowski swore. "You cold-cocked him."

Jose crawled into his truck and drove off. At home, he stripped, dropped his clothes where they fell, and crawled into bed without turning on the light. Most of the night he tossed fitfully, hanging onto a mattress that seemed to roll and buck like a canoe in white water.

The next morning, he discovered Consuela had paid him a visit during the night. His shirt and trousers were folded at the foot of the bed. His keys and billfold lay on the kitchen table. Two wrinkled dollar bills were all that remained of his paycheck. Consuela had left cigarette, gas, and eating money. She was good that way.

****

Saturday morning Jose dressed and drove to the jobsite. He needed that overtime bad enough to work through his hangover. After wasting five minutes looking for the little card with his name on it, he asked about it at the trailer, and was told to go see Pulkowski. He found the foreman at the jobsite.

"Yeah, Chief. What is it?"

"My card, Mr. Ski. It ain't at the clock."

"That's right. You been canned. Fired."

His jaw fell. "What for? I ain't no skater. I work hard for you."

"What for? Christ! You near kill one of our best equipment operators, and you ask me what for? That man's been with this outfit for over five years."

"But I was drunk!"

"Look, Geronimo, I don't play no favorites. I ain't got nothing against you.

You can believe that or not, but I really ain't. Take it like a man, kid."

"But I was *drunk!*" Didn't these white men understand anything? Hell, they'd covered for one another in the Corps. "A drunk man can't help what he does. Everybody knows that."

Pulkowski flushed. "What the hell kinda excuse is that? I swear you people are something else. Ain't never seen a skin who can handle alcohol. And if you can't handle it, you damned well better leave it alone. Ain't got time to stand here and argue. You're canned, and that's it. You got a week's time coming. Pick up your check at the office." The big man hesitated. "They gonna hold out the five you owe Stephens. Only way to keep him from calling the law. Look at it as the cost of busting his head open."

Jose gaped as the big man walked away. His head felt as if it would explode when he went to the trailer to collect his money. A pudgy clerk with soft hands made him wait before bringing his check.

Harry's Bar was practically deserted. The owner looked at the draft shrewdly. "Canned, huh? Happens to everybody, one time or the other."

Jose collected his cash and shoved a quarter across the counter. "Gimme a beer."

"Sure, Chief. But take it out back."

Chapter 7

On his way out of the *gowa*, Ro brushed the P-51 Mustang suspended from the roof by a thread of horsehair. The morning was bright and sunshiny; the paint, cranky.

"You oughta been born a jackass. Colorado wouldn't carry on like this." He bit his tongue at the mention of the big red. Two weeks of shying clear of the Chandler ranch hadn't shaken the pony from his mind.

He hung around the schoolyard long enough to earn a turn at bat, but softball wasn't getting at what bugged him. Where was Clarence Wolf? A good fight was what he needed, even if he took an ass whopping.

Ro took to the back of the paint and kicked the animal into what passed for a trot. He didn't think he was headed anywhere in particular, but he soon ran into the gate where they'd crossed over onto the rez that night he led Mr. Chandler to Blind Man's Arroyo.

As he drifted aimlessly along the wire, noises from over the next rise caught his ear. He dismounted and crept to the top of the hill. Two cowboys running fence in a pickup worked a stretch of loose wire. One man was so short he made the other look tall. They worked with a minimum of effort and a maximum of conversation. Often as not, they talked at the same time.

Taking advantage of natural cover the way Child-of-Water learned from Lizard, Ro settled down to watch and listen to the men bitch about the shortage of tobacco and chocolate and things. The short one griped about gasoline costing fifteen cents a gallon.

At length, the tall man straightened up and looked around. "Where's that kid?"

Startled, Ro froze.

"Damned if I know." The smaller man hit the horn on the pickup. "You'd think that cast would tether him. Paul's a pest one minute and a ghost the next."

The short honk drew the Indah boy out of a wash fifty yards up the fence line. Heaving his walking cast awkwardly, he shambled to the truck where the two men worked. He'd shed his crutches but carried a stick like a staff.

Ro slipped away, but he returned the next two days to stalk the crew again, now working rougher country by horseback. He learned the big, tow-headed man carried the named Wade. The feisty one was Pete.

Today, Paul didn't seem to be around, which killed the better part of Ro's interest. After a few minutes, he climbed aboard the paint to scout the area ahead of them. About fifty yards up the fence line, something caught his eye. In a small clearing on the ranch side of the fence, he spotted a red pony tied to a cottonwood. His red pony.

He reined in and called softly to Colorado. The pony danced and snickered. "Hey, boy! Was Paul riding the red? If so, where was he? Ro moved in on the pony like a prairie wolf stalking a lamb. The horse was just beyond his reach; the temptation, too great. He scaled the wire and laid a hand over Colorado's nose.

"Climb aboard and ride him." Ro looked up to find Paul perched on a limb.

"How'd you get up there in that cast?"

"Wasn't easy. Steady Colorado, will you?" Paul dropped from limb to limb, his heavy cast swinging like a pendulum, until he eased onto the horse's back and slid to the ground.

"How come you rode Colorado today?" Ro asked.

"The guys said somebody was hanging around and thought it was you. Why didn't you come over?" Ro shrugged. Paul shook his head. "You're an odd ball, you know that?"

Ro hopped aboard Colorado while Paul stomped away to recover Pedro. They rode aimlessly until noon, and then Paul talked him into going to eat with Pete and Wade.

"Caught him, I see," Pete said. "A feller can catch anything with the right bait. Glad to see it weren't no hostile scouting us. My scalp was starting to itch."

"Reckon they might both get a bit hostile, we don't offer 'em some grub."

Ro crammed down two sandwiches and would have tackled another, but strangers put a damper on his appetite.

That set a pattern for the next few days. Early each workday morning, Ro made for the ranch to tether the mare and change over to Colorado. The paint seemed content at her desertion.

Since Paul was supposed to be working, they often lent a hand before wandering off by themselves. Paul aped the two men, adding his voice to theirs. They jawed about everything: a big tsunami that hit Hawaii last April and killed over a hundred people. Some Japanese general who got executed in the Philippines. He'd apparently led the Bataan Death March, and that was a big deal in New Mexico because lots of their soldiers were in it... even some *Tinneh.*

Before long, Ro was an unofficial member of the crew. The men declared they couldn't have gotten along without him and flipped loose change his way.

At first, he stuffed himself with candy and soda pop, but before long, he began to think in a different way. Cane-woman had taken the turquoise ring to the trading post near White Pine. It was a fine ring, but sometimes even good jewelry stayed for a long time.

****

Saturday morning found him stalking the aisles of the barn-like building. He scanned the case of Navajo and Pueblo jewelry, and there it was, the finest of all the rings in a counter crammed full of them.

"What can I do for you, sonny?" A deep voice startled him. "Candy's over on the other side of the store."

He stared at the fat white man behind the counter. Round, rimless glasses made the trader's eyes look too big for a face made up of eyes, jowls, and mouth. His nose, a tiny tube of flesh, looked like an afterthought.

Ro pointed. "That's my ring."

"Whoa. Alla them rings belong right where they are. Which one you talking about?"

"That one." He tapped the glass counter with a fingernail.

The trader pulled out the ring and adjusted his glasses, furrowing his brow while he studied a tiny slip of paper attached to it. "This ring just came out of pawn. You say it's yours?"

He nodded. "But my grandmother took it away."

"You're Cane-Woman's grandson?"

He nodded again, surprised this *Indah* knew her Indian name.

"You don't say. Well, sonny, you gotta understand it ain't your ring anymore. You want it back, you gotta pay for it. I got it marked at twenty dollars. But seeing it was yours, you give me six, and I'll let you have it back. Lowest I'd go for anybody else is fifteen, cash money. And that's a good price too. It's an expensive ring. You got six dollars, boy?" The man studied him. "I see. Well, how much you got?" His gross hand cupped the coins Ro dropped into his palm. "You about four-fifty shy, son. What's your name?"

"Ro, uh Román."

"You ain't got enough money, Román."

"I'll get some more, but I gotta have my ring back."

"You got some kinda job?"

He nodded. "I help some cowboys fix fences, and they give me money for it."

"Tell you what. You leave this dollar-fifty with me, and I'll keep the ring for thirty days. Won't sell it to nobody else. I'll just keep it safe. You bring the rest of the money inside thirty days, and it's yours."

The man laughed, and the wooden floor squeaked in protest. "I'm not gonna do you outta your money. Look, I'll make a note right on this tag. Received from Román one dollar and fifty cents on account." He took a pencil from his pocket and wrote on the slip.

40

****

Ro stayed close and worked with Pete and Wade for the next two weeks. On the weekends he took what the cowboys gave him and managed to increase his money by winning half a dozen foot races. By the time Paul was out of a cast and into a brace, Ro had the money he needed. Lucky, because once Paul was liberated, the white boy insisted on riding and climbing everything in sight.

A few days later, Paul reached inside Ro's shirt and drew out the ring strung on a string around his neck. Then he pulled out his own and held it beside the other one. Silver winked in the sunlight; turquoise glowed.

The next morning, Pete called them back as they were about to ride off and tossed over a new bar of Benchley's. "Ro, the boss said to give this to you."

He grinned. "Come on, we gonna have some fun." He dug his heels into Colorado's flanks and made straight for the nearest water tank with Paul close on his heels. Ro dismounted and jerked off his shirt. The soap was almost too pretty to put in water. The pale green cube was hard and sleek with fancy letters and a man's profile embossed on each side.

"Soap!" Paul said. "For cripes sakes, it's just a bar of soap."

Ro dunked the bar and started lathering. "Come on, you can have some fun too."

"Fun? All you're doing is taking a bath. Some fun."

"It is. Me'n Mr. Chandler had real good fun the other day."

Paul's jaw dropped. "*My* dad? When?"

"The day we flew the airplane." His head and torso a solid mass of white foam, Ro kicked off his sneakers and shinnied out of his pants before hopping into the water.

"He do that too? Get in the tank?"

"Uh-huh."

"That blows me away." Paul removed his brace, stripped, and crawled into the tank. Disdaining the soap, Paul spread his arms and floated on his back. Like his father, he was two-toned.

Ro soaped up and splashed the suds off a couple of times, grinning like he was showing off a new set of store-bought teeth. Bored, Paul dunked Ro, kicking off a water fight.

The Chandler boy crawled gingerly out of the water and dried off with his shirt. Ro had to help him with his brace. "Come on, I'll show you my favorite place," Paul said.

Harrigan's Butte began as a gentle swelling of the desert, growing so that sweat shone on Colorado's flanks before they reached the mass of bald rock

41

jutting into the sky. The fifty-foot climb was almost too much for Paul's weak leg, but he kept at it.

The top of the mesa, flat and practically free of vegetation, covered roughly the size of two football fields. This afternoon, it became an aircraft carrier defending against a Japanese kamikaze attack. Later, they sprawled near the rim of the butte to rest.

"Your people have a name for this place?" Paul asked.

Ro nodded. "Sleeping Turtle Mesa."

"I like that better. Wonder why it's Harrigan's Butte on the map?"

"It's a white man's map."

"Yeah, guess it is." Paul poked at twin rows of busy ants. "How'd they get up here?"

"Same way we did, I guess," Ro said.

"Man, it would take a couple of generations to climb up here. Busy little devils. I wonder if they're pissants? I think I'll see. I need to go anyway."

Ro sat up quickly. "Don't do that!"

"Why not?"

He squirmed beneath Paul's curious gaze. "Just don't."

"That's no answer." The older youth stood and popped the buttons to his Levis.

Ro scrambled to his feet, his hands balled into fists, his stance stiff. "It's bad luck!"

Paul turned away from the ants to urinate. "Never heard that one before," His back to Ro, he shook himself off, buttoned up, and addressed the double row of busy insects. "You guys better be thankful he's superstitious. I'd have drowned half of you."

As they sat studying the palette of vivid colors building in the sky to the west, Paul picked up a rock and made marks in the dirt. "What you wanna be when you grow up?"

Ro opened his mind, but no image came. "I dunno."

Paul lay on his stomach and rested his chin on the backs of sun-bronzed hands. "I'm gonna be a lawyer and help people. Even your people. Lawyer. You know what that is, right?"

"Sorta like a policeman? We got a couple of them on the reservation, but they don't help you much. They might bust your head for you."

"Not like that. If you sue someone in court or someone sues you, you do it through lawyers. They make lots of money and run the state and everything. They've got a fancy name too… attorney. Attorneys-at-law, they call them. Why don't you be a lawyer too?"

The white man's court wasn't any place Ro wanted to be. "Maybe I'll be a rancher and have a big herd… big enough to feed the whole reservation. I'd feed everybody. Except, Clarence Wolf."

"Who's that?"

"My enemy. I call him Clare-Ass."

"You have a sworn enemy? How big is he?"

"As big as you."

"I'll take care of him for you," Paul promised. "How come he doesn't like you?"

"Cause I'm littler'n he is. He's a bully. I put up a fight, but when he gets me cornered, I'm a goner."

Paul grimaced and returned to the subject of the future. "Gee, you really want to be a rancher? Anybody can punch cows, but if you want to help your people, a lawyer's just the thing. You guys wouldn't have lost your land if you'd had a few good lawyers."

"More providers woulda been better."

"Providers?"

"You guys call them warriors," Ro said.

"Nuts! One good lawyer's worth a hundred warriors, any day."

"Probably takes a lot of school learning, and I'm not good at school."

"Man, you gotta get in there and hustle. Schooling's the answer to everything." Paul frowned. "Crap, I sound just like my mother."

Ro turned inward. The whites always wanted to teach you something, and Paul was as white as last year's schoolteacher. "You're an *Indah*. Why would you help my people?"

"I'd help anyone who wasn't being treated fair whether they could pay me or not. *Pro bono* work, they call it." Paul squinted. "What do you mean I'm an *Indah*? What's an *Indah*?"

"An... outsider. Can somebody who's not *Indah* be one of those lawyers?"

Paul chuckled. "*Indah*. That's like calling us whitey so we don't know it. That's rich. But sure, anybody can be a lawyer if he tries hard enough."

Paul turned on his back and cradled his head in clasped hands. "The way I see it, I'll fool around until you graduate so we can go to college together. Even room together."

Ro's stomach flip-flopped, but he didn't know why. "Does it cost a lot of money?"

"I guess it does." The setback was only temporary. "I'll bet dad would lend it to you."

"Why would he do that? But maybe I can work for him. You know... for money."

"Sure. Okay, after college we'll open a law office and be lawyers together. Anybody who'd fight me over pissing on pissants has gotta make one hell of a defense attorney."

Chapter 8

A weather front rolled east across the desert spilling virga—streaks of evaporating moisture. Once across NM35, the rising landmass slowed the wet, black clouds, allowing ragged mountain peaks to gouge holes in vaporous undersides. Firmly impaled, they cried themselves into oblivion in torrents of rain.

Ro lay wrapped in a blanket listening to the storm moan over its approaching doom. Orange flames in the firepit released the pungent aroma of stew, making the *gowa* warm and sapid. The rattle of rain against the roof made his eyes heavy, but thoughts of yesterday's visit to Sleeping Turtle Mesa kept him from slipping over the edge.

Paul claimed they were friends and that seemed too fast. Was the *indah* boy a wizard? Paul had given him a new name. Did that mean Román was gone? No, that's who he was on the reservation. Román was still around, but so was Ro. Had the white boy split him in two? Course, he had another name. Roan Orphan, the one given him at birth.

"Grandmother, does God have a son?"

"The *Indah* ain't talking to you about their god, is they?"

"No, but the ranch hands are always calling Jesus Christ. They claim he's God's son who died but got up and came back. He sure looks dead hanging on that cross down at the church."

Suddenly aware they'd called this spirit by his true name, Ro put ashes to his forehead and ears. The old woman dropped a clump of sacred sage into the fire. Jesus had been gone a long, long time, but better safe than sorry.

He pursued his line of thought. "Does God damn everything they ask him to?"

"For them that's got the power, he's apt to," Cane-Woman said. "Like them black robes at the church. They got black souls, you know. *Indah* are little people on the inside."

"Can little-on-the-inside-people make cars and build big buildings and fly and...."

She stared at him so hard he shut his mouth.

"That's what's big to you, then you ain't *Tinneh*. Our ancestors was big people. Our leaders listened to everybody, and after they listened enough, they had their say on the matter. Their words was true because they was right thinking and right talking men. Wouldn't nobody follow them if they spoke false."

"My schoolteacher says anybody can say anything and be anything he wants."

"Them's words for white skins. They don't touch us. But hear *these* words. The time'll come when you set off down a path and find it closed because you are *Tinneh*."

Seemed like they'd strayed from the subject just so she could preach at him again. Outside, the wind eased. Heavy raindrops fell straight from the sky. Some found the smoke hole and sputtered in the fire. He listened to the rain until he floated toward sleep, vaguely wondering why she hadn't pestered him about the red horse. Likely because the saddle had fetched a good price. That meant the animal was like money in a white man's bank waiting to be spent.

****

The next morning, he cleaned up after his run in the wet, clay-heavy mountains, ate, and sneaked off to the ranch where he and Paul found a muddy arroyo with running water that needed wading in. When Paul got hungry, they took off to catch up with Pete and Joe.

After stuffing down some smoked beef sandwiches, they worked fences for a couple of hours. Ro needed some money. He was walking out of his worn sneakers and wanted a pair of cowboy boots. But the silver shower of earlier in the summer had slowed the minute Paul got unshackled from his cast and insisted on playing instead of working.

Mid-afternoon, Paul talked Ro into going to see his new model B-17 bomber. Paul's sister came out of the house as they rode up to the corral.

"Mother, Paul's back," she yelled over her shoulder. "And that Indian kid's with him."

"He's got a name, you know," Paul snapped. She stuck her tongue out and vanished inside. "Brat!" he muttered.

Paul slammed the bedroom door, but they barely had time to examine the model airplane before Teresa barged into the room.

"Mother said for you to let me play too,"

"Buzz off. Don't you know what a closed door means?"

"Not supposed to close it when you have company."

"Oh, go—"

"Ahmmm! You better not say a naughty word."

Paul gave up in disgust. "Come on, Ro, let's go outside."

Teresa clapped her hands. "Goodie! I'd rather play outside."

Paul scooped up an air rifle on the way through the door. Teresa stuck like a goathead to socks. "You ever shoot one of these?" Paul asked when they

45

were in the front yard.

"A BB gun? Sure," Ro said.

"Uh-uh. It's a pellet gun. You pump it before you shoot it. The more you pump, the harder it shoots. Lots stronger than a BB gun and shoots straighter too. And it's quiet. Good weapon to ambush commies with. You know, those red b—" He eyed his sister. "Those Russians trying to take over the world."

Teresa jumped up and down. "Dibs on first turn!"

"First turn, my ass," Paul said with a sneer.

Her mouth fell open. "Paul Ryan Chandler! I'm gonna tell."

He grabbed her arm. "Okay, first turn, but you better not tell, or I'll pound you in a hole."

"I oughta get three first turns," she said.

"You have to pump it yourself."

"You know I can't."

"Tough ti—" Paul bit down on his tongue.

Teresa squinted. "Four turns."

"I didn't say nothing."

"You almost did. That meant you were thinking it."

"But I didn't say it, so you can't prove it. Pump your own gun, smarty."

"I'll do it for her," Ro said.

Paul pulled a face. "Let me handle her."

He handled her so well she got an even dozen first turns. As Teresa popped cans with fair accuracy, Ro lifted his shirt and unwound the leather slingshot he carried whenever he could remember. Together they kept the targets rolling across the ground.

Teresa dropped the rifle in the grass and pointed to the sling. "I wanna try that."

Paul struggled for self-control. "Oh, go…suck an egg. You've been a pest for long enough. Go practice being a witch on somebody else."

Ro looked from brother to sister. Now was a good time to be somewhere else.

Teresa fixed Ro with a stare. "Show me. Pretty please."

"Oh, for cripes sake, go on and get it over with." Paul started pinging away with the rifle.

On Teresa's first try, the stone went straight up in the air, scattering everyone as it fell. When she was less of a menace, Paul handed the air gun to Ro. The weapon felt good against his shoulder. Heavy and solid, the rifle fired with a hissing noise. Shooting the thing was great, but pumping it was a pain. A sudden ruckus distracted him.

Paul tugged on one end of the sling; Teresa hung onto the other. "Dammit, let go!"

"You...took the name of...the Lord...in vain!" the girl said in an unsteady voice as she flew over half the lawn. "I'm—"

"Oh no! No more blackmail. You let go. I wanna try it now." He jerked hard, pulling her against a small poplar. Turning disaster into triumph, Teresa wrapped the end of the leather sling around the sapling.

"Now, smarty! Just try and take it away from me." She snatched a sharp rock from the border of a small flowerbed at her feet. "You take one step, I'll cut it up!"

Paul froze. "Grab her, Ro."

He had no intention of grabbing anybody, but Teresa didn't wait to find out. She slashed the leather thong and ran for the house.

"Aw, gee. I'm sorry." Paul picked up the ruined sling. "Can you make another one?"

"Sure." He had no idea where he'd find a leather strap.

"Why didn't you grab her arm? She won't break. Come on, there's some leather in the tack room."

Mr. Chandler rode up and dismounted as they were working the stiffness out of the new leather. Paul nudged Ro. "Now's a good time to talk to him about working."

"What's up, fellas?" Mr. Chandler paused a moment. "Paul, your mother's calling you."

Paul looked like he nursed a sudden gas pain as he left. "Ro wants to talk to you."

"Let's go to the office where we can relax. I've been on that bronc too much today."

The place Mr. Chandler called his office had an outside door with a brass knob so shiny Ro could see himself in it. But it made his nose too big and his chin too little. The room looked like a man's room, with a walnut desk, a metal cabinet, a small couch, and two leather chairs.

"Sit down." Mr. Chandler dropped into the chair behind the desk and filled a pipe from a humidor. In a few minutes, a pleasant aroma tickled Ro's nostrils. Nothing like Cane-Woman's stinky tobacco. "Pete and Wade tell me you've been helping out." When Ro nodded, he went on. "They tell me you've been a big help."

He wished the man would keep talking. Sounded good in his ears and felt good in his heart. But it came to an end. "Paul said you wanted to talk to me. What about?"

Ignoring the invitation to sit, Ro stood before the wide desk, one finger timidly caressing the oiled grain. His head rattled emptily. Were his shoes getting Mr. Chandler's bright Navajo rugs dirty?

"I hear you've been riding Colorado. Like him?"

47

Ro nodded. He could talk about the big pony. "He's a good horse."

"The best," Mr. Chandler agreed. "We'll keep him healthy for you. Or is that what you wanted to talk about? Are you ready to take him home?"

"No!" Had he betrayed his fear? He opened his mouth. Nothing came out. His eyes fixed on the huge painting of a brooding warrior hanging behind the desk. Wasn't Apache. Comanche or Kiowa, maybe.

"Go on, don't be nervous." Mr. Chandler pulled on his pipe and rested the curved stem in the corner of his mouth.

"Paul...Paul and me...." His lips went dry; his heart hammered. "He was telling me about school."

"School? You mean high school?" Ro shook his head, and the man went on. "College? Any particular college?"

Was there more than one? He shook his head again. "Do you... do you think I can go too?" Muscles on either side of his mouth pulled his lips into a frown.

Mr. Chandler leaned forward, elbows on the desk. "I think you can do anything you want if you're willing to work hard. I mean give it a really good try. It isn't easy. And you have to start right now so you'll be ready when the time comes."

He swallowed hard. "It takes money, I guess." He tried to wet his lips, but his tongue was dry. "Uh... I was thinking... if I could work for you, I could save some money so I can go to school." He dropped his gaze to his hand resting on the rancher's desk. He snatched it away.

The man nodded. "I can use some more help around the ranch. Of course, you'll need your grandmother's permission. But if she says it's all right, we can work something out."

He felt weightless.

Paul was boiling when Ro came outside. "That Teresa! After all those free turns, she snitched. Well, did you ask him?"

He told Paul of the conversation.

"She oughta be okay with it. Your grandma can't object to you making a little moolah."

Ro kept his mouth shut. She'd shown signs of impatience lately. She hadn't said anything—and he wasn't about to ask—but he figured she was fed up with his ranch time. She'd found out he rescued his ring but hadn't said anything about it... yet.

Paul slapped him on the back. "That's it, then. We're on our way. We're gonna be lawyers. Man, think about it. Lawyers."

****

Ro didn't get Cane-Woman's permission, but Mr. Chandler never asked about it, so he didn't have to lie. He did his run each morning before going to the ranch. Mr. Chandler put him to work running fences with Pete and Wade just like before, but now Ro was getting paid. At night, he buried cramped fingers in his armpits to ease the ache. The old pair of leather work gloves Pete gave him made things better, except they fell off when he wasn't paying attention. Paul joined the crew occasionally but always showed up around quitting time so they could play.

One day, they worked together on a come-along jack stretching wire when Paul froze. "Varmint," he whispered. "Other side of the fence. Hold on." Paul walked to Pedro and pulled his pellet gun from a scabbard he'd taken to carrying on his saddle.

Ro scanned the far side of the fence, seeing nothing but hearing movement. Out of the corner of his eye, he saw Paul raise the air gun.

"Wait!" he yelled.

The gun hissed as Ro's mare walked into the open. She squealed and shied into a tree.

Ro dropped everything and scooted through the fence to take off after the pinto on foot.

Chapter 9

When Ro didn't show up for work the next day, Paul went to his father and explained what had happened. "What if he doesn't come back?" Paul asked.

"Would that matter?"

"Yeah, it would. I like him, Dad."

"Why?"

"He's different from my other friends."

"He comes from a different culture. Is that it? You're the Lone Ranger, and Ro's your Tonto? Someone you can wrap around your little finger."

Paul snickered. "Ro's not anybody's Tonto." He went serious. "He's flexible, but I don't see him as wrappable. I get the feeling we can teach one another a lot. And he'll be a friend a fella can count on." He shot his father a look. "You like him too."

"I do. I see a kid who's floundering. A good kid worth helping... without smothering."

"Think I oughta go look him up? You know, over there?"

"Couldn't hurt. If the mare's injured, we need to get her to a vet."

"Can somebody drive me? Or maybe I can drive myself... you know on the back roads."

"Afraid not. You and your pellet gun got you into this. You have to get yourself out. But I'll give you the key to the padlock on the gate, so you don't have to take the long way."

****

Uncertain how badly Ro's mare was injured, Paul saddled both Pedro and Colorado and set off for the reservation gate with the big red in tow. Ro had talked about Rising Rock several times, so Paul had little trouble locating the bluff a mile east of White Pine.

Upon entering the grove below the cliff, Paul ignored a tipi and a small frame house, making straight for what appeared to be a big pile of brush. He didn't know what he'd expected, but this wasn't it. No one was in sight, yet a pot boiled over a small fire near the brush shelter.

"Hello! Anybody here? Ro?" No answer. Movement in the teepee across the clearing drew his attention. When he turned back to the wickiup, Paul almost jumped out of his boots. A woman stood at the entrance leaning on a stout, black stick—a woman so old and wrinkled and emaciated he thought of a cadaver. His pulse raced. He swiped at the sudden moisture on his upper lip. "How do, ma'am. Name's Paul Chandler, and I'm looking for Ro...uh, Román Otero."

Hooded black eyes scanned him from head to toe. The woman was so infirm she trembled. Or maybe she was mad about the mare. His buttocks pimpled.

Her stare fixed on the big red for an instant. "He ain't here."

"You know where I can find him?" She shuffled forward to drop something into the pot over the fire. Eye of newt? Toe of frog? "Uh... Ro didn't come to work today, and we got worried. Will you please tell him Paul came by?" Despite the old woman's obvious frailty, he sensed strength. His hands shook as he left, and that both puzzled and pissed him off.

He rode the wagon track back toward the settlement, Colorado still in tow. A quarter of a mile out of White Pine, he met Ro walking along the dusty road carrying a shoebox tied with string. Ro stopped and stood his ground until Colorado nuzzled his shoulder.

"You decide to take the day off? Where's the mare? Dad said he'd take her to a vet."

Ro shrugged. "The man at the store knows about things like that. Said she won't be no good anymore. He gave me a dollar and a pair of tennis shoes for her."

Paul tossed Colorado's reins over. "You shoulda called to say you weren't coming in."

Remaining mute, Ro mounted, and they headed back to Rising Rock.

Paul sighed. "Look man, what happened was my fault. I'm really sorry."

Ro slid off Colorado's back and walked into the forest.

"Wait!" Paul dismounted and caught up. "It's not so bad. You've got Colorado. Ride him to work instead of the mare."

"No place to put him. Colorado's too good. Somebody'll steal him if I let him run loose."

"We can build a corral right near your hou... wickiup. I'll help you. You got an axe?"

"Hatchet and some rope."

Ro's grandmother was nowhere in sight as they trimmed brush and strung rope between saplings behind the wickiup. Finally, Paul cast a critical eye on the corral they'd rigged.

"Oughta hold him. Later, we can make it more permanent. Add a shed. Man, I'm thirsty." He sat down with his back against a tree.

Ro took off and returned with a bowl of water and a couple of jerky strips. While Paul drank and gnawed on a piece of dark meat, his companion flopped down in the dirt and hacked the ground with the hatchet. Paul tried to wait him out but failed.

"You're coming back to work, aren't you?"

Ro shrugged.

"For Pete's sake, you gonna crap out on me? Fine best friend you turned out to be." The anger building in Ro's eyes died. "Didn't you know that? Hell, we were going to be *lawyers* together." Ro kept chopping the ground, but Paul figured he'd scored some points. "Well, are you?"

Ro exhaled audibly. "Too late today."

"Yeah, Pete and Wade'd start yelling about Indian time."

They got up and brushed off their jeans. Ro buried the hatchet blade in a sapling. "I guess you're mine too. My friend."

Paul fixed him with a stare and experienced a flash of insight. "That was hard to say, wasn't it."

"Not good at it. Anytime I've tried to have friends, it didn't work out too good."

"Well, you got one now… for life. Let's do something to show we're really friends. I know, we'll be blood brothers. Mix your blood with mine like they do in the movies."

"I guess. Sometime."

"Not sometime. Now." Paul held up his pocketknife. Slowly, as if it were some kind of ritual he held the blade against his thumb. Closing his eyes, he jabbed. Ro took the knife and did the same thing. Then they hooked thumbs.

Something moved in Paul's chest. "It's done, buddy. We're bound. Whatever happens to one, happens to the other. Only death can release us."

Chapter 10

Ro finished his morning run and filled five one-gallon tins from a freshet called Rising Rock Spring at the base of the yellow bluff. Cane-Woman boiled their clothes and blankets in a black cauldron, but Ro cleaned up in cold water every morning, except when he occasionally heated a tin of water and took it into the *gowa* for a warm-water bath.

The new school year would start Monday, and while that was going to seriously get in the way of work, it might make cleaning up easier. Last year, the showers in the boy's locker room were usually empty after class. Maybe he could sneak in and use some of their hot water. Other than that, there wasn't anything he liked about school.

His mind turned to heavier matters. He wasn't going to be able to hide his pay from Cane-Woman much longer, but when Mr. Chandler gave him fifteen dollars for the loss of the mare, the solution slid uninvited right into his mind. He asked the rancher to hold onto it for him. After coming to grips with the upside-down fact he trusted the *Indah* more than Cane-Woman, he built on the idea and asked the rancher to keep half his weekly pay as savings. He'd turn the rest over to his grandmother... except soda pop and candy money.

Pretty soon, his pay was gonna take a hit. Sunset was a long time coming in August, but darkness showed up earlier and earlier as the year got older. Soon, he'd barely get in enough hours to make the ride to the ranch worthwhile.

****

Like it did every week, Monday morning rolled around, and twenty-four fourth graders and nineteen fifth graders crammed into a single room at White Pine Elementary and shared the same teacher. Ro liked the fifth grade even less than the fourth. Miss Alicia Penny—the teacher quickly dubbed Miss One Cent—was new. The old ones were better because they'd given up trying to change everyone.

Each hour he sat at the hard desk-chair—which made his bottom itch—was an hour he wasn't at the ranch where he was out in the open. The school room was crowded and stuffy. The only relief they got was by opening windows.

This teacher didn't mess around. She started right off with a test to find out what everyone already knew. By then, they'd learned a couple of things about her too. She didn't understand *Tinneh* and wasn't too strict about enforcing the ban on speaking it at school.

His unusual name meant he'd be called upon to read aloud more often.

When his turn came on that first day, he stood, shuffled his feet, and stammered so the teacher wouldn't think he was someone special. That brought him face-to-face with a perplexing problem. He had to learn if he was going to college, but he wasn't about to get labeled teacher's pet. Especially by this woman who squinted through glasses shaped like rain drops laid sideways. He'd have to learn without letting it show.

Ro hurried through a shower after last class, and was about to rush out of the locker room when voices outside the door stopped him.

"Well, how was your first day?" someone asked.

"Hectic," a voice that belonged to Miss One Cent answered. "But they're beautiful children."

"About a third of them I'd like to hug," the first woman said. "About a third I'd like to strangle. And the rest I'd like to strangle with a hug. They're adorable children, but by the time they're ten or eleven, they're so far behind it's hopeless. Sixty percent of them will never finish high school. I doubt if a single one graduates from college. We need more Native teachers."

"What difference would that make?" Miss One Cent asked.

"Trust. We haven't earned much of it. All they see is us trying to take their children away from them. Turning their minds around, they call it."

"What a pity. Well, thank you for the talk, Mrs. Goodert."

So old Miz Thin Nose was talking to the new teacher. He waited until he thought both women were gone and darted out the door, almost colliding with Miss One Cent, who stood tapping her folded glasses against her lips like she'd been thinking.

Well, hello there! Don't I know you? Aren't you one of my students?"

"Yes, ma'am." He tossed the words over his shoulder and ran as fast as he could for the exit. He made it outside without anyone calling him back. A narrow escape.

****

As soon as he walked into the classroom the next morning Miss One Cent fixed him with a stare. She'd figured out he was the kid running in the hall yesterday, so he was in big trouble. She'd send him to the office where they had a paddle with holes drilled in it.

She fooled him by asking her students what they wanted to be when they grew up. Ro lost his head and said "lawyer" when his turn came, earning him a strange look from the teacher. All the other boys had said they wanted to be cowboys and loggers and rodeo hands. But dumbass him had said lawyer. That was a white man's job. Now, for sure, he was in trouble.

The long day ended without a trip to the principal's office, but as he started to leave after the final bell, Miss One Cent stopped him to say there was a book in the library about lawyers he could read. He shook his head and kept on walking.

Ro headed straight to the ranch and pitched in to help. Before long, Paul hauled up on Pedro and dumped a heavy sack at his feet.

"Feed. Colorado's gonna need it."

Nuts. He'd have to hold out money to feed his pony. Darkness fell before Ro got home.

"Where you been?" Cane-Woman asked. "That stupid school was over long time ago."

"Went to work."

"Don't the one foolishness put an end to the other? Ain't you got your fill of whites?"

"I gotta work so I can bring you money. We got more to eat now. And I got pants and stuff for school. And clothes for you too."

"If I'd a wanted it easy, I'd a left you on an anthill when you was born. Don't claim you working to make it easy on me. You're a fool. How come you don't listen when I talk? They wanna make you act like a white, but you ain't one. They'll hold it agin you one a these days."

****

Ro fell into a pattern that wasn't broken until October when it was time to gather the J-Bar-C yearlings steers for sale. On the Friday morning the gathering was to start, he told his grandmother he was going camping, rolled up his blankets, and mounted Colorado. He skipped school and rode through the pre-dawn darkness straight for the ranch.

Mr. Chandler gave him a long look, and Ro thought sure the man was gonna send him to school. Instead, the boss motioned him over to the stable. They were only taking four spare horses, hardly a real remuda, but he put Ro in charge of them, and that was reason enough for pride. The crew— augmented by two cowboys hired for the gathering—spent the remainder of the day in the saddle. They emptied out three pastures and collected a sizeable herd by the time sundown overtook them.

Everyone saw to his own gear and personal mount after supper. Ro fed and watered Colorado and the spare animals and hobbled them on a short string. By the time he was finished, the men had collected around the campfire. He settled down in his bedroll. Although tired and chock-full of beans and chili, he kept his ears open. Tales tossed around the campfire were like cones on a pine, they made it perfect. He didn't even care he'd been eating dust behind the remuda. One day he'd be a drag rider, and then a line rider.

Ro drifted off to sleep with voices warming his ears and a campfire toasting his toes. The herd shifting about midnight and the nighthawk singing

55

to calm the cattle half-roused him. He was so beat the thought of owls and whippoorwills and ghosts didn't ruffle his feathers.

All was oblivion until Chuck Griggs rousted everyone before dawn. Ro tumbled out of his warm blankets into the cold air to gulp a quick breakfast and help the cowboys pick their mounts for the day.

The camp was in full swing by the time Mr. Chandler and Paul rode up. Then they cleared the rest of the pastures and reached the pens alongside the highway late in the afternoon where the agent for some Texas feedlot was waiting. Paul and Ro joined the cowboys hazing the bawling cattle into loading pens and prodding them up ramps into long trailers. The sun was low when the last gate slammed and heavy diesel motors throbbed to life.

As the big trucks followed the buyer's dusty sedan down the highway, the rancher reined in beside Ro. "Well, how was your first gathering?"

A broad smile split his face. "Great, Mr. Chandler."

"There'll be lots more of them."

Ro watched him ride away. He hadn't known a man's back grew so broad.

Chapter 11

Jose's mocking of Eagle drove Consuela away for a whole month. He stood in the kitchen in his shorts one afternoon when the screen door banged. He turned to see a nervous Consuela holding Mary Sue. His heart took a leap, but his tongue turned sour.

"What you doing here?"

She flinched. "I can go if you want me to."

He walked over and hugged the two of them. Consuela felt good against him. She moved away and put Mary Sue in the crib. Then he gathered her in his arms and took care of his craving. Hers too, from the way she reacted to him.

But it didn't take long before another argument over Cane-Woman drove him out of the house and into town to look for work. Finding none, he did a few chores at the bar for Harry, earning enough to take Consuela and Mary Sue to a doctor in Terreon.

After waiting an hour for a ten-minute session with the medicine man, they left only half-understanding what the tall, spare medic told them. All Jose knew was, he needed to buy medicine for something called bronchitis. Once they left the drug store, he was broke again.

The next morning, Jose went on another fruitless job-hunt in Estrella, the only other nearby town of any size. By the time he got home that afternoon, his wife had given the baby half the medication in the bottle. If a little was good, a lot was better. The child was so listless Consuela refused to touch the medicine again. After that, he dosed the baby.

Mary Sue got worse, but without money for the town doctor, he bent his neck and took the girl to the clinic at White Pine. The wait was longer than it had been at the white doctor's, but the silver-haired medic fussed over the baby at least an hour before sitting down with them.

"Mr. and Mrs. Peyote, I don't have good news. Mary Sue has a disease called tuberculosis. We need more tests, and those have to be done in a hospital. The sooner the better."

Jose's blood ran cold. Consumption had taken his two brothers.

"Where?" he heard his frightened wife ask.

"Albuquerque. The agency will make all the arrangements and provide transportation. I can't tell you how important time is."

Mistrust infected Jose's mind. White doctors had saved *Marines*. "How come the doctor in Terreon didn't tell us that?" he asked.

"I can't answer your question, but if you wish, we can get another opinion."

Jose closed his mind and took his daughter home where Consuela cried herself to sleep. The baby just cried.

He went to see Harry and begged for work so he could take Mary Sue to the Terreon doctor again. The barman made it plain Jose was becoming a pain in the ass. The blood drained from his face when he got home. Consuela and Mary Sue were gone. With his heart in his stomach, he defied convention and went straight to his mother-in-law's house, confirming his suspicions. Consuela and her mother had taken Mary Sue to Cane-Woman.

He drove to Rising Rock, but the witch's hut was deserted. Jose stifled his panic. If Consuela and her mother were looking from a healing from Cane-Woman, the old woman would need time to set it up. Sometimes it took weeks of preparation. But if *any* kind of a healing was taking place, someone would know about it. It galled him Beaver was the one who told him where.

"I hear it's a rush-job, man. Grabbed a drummer and a singer, and headed for the bushes," his friend finished. "You didn't know nothing about it?"

Drumbeats reached his ears a mile from the ceremonial tipi. Halfway there, two of Consuela's brothers and one of her cousins blocked the road with a pickup. He got out of his truck and tried to argue his way past them. When that failed, he took them on. He fought savagely, but they overpowered him, beating him until he didn't have the strength to resist. He tried to run them down with the pickup, but they pulled him out of the cab and left him unconscious.

Somewhat recovered, he drove to the police station in White Pine. The officer—a chubby ex-schoolmate he'd never liked— went round-eyed when Jose told him what he wanted.

"You want *me* to go break up that old woman's ceremony? No way, brother. I don't got a death wish. Besides, your wife can take the girl anywhere she wants."

He tried to file an assault complaint against her brothers and cousin, but the policeman just smirked. Jose remembered the man belonged to the same clan as his in-laws.

****

The next day, he learned the health people had come for Mary Sue at his mother-in-law's house and took her away. Consuela came back home, but they were strangers. Neither gave the other what was needed. The agency people made them take tests to see if they had the disease. They weren't infected, but Jose felt sick just the same. The house was empty without the baby.

Two weeks later, an agency man came to say Mary Sue was dead.

Jose's mind went away. He found himself up on Wandering Water where he fasted and prayed and took ritual baths in the river. During the night, he heard sounds of war and relived the terror of Peleliu. In the daylight hours, he thought about his daughter without calling her name aloud. His last night on the river, an owl kept him awake. A loon's wail sounded like a baby's cry. Goosebumps washed over him. Was his little girl coming for him?

When Jose returned home after the fourth day, Consuela didn't even ask where he'd been. She just sat like a stone. Did she expect punishment for taking the baby to Cane-Woman? Her meddling mother was to blame for that.

Jose hated his mother-in-law, loathed the reservation, and despised the settlement. He had to get out of there or he'd throttle the old woman and take a knife to his wife's brothers. The only period of his life he could recall with any pleasure was in California when he was in the Corps. It was good then, so it would be good now. Time to head west.

He had no money for the trip, so he spent the afternoon trying to wheedle some from Harry. After stringing him along for hours, the barman forked over a five-dollar bill. Not nearly enough to get to California.

As he sat on a boulder behind the bar trying to figure how to come up with the rest of the poke he needed, an Air Force enlisted man staggered down the path to the outdoor privy. When the man failed to return, Jose found him passed out beside the toilet. The temptation was too much. He eased the drunk's billfold out of his pocket and took the ten singles tucked inside.

He didn't know anything about the Air Force, but if they paid like the Marines, the air jockeys oughta have enough loot to finance the trip. He drove to a bar east of Terreon that snagged the flyboy trade from the White Sands Missile Range.

Like Harry's, the "Missile Inn" had a "No Indians Allowed" sign, so he hung around outside, approaching people as they arrived or left the joint. There were no easy pickings; he had to work for the money. He'd managed to panhandle another five dollars before running into a squat man with a bunch of chevrons on his arm who got in his face and called him a bum.

He saw red. "I ain't a bum. I'm a Marine." When the sergeant threatened to whip his ass for lying about serving, Jose lost his head and slugged the man in the throat. Then he took what the airman had… which was plenty. Almost a hundred dollars.

****

Jose's old Ford pickup rattled past the schoolyard where his little girl would have played one day. He glanced at Consuela sitting beside him like a turtle shell—hollow on the inside and hard on the outside. Her burnt-out eyes made him uneasy. Did she blame the baby's death on his mockery of Eagle? Could it be true? Goosebumps rolled down his back.

Jose headed south to pick up the highway out of El Paso. He figured on being in Phoenix before morning, but they barely made Arizona before steam boiled from under the hood. He managed to get it fixed, but they arrived in Los Angeles days later with just enough money to pay for a room at the Shoreside. What kinda name was that? The fleabag place was twenty miles from the nearest water. But it was cheap. Jose'd been broke lots of times, but he'd always belonged to something... the Corps or the *Tinneh*. Now, he was exposed. Vulnerable.

They needed food and gas and pocket money... and enough to buy a couple more nights in the motel. Leaving Consuela in the room, he tucked a short length of pipe from the pickup bed up his sleeve for protection, and hiked until he located a street lined with bars. The alley running behind the buildings was only half-lit. The city's night voices washed over him. Millions and millions of outsiders in every which direction intimidated him.

By then he knew why he'd brought the pipe. His skin crawled at the realization. This was different. The others had been passed out or in his face. He squared his shoulders. He'd do what he had to... but only until he got a job.

As Jose grew more nervous, his kidneys reacted. After he emptied his bladder, a man came into the alley and slackened his pace as Jose refastened his trousers.

"Well, if you're out for a little fun, there's no need to do it by yourself. Especially such a good-looking hunk as you." The man moved closer. "My God! You *are* a looker."

Did this faggot believe he was like that? He swallowed hard. "Buy me a bottle?"

"Sweetheart, I'll buy you a case. My car's right down there. Now look, no funny business."

"How about cops?"

"Police don't come around here." The man took his arm and led him down the alleyway. "Are you an Indian? I hope so! I've never had a Native American before."

Could he do this? Jose tensed as a hand caressed his thigh. When the man covered his groin, he knew he couldn't go through with it. He let the iron pipe slide down his sleeve and struck. The queer's money clip held exactly ninety dollars. Jose took it all, as well as a gold watch for himself and a fine gold chain for Consuela. She brightened at the gift, and he was a man again.

Chapter 12

Miss One Cent wouldn't get off Ro's back. She constantly singled him out, calling him "RO-man," like those old soldiers with skirts and helmets with upside down brushes on top. If he wasn't answering questions, he was running errands. Some of the boys made obscene gestures and teased him about the toothed vagina, claiming she was sweet on him.

Sweet on him? She hated him! He gave wrong answers on purpose, but that didn't do any good. She hauled him up before the class until he said something that satisfied her.

"See, you knew the answer all along, didn't you? You just needed to reason it out."

She was messing him up with the kids. Not a week went by without a fight. Nobody called him teacher's pet without paying for it. Size made no difference. More than once, Cane-Woman smiled over his welts and bruises, but she never asked about them.

****

Teachers usually wore down as the year went on, but not Miss One Cent. She came back from Christmas holiday more charged up than ever. Spring took a long time arriving. The snow melted and the plants budded, but an inevitable late freeze sneaked in one night and pinched the life out of the blossoms. Finally, the wind—the true herald of spring—showed up to blow grit in his eyes and ears. While March gusts busily blasted winter off mountaintops, the pace of work on the ranch picked up. A good spring rain put green on the grass before the hands made ready to receive cattle.

Once again, he skipped school on Friday to line up with the rest of the crew for the delivery. Mr. Chandler called him over, and Ro about went giddy when the rancher took time to explain he sometimes bought stock from the sale barn but mostly got his calves from a couple of reputable cow-calf ranches in the area. He liked weaned animals already vaccinated, dehorned, and castrated. Transporting and branding them was traumatic enough without adding to the mix. The less stress on a calf, the faster it gained weight. Even so, a few uncut bull calves slipped through, so there was always some of that rough work to be done.

The first day, Ro learned to toss a lariat, boil coffee, and haze balky animals. The rope was the hardest. Wade did the Texas tie-down while Pete dallied his rope—anchoring one end by snugging it around the pommel a couple of times. The first time Ro managed to drop a rope over a steer, he forgot to do either and got yanked from the saddle and dragged until he remembered to let go. One irritated animal butted him in the air, injuring nothing but his pride. Another mangled the coffee pot he was carrying when the woolly tried to trample him. He finished the first day bruised and battered but happy.

That night, he sat around the campfire listening to Pete tell about his champion hound that could always find a raccoon to fit any pelt board showed him.

"Come on, Pete," Wade said. "You telling me you just show that dawg a board, and he'd go off and hunt up a coon that fit it?"

"Wouldn't come back till he did."

"What happened to him?"

"Dunno. We ain't seen hide ner hair a him since the night my ma left the ironing board out on the front porch.

****

Monday, Miss One Cent rounded the corner and bore down on him with her mouth already moving. He scooted into the boy's restroom two steps ahead of her and cut through a bank of cigarette smoke to reach a wash basin. He doused his head and patted down his unruly hair until a rapping on the door froze everyone.

"RO-man? Roman Otero? I need to talk to you.?"

One of the boys held up a cigarette. "Get outta here. We trying to finish our butts. Just a minute, Miss Penny," he yelled. "He's almost finished piss...er, uh. He's almost done."

Ro flipped them off and went out to face the music. Miss One Cent stood squarely in the way so he had trouble closing the door behind him.

She squinted through the thick lenses of her raindrop glasses. "Was that tobacco smoke? Better have the coach check the boy's room." Several commodes flushed simultaneously. Apparently satisfied she had seen to her duty, she turned to him. "Did you wash your hands?"

"Yes'm." He started down the hallway. She fell in beside him.

"I want to talk to you, Roman, but I'm on library duty. You come along with me. It won't take long." He followed her to the deserted library and took the chair she indicated. "Now then, young man, you missed school Friday. Were you ill?"

He put his hand over his mouth and coughed. "Uh-huh, but I'm all right now. Mostly."

"Of all my students, I have the highest hopes for you. The law is an

62

admirable ambition, but it requires a great deal of study and effort. You are a much better student than your grades show. I don't know why yet, but I suspect it has something to do with peer pressure."

He blinked. Was she going to talk all afternoon?

"I want you to know I will gladly do whatever I can to assist. After classes are over, I staff the library for an hour. Why don't you join me so I can work with you?"

"I have to work."

"Yes…yes! That's the spirit."

"No, I mean I have to *work*. On a ranch."

"You work every day?" At his nod, she frowned. "Oh, dear. That makes it difficult. Well, we *must* do something to bring your grades up. Universities equate school records with ability. Very well, I will open the library half an hour early each morning. You report to me here. If nothing else, you can learn to use a library properly. Research is important to an attorney."

He left in a daze. What had he done to deserve more school time? Next year if anyone asked, he was gonna say he wanted to be a cowboy. Nonetheless, he started showing up half an hour earlier than anybody else. No telling what the kids would say about that.

When he got to the ranch Friday afternoon, Paul wasn't with the crew, but he'd left word for Ro to come to the house after work. He wasn't keen on the idea but went anyway.

Mrs. Chandler sent him to Teresa's room across the hall from her brother's where Paul straddled a chair backwards and stared out the window while reciting a fairy tale in a monotone. Teresa, obviously fighting a cold, fidgeted on her bed when Ro entered.

"Tell me some stories. Paul's no good at it."

"Well, thanks a heap, Miss Prissy. If that's true, why'd you keep me here all afternoon?"

"You're better than no company at all."

"Ro, take over my nursing duties, will you? I'm gonna go get a soda. You want one?"

Teresa piped up. "I want a Grapette."

"Me too, I guess."

The girl sighed. "I like Grapette. It's such a delicate drink."

Ro changed his mind. "I'd rather have a strawberry."

After her brother left, the girl turned to him as he claimed Paul's chair. "Tell me a story."

"Don't know any."

"Sure you do. Paul tells dumb stories. Well, the stories aren't bad, he just tells them dumb. Tell me some Indian stories. I like Indian stories, or I'm sure

63

I will when I hear one. I know the one about Hiawatha. He was so romantic! Are you going to tell me a romantic story?"

He squirmed in his seat. "I dunno. About Child-of-Water, maybe."

"Who's that?"

"The son of White-Painted-Woman. She's the mother of our people."

"That's a funny name, but lots of Indian names are funny. Yours isn't though. Román. That's a good name. But go on, tell me about Child-of-Water. Was he a handsome prince?"

Ro wrinkled his nose. "He's the son of our mother and Water."

"Water? Water isn't a person, it's a thing."

"A long time ago all things were like people. They could even talk."

"Oh, my!" Teresa said. "It *does* sound like a fairy tale. Well, if he wasn't exactly a prince, was he handsome like you? You're pretty, you know." Her eyebrows drew together. "Except it's a different pretty. Not like a girl."

He felt his cheeks tingle. "Guess he was. A prince, I mean."

"Oh, goody. Now go on and tell me about him."

"Well, the first of the *Tinneh*—"

"The who?"

"The *Tinneh*… the People."

"What people?"

"*My* people. The first People after the flood—"

"What flood?"

"Same flood as in your bible, I guess. How am I gonna tell a story if you keep asking questions? Anyway, the flood dried up after four moons and left two men and two women and the monsters living at Standing Mountain."

"Moons? Monsters!" She clapped her hand over her mouth and settled back on the pillow while Ro told her the legend of Child-of-Water as he'd heard it all his life.

Whenever the women had a child, the monsters ate it. Usen, the Creator-of-All-Things, told White-Painted-Woman to go to a place where ice cold water fell from the mountainside onto a rock. Some of the water dripped on her head, and White-Painted-Woman knew she would have a son who would stand against the monsters and prove man was master of all things.

After Child-of-Water and his brother grew up, Coyote helped them get mulberry wood from a forest guarded by bears to make bows. Coyote tricked the bears into going to the other side of the mountain by telling them the juniper berries and other fruits he'd defecated came from there.

Child-of-Water challenged Giant, the fiercest of the monsters, to a death duel. He stood in the east while Giant stood in the west. Giant fired a pine tree from his bow. A rainbow deflected the arrow—that's why the rainbow is a sign of protection. Child-of-Water's fourth arrow pierced the giant's white flint coat. The monster cried out that he was killed, and fell over four ridges and four canyons.

"That was beautiful!" Teresa said when Ro finished. "He was so brave he *must* have been a prince. Where was the pretty maiden? All stories have a pretty maiden."

"Quite a fairy tale," Paul said from the doorway. "How come everything's in fours?"

"And what does de-fe-cate mean?" Teresa asked.

"You don't wanna know," her brother said.

"I do too, smarty pants. I want to know right now."

"If I tell you, you'll go running to Mother."

"Won't. I promise."

Paul smiled. "Shit. It means to shit."

"It does not! You made that up. You said a dirty word, and I'm gonna tell."

"You promised. You gave a solemn vow, so you can't tell."

"I can if you fibbed. It doesn't mean that, does it, Ro? You can't make berries that way. Conjured!" the little girl decided. "It means conjured. Coyote conjured up those berries. That's a perfectly good fairy tale word." She turned her big eyes on Ro. "Tell me another one."

"No soap," her brother said. "And no Grapette either. Mom says dinner's ready. Ro, you're gonna eat with us. Why don't you stay the night. You can sleep in my room."

This was a new wrinkle—a couple of new ones. On the rare occasions he'd stayed on the ranch before, he'd eaten and slept in the bunkhouse.

Ro had learned to use silverware at the school cafeteria, so he made it through the meal okay. Wasn't like at the *gowa*. These people talked while they ate, chatting about a Black Dahlia murder in Los Angeles and communists taking over Poland and a black ballplayer named Jackie Robinson playing in a national league. Ro felt like he was back in class.

After dinner, the family moved to what they called the den. Mrs. Chandler found soft music on the radio, then she and Mr. Chandler shared a newspaper while Teresa went back to her room. He and Paul played chess until Mrs. Chandler said it was bedtime.

After Ro's bath, Paul loaned him a pair of pajama bottoms. They crawled into the big bed, and Paul turned the radio to something called "Mr. District Attorney." Once the mystery program was over, Paul asked how school was going as he snapped off the light.

"Not too good. I've got this teacher who's got it in for me. All week, I hadda go in thirty minutes early every day and do extra work in the library. For the rest of the year, I guess."

"What'd you do to deserve that?"

"Dunno." He didn't let on he'd brought it on by claiming he wanted to be a lawyer.

Paul went quiet, but Ro was too tense for slumber. The high-ceilinged room was like a church. The bed was too soft, but the sheets felt good. What was he doing here anyway? What crooked trail brought him to lie on a bed with an *Indah* boy? He sighed audibly, and Paul stirred.

"Ro, you asleep?"

"No. You?"

"Course not, dope. I'm talking to you, aren't I?"

They giggled, and everything was all right.

****

The year-that-never-ended—the school year—finally ran its course. And this summer was different from all the rest. He had a job to fill his day and a friend to fill his heart. Both were new experiences, and they helped the summer speed by. Mr. Chandler gave him different jobs like taking care of the tack room, milking the ranch's cow, and cleaning the stable. He wondered how many other eleven-year-olds got paid to do that stuff. Paul was usually at his side... except when it came to mucking out the stalls.

He came to work one July day to find his blood brother goggle-eyed and hugging a portable radio. "Did you hear?" There's an alien invasion. And one of them crashed down by Roswell. They've got the wreckage and the bodies and everything. A real UFO." Paul looked at him and added, "You know, Unidentified Flying Object."

At first, the radio said Roswell Army spokesmen confirmed it all. Then they backed up and claimed it was just a crashed weather balloon. That was bullshit, Paul argued. The army wouldn't move in and isolate the place to recover a weather balloon. And why was Highway 285 closed for a day and a half? Uh-uh. It was a government cover-up.

Ro was surprised to learn Cane-Woman had heard about the crash. When he asked about it, she studied the flames in the fire pit before smacking her lips.

"Eagle says it's all a lie. The white man's trying to scare us so we'll run away. Then he can take all our land and we won't have nothing left."

66

Chapter 13

Jose found Long Beach and Los Angeles nothing like his liberty days in the Corps. Something called the Public Employment Commission got him work as a janitor in a downtown building. That lasted until the manager's nephew needed a job.

He took care of a swimming pool and the grounds at a big house out in Beverly Hills until the teenaged daughter showed too much interest in him.

Out of work again, Jose was pissed. Consuela was so terrified of the city she was unable to look for work. She spent every dreary day in their small boardinghouse room, refusing to set foot outside the door, constantly begging to go back to the rez. He wasn't interested until she got pregnant again, and that started him thinking about the White Mountain country.

As usual, he was broke, so he prowled the alleys one final time. Around midnight, a man walked past him in the alley a couple of times, before approaching and asking if Jose had a cigarette.

"Sorry, man. Give you one if I had any. Broke."

The middle-aged man licked his lips and dropped his gaze below Jose's belt. "I know how you can make a buck or two." When Jose didn't respond, the mark moved closer and dropped his voice. "How proud are you of that?" He flicked Jose's groin.

Willing himself not to flinch, Jose smiled and said fifty bucks.

The man's eyebrows rose as he turned to walk away. "I don't care how fucking handsome and hunky you are. Back-alley cock's not worth that kind of money."

The scorn in the man's voice got to him. He swung the length of pipe he'd been hiding behind his leg more viciously than usual. It made a strange, sickening sound on the queer's head. Jose stripped money from the man's wallet and ran straight to the boardinghouse, only stopping to count his loot with a locked door behind him. Fifteen tens. Three times the fifty dollars he'd asked for.

The old pickup had long since given up the ghost, so Jose and Consuela stayed at the boardinghouse until city buses started running the next morning.

****

When they arrived back home on the rez two days later, Jose found a small cabin where they could live until the baby was born. Willie Peyote had his father's eyes, his mother's small hands, and his sister's health. He was dead within six months. Consuela went to live with her mother after that.

Jose wasn't sure when he got fed up with the life he was leading, but one day he heard old man Chandler was looking for a hand. The J-Bar-C already had one Apache cowboy, so maybe it could use two. Jose'd done a little rodeoing and could handle a horse. Hell, why not give it a try? He hitched a ride up NM35, walked down the long gravel drive to the house, and hung out at the corral until the rancher came in from the field.

Mr. Chandler shook hands like a man and talked to him straight, asking right up front if he liked whiskey. Sounded just like one of his Marine drill instructors. Probably why Jose didn't get his back up. Instead, he owned up to it and figured he'd walk away empty-handed. The rancher threw him a curve.

"You drink on your own time, that's your business. You drink on mine, I'll can your ass. You can stay in the bunkhouse. I'll furnish a mount. You start tomorrow morning."

Son of a bitch! He had a job.

Chapter 14

J-Bar-C Ranch, Five Years Later - Friday, March 9, 1951

Jim Chandler surveyed the group at the dinner table. Judith was as beautiful as ever. That day he'd spotted her in the university Student Union Building was the luckiest day of his life.

Paul's honey hair, blue eyes, and broad shoulders would make him a force to be reckoned with when arguing before a jury. Learning came easy to him. He handled himself well and never took a blessed thing seriously. They'd had to talk him out of trying to go fight over in Korea.

A grin tugged the corners of Jim's mouth as he eyed Teresa—talking, as usual, and waving a fork to emphasize a point. A gangly, gawky, irrepressible pain in the ass, she was his pride and joy. Unruly black hair spilled around a thirteen-year-old, heart-shaped face with green eyes and a pouty mouth that could stun with a sudden smile. He'd always envisioned a dark-headed son and a golden replica of Judith for a daughter. Nature had a quirky sense of humor.

Jim leaned back in his chair and pushed away his plate. Ro sat immediately to his left. In the last five-plus years, he'd spent more time with this boy than with his own son. Ro worked harder at being a ranch hand than Paul ever would. Ro's raven hair, long by most people's standards, shone like a high-gloss photograph. Thin features, except for huge eyes beneath gracefully arched brows. The boy's chest was deeper than Paul's—the result of running five miles daily—even though at sixteen he was more adolescent in his build. The boy was a good worker who lived by a mantra Jim had heard him express countless times over the years.

"A man's gotta own his words," Ro would say, meaning that if someone gave his word, he damned well better keep it.

Turned loose on the ranch, Ro was a graceful antelope, but Jim suspected classes were hateful labor. At least, he'd outgrown the reservation school and now attended classes over in neighboring Estrella High. Yet the boy's grades still gave little hint of the sharp mind that lay behind those piercing eyes the color of weathered acorns.

Ro's grandmother was a good part of the boy's school problems, constantly reminding him he was different. Horsefeathers. The boy was a boy and would be a man. Many a night he'd seen a dog-tired Ro ride back to the reservation after work just to be with the old woman. The lad's determined struggle to meet his obligations to two different worlds, kindled twin feelings of admiration and affection.

How would the boys fare when Paul was at school up in Albuquerque? Jim suspected it would be a rough transition for both. They'd made some cockamamie pact for Paul to dawdle around until Ro graduated high school, but the war in Korea had put an end to that foolishness. Paul would go to college or else become draft bait when he turned eighteen at the end of August.

Jim's mind wandered back to *his* war. For the Americans, World War II had broken out in his third year on the J-Bar-C. Despite the fact it was a crucial time on a struggling new ranch, he enlisted in the army in early '42 and saw service in some of the worst fighting in Europe at the Battle of the Bulge.

In early '46, he'd mustered out and returned to the ranch to discover how well Judith had tended their enterprise while raising two children. After that, the years rolled by. A miracle they'd made a success of it, but they had. Last year he expanded again, bringing the spread to 75,000 acres of fee land and another 125,000 of Taylor grazing and leased state land.

Cattle started him on the way to security, and more recently investments in Texas oil and Arizona minerals had added to his fortune. He'd even put a little money in the stock market back in '46 when the Dow Jones stood at 177. Today it was 269, but Lord, the time and effort required staying on top of everything.

Chapter 15

Paul kept a wary eye on roiling black clouds as he replaced a windmill blade. Flickers of light playing at the edges of the approaching storm sent him scrambling down the platform. They needed a good spring rain, but not while he was standing on top of a metal tower.

The restless weather had drifted north without dampening the ranch by the time he reached the house. After a quick bath, he brushed his hair into a gleaming halo and pulled on fresh clothes. He'd wrangled the jeep for the night and was anxious to be off. Paul tripped down the stairs to see if Ro had come in yet. His brother—that's the way he thought of Ro now—had gone with Pete to move cattle to one of the high pastures.

Darkness threatened before the stock truck pulled in beside the corral. He went outside to find Ro already heading for the stable to saddle Colorado.

"Hey man, let's hang this evening."

Ro glanced down at himself. "Look at me. I'm grungy."

"You know where the shower is. I think I can even dig up a bar of Benchley's."

"They stopped making it three years ago. Rumor is they only had one customer, this rancher fella down in the Southwest. Hell of a way to trick a kid into taking a bath."

"Actually, it was a pretty cool way. Go wash up. Saturday night's getting away from us."

"I don't have any clean clothes, and I've got a theme for English class due Monday."

"Who're you trying to snow? You're not gonna work on any theme tonight. I'll scare up clothes while you shower. We'll grab a bite, catch a movie, and I'll have you home early."

Thirty minutes later, they pulled out onto NM35. Paul switched on the radio even though the Mills Brothers' "Hoop-De-Do" was lost in a rush of wind.

As they approached Snowflake Pass, Terreon's lights beyond the horizon lit up the sky like a poor man's Aurora Borealis. Upon entering town, Paul circled the square around the old mission church and parked at a popular drive-in restaurant, swapping friendly insults with a carload of boys while the joint's loudspeakers wailed Mario Lanza's "Be My Love." They both ordered chili cheeseburgers and french fries. Paul had Coca Cola; Ro, strawberry.

Paul settled back in the seat. "How'd the grass look up there?"

"High country looks good. Coulda moved the stock last week."

Paul shook his head. "Those afternoon clouds better piss harder if it's gonna stay that way."

"My vast store of ancient Indian lore tells me it's going to be a wet spring."

"Hey, let's go camping on spring break. Do a little fishing."

"We'll see," Ro said.

"Yeah, we'll see the spring break come and go with Chandler and Otero working their butts off as usual. Hey, that sounds pretty good. Chandler and Otero, Esquire. Make a great lawyer's shingle, won't it?"

Ro toyed with the silver and turquoise band on his ring finger. "Yeah... guess so."

The waitress delivered their order and flirted a minute. After she left, they tackled their burgers in silence until Paul dived headfirst into the subject at the top of his mind.

"You gonna be all right with me up in Albuquerque while you're stuck here?"

Ro grinned. "I'll admit you've become a bad habit. Might have some withdrawal pains, but I'll survive."

"What I'm thinking is, a guy just needs a two-year pre-law course. I'm going for an undergraduate degree, and that takes four years. You can do the pre-law, and we'll still enter law school together. Sound copacetic?" When Ro hesitated before nodding, Paul pressed. "You wouldn't bullshit a blood brother, would you?"

"No way, White Injun."

Paul punched Ro's shoulder. "Man, we got all summer in front of us, and as for next year, you're not going to have the opportunity to miss me. You're going to be so busy you won't even notice I'm not around. You gotta get with it and haul those grades up."

"I was trying tonight, but you talked me out of it," Ro said.

"I was testing your moral fiber. By the way, it's lousy."

Paul dumped their garbage in a trash can and went in search of a gas station. Filling the tank was his rental fee for use of the jeep. He pulled into a neighborhood station where the gas was *nineteen* cents a gallon. Highway robbery.

After leaving the station, they took in *Rio Grande* at the Grand. Paul liked John Wayne; Ro wasn't so gung-ho about the guy. But Maureen O'Hara alone was worth the price of the ticket.

****

A little of their camaraderie slipped as Paul became increasingly wrapped up in the tail end of his senior year... parties and events where Ro wasn't involved.

Paul took to the saddle every day, usually working alongside Ro. Whenever they teamed up with Jose Peyote, Paul was struck by the similarities between the two. Both had a secret side. Ro's wall, Paul was convinced, was rooted in his grandmother's suspicion of whites. Jose, on the other hand, fit in. The men liked him. He carried his part of the load and dealt, as well as received, his share of bullshit. His barrier seemed rooted in alcohol, and that was darker.

The crew put in hard weekdays and rotated Saturday and Sunday chores. Jose worked like a squirrel storing acorns for the winter five days in a row and drank his ass off the other two. When he pulled weekend duty, he was there, but he was hung over. And when he was hung over, you didn't screw around with the man.

Paul opened the gate to a pen and watched the two Indians haze cattle into the enclosure. Two peas in a pod. Lean and rangy, and both damned good-looking men. Paul blinked. Ro wouldn't even be seventeen until October. But he already moved and looked like a man.

****

Saturday night Paul intended to get laid. He'd swapped lies with the guys in the locker room, but he was a virgin like most of them. Sara Jane Elkins had brought him to the edge a couple of times, and tonight she was going all the way if it killed him.

By the end of the evening, he'd decided Sara Jane was a tease. He had her on the brink when she suddenly announced she had to go home. Insisted on it. Now he was headed back to the ranch shot down and pissed as hell... and a little high from a bootlegger's bottle. Paul eased up on the accelerator. The heat didn't often patrol the road past the turnoff to White Pine and the reservation, but you never knew.

He turned down the drive to the house without picking up any traffic violations and killed the lights before stopping in front of the garage. He got out of the Jeep and started for the back door, hoping to avoid the den and risking the folks smelling alcohol on his breath. Dad would be in bed, but Mom might be waiting up. As he went around the side of the house, he stopped in his tracks. Someone was peeking in the windows. Ro? No... Jose. Son of a bitch!

Paul rushed forward, grabbed the man's shoulder, and threw his weight behind a punch, jerking away when something wet splashed across his legs. Crap, the guy'd been peeing. Pissing right in the begonias. Paul hauled Jose to his feet. "Keep away from our windows, you hear?"

He headed for the kitchen door trying to hold wet pants away from his skin and praying Jose was so soused he didn't know what had happened. He got that way sometimes.

****

To Paul, the high school graduation ceremony was just something standing between him and the dance that evening. And the ball was important, because he damn well intended to get laid before the night was over. So far as he was concerned, that dance was a mating ritual.

The disk jockey—a local hep cat—played last year's favorites and this year's pop tunes. Nat "King" Cole's "Mona Lisa," one of Paul's favorites, was a great dance tune. Red Foley's "Chattanooga Shoeshine Boy" was okay, but he preferred dancing slow and close.

Around midnight, he picked up a bottle of moonshine from a guy in the parking lot and bundled Sara into the Lincoln. Parked ten miles from nowhere, he opened the Mason jar and sampled its contents, struggling to keep from gasping. God, it was the worst homemade booze he'd ever tasted. Sara handled a sizeable gulp with no apparent problem.

Once the level in the jar dropped below midpoint, things got quiet in the car. The radio crooned romantic melodies absolutely perfect for making out.

He couldn't believe some of the bawdy goo pouring out of his mouth into Sara's cute little ear. Some of it was gawd-awful. Paul took liberties. Sara laughed and pushed him away, but that was part of the game. When things got intense, he felt stifled in the car.

"Hot in here. Wanna go for a walk?"

"Why, of course, darling."

They navigated an uncertain course, his hand resting on her hip. Her thigh moving against his distracted him, and he blundered over the edge of a shallow arroyo, pulling her with him. On his belly, his mouth gritty, he looked over at Sara. Had he screwed everything up? "You okay?"

She lay on her side, her features hidden in the darkness, and giggled. He exhaled explosively and wiggled over to her side. She turned on her back and pointed to the sky.

"Why are there so many more stars out here than in town?"

Like a dufus, he explained light diffusion. Crap! Sounded like a complete imbecile. He bent over and kissed the hollow of her neck. His tongue went exploring. She moaned. He fumbled with her buttons. Completely sure of himself now, he moved to her exposed breasts. She inhaled sharply. His hands sought other goals. She reciprocated, and it was his turn to gasp.

****

74

On the way home neither of them talked much. Paul was at a loss. What was there to say? Thank you, ma'am. It was nice. After dropping Sara at her front door, Paul relived the evening without paying much attention to the road but somehow found himself turning down the gravel drive. He parked, killed the lights, and sat in the car trying to reclaim that moment of rapture when his muscles had convulsed with electrical impulses, but it was just an academic exercise without meaning.

Paul crawled out of the car and started for the veranda. A sudden noise brought him out of his trance. He half-turned before something struck him on the side of the head. He hit the ground and tried to rise. A second punch drove his face into the gravel. He clawed his way to his feet. An amorphous, moving shadow caught him in the stomach. He toppled over. Every time he tried to get up, someone sent him back to earth. Finally, he didn't want to get up anymore. He lay spread-eagled on the lawn, sick and weak. He threw up all over himself and passed out.

Chapter 16

Jim bounced up in bed as Judith threw back the covers.

"Downstairs!" she said.

Jim met Teresa rushing into the hallway and sent her back to her room before slipping cautiously down the stairs. When he snapped on the hallway light, his heart almost stopped. Paul sagged against the open door, banging it against the doorstop as he swayed uncertainly. Drunk? His face was bloody. Paul took two halting steps and collapsed.

Jim rushed to him. The kid had taken a beating. Judith gasped as she flew down the stairs. He warned not to move the boy and sent her to call for a medic before looking around outside.

Finding nothing, Jim returned to the house and sat on the floor with his unconscious son while Judith huddled on one side, a tearful Teresa on the other.

****

Shoulders tense, eyes smoldering, Jim watched the sedated form on the hospital bed. He and Judith spelled one another keeping a distraught Teresa busy. The girl and her mother were downstairs at the cafeteria getting something to eat when a slight movement on the bed brought Jim to his feet. Paul's lids fluttered. A brief, blank stare and then alarm.

"I'm here, son. How do you feel?"

"Like... horse stomped me."

"The doc says you'll be okay. Thank God you don't graduate every day. Not sure you could survive it."

Paul tried for a grin. It disintegrated into a grimace.

"What happened?" Jim asked.

"Parked in front of the garage. Dark. Got out. Somebody hit me. Dunno who."

"Right in our driveway? Been in any scrapes lately?"

"No... yes." His words coming hard, Paul related what had happened outside the den window a week earlier.

Jim struggled to keep reproach from his voice. "Why didn't you tell me?"

"Saw Jose was pissing... wasn't sure."

"Get some rest. I'll take it from here."

Jim met Judith and Teresa coming down the hallway. He paused to relate what Paul had admitted before starting for the entrance.

Judith snatched at his arm. "Jim, let the authorities take care of this. Call the sheriff."

"I'll handle this my way. Stay with Paul. I'll send for you later."

Upon arriving at the ranch, he raised his foreman on the radio. "Chuck, where's Jose?"

"Ain't out with the crew today, Jim. Drunk as a coot. First time I ever known him to miss work. Still at the bunkhouse last I saw. How's Paul?"

When Jim assured Chuck his son would be all right, the man said he'd pass the word to Ro, who was jumpy as a jackrabbit.

"Boss," the foreman's tone indicated he had put two and two together, "I'm on my way. Be there inside of ten minutes. Hold off till I get there."

"Over and out, Chuck."

Jim made straight for the bunkhouse. Neat beds lined either side of the large room except for one in the far corner. Jose's bunk stood rumpled and empty. The sound of running water from the washroom stopped. Jose appeared and leaned against the doorway as he dried his face on a towel. Daubs of blood on his rumpled shirt fairly glowed, providing the confirmation Jim needed. He stalked over to the unsteady man.

"You put your hands on my boy, and now you're gonna pay for it," he said.

Jose blinked and made no effort to protect himself. Jim's blow bounced him off the wall. The Apache straightened up warily. Jim moved in fast. A jab to the mouth missed. Jose was quick for a man in his condition, blocking blows with his arms. Jim's fury got the better of him.

Jose took advantage of his wild flailing and stung him with a glancing blow to the right eye.

Jim's anger gave way to cold, calculated determination. He pressed Jose, forcing him back. Jose launched a long right that slid off Jim's shoulder. Jim's counterpunch missed as Jose bobbed and gave him a short one beneath the armpit. Some of Jim's wind deserted him, but Jose failed to follow up. Two sharp raps to the stomach brought Jose to his knees. Jim threw his body behind a wicked smash to the cheek. The cowhand collapsed.

Jim unclenched his fists and walked to the fallen man. Mistake. Jose's boot caught him under the chin and sent him reeling against a bunk. Jim fell forward on his hands and knees. Jose chopped him on the back of the neck. Jim went to the floor. A boot dug into his side. He twisted out of the way and regained his feet.

Jose rushed. Jim sidestepped and smashed a right to the jaw. He got through the man's guard to the heart and stomach. Jose's knees sagged. As Jim moved in for the finish, Jose suddenly caught him in the throat. Jim staggered, gagging and gasping and rubbing his swollen right eye to clear his vision. Jose shook his head like a wounded bull and slowly advanced.

Jim took repeated blows to his arms and shoulders. Age and wind got to him. He gasped for each breath. His arms grew heavy, his movements sluggish.

Too tired to be effective, Jim knew he was finished. Jose knew it as well. The smaller man closed the distance, a gleam of pure hatred in his eyes. Jim backed the length of the room and rammed against the wall. He had nowhere to go. He caught a quick breath. Something brushed his shoulder. Pete's Winchester. As Jose charged, Jim jerked the weapon from its rack and slammed the barrel on the man's outstretched arm.

Something snapped. Jose grunted and fell to his knees, cradling his right arm against his chest. Jim brought the rifle's stock weakly across the side of the cowboy's head, and it was over. Jose lay slack-jawed on his back, his glittering eyes fixed on Jim.

Leaning on the rifle like a crutch, Jim clawed money from his pocket and dropped it on the floor. "Want you... off this ranch. Touch my boy, I'll... kill you! Now get out."

Jim took the Winchester with him but ran out of steam at the corral. Hooking an arm over the rail for support, he sagged against the fence and bellowed for Chuck.

Chapter 17

Paul examined his face in the mirror. The bruises were bad enough, but his swollen, lumpy nose was really grody. He and his dad couldn't stand side by side in public or their matching bruises and shiners would tank the family's reputation.

The doc assured him the nose wasn't broken, but it sure felt like it. Riding a horse was pure misery, so he'd taken a summer job at the Rio Chacon Cattle Barn in Terreon. Appearing in public looking like a giant bruise embarrassed Paul, but he'd spun a tale that kept them laughing… and guessing. The Barn held sales on Wednesdays and Saturdays, drawing cattlemen from all over southern New Mexico. The Saturday auction tore up the weekend.

He woke one day with half the summer gone to realize he'd seen very little of Ro. His brother was at work before Paul got up in the morning and had left for the reservation by the time he got home in the evening. Sundays and Mondays, Paul's days off, were about the only time they saw one another, and Ro generally worked one of those days, and sometimes both. Paul left the Barn early one Saturday and made it home just as his buddy headed for the corral.

Ro leaned in the window of the ranch pickup Paul used to go to work every day. "You're early. Get fired for stump-breaking cows?"

"Not a firing offense. Came home to catch you. Time to howl and prowl. You game?"

Ro smiled. "Sure. What do you have in mind? A picture show?"

"You can have *Sunset Boulevard* at the Rialto or *All About Eve* at the Grand. Swanson or Davis, take your pick. But first, we gotta round up a couple of dates. And don't go bellyaching you don't know any girls. I'll take care of that detail. Go put Colorado away and clean up while I get on the horn. You okay for bread?"

Paul pulled the upstairs hallway phone into his room and closed the door as far as the cord permitted. Bucky Hanson's sister Kate agreed to a blind date with Ro. Paul replaced the receiver and took a deep breath. A few minutes later, his pulse dot-dot-dotted Morse Code to his libido when Sara condescended to a date.

****

Kate Hanson, lively, petite, and very blonde, dimpled prettily when he introduced her to Ro. On the way to pick up Sara, a one-sided conversation developed in the back seat. Ro only spoke to answer questions. "Just finished the tenth," he said in response to one of them.

"Me too. But I don't remember you at school."

Paul tensed. Might as well get this over with. Some of the Terreon kids considered Estrella guys as hicks… or worse. "Ro goes to Estrella," he said over his shoulder.

Kate didn't seem to know it was a tense moment. "Really? What's school like there?"

"Like any place," Ro said.

When Sara answered the door, Paul's tongue curled into a dry piece of leather. "You look crazy cool."

"Why thank you, darling," she cooed. "Can't say that about you. What happened?"

"Thought you'd heard. I got in a fight."

"Hope you lost, or else the sheriff's hunting you down for murder."

He felt his ears burn. "I was blindsided."

After what seemed an interminable movie—Davis, not Swanson—Ro suggested a malt. Paul barely touched his drink. Sara's leg pressing against his thigh killed his thirst.

****

Terreon's jeweled lights dimmed and blurred as Paul sent the Lincoln over a maze of back roads. Sara rested her head on his shoulder and hummed "If" along with Perry Como on the car radio. In the back, the monologue droned on. Paul stopped the car and killed the lights.

Sara snuggled more comfortably against him. They exchanged a few awkward kisses… thanks to his sore nose. He suggested a walk when the gab from the rear seat became more than he could stand. They got out and laced arms, strolling aimlessly. When they reached the lip of an arroyo, she stopped.

"What if I don't want to go down there?"

She was going to get it, whether it was down in a ditch or on top of the car. He gave a false grin. "Just thought sitting against the side and watching the stars would be kinda rad."

"How sweet, darling." She seemed to have appropriated the word "darling."

He steadied her as they slid down the side of the gully. At the bottom, he spread his windbreaker for them to sit on. Beneath it, the sand had begun to cool. He sat with his back to the wall of the arroyo; she cuddled against his shoulder. The pressure on his bruised ribs about drew a groan from him. Awkward. His fingers trembled. His palms leaked sweat. Man, what he wouldn't have given for a slug of moonshine, even the bad stuff.

80

He caressed her face and tilted her chin. Her lips were soft and pliant. He reached for her breast and squeezed. The kiss heated up, but he dallied, prolonging the moment.

Chapter 18

The girl beside Ro in the darkened Lincoln was as pale and indistinct as the surface of the big moon hanging in the sky. Too fair to be really pretty, he'd nonetheless been drawn to her blue eyes. She talked and asked questions endlessly, but that's just how the *Indah* were. The *Tinneh* way was better. Don't talk until you've sized up the other person.

Then it hit him. She was nervous. When he was edgy, he went as quiet as a fence post. The quieter he got, the more vocal Kate grew. Once when she paused, presumably to catch a breath, he thought of kissing her, but his muscles were as frozen as his voice box.

The back seat of the car was too confining, too intimate. Kate seemed relieved when he suggested they get some air. He scrambled out and ran around to open the door for her like he'd seen white boys do. They leaned against the trunk of the car. This was better.

She turned to look at him. "Do you ever get the urge to see some other part of the world? You know, see different things and different people?"

His Adam's apple bobbled. He focused on her smooth neck. Did girls have Adam's apples? "Maybe California and the ocean."

"It's nice, and I like it for a change. But the quiet up here is better than the noise down there. Can I ask you something? What's it like living on the reservation?"

"Like anywhere else. You know… food, clothing, shelter. Grow up, get married, look for a job. Just like the *Ind*…uh…just like people off the reservation."

"But your customs are different, aren't they?"

"Well, for one thing, we don't wear out one another's names."

"What do you mean?"

"Instead of saying 'Hello, Kate,' for instance, we'd likely say 'Hello, Cousin' or "Hello, Cuz.' That kinda thing. Except for me, I don't do that much."

"Why not?"

Her question hit him between the eyes. Why didn't he? Maybe because Cane-Woman didn't. He shrugged. "Dunno. Just don't."

"And that's it?"

"Except for the gray hairs. The old folks. They still live in the past a lot. Not so much for the young guys since the war."

"What a shame," Kate said.

Ro blinked. "What do you mean?"

"Someday the older generation will be gone, and so much will be lost. Do you speak your language?"

"All I talk at home." Stupid. Now she'd want to know about his home. "But they didn't let us talk it at school on the rez."

"Can I ask you something else? I know how we think the world got started."

The scent of wildflowers drifted in on a dry breeze. "Like Adam and Eve, you mean?"

She nodded. "Uh huh. How do your people explain it?"

So he told her how the Jicarillas said there was only darkness, water, and cyclone in the beginning. How the Hactcin, their gods, made the earth, the sky, and the underworld. Everyone lived in the underworld. White Hactcin hung the sun, and Black God the moon. First, they created animals. Then Black God fashioned man in his own image out of pollen and turquoise and white rock and white clay and jet and abalone.

"Goodness, everything's so hard," she exclaimed.

"Had to be. Life was tough back then."

He told of the Emergence when the shamans chased the sun and moon out of the underworld through a hole and people following on ladders of spider webs and sunbeams.

"That was beautiful. But why did you tell me what the Jicarillas believe?"

He shrugged and pushed away from the car. "It's not so different."

Kate squinted at her watch in the moonlight. "It's getting late. I have to get home soon. I catch the blue blazes when I'm late."

"I'll go see if I can find Paul and Sara."

As he set off following faint footprints by moonlight, his reluctance to leave Kate's side surprised him. At the edge of the arroyo, he decided to give warning, but when he glanced down, the sound died in his throat.

Ro turned back to the car. He was no prude, nor was he ignorant of such things. He'd seen animals on the ranch. Although he had no grandfather of his own, he'd heard other boys snicker over their elders' instructions on being a man with a woman. Yet that glance into the gully troubled him. His brother had a need he couldn't share. Paul was being a man while Ro'd never even kissed a girl. Was there something wrong with him?

He gazed at ghostly shadows on the moon and admitted another truth. Paul's leaving for school wasn't what would change things between them. Things had *already* changed. Why was he surprised? That's all there was to life. Change.

He returned to find Kate standing in the road watching him. "Did you find them?"

He shook his head. "Fine Indian tracker I turned out to be. If they aren't back in a few minutes, we'll honk."

They leaned against the hood of the car. Her shoulder touched his. "Kate, I'm kinda new at this. Have you had a good time? I wasn't sure I'd be good company."

"Of course, you are. I'm glad Paul introduced us." Her soft hand touched his arm. A magical moment. He turned and lifted her chin with nervous fingers. He searched her face before touching his lips to hers.

Both embarrassed and excited by what he'd done, he mumbled, "I'm sorry."

Her voice was small. "It's all right."

He laughed deep in his throat. "Would you believe that's the first time I kissed a girl?"

"Really? You're not serious, are you?"

He flipped a hand. "I own my words."

She glanced at him. "What do you mean?"

"When I say something, I mean it."

Her large, serious eyes studied him. "Then I'll own my words too. That was my first time, as well."

"Thought maybe I was retarded."

She stifled a giggle. "Oh, Ro!"

Her first kiss, and it was with him. The second kiss was longer.

"What's going on here?"

They jerked apart. Paul and Sara stood at the side of the road laughing. Ro considered throttling his brother.

The ride back to town turned quiet. The motor hummed, dash lights glowed, and pop tunes drifted from the radio. Sara rested her head on Paul's shoulder. Ro and Kate held hands in back. Even after they dropped the girls off and Ro got into the front seat, neither felt like talking. Since it was late, Paul prevailed upon him to spend the night. After a snack and quick showers, they turned in. Ro lay on his side of the bed and haltingly confessed coming to look for Paul.

"You didn't say anything to Kate, did you?"

"No! But… I sorta watched for a minute."

"Did I put on a good show?"

"Shoulda charged admission."

"I will. Fork over a quarter."

"Worth at least half-a-dollar."

"Wow! Was I that far out?"

"Sara wasn't complaining. So you don't mind?"

"That you saw us? Naw, it's cool. You ever had a girl, Ro?" He didn't wait for an answer. His voice took on a hushed quality. "You oughta. It's the greatest thing in the world. When you start doing it, you're cranked. Something builds up inside. It's all happening inside. Man, you want to drag it out forever, and at the same time you wanna punch it and get there. Getting there's what it's all about… but it isn't either. Aw, it's for doing, not for telling."

They fell silent, and soon Paul's breathing indicated he was asleep. A bird nesting outside the window twittered and fluttered restlessly. An owl hooted nearby. Then a rush of wings against the foliage chilled Ro from head to toe.

Chapter 19

Naked to the waist and bent almost double over a narrow trench, Ro plucked corn sprouts Cane-Woman had planted earlier and carried the seedlings back to the wickiup. She was no longer strong enough to do everything, so he had to help. Before grinding the corn on a *metate*, he checked to make sure no one saw him doing woman's work. He didn't need another fight.

His grandmother nodded approval. "That'll make fine gray water."

He put the corn meal in a pot of water and set it over the fire. She ought to quit drinking *tulapai*, but that was like asking Colorado to give up oats. Ro settled down to wait for the mixture to boil and lament the misuse of his free Sunday. He glanced at the frail woman and was contrite. He saw little enough of her; he shouldn't begrudge helping her.

Cane-Woman, never large, had shrunk even smaller, but was an unlikely candidate for pity. Her sunken eyes were as alive as anything he'd ever seen. Besides, his grandmother didn't suffer misery—she dealt it.

The old woman gave him a sharp look. "How long you worked on that white ranch?"

"Five years."

"Ain't that enough?"

"Aren't things easier? The cot I bought you is better than sleeping on the ground. The sleeping bag keeps you warmer than blankets. We always have food in the wickiup now."

She hissed. "Things! You talk about things! You getting to be a man, but you growing to a man who don't think about nothing that counts. It's that school they send you to. It *makes* you a thing. The white man's thing—like one of his cattle. You ain't never opened your mind to the learning I give you. You gotta be *Tinneh* on the inside. Just on the outside ain't enough. You oughta sing Eagle's songs."

"Can't. Gotta work. And school starts soon. That takes time."

The old woman's eyes scanned the sky. "The sun still walks at its own pace. Time is the same. That ain't why."

His white man's education failed him. No response came to mind. Having no reasons to satisfy her, he fell back on what made sense to him. He threw a hand in the direction of the ranch. "The more I learn out there, the better it is for both of us."

Her head trembled as she regarded him for several moments. "One a these days, you'll get your real education."

"You talk in riddles."

"If I tell you the words straight out, you ain't gonna hear them."

He tried to be as eloquent as she sometimes was. "As a riddle or straight out, I hear your words and try to make them my words. But sometimes my heart goes looking for its own truth."

"Pretty words, Román Otero," she said.

Something moved in his guts. Was he no longer Roan Orphan?

"You listen, boy, your due's already walking down the track. And when it gets here, it's gonna knock some sense into your head, or it's gonna knock you loose from your sense."

Time for deep thought was over. "I'd better get more firewood to finish your gray water. You got enough sugar and oak chips… you know, for flavor?"

When she nodded, Ro gathered wood before saddling Colorado to ride into White Pine. The children swarming the schoolyard could have been ghosts from his past. He thought of Clarence Wolf who'd dropped out of school, lied about his age, and joined the army. They said he was over in Korea.

Ro rode past the general store, closed like everything else on Sunday. The tap he drank from when he was a kid still leaked and puddled water at its base. Jose Peyote and Tomas Wingfield sat on the back steps. Jose held a paper bag hiding a bottle and motioned with his right arm wrapped in a dirty bandage.

"How you doing, Cuz?"

Ro judged him leaning toward drunk. "Good. How about you? How's the arm?"

Jose flexed his fingers. "Cut the cast off last week. Just wrap it up now." He held the bottle out to Ro, who shook his head. "Fucker took a gun to me. Clubbed me with the barrel."

"Mr. Chandler carries more years. Guess he had to even it up somehow."

"Why'd he start that shit, anyhow?" Jose groused.

"'Cause you waylaid his son."

The man stood. "I'm a Marine. Nobody steps on me. That shithead bushwhacked me."

"Aw, Paul thought you were window peeping. He'd have apologized if you asked."

Jose hawked and spat. "What would that of got me?"

"Saved you a job and a broken arm. Hell, Jose, you were a good hand."

"To hell with their job. I forgot the way things are. Just like you do. But I reconned the position and got the lay of the land." He thrust his arm toward Ro. "This is what it cost me. Old man Chandler don't know what it's gonna cost him yet."

"Don't screw around with the man. You can't win."

Jose laughed and glanced at Tomas. "Brother, you oughta see this kid haul ass when the white man barks. This Injun's the whitest hand on that ranch."

"Knock it off," Ro snapped. Why did the words cut so deeply?

"Come down offa that horse and make me."

"Shit, Cousin," Tomas mumbled. "Leave the kid alone. You ain't mad at him. But if you gonna duke it out with Roan Orphan, I'll mosey off and finish up the bottle."

"Hell you will! Half that's mine."

"Well, come get your half." Tomas held the bottle just out of reach as he sauntered around the corner of the building. They argued as they made their way down the dusty road.

Ro leaned over the saddle horn and mulled Jose's words.

****

The summer, dominated by news of the Korean war, slipped away. One Friday afternoon in August, Paul packed for college. Ro itched to run away and hide like a little kid. At the same time, he wanted every minute with Paul he could get. His throat closed up. Long time till spring break.

After the Lincoln turned north on NM35, Ro faced the empty house he'd promised to watch until the family returned from Albuquerque. He wished he were back at the wickiup and had never heard of the Chandlers. The next two days and nights spanned eons. Did he really miss the Chandlers that much?

Sunday morning, he went to check on his grandmother, quickly regretting his decision when the old woman gave him a tongue lashing for failing to come home the last two nights. He accepted the harsh words even though he'd warned her he'd be away for a while. When he told her he had to go back to work, her flesh turned dark. Promising to be home later that night, he backed rapidly out of the wickiup. Her tirade followed him.

"Where is home? Do you know? Or does the eagle figure he's a dove now?"

"Won't be gone long," he promised over his shoulder.

"Ain't how long. It's how far."

She crazy-talked a lot these days.

The sight of the Lincoln in the driveway made him forget his troubles. The Chandlers were home, and already the house looked happier. He looped his reins loosely over the corral and went to the kitchen door.

Mr. Chandler answered his knock. "We're having a bite. Want some?"

"Yes, sir." His belly rumbled for the first time in two days.

****

When Chuck Griggs accepted a job with a big Texas ranch, it seemed to Ro that Mr. Chandler leaned on him harder. He took it all in stride. Work became a balm. Long hours and tired muscles made things acceptable. He was most vulnerable to missing his *Indah* brother on the lonely rides home at night.

Friday night he finished work early and watched some television in the bunkhouse. On CBS, Douglas Edwards talked about President Truman firing General MacArthur over in Korea. When Pete asked if anyone wanted a ride to town, Ro accepted on the spur of the moment. Once there, he wondered why he'd come. He had a milkshake and wandered the streets aimlessly. Early evening, he turned his footsteps north to hitchhike home.

Near the edge of town, he passed Kate Hanson's house. Hesitating on the corner, he stared at the neat stucco and hoped for a glimpse of her. The place leaked yellow light from a half-closed window. If only he had the nerve. Hell, why not?

Despite legs that threatened to balk, he made it to the door and rapped lightly. A big, straw-headed youth answered his knock and told him to wait.

Kate beamed as she opened the screen and stepped outside. "Ro, how nice."

"Passing by and remembered this was your house. Hope it's all right...."

"Sure it is. I'm glad you stopped."

She declined his invitation to a movie but proposed a walk. They strolled in comfortable silence until she spoke. "I like to walk. Don't you?"

"Tell the truth, I'd rather ride. My legs weren't made for walking."

"It's those cowboy boots. Do you always wear them?"

"Wore sneakers until I started working on the ranch. Never had a pair of boots until five years ago. But I wear my sneakers when I run most mornings."

"You run, but your legs aren't made for walking?"

"I have trouble with that one too."

They made their way through the town's park, walking easily, occasionally skipping pebbles in the small lake or taking detours to inspect something interesting. Finally, they sat on a stone bench near water's edge.

"I thought about you a lot," he said. "Figured you'd forgot about me. Probably ask me who I was when you answered the door."

"Silly, I had a nice time that night. You're good company. And anybody who's ever looked into your eyes would remember you. You've got wonderful eyes. They're so big and soulful."

His cheeks tingled. "You're the one who's good company. And talk about eyes, yours are so blue I keep looking for a big white cloud to float across them."

"How sweet. You have a way with words."

He snickered. "When I can get them out of my mouth. But you gotta be

89

satisfied with that 'cause I got nothing else. Except that you sure are pretty."

A silence grew while he pumped up his courage. "I thought a lot about, you know, kissing you." His boldness rendered him woozy. Sitting close with his arm around her, he hesitantly tried another kiss. Then he was content just to stare across the water. "We shouldn't do this, you know."

"Do what?" she asked.

"Look at the reflection of the moon. It's all right to look at the moon, but not its reflection. Gives you stomach trouble or heart trouble. Every Apache grandmother knows that."

She started to giggle but stopped. "I'm not laughing at you."

"I know. That's why I like you so much." He leaned over and kissed her moist lips again.

"Ro, I have to go home," she said. "Sorry, but I do."

"Can we go to the picture show tomorrow?" he asked.

"Do you like to swim? We could go to the city pool first and the flick later."

"Okay. I'm not sure what time I can catch a ride, but I'll make it as early as I can."

He walked on air and didn't even remember who gave him a ride back to the ranch.

****

Ro rushed through Saturday morning chores so fast the hands eyed him suspiciously.

"Ain't but two things make a kid work like this 'un," Pete said. "He's going after a little gal this afternoon, or else she give him the brush last night, and he's trying to forget."

Ro held his tongue but couldn't hide a grin.

"By doggies, he's blushing. It's a rare sight, but here's living proof a Injun can blush. Know what that means? He's going for her this afternoon. Sic 'em boy!"

Turned out, he was lucky. Mr. Chandler was headed for the Cattlemen's Club and gave him a ride into town. On the way, they talked about missing Paul and the shaky truce over in Korea, and President Truman telling Congress they'd have to build up the armed forces.

The rancher cleared his throat. "Son, your birthday's coming up soon, isn't it?"

"Yes, sir. Number seventeen. In October."

"Looking forward to getting your driver's license, I imagine."

Ro gave one of his grunts and looked sideways at Mr. Chandler. Where was this going? Had the man found out the hands had been letting him drive pickups for the last six months?

Mr. Chandler laughed. "Yeah, I know about it. Wade asked me before they ever put a set of keys in your hands. They tell me you can put a truck about anywhere you want, but I'll bet you aren't ready for the written test. I'll pick up a booklet so you can study for it."

Ro was daydreaming about that driver's license when he walked into Reaper's Department Store to buy a swimsuit that afternoon. Scandalized at trunks resembling his jockey shorts, he settled for a loose-fitting suit the clerk claimed was last year's style.

When Ro knocked on Kate's door, she about unhinged him by leading him inside to meet her parents. But she kept it short, and they were soon hiking to the municipal swimming pool. Once there, they changed into their suits and met by the diving board. Ro liked Kate-s one-piece, lime-green swimsuit. It was a great color for her. She shouldn't ever wear any other color. He flushed slightly at the thoughts rattling through his head. Made her look interesting without seeming too... forward. His flush deepened as he squirmed beneath her stare.

After the awkward glances, they jumped feet-first into the water. Kate was a strong swimmer. Ro had to work to keep up with her. They swam for almost an hour before sprawling on a beach towel to soak up the sun.

"But just a little. I look like raw beefsteak if I stay out too long." Kate ran a finger over his brown shoulder, sending a shiver up his spine. "Bet it doesn't bother you though."

Later they stopped at the malt shop where Kate confessed to a gluttonous appetite and said she always brought her own money on a date so she could pig out.

Was this a date? "You're shaped too good to be a pig. Anyhow, I hardly ever get to spend any money, so don't worry."

She took the last bite of her burger and glanced at the door. "Oh, look! There's my brother." She waved to the guy who'd answered the Hansons' door yesterday and introduced him as Bucky. The youth had him by a couple of years and was considerably bigger. He looked like a jock. Bucky sat down and asked what they'd been up to.

"Swimming."

"Why did I ask?" Bucky said. "This girl outswims everyone in school."

"Not Ro," Kate said. She was being generous.

"Then you oughta go out for the swim team. We could use a little help."

"Ro goes to school over in Estrella." Something flickered in Bucky's eyes. Kate spoke into sudden silence. "Would you think me terrible if I had another hamburger?"

Her brother stood. "Come on, Kate, I'll give you a ride home."

"We're going to the show after my burger, I'll be home early though."

Kate's sunshine personality soon pulled Ro out of the mood her brother had put him in. On the way home later, they detoured through the park and talked about the movie, Hitchcock's *Strangers on a Train*. Kate thought Farley Granger was handsome and Robert Walker baby-faced, but properly sinister.

"It's so quiet here," she said as they halted by the park's lake.

"Uh huh," he mumbled before he kissed her. Wild, crazy thoughts filled his head. She sought to pull away, but his arm was around her waist. Their hips pressed together.

"Maybe we'd better go," she said.

"Minute," he rasped. He kissed her again and slipped a hand between their torsos. She stiffened, but submitted to his timid explorations. His blood pounded; his extremities throbbed.

After a long minute, she pulled away. "Really, I've gotta go."

He boldly clasped her hand as they walked to the house. Before they parted, she noted her brother's car in the driveway and offered to have him take Ro home.

He shook his head. When she started to insist, he cut off her words with a gentle kiss. Then she danced away and waved to him from the porch.

With Kate gone, the night was no longer silent. Cars rumbled and horns honked and radios rattled window panes. An occasional voice came from somewhere in the darkness. NM35 north of town was quiet enough to try and recapture the mood they'd shared.

Nothing much moved on the highway. A couple of cars flashed by without slowing. Ro had decided he'd spend the night walking when an older model Frazer Manhattan rolled to a stop. A car door banged as the driver got out.

"Hey, kid!" Bucky Hanson cut through his own headlights. "You leave my sister alone."

"Am I bothering her?"

"Damn right you are."

"Excuse me." He brushed past the bigger boy.

A hand on his shoulder spun him around. "Don't walk away when I'm talking to you."

"Get your hands off me."

"Don't bite off more than you can chew, kid."

"I'm not biting anything. I'm minding my own business."

"My sister is *my* business. Leave her alone. Estrella kids aren't welcome in Terreon."

"Now that bullshit's out of the way, give me the real reason."

"Really get off on punishment, don't you? Kate goes out with a better class of people."

"Meaning whites?"

"You got it. You reason things out pretty good for an Indian. Except you aren't even that, are you? You're a breed. Guess that's what had me fooled."

Ro took a breath. "I'm picking her up tomorrow afternoon to go swimming again."

"No you're not. You try it, I'll kick your red ass all over the countryside."

"Then you better get at it, because I'll be there tomorrow."

"Any way you want it, buddy!" Bucky lunged unexpectedly.

Ro stumbled backward too slowly to elude the bear hug. He folded his legs and dropped to the ground, breaking the hold. Before he could scramble to his feet, Bucky caught his left eye with a fist. Ro lashed out. His knuckles ground against teeth.

"You little snot!"

They rolled and wiggled in the dirt until Bucky's weight gave him the upper hand. He pinned Ro to the ground. "You gonna behave?"

Ro growled through clenched teeth. "No!"

An open hand slapped his face. "Now?"

"No!" Another blow. Ro saw stars.

"Cripes! You aren't as bright as I thought. What does it take to make you see the light?"

"She's gotta tell me," Ro snarled, spitting blood.

"I'm gonna let you up, kid, but no funny business, or I'll turn you inside out."

The pressure on his arms lessened. Feeling flowed back into his numbed hands. As soon as he was free, Ro gave Bucky a knuckle sandwich. The youth cursed and landed a heavy blow to Ro's jaw. The world whirled. After a long moment, Ro regained his feet. Bucky's car spun in a tight circle and roared away, spraying gravel from the shoulder.

An hour later, a pickup came by and screeched to a halt. Wase opened the door and gawked. "Jiminy Christmas, Ro, that you? You drunk?"

He shook his head. "Another fellow and me had a disagreement."

Ro wasn't up to the ride to Rising Rock, so he bedded down in the stable with Colorado.

****

Ro got the ribbing he expected the next morning. Of course, Pete started it.

"Lordy, Lordy! Our rooster done got his crown trimmed. I told you a hunnert times, there's them that will and them that won't, and you gotta learn the difference."

"And if that was one that will," Wade offered, "I'd sure like to meet her."

93

"Next time," Pete continued, "pick on one littler'n you, case you miscalculated."

"Ain't no gal done that damage," Wade said. "More like a jealous boyfriend or a husband. You don't suppose our new barnyard cock goes for setting hens, do you?"

Mrs. Chandler learned of his condition and plopped him in a kitchen chair to apply a red medicine that stained his skin and stung the open cuts. Thankfully, she didn't ask questions.

Mr. Chandler gave him a long stare, but Ro figured the crew had already satisfied the boss's curiosity. As soon as he could, he grabbed his swimming suit, caught a ride into town with Pete, and walked to the Hanson house. Bucky answered his knock.

"Didn't think you'd have the balls," the older boy said through mangled lips.

"Is Kate here?"

Bucky disappeared, and Kate replaced him in the doorway. She wouldn't meet his eyes.

"Hi!" Ro tried to sound cheerful.

"Let's sit out here," she suggested in a trembling voice. Seated on the front steps, she touched his bruised face. Tears pooled behind her eyes. "I... I can't go this afternoon."

"I know. I shouldn't have put you through this. It was selfish of me."

She cried at that, spilling big tears down her cheeks. "I would have looked you up somehow if you hadn't. I wanted to let you know it's not me. It's Bucky... and my folks. They don't understand." She stopped him as he started to rise. "Did he hurt you?"

He touched his swollen eye gingerly. "It looks worse than it is."

"I'm glad you didn't let him off without a scratch. Maybe those old Apache grandmothers were right about the moon's reflection. I've got heart trouble, kind of."

Chapter 20

The beginning of the school year gave Ro something to despise besides the Hansons. Unwilling to leave Colorado in the pasture near the reservation school while he was in Estrella, he walked the mile to the White Pine Agency parking lot each morning to board a yellow bus bound for a bleak, two-story structure resembling a prison more than an institute of learning.

He knew from last year the top grades belonged to the *Indah*, but he'd come to understand it wasn't a matter of discrimination. As a group, the whites sought to excel in school. They coveted the approval of their teachers, whereas Ro and others like him did not.

****

October 17, his seventeenth birthday. He doubted Cane-Woman even remembered the occasion, but Mrs. Chandler baked him a three-tiered chocolate cake, and he blew out candles the same way Paul and Teresa did on their birthdays. Mrs. Chandler gave him a fine sheepskin coat. Teresa presented him with a Motorola portable radio. Mr. Chandler gifted him with a lever-action Winchester thirty-thirty rifle. Pete and Wade contributed a saddle holster and a box of cartridges, and Paul sent him a Timex, one with numbers and hands that glowed in the dark. Ro didn't have words to adequately thank them, so he grunted a little and grinned a lot.

****

Mrs. Chandler's fleece-lined coat came in handy when an early winter set in. A snow squall hit the Capuchas before the month was out, and by December they'd seen more rain, sleet, and snow than usual. Good for grass; hard on cowhands.

Shortly before school broke for the Christmas holidays, a snowstorm hit the rez. He struggled through deep drifts to the bus and sat in soaked trousers all day in classrooms either too hot or too cold. The bus got stuck in a drift on the way back to White Pine, so it was pitch dark before everyone piled out in front of the agency building. Hugging his new sheepskin against the wet wind, Ro set out afoot for Rising Rock.

He found the wickiup deserted and the fire pit cold. Puzzled, he fed Colorado and saw him snug in his shed before tromping through the wet snow to scratch on Big Tom's tipi. No one answered, nor did anyone respond to his knock at the little house.

Uneasy now, he built a fire to warm the *gowa* for Cane-Woman's return. By the time his new watch read ten o'clock, fretting had turned to worry. An owl hooting outside the hut did nothing to calm him. The bird was a bad sign. He slipped the strap of Mr. Chandler's flashlight over his wrist and used the torch to find a great snow owl in a nearby tree. When he couldn't scare the creature away by shouting, he dug through thick snow for a rock to flush the bird.

By the time he got tired of chasing the big raptor, he was well on his way to White Pine, so he slogged through snowdrifts all the way to the police station. Maybe a policeman could help find his grandmother.

As soon as the door closed behind him, Ro regretted coming. The glowing stove in the corner made the office stuffy. A stocky young man with a short, military-style haircut turned to glare at him. Pock-faced and thin-lipped, the lawman's small eyes made Ro think of a javelina.

The officer was the nephew of a man who'd been a judge for as long as Ro remembered. People claimed the old man used witchcraft to win elections, and there were bad stories about this policeman, who'd recently returned from the white man's army. Coyote, they called him, because he was as full of tricks as the four-legged kind.

"You're Román Otero." It wasn't a question. The cop was making an identification. "You here about the old woman?"

Surprise overcame uneasiness. "You know where she is?"

The man motioned with his lips toward the door leading to the cells. "Back there."

"How come?"

Coyote laughed. "She'n some other old women got in their *tulapai* too much. She took after one of them with a hand axe."

"I'll take her home now."

"Not so fast. She'll go up before the judge tomorrow."

His breath caught in his throat. Bad blood between Cane-Woman and the judge made that dangerous. He figured each was afraid of the other's magic, but having her under the old man's jailhouse power was bad.

"I've got a few dollars on me…." He ran out of steam as the officer's look turned mean.

"Brother, you just earned yourself a cell beside the old witch."

Ro's eyebrows climbed. "What for?"

"For trying to bribe me."

"Wasn't a bribe. Money for a fine. Can I talk to her?"

"You can talk to her all you want… from your cell. We'll let the judge take care of both of you nice and legal-like in the morning. Now take off that coat and spread-eagle against the wall. Gotta search you for contraband."

He did as he was told while rough hands clasped him beneath the armpits and slid down his sides, hips, and legs. They examined his ankles and traveled back up the inside of his legs.

"Hey!" Ro yelped.

"Shut up and turn around. What's your real name, boy?"

"Roan Orphan." Ro bit down on his indignation. It was over. Let it go. He reached for his coat. "Forget it. I'll come back tomorrow."

Coyote shoved him back against the wall. "Too late for that. You gonna spend the night in the other cell. But first I gotta check for eagle parts. That old witch gets her hands on eagle parts, no telling what might happen. Take off that shirt."

Ro had managed to shuck the coat without taking the flashlight strap off his wrist, but now he had to remove it, slipping the leather strap back on while Coyote examined his shirt pockets before dropping the garment on the floor near the sheepskin. Ro's throat tightened, and he stood mute when the cop told him to empty his pants pockets.

When he didn't move, Coyote cuffed Ro's jaw and did it himself, holding up a pocketknife. "You brung a dangerous weapon into my jailhouse. That's a crime, Cuz."

"J… just the knife I use at work," Ro sputtered.

"That's what you claim. All right, let's go. Through that door back there."

Why was this happening? Then it hit him. This was serious. The old judge wanted his grandmother under his power, and they didn't know if she'd taught him to speak to Eagle. So Coyote needed them both in jail.

The cop slapped him again and drew back for another blow. "Move when I say move."

Cornered, Ro took a swing at the man. The flashlight hanging from his wrist shattered against the cop's left temple. Coyote dropped and lay still.

Stupefied, Ro let precious seconds pass before dropping the broken torch and grabbing for his shirt. But the garment was trapped beneath Coyote. The policeman groaned. Panicked, Ro searched the desk and came up with a ring of keys. Cane-Woman—the only occupant of the cells—lay motionless on a bunk. He fumbled for the right key.

The steel door screeched open, and he rushed to his grandmother. An ugly welt beneath her left eye took his breath away. The son-of-a-bitch had hit her! Ro scooped her into his arms and carried her into the office where Coyote struggled to sit up. On the way to the exit, Ro managed to grab his coat but had to abandon his shirt. Expecting an explosion from a handgun at any moment, he rushed outside and fled into the cold, wet night, pausing only long enough to wrap the sheepskin around Cane-Woman before running as fast as he could.

Snow fell in huge flakes. A frigid breeze puckered his naked back. His grandmother in his arms, he headed for the nearest woods. Halfway to the wickiup, his pace slowed. He staggered. The wet snow sucked at his boots. Icy flakes melted on his bare skin.

Ro skirted the meadow before the pine grove, afraid of open spaces even though his path was clear for anyone to follow, even by moonlight. A miracle the policeman hadn't caught up already. A different sort of chill seized him. What if the man went to the wickiup and waited in the darkness. Still, Ro had nowhere else to go, so he kept putting one foot in front of the other.

He remembered Big Tom's bear trap at the last moment. Tom, who had no regard for the medicine animals, insisted a wolf stalked the grove and had set the only trap he owned, a massive, steel-jawed thing. Ro's boot was almost on the trigger before he realized where he was.

Halting his momentum threw him off balance. He fell against a sapling and lost his grip on Cane-Woman. She rolled free. A heavy shower of snow spilled from the branches overhead, all but smothering them. Shivering with cold and fear, he struggled to his feet and picked her up.

Ro lurched into the wickiup not really caring if a pistol waited in the darkness. He laid her on the cot and fought to keep his hands from shaking long enough to build up the fire again. That done, he stripped his grandmother, dried her as best he could, and bundled her into a heavy sleeping bag. She choked on the *tulapai* he fed her, letting him know she was alive.

After seeing to her, Ro shrugged into dry clothing and pulled on his sheepskin in an effort to get warm. With warmth came fear. He was defenseless. His only weapon, a hatchet. His rifle was at the ranch.

Big Tom had a rifle. Ro stepped out into the weather once again, making for the tipi. At any moment, he expected a bullet to rip through his flesh. Tom's place was abandoned, as was the house across the clearing. He entered and set the fireplace ablaze before heading back to the wickiup. On the way, a fit of coughing seized him. Not daring to remain in the *gowa,* he lifted Cane-Woman, and struggled through the snow to lay her before the fire in the old couple's house.

Satisfied she was okay, he staggered back outside to search for signs of an intruder. Coyote would come. Why wasn't he already here? Then he heard what he'd been listening for. Gunshots, but they were distant. He coughed again, a sharp brittle sound in the night. Before long he was hacking and wheezing uncontrollably. Concealment was impossible. He built up the fire in the wickiup as a diversion and returned to the house. Cane-Woman slept, her breathing normal. Her skin was dry to the touch; his, searing hot.

Weak and woozy, he sat through the night at the front window, but Coyote didn't show. While waiting, Ro tried to sort things out. Big Tom and the old couple believed in witches, and as soon as word went out Cane-Woman was in jail, they must have cleared out of harm's way.

His coughing grew worse, his thinking fuzzier, his breathing raspier. He held onto one thought… he was in trouble with the law. An angry policeman with a powerful protector would come for him. How would this thing end? He shuddered and drifted in and out of awareness.

By morning his breath was hot and labored. Cane-Woman roused and seemed all right physically, but her mind wandered from time to time. No more than his own, he realized in a lucid moment. When she was conscious, she muttered dark depredations against her jailor; when out of her head, she conversed with Eagle.

Gasping for each breath, Ro staggered outside at first light. The only tracks marring the snow were his own. No one had approached the wickiup. Despite his weakness, he backtracked and discovered why Coyote hadn't come. When Ro had sidestepped the bear trap and fell, he knocked enough snow from the overhanging trees to cover the trap, and the policeman had blundered into it. Lots of blood. Those gunshots had been signals for help.

Ro moved Cane-Woman back to the wickiup and got some stew down her. Sick and exhausted, he climbed into his own bedroll and passed out, waking once as she sponged him with rags. He was drenched; his clothing, soaked. Alternately shivering and sweating, he tried to get up but collapsed. His mind went away.

Chapter 21

A beam of sunlight pestered Ro into consciousness. His environment revealed itself slowly. Bed. Big room. Cane-Woman dozing in a chair. Damn! He was in the White Pine clinic.

Over the next few days, as he lay abed regaining his strength, Ro learned Mr. Chandler had sent Wade to check on him when he failed to show up for work. Cane-Woman refused to allow the cowboy to take him to a hospital. Ultimately, Mr. Chandler called someone at the Indian Agency. Shortly thereafter, tribal policemen moved him—still unconscious—to the clinic. Cane-Woman, weakened by her own ordeal, moved into a chair beside his bed.

Alicia Penny, Ro's reservation schoolteacher, showed up at the clinic with books and lessons and returned every day after her own classes to tutor him, even though he was now enrolled in Estrella. She had matured. She even pronounced his name correctly now. Work might suffer at the ranch, but Miss One Cent was going to see he stayed current with his classes. He considered her a pain, but on sober thought, it was good of her to help. Cane-Woman muttered every time the teacher showed up but didn't interfere.

****

Ro knew the *Tinneh* calculated everything that followed as Cane-Woman's retribution. The cop—Coyote—lost his mangled leg, but that wasn't enough for the old witch. She demanded his life. That was why he jumped off the balcony of a hospital in Albuquerque.

The reservation awaited the inevitable clash of giants. The judge couldn't ignore a direct challenge to his power, but whatever his plans, they counted for nothing. His bailiff found him dead in his judge's chair four mornings after his nephew died. Riddled with witches arrows, people whispered.

The judge's surname had been Red Fox. The animals became "small dogs" lest someone unintentionally summoned the warlock's *ashee*. She-Who-Walks-With-A-Cane had proven the power of her *en ti*, but the effort had left her too weak and wasted to cure her own grandson.

Ro heard the rumors but was unable to put words to what he believed. Wounded men committed suicide. Old people died. All without benefit of witchcraft. But how could everything she wanted have come to pass without help from somewhere?

****

The law failed to come for him, so Ro resumed his life, more or less as it had been. That night in the police station moved to the basement of his mind. When school ended, he had no regrets. He'd had his fill of cold books and dry lectures and longed for sunshine and Paul's return. But the Korean thing was still going strong, so his brother attended summer classes in case the army got desperate for cannon fodder.

Shortly after school ended in May, Mr. Chandler joined Ro to ride a section of fence in one of the pickups. He drove while his boss talked of big things: Ro was carrying a man's workload and was entitled to full pay this summer. The savings Mr. Chandler was holding for him was growing into a healthy nest egg.

As Ro braked beside a stretch of wire needing attention, the rancher spoke again, "You're the only one around here who calls me Mr. Chandler. Call me Jim like everybody else."

Ro's chest swelled. "Okay."

They finished the task and got in the truck again. "You feeling all right, son? Pneumonia's nasty stuff. It can come back on a man."

"I'll quit running around in the snow with my shirt off." Ro flushed and bit his tongue.

Jim glanced at him, but let it drop… something that made him different from other white men. A hundred yards down the fence, the rancher spoke again. "You know, it's high time you go take that driver's license test. Do that, and you can drive one of the ranch vehicles to work and school. Leave Colorado in the stable and drive my old Jeep… the one Paul used."

His pulse raced. "That'd be great. I can get in a lot more work time when school starts again. Thanks, Mr.… uh, Jim."

"Hard to believe it's your senior year coming up." Jim dumped a roll of wire in the back of the pickup. "Son, when's the last time you went to town and fooled around or went to a movie or did whatever young folks do these days? If you don't already have something planned, how about you take Teresa to the Rialto tonight? She's been bugging me to go. That's providing you can stand her for that long. Okay?"

Ro shrugged. "Sure, if she wants to go."

"Good. Someone'll drive you to town. Get your ass in gear about that license, and next time you can drive yourself."

****

Teresa, dolled up in a dress and shoes with a bit of a heel, a hint of color on her lips, sat with him in the back seat of the Lincoln. All the way to town, they listened to Wade do what he did best… talk.

An American in Paris was okay. Leslie Caron was cute. Of course, Teresa liked it because it was romantic. *Fox Movietone News* filled them in on the latest horrors over in Korea while a Donald Duck cartoon made them laugh. Whenever Teresa liked something, she shared her pleasure by clutching his arm. They hit the malt shop afterward where she slipped into the same booth he and Kate had occupied. A girl laughed, drawing his glance. When he turned back, he caught Teresa's arched eyebrow. At fourteen, she seemed older than he was.

"I've wondered about you and girls. Paul's are always easy to spot. Loud and brassy and willing to make mush all over the place. Is that the way you like them?"

He grinned. "Don't most guys?"

"Hope not. Someday I want a boy to be interested in me, and that doesn't describe me."

Teresa wasn't a little girl anymore, but neither was she a woman. He hadn't realized how pretty she turned out.

"Just wait," he said.

"Why do you do that?" she demanded.

His eyebrows climbed. "Do what?"

"You never look directly at anyone. You always take little peeks. You hide your eyes with your lashes. You have lashes like a girl, you know."

Disconcerted, he answered the original question. "Because it's not polite to stare."

"You look sneaky when you won't look anybody in the eye."

"Where I come from, it's rude to glare... like you do."

"I don't glare," Teresa snapped.

"Ha!" he said. "You're the champion glarer of all time. That first day I came to the house, you about glared me off the place."

"I'd never seen a wild Indian up close before. You were pretty scary."

"Not half as scary as you," he said.

"You know," she observed, "in six years, this is the first time we've been alone together. Well, except the time I was sick, and you told me about Child-of-Water."

"You still remember that?"

"How could I forget? For two years, I ran around thinking defecate meant conjure. The whole school laughed at me behind my back."

Ro swallowed a snicker. "Wondered why Paul didn't straighten you out on that."

He learned new things about her that night. Her favorite color was yellow; roses, her preference in flowers. Yellow roses were perfection. She still liked Perry Como.

She went pensive. "I hate to think about you leaving for school. You always run away with Paul and leave me behind. He never wanted his sister around. It was always Paul and Ro."

His finger traced a rip in the plastic tablecloth. "Were you close before I came along?"

Teresa tossed her head. "I was such a brat nobody could stand me. But Paul was no angel either. I often wondered why you two hit it off so well."

"Not sure we did. He just overpowered me."

She laughed. "I wasn't sure you recognized that. Paul's terribly charming when he wants to be. And so good-looking." She eyed him. "Is this lawyer thing what you really want, or is it another case of Paul overwhelming you?"

"Something wrong with wanting to be a lawyer?" When he saw Wade ease the Lincoln into a parking space outside, Ro stood. They were quiet on the way back. As they climbed out of the car Teresa turned to him.

"Thanks, Ro. I enjoyed the evening." Her hand rested briefly on his arm before she gave him a peck on the cheek and disappeared into the house.

Ro was tempted to stay overnight in the bunkhouse, but he saddled Colorado and started for home in a peculiar frame of mind. He'd had fun tonight, but somewhere down deep, he'd worried about seeing Kate with another guy. Something hurtful shuffled through his guts.

A shooting star fell toward the moon-lit mountain peaks occasionally visible through the trees. Silent and intimidating, they were the home of his grandmother's gods. As he neared the pine grove, a whippoorwill swooped low over him, uttering its strange cry.

He caught the glow of a fire though the skin of Big Tom's tipi and a feeble light in the window of the little house. His neighbors had come back after last winter's scare. The hooting of four different owls raised hair on his neck. His heart fluttered. He dropped Colorado's reins and slipped through the opening of the wickiup. The fire inside was low, but provided enough light to make out Cane-Woman on her cot. Her breath came in heavy, painful gasps. He knelt at her side.

"Grandmother?" He shook her. "Mother? Are you all right?" An ember flared. In the thin light, he saw her gaping mouth. Glazed black eyes stared, unblinking. He tore out of the *gowa* and called Big Tom from his sleep. Together, they lowered the old woman to the blanket on the ground so Ro could cradle her head in his lap. After Big Tom stirred the fire to life, he stumbled out of the hut with a look of stark terror, mumbling he'd go for help. Ro understood. Tom didn't want to be anywhere near a dying witch.

One thin, bony hand plucked at Ro's wrist. He understood. Cane-Woman didn't want to die inside the wickiup. He'd have to abandon his home if she did. He started to rise, but she went quiet, so he settled back. She whispered a few unintelligible words in a strange rattle. Her concern, even now, was for him. He knew all the words she was trying desperately to say. He bent low to her ear and muttered his own liturgy.

"I hear, Grandmother. I hear. Roan Orphan understands."

From outside came the rush of giant wings. Twigs and dust settled on him as something struck the brush shelter. Crows, disturbed from their sleep, raised a raucous cry. Every owl in the forest screeched. Whippoorwills screamed and jays hawked. Bedlam reigned while he sat frozen in awe. He didn't know the moment she left, but when the forest grew quiet—unnaturally so—she was no longer with him. In the silence, he heard Big Tom returning with a medicine man, who poked his head into the *gowa*, sniffed, and backed out quickly.

"Why are you afraid?" Ro shouted. "She's not a threat to you." The wind grew behind his words. "She can't hurt you now. Why are you afraid of an old, dead woman?"

A rifle shot rent the night. Two more followed. Big Tom was letting other camps know there had been a death. Moments later the mourning wails of Big Tom's wife echoed through the pine grove. A weak voice joined her from the little house. The women cried in sympathy for him and respect for—or fear of—her.

Old women usually prepared a deceased's body, as they were less susceptible to harm from a cadaver. Elderly people passing to *ni goya*, the earth below, normally represented little threat to the living. But Cane-Woman wasn't just any gray hair. She had been a great shaman who practiced her medicine for evil as well as good. A witch had died, and a dead witch was dangerous. He—not women—would wash and dress her in her best clothes and dust a cross of pollen on her head.

So he became Roan Orphan and set about doing things in the old way. Finished with preparing her, he hacked the hair from his head until it was as short as the *Indah* boys' at school. The cuttings, he would hang in the limb of a tree outside the entrance at first light. After he drew blood from each arm with a knife, he sat recalling his life journey with this woman who had been his only family. His teacher and healer... his everything.

Little memories from childhood rose. The tail of a ground squirrel tied at his shoulder to keep him from harm. Fox grease daubed on his skin so he wouldn't grow up to be lazy. Throughout the long night, he relived their life together. Her stories with hidden lessons. Cane-Woman going hungry so he could eat.

Without warning, tears stung his eyes and spilled down his cheeks as he recalled his impatience with her. He made no sound. He was safe from prying eyes but not eager ears. The entire reservation would know of her death by now, and some reckless souls doubtless hovered at the edge of the grove, titillated by their own fear.

She had done her best for him. Why had he let the Chandlers rob her of his presence? Tears leached shame and fear and weakness away, so he was able to mourn her from a sense of love and loss. The night passed as a serpent crosses the desert, slowly but with purpose.

At first light, he drew on a shabby pair of Levis and went outside to saw off part of Colorado's tail so his horse could share his loss. He ignored the cemetery where the agency said the People must bury their dead. She had lived as *Tinneh*, and she would rest that way.

Big Tom's tipi lay on the ground. The man would soon leave, making certain a stream of running water lay between his new home and the place where the witch died. The old couple in the house would leave too, but you can't move a house, so they'd have to return after four days. If anything happened to either of them, She-Who-Had-Been-Cane-Woman would be blamed for one more dark deed.

When Ro was ready, Big Tom led Colorado to him. The man eyed his ragged locks and tattered jeans with approval. He fingered the cuts on each forearm.

"You're doing everything right, Tall Rider."

Ro needed a new name, and Tall Rider seemed as good as any. He nodded acceptance. From this day forth, Tall Rider would be his *Tinneh* name. Roan Orphan would pass on with the woman who had so named him.

He loaded her possessions aboard the pony, rolled her in the best blanket they owned, and gently laid her across the saddle. Colorado shied, but settled beneath his touch. As he led the pony through the clearing, Big Tom's family and the old couple turned their backs. The women wailed politely. Others who had gathered to witness the departure of a great witch did the same. Occasional rifle shots marked their passing.

Ro walked far into the mountains to a spot in Dead Scout Canyon. Secure in the knowledge no one would have dared follow, he enlarged a hollow place in the rocks with his hatchet, checking four times to make certain it lay from east to west. He spread her sleeping bag over the bottom of the grave and laid the blanket-covered body on top with her head to the west. Before closing the grave, he arranged her most precious possessions around her. A brass button, all she had left of her first husband. An old, blackened pot lugged all the way from Bosque Redondo during the time of confinement. A lead bullet removed from her hip and strung on a string.

The remainder, he broke beyond repair and scattered around the site. His final act was to trace the image of a cross on his bare chest with a clump of sage and place the sacred plant atop her grave. He would never again come to this place.

Straight and unbowed—but hollow on the inside—he led Colorado out of the canyon and made for the river. Somewhere along the way he picked up a shadow, but he paid no attention. At the bank of Wandering Water, he built a small fire and stared into the purifying flames.

The Owl had called her name, changing *his* world forever. But *the* world was the same. Fire was still blue and orange; smoke still stung his eyes and turned acrid in his nostrils. If he glanced up, the sun would be a white orb in the blue heavens. Yet if he returned to the wickiup she wouldn't be there. He'd never again eat a meal she prepared. If he failed to come home at night, no one would be there to scold him.

He rose and stripped, feeding his clothing to the flames. The fire gnawed and chewed the rough denim, leaping toward him, greedy for more. Naked, he bathed in the purifying smoke before leading a jumpy Colorado through the gray curtain. Then he curried the horse with a clump of sage. Afterward, he gave himself over to the shocking embrace of the river.

Upon emerging, he donned a buckskin breechcloth from his saddlebags, touched ashes to his ears, and traced a dark cross on his forehead. Mounting Colorado, he returned to the wickiup, ignoring an indistinct form paralleling him in the trees.

Big Tom was gone, leaving only a smoldering campfire. Ro picked a brand from the ashes and fanned it to life before casting it atop the *gowa*. Within minutes, a raging fire consumed the mass of canvas and brush. Heat withered the overhanging pine branches and seared his soul. His last tangible tie with She-Who-Had-Been-His-Grandmother sagged and fell in upon itself. The flames, destroyed by their own violence, turned pitiful. He moved away and discovered Ruby Chinol, the dark girl who had shadowed him as he completed his ritual.

He dropped his gaze away, loaded his things aboard Colorado, and found a quiet, uninhabited thicket with a clearing in the center. The *gowa* he fashioned was crude. That was woman's work, but he had no woman. The onerous task done, he stretched full length before a fire outside the hut and considered important things. Today he had acted as a son of White-Painted-Woman. Had he done so out of belief or out of respect? Did it matter?

When he had closed that rocky grave, he literally buried a part of himself, a length of his umbilical cord in a medicine bag around her neck. He had handled a corpse, so the old customs dictated he must remain apart from others until he was safe to be around. He was not sure he could do that. He had his work to think about. But why would he travel part of the way according to her canons only to balk now?

Darkness approached. Choked by a myriad of emotions, he moved solely to feed the flames of a small fire. What was he? Eagle... dove? Who was he?

Tinneh… Indah? Schoolboy… man? He was pieces of all those things.

He longed for Paul to talk him out of his confusion. Where had that come from? The answers he found now had to be from his mind and his soul, not those of his white teachers or *Indah* brother.

He pulled in a deep breath and sought solid ground. The sun had gone down. Tomorrow, it would rise on a new day, and he'd begin a fresh life. Was anything left for him in this place now she was gone?

A polite rustling came from the brush, and Ruby stepped into the clearing to hold out a basket. "I brought food."

His blood rose. Suffering was a private thing. "I'm not hungry." His breath caught in his throat. He was wallowing in his sorrow like a boar in a sty. He erased the resentful tone. "You shouldn't be around me right now."

"Someone has to feed you." She sank down beside him and placed the food in his hands. He gave in and gnawed a rabbit leg without tasting it. "You did everything right today, Tall Rider. The whole reservation says so. She-Who-Was would have been proud."

"Thank you," he said less sulkily.

"I called that ranch and let them know what happened. They sounded concerned for you."

Uncertain if he was pleased by her thoughtfulness or upset by her impudence, he nodded.

"After you left this morning," she went on, "a government man came with the police. The white man was mad when he found what you'd done. He tried to talk to the old man in the house but got the door slammed in his face. Even his *Tinneh* policemen ran off when he kept calling a name that oughta be forgot. He'll make trouble because you didn't use their cemetery."

"Doesn't matter. What can they do to me?"

"Put you in their jailhouse. Why'd you burn the *gowa*? You'd already moved out." She hesitated when he didn't answer. "I don't know if you believe in the Old Way or if you only did it for her, but you'll be careful, won't you?"

He indicated the cross of ashes on his forehead. "I'll remember not to whistle at night or pick my teeth or put a knife blade under my fingernails and all the rest."

"For four whole days and four whole nights," she added. "I don't really believe in it either, but you're better off safe than sorry."

He had gone to school with Ruby Chinol all his life, paying no particular attention to her. She was tall for a girl… nearly as tall as he was. Her black hair fell around a wide face with deep, glowing eyes. From the way those orbs caught the fire and threw it back at him, there must be something of the mountain cat in her. She went to school over on the Mescalero Reservation and worked at the trading post where She-Who-Was had pawned his turquoise ring.

After he ate, the two of them sat silently by the fire. Her quiet company helped him in a way he couldn't explain. An hour passed before she spoke again.

"You gonna go back to work for the whites? I think you will. What else would you do?"

"Join the Red Hats." He spoke of a team of firefighters made up of Mescalero and a few *Tinneh* men. Competition for available spots was fierce because battling forest fires was dangerous work… man's work.

"They don't take seventeen-year-old boys," Ruby said.

"Who says I'm seventeen?"

"My mother says you were born a month before I was."

"Okay, so I'm seventeen and a half," he said, calculating the passage of time. "You talk about me with your mother a lot?"

"Don't talk about you at all, smarty. But women talk and girls listen. You're seventeen… and a half."

"All right, they won't take me. But the army might. They took Clarence Wolf."

"Clarence is twice as big as you are, and he lies better."

"Okay, probably keep working for the whites."

"You gonna move to the ranch?"

"No." His answer surprised him. He'd practically decided to do just that before she asked. "I'll live here where I belong."

He rose with her, aware she'd seen him naked by the river this morning. The thought gave him a little rush. After she was gone, Ro settled on his blankets in the hut to stare at a cold white star centered in the smoke hole. Ruby had caused things to fall into place. He would work for the *Indah*, but he would come home every night. He would do that for She-Who-Had-Been. He would remain *Tinneh* for her. His decision made, he should have rested more easily. Yet, an ache in his chest kept him awake most of the night.

Chapter 22

Ro strayed from his rude hut only to trap rabbits and gather edible roots for the next four days and nights. Colorado, loosely hobbled, foraged for himself. Saturday morning, Ro cleaned up in the J-Bar-C bunkhouse and went to work. The Chandler women loaded him up with condolences, but Jim and the crew nodded in sympathy and continued to work.

Each day he went to the ranch early, and each night he rode back to the reservation to suffer through his loss as keenly as the day his grandmother died. He accepted living in a hollow body with a seared soul as his merit.

****

Miss One Cent sent word she wanted to see him at the school library at two o'clock Thursday afternoon. He left work early to keep the appointment. He owed her that much. A tall, stooped figure sitting at a library table caused his nostrils to flare. Fair skin. Brown freckles gone splotchy. The white man who'd been hunting him. Ro squelched his flight impulse.

As Miss One Cent introduced Mr. Frawley from Indian Affairs, she colored slightly beneath Ro's venomous glare.

"We've met before," the man said. "Who'd have thought that skinny little kid who wrestled the lawnmower at the agency would grow into such a fine young man?"

Ro stood silently until Mr. Frawley spoke again. "I left messages at your new wickiup, but obviously the wind blew them away. So I asked Miss Penny to arrange a meeting. I understand there's a great deal of mutual trust and respect between you."

Maybe at one time.

The agency man stepped into the awkward pause. "I believe your grandmother, Tonia Otero, passed away on June the second or early on the third. Is that correct?"

Ro grunted. This Mr. Frawley had been on the rez a long time and still didn't know any better than to speak names that shouldn't be spoken. At least, he used her Spanish name.

"It's come to our attention that you removed the body early the next morning without waiting for a death certificate by the proper authorities." Another pause. "We also understand you made your own disposition of the remains outside of the local cemetery. Son, this is highly illegal." Mr.

Frawley's smudged eyes blinked. "Please tell me what you did with her."

In spite of himself, Ro allowed a muscle to contract in his jaw.

"Román, it's a matter of health," Miss One Cent said.

"She's dead."

Mr. Frawley spoke up. "Son, the dead must be buried carefully. What if she died of a communicable disease? What if others fall ill? How would you feel then?"

Like she was doing what everyone believed she would. But he turned his growing anger inward and said nothing.

After repeated questioning, the government man leaned back in his chair, his frustration evident. "I've done my best. Now the legal authorities will become involved."

Miss One Cent tried again. "Do you understand what Mr. Frawley is saying? Your ambitions... your plans. Will you jeopardize them over this?"

He almost felt pity for her. How could she understand what they were asking? He bowed his head silently.

"So be it," Mr. Frawley said. "In the meantime, there are decisions to be made in the case of the minor child, Román Otero."

His head came up. "I'm eighteen."

"According to agency records you are seventeen. As such, you're a ward of Indian Affairs. I cannot allow you to live unsupervised. Do you have relatives who'll take you in?"

Ro claimed an uncle with a name so common it would take time to check out.

"One final thing. Since you won't cooperate in the matter of your grandmother, you need to report to the Public Health Service. They'll examine you and perhaps keep you in isolation until they're satisfied you weren't exposed to an infectious disease."

"I wasn't."

"Then why did you burn the wickiup?" the man asked.

So that was what was bothering them. Fire meant purification to him. To the *Indah* it meant sterilization. "Because—" A little of what he felt percolated to the surface. "—the only mother I ever knew was gone, and I wanted everything to go with her."

The agency man nodded. "I believe you, but unfortunately, that's not enough. You'll have to report to PHS for a thorough examination tomorrow morning." Mr. Frawley apparently read his body language. "I'm not asking you, Román. I am explaining as patiently as I can this is something you must do. If necessary, I'll have the tribal police escort you there."

"Please, spare yourself this," Miss Once Cent said. "There are valid reasons for what Mr. Frawley asks. It's for your own good. Trust me." She flinched at his look. "When you've thought this over, you'll realize Mr. Frawley had to ask his questions. Sooner or later he would have had the police detain you. I wanted to spare you that. I know your experience with them in the past has not been... pleasant."

Blood rushed to his head, but he agreed to show up at the clinic. Escaping Rainbow House was more difficult. He probably could not have managed it if the agency man didn't believe everyone on the reservation was related to someone.

****

Outwardly calm when he reported to the Public Health Service clinic Friday morning, he raged on the inside as he stood before a medicine man wearing a long, white coat. He'd thought about not showing up, but he'd given his word, and a man had to own his words... when truly given.

The examination was nothing. He didn't even mind when they poked a needle in his arm to draw blood, but he felt silly handing a bottle of warm urine to a nurse. The clinic kept him waiting until the test results came back before deciding against placing him in quarantine. As he left, they made him promise to report back in a week for follow-up tests. He made a sour face. More of the same.

****

The next morning, his mind dwelt so much on She-Who-Was he suspected her *ashee* hung around. Driven out of the wickiup by his imagination, he saddled Colorado and rode into White Pine, but the sight of the police station drove him away. On the road back, he saw the J-Bar-C jeep approaching ahead of a storm of white dust. Wade slid to a halt beside Colorado, setting the pony to dancing uneasily.

"What in hell's got into you? You take off early Thursday, and don't bother to show up a'tall since then. You got everybody worried to death! You all right?"

Another *Indah* telling him what a worthless shit he was. "Fuck you, white man!"

Wade turned two shades of purple. "Why you little shit! I'm the one's gotta take my Saturday to go hunt you down and make sure you're all right, and that's the thanks I get. Well, you can just go to hell!" He threw the Jeep in gear.

"Wait!" Ro swallowed his resentment. He should have sent word to the ranch. The burning in his belly rekindled as he explained he'd had to go to PHS for an examination.

"That all? Hell, kid, that ain't nothing to be ashamed of. Happens to a man

111

ever once in a while. You lucky they got a handy place to take care a something like that. You catch it early enough, them new drugs'll cure it right up. Just make sure the gal goes in too."

Let Wade assume what he liked. When the cowboy said he was on his way into Terreon, Ro put Colorado in the school pasture and bummed a ride. But the town did nothing for him. He went to the swimming pool hoping to find Kate. Half glad he didn't, Ro hiked to NM35 to thumb a ride back to the reservation.

Jose Peyote picked him up in his old Ford pickup and yelled over road noise coming from a hole in the floorboard, "I hear Owl come while I was gone."

"Where you been?" Ro shouted.

"Tried my hand in the Texas oil fields. Work ain't no good, but pay sure is."

"Why'd you come back?"

"Why does anybody?" Jose's gaze slid to him. "Hear you're having trouble. That government man can't seem to find no kin of yours. Another thing," he added, "the white man's got trackers out."

"They won't find her."

"Already did. You shoulda buried her *tulapai* jug instead of busting it. Ain't another one like it around. Don't worry, nobody's gonna tell the *Indah* nothing. They'll keep on playing like they're looking till the white eye gives up. Hell, they admit to finding her, they'd have to dig her up. Ain't *nobody* gonna bother that one."

Ro saw the truth in that.

"How's everybody at the J-Bar-C? Paul home?"

He went on guard. The questions seemed innocent, but Ro was glad when Jose dropped him to pick up Colorado and head home. After scouting the area around the wickiup for signs of Mr. Frawley, he collected his belongings and spent the rest of the day preparing a new home a mile to the north.

****

Monday didn't start out right. Jim kept him in the office going over paperwork most of the morning. Ro wasn't in any mood to cope with numbers and kept making mistakes.

Finally, the rancher looked up from what he was doing. "Son, whatever's bothering you, let it out where we can deal with it."

"Nothing."

"Either something's wrong or somebody else is sitting over there in your skin. You haven't been the same since your grandmother died. Is that at the bottom of it?"

Ro picked up a pencil and doodled in the margin of a ledger sheet. "Probably."

"You once told me she was your only family. Who's taking care of you now?"

He examined the rancher frankly, something he rarely did. What he saw in Jim's face made the man's questions less offensive. "I take care of myself."

"You're the most self-sufficient teenager I've ever known, but that's not right. No seventeen-year-old should have to live by himself. You're welcome here. I'd feel better if you moved in tonight. The bunkhouse or the big house, either way you want it."

Ro squirmed in his chair. "Can't. Made a promise… to her."

"I respect a promise more than most men, but a promise made under those circumstances? She'll understand if you change your mind."

Ro's mouth went stubborn. "She always told me a man has to own his words."

"Meaning, I take it, he has to honor his word." Jim rubbed his eyes. "I won't push you on it, but the invitation stands. You ever want to move, just do it."

Ro looked away from the man he respected above all others. "Thanks. I'll remember."

"One more thing. Judith and I have been planning to help you through college. We didn't tell you because we didn't want to kill your initiative. There's a bank account with enough money to take you through college and law school. That probably doesn't mean much right now, but at least it lets you know there are others who care."

Ro dropped his head. "Dunno what to say."

"Son, you've earned a helping hand, so there's nothing for you to say. Just work hard and make something of yourself."

They pretended to go back to work, rattling and shuffling papers until Ro laid his ledger aside. "Can you do without me for a while?"

Ro saw the uncertainty etched on the man's face, but he couldn't help himself. He had to get out of there. Fleeing to the stable, he straightened out tack gear until he sensed someone behind him. He turned and caught Teresa frowning at him. "What are you doing here?"

She made a face. "What a grouch! I was looking for you. Go riding with me. Please."

"Okay, but it'll be on your conscience if I get fired. Go tell your dad while I saddle up."

Minutes later they mounted. "Where to?" he asked.

"The place you and Paul used to go all the time. Harrigan's Butte."

Neither of them spoke on the ride. They tethered their horses at the base of the column of rock and started up. He went first, offering a hand when the going got rough. As they stood on top looking out over the landscape, Teresa leaned against him trying to regain her breath.

"It's beautiful! Paul used another name, uh...."

"Sleeping Turtle Mesa."

"That's so poetic." She linked her arm in his. "Ro, do you believe in God?"

"Guess so. God and Killer-of-Enemies and White-Painted-Woman and-"

"I'm serious. Do you believe He causes things to happen? Do you believe in fate?" She removed her hat and pulled her windswept hair back as he led the way to a rock ledge. They sat beside one another. "I do," she went on. "I believe fate sent you to the ranch."

"Deep."

"You were supposed to meet us. Your fate is tied to the ranch."

He laughed without humor and rose. "Way deep."

She caught his wrist. "What I'm trying to say is, you were supposed to meet us and come work on the ranch. You did what you should have done. So don't feel guilty about being in town with me the night your grandmother died." He stiffened as she rushed on. "She lived a long, long time. She had a full life. It was time for her to go, so she went. It wasn't your fault... it *wasn't*!" Teresa hid her face in her hands. "And it wasn't mine either."

He sat back down. His heart reached out to her, but his hands gripped his knees. After a moment, he put an arm around her shoulders and pulled her close.

"Why do you think I blame you?"

She swiped at her eyes and raised her chin. "Ever since it happened, you're so... cold."

"Oh come on." He dry-washed his face. "Maybe I'm not worth—"

She plugged her ears. "Stop it! Stop it! Stop it! Don't say stupid things like that. You're just feeling sorry for yourself."

Were his imperfections so evident? He pulled her back to his side. "Guess I took it hard." He drew a deep breath and exhaled. "I'd never seen her helpless before. She couldn't move or talk. I dunno how long she'd been that way. All she could do was look at me when I finally got there. She was holding on until I came. She tried to say something, but just clunks and clatters came out. Just noises. If I'd been there, maybe I could have saved her. Gone for a doctor. *Something*."

He drew a breath and continued. "I shoulda been there, anyway. My place was with her, not off somewhere with the whites." He swallowed. "Sorry, didn't mean it that way. But I neglected her, Teresa. I was all she had in this world, and I practically deserted her. When I was little, I was with her all the time."

114

"You were growing up," she said. "It's the way things are when you grow up. If I know that, she knew it a hundred times better."

"She hated you whites. She didn't want me to go back to the ranch after that first day. Just wanted me to go get some kind of reward and help her butcher Paul's pony, the one that broke his leg, and be done with it."

Her eyes widened. "You *ate* Pedro?"

He grinned. "Fed the neighbors and us for weeks."

"Ugh!" She looked thoughtful. "Why did she hate us?"

"You'd have to live in her moccasins to understand that. She lost three husbands to whites. She limped and walked with a cane because they shot her. She spent her life running from soldiers or being penned up by them or being told what to do by agency people."

He paused. "I'm Apache, Teresa… *Tinneh*. She knew it, and now I know it." He wrinkled his brow. "I didn't for a while. Maybe I wanted to be white. She knew that would happen. She knew everything. A long time ago she said something I understood in my head, but not in my heart. She said the eagle's claw doesn't make the track of a dove."

Teresa gasped. "That's beautiful. Wish I could say things like that. I understand what she meant, but it doesn't matter what you're called. You're a human, that's all."

"Oh, it matters. Believe me, it matters."

"It hasn't to me or to Paul or my parents or the men you work with."

"Not everyone's like you. And it's not all one-sided either. White eyes, we call you. *Indah*…the enemy. Guess it means we're saying *you're* different. How does that sound? You're the ones who're different." He rested his head against her black tresses. "Thank you. It helped to talk about it out loud."

"I had to get you better so I could get better."

He glanced at her. She was beginning to sound like a sister. "It's getting late. Time to go."

At the edge of the mesa, she paused. "Funny what the desert means to different people. Wonder how Paul felt when he was out there with a broken leg? But me, I love it!"

****

Mr. Frawley was nothing if not persistent. He left notes at Ro's new *gowa*. After he ignored several, Miss One Cent sent a message asking for another meeting. He paid no attention to that one either. So it was no surprise when the agency man showed up at PHS the following Friday.

The pale *Indah* stared at him while a woman in white wrapped a strap around his arm and pumped it full of air. After a minute, Ro's fingers felt as if they were blowing up like balloons.

115

The man squinted at him. "I don't think you leveled with me. Haven't been able to locate this uncle of yours."

"He moved," Ro said. "We do that a lot."

"Yes, you do seem to be a bit nomadic, even now. Román, you understand I can't let you get away with this, don't you?"

The woman returned his arm and said Ro was free to go.

"Get away with what?"

"You are a seventeen-year-old minor living in a brush hut. You'll have to move into Rainbow House."

"I grew up in a brush hut. Excuse me, sir, right now I've gotta go to work."

"You're not going anywhere until I verify a few things."

"Look, Mr. Frawley, I'll be eighteen in just four months. Not worth bothering with."

The white man shook his head. "Sorry, but legally it is."

Desperate, he blurted out nonsense. "How about I bring my uncle to your office next week sometime."

"How about you bring him to my office Monday morning at nine a.m. Otherwise, you've run out of rope."

"Okay, Monday... at nine, or maybe a little later."

Mr. Frawley's words brooked no nonsense. "Nine. Sharp."

"I... uh, we'll be there."

His world was shrinking like raw wool in boiling water. Rather than going to work, he decided to dither over his problem. But this time, he phoned the ranch from the trading post outside of White Pine.

****

Ro sat in front of the *gowa* to think about his problem. That agency man wasn't going to let go. If this thing ended up on the trail it was traveling, he'd be penned up in Rainbow House. His work would suffer, and he'd have to leave Colorado at the ranch. He had to do something, but what? Maybe he oughta talk to Jim.

No, the big man would jump in with both feet, and he'd be caught between the rancher and the government. Either way, he'd end up doing what someone else decided. Besides, he wasn't ready to move to the ranch. Crap. She-Who-Was hadn't been gone two weeks, and already he was having trouble holding his life together.

Deciding he needed a few things from the store in White Pine, Ro boarded Colorado and rode into the settlement. As he entered the store, he met Big Tom leaving, and an idea hatched full-grown in his brain. He hailed the man and accepted an invitation to coffee. Somehow, Ro found himself walking and Big Tom riding Colorado on the way to the Bearclaw camp.

116

The tipi looked just as it had when it stood at Rising Rock. The man's wife also looked the same, sobersided and pregnant. Big Tom took a seat on a blanket before the tent, two steaming cups of coffee in hand. He passed one to Ro.

"How goes things with you, Cuz? Hear you moved across the meadow."

Desperate to solve his problem, Ro decided he neither felt like nor had time for polite chatter. Today, he would act like a white man. "What else have you heard?"

Big Tom gave him a sharp look. "What else is there? The *Indah* at the agency is making big noise about you."

"What does he say?" Ro was rushing things, but he had to settle this matter.

"He give up looking for where you put She-Who-Was, but now he's hunting for your uncle. Hell, Román, I didn't know you had one."

He noted the failure to use his personal name. Big Tom must figure Ro's white blood was rising. "It's important I find one."

"Hear it ain't so bad at Rainbow House. They feed you good."

"I keep my own belly full." His stomach growled, making a liar out of him. "I don't want nothing to do with Rainbow House. I gotta find me an uncle, Big Tom."

"Where you gonna look?"

"I'm looking right now." A series of noises came from inside the tent, but Ro ignored them. "It's important to me. Nothing I've got's more important… except my horse," he hastened to add when the man's eyes slid to the chestnut.

"He's sure a good-looking animal. Be a mighty fine thing for a family to have. But come to think on it, an uncle'd probably like to have a good strong mare."

Ro tried to keep relief out of his voice. "That's the way I figure it."

More clucking from inside the tipi. Was Tom listening to his wife?

"A uncle of yours would probably have a two-burner Coleman stove and one of them big Coleman coolers."

Ro sighed. Yes, the man was listening to the voice from inside the tent. And because he had rushed into things like an *Indah* panting after a dollar, he was gonna pay.

Big Tom went on, "And he'd have some kind of money coming in the first of every month too. Probably twenty-five dollars."

Time to put up a fight. "Don't believe any of my family was ever so rich."

"Kin of yours sang to Eagle. They did right well."

"No better than five dollars."

"Lots better'n that. Twenty, at least."

Ro hardened his tone. "None of them ever did better than ten. Ten was tops."

117

"Was that cash money?" Tom wanted to know. "Not some of them checks I seen?"

"Two five-dollar bills."

This time, Big Tom tilted his head back in order to hear his wife better before speaking. "I never told nobody, but there was some of He-Who-Used-To-Be-Your-Uncle's blood mixed up in my family. But this uncle'd probably rather have ten of them one-dollar bills."

Ro would have laughed if he hadn't just been snookered. Big Tom didn't claim kin to She-Who-Was even though she and her brother came out of the same stock. "This Mr. Frawley said I have to bring my uncle to see him at nine o'clock Monday morning. White man's time."

"How would your uncle get there?"

"His nephew would bring his new mare and go with him to the agency building."

"And would your uncle have a saddle for his new pony?"

"Not unless he got it himself. There's an end to how much my uncle owns."

Big Tom grunted and offered another cup of coffee.

****

Ro went to work the next morning and slept over in the bunkhouse because he worked late. Sunday, he bought a mare from the ranch's remuda and lied himself into believing he was too tired for the ride to the reservation.

Monday morning dawned bleak and cloudy. The air was heavy and smelled damp. A good day for ghosts. She-Who-Was had always looked for them on cool, wet mornings when mists played across the mountains. As he led Colorado and the mare outside, movement high in the rafters distracted him. He halted in his tracks. An owl sat on a crossbeam at the apex of the roof, its great, yellow eyes glowing in the near darkness.

"I'm going back." His own voice raised a chill on his neck.

Chapter 23

As the meeting with Mr. Frawley progressed, Ro suspected his "uncle" came to regret the bargain he'd struck. The white man peppered Big Tom with so many questions, he tried to dump the problem in Ro's lap by suddenly having trouble understanding English. Mr. Frawley countered by bringing in an interpreter.

Just when things looked darkest, Ro came to understand the interrogation was to impress Big Tom with the seriousness of assuming responsibility for a minor. His "uncle" was getting the drift too. Tom's English returned enough to ask if there was compensation for feeding an extra mouth. Mr. Frawley didn't rise to the bait.

Ro argued against moving in with the Bearclaws, and the burning in his belly eased when Mr. Frawley agreed he could move his wickiup to the family camp, although he didn't understand why living in a brush hut on his own was wrong but okay simply because he had an uncle nearby. He kept a straight face as the *Indah* instructed him to obey Big Tom. He had no intention of paying the slightest attention to what the man said, and his new uncle likely had even less interest in wet-nursing a nephew.

Mr. Frawley informed him the PHS doctor had declared him in good health. As a bonus, the legal authorities didn't intend to pursue his refusal to divulge the resting place of She-Who-Was. His problems on the reservation were contained, if not resolved.

Ro's nervous stomach disappeared when he arrived at headquarters to learn Jim was taking him to get his driver's license. Afterward, his boss kept his promise and handed over the keys to the ranch's Jeep.

Thereafter, Ro drove back and forth to the *gowa*, which he wasn't about to move to the Bearclaw camp. In fact, he didn't see Big Tom until the first day of July when his "uncle" popped over the horizon to collect his ten dollars and the Coleman equipment he was due.

****

Paul returned home after summer classes ended mid-month, and Ro thought he was looking at a stranger. His blood brother was taller, thinner... and different. He shaved every day or else raised a golden stubble that caught the sunlight.

One day, after they finished repairing a holding pen in one of the pastures,

Paul decided he wanted to go swimming. They stripped at the riverbank and waded chest-deep into a pool in the otherwise shallow river. While frolicking like kids in Wandering Water, the magic returned enough for Ro to haltingly tell Paul about his summer. Almost getting arrested. His flight in a snowstorm. She-Who'd-Been's death. Mr. Frawley… everything.

"God, Ro! Why didn't you call or write? Or talk to Dad? To someone."

"You couldn't come back, and your dad doesn't know. Promise you won't tell."

Paul clapped a hand behind Ro's neck. "Okay, I promise. But if Teresa needed me, I'd be here in a flash. Don't you think I'd do the same for you?" Paul grinned. "Still the goof ball I left behind. For a while, I thought you weren't the same guy."

Chapter 24

Things didn't work out the way Paul envisioned. Ro worked long hours and made a fetish out of going back to the reservation at the end of the day. They managed one overnight fishing trip to a nearby lake. The water was clear, the fishing good, and sleeping under the stars relaxing.

Tonight, Pete and Ro had gone to check on Brutus, one of the J-Bar-C's bulls, that had tangled with some loose wire, so Paul drove into Terreon alone. Rumor said Sara was in town, but rumor was wrong. Mrs. Elkins explained her daughter was visiting an aunt in Dallas.

A couple of swings around the main drag turned up nothing of interest. The town was dead. Giving it up as a bad venture, Paul popped the clutch on the pickup and headed up NM35. Just north of city limits, a neon sign, its once gaudy letters now faded to a sickly pink, proclaimed to the world this was Harry's Bar, as if the world gave a shit. Judging the place disreputable enough to serve a man without demanding an ID, he pulled into the lot.

Surrounded by a carpet of bottles and broken glass, the tavern backed up to a cluster of boulders and a few stunted pines. The building, a one-story cracker box, had been a flashy green once upon a time. Now, hunks of broken stucco reminded him of a rotting carcass.

Inside, a crowd of Anglos and Hispanics talking, arguing, drinking, and playing pool filled the bar. A blend of two languages rode clouds of cigarette smoke up the walls and across the ceiling. The pudgy man behind the bar gave him a mildly searching look before selling Paul a brand of beer he didn't recognize.

He claimed a table in the corner, and by the time he finished his second brew, his lungs, blood, and brain cried for oxygen. After elbowing his way into the parking lot, Paul froze as two men came around the back of the building. Jose Peyote halted in his tracks. Paul didn't know his companion.

"Lookie here, Tomas. Here's a man can buy us some drinks."

Paul shook his head. "Sorry, Jose. Against the law to sell alcohol to Indians."

Jose made a noise through his nose. "Wouldn't be selling to Indians. Selling to you."

"Afraid not. Gotta go."

Jose nudged his companion. "His mama's looking for him. You oughta see his mama."

"Knock it off, Jose!"

"Don't go getting stiff-legged, man. Don't mean nothing. Mean it nice. She's a fine lady. That's all I was saying. Didn't know no better, I'd say you don't like Jose." His voice dropped an octave. "Or maybe you scared when your old man ain't around."

Paul stared straight into the man's black eyes. "It'd be a blast to handle a drunk like you."

"Whew! White boy sure talk a good fight," Tomas said.

Paul stabbed a finger toward Jose. "If he can't hit somebody from behind, he doesn't want any part of them."

Jose planted his legs and rolled his shoulders. "Come on, white bread, let's go."

He matched the bastard's taunt. "How's your arm? Wouldn't want to take advantage."

Jose didn't move a muscle, but he sounded hoarse. "That bill ain't been paid yet."

"I'm leaving now. Haven't got time to waste trading four-letter words with you."

Paul spun on his heel and walked toward his pickup. A spot in the small of his back itched. Sweat beaded his forehead, and he fought to keep from checking his rear. Wouldn't give the son-of-a-bitch the satisfaction of seeing him squirm. He slid into the driver's seat, kicked over the motor, and pulled out of the parking lot.

A week later, he left for school.

Chapter 25

A yen, an itch… *something* crawled up inside Jose and wouldn't let go. He couldn't eat. Couldn't sleep. Gave up looking for a job. The few chores Harry gave him earned a pittance. Not enough to raise a good drunk. Relatives fed him, but nobody handed out booze.

He jumped an airman on a side street directly beneath a lamp post in Terreon. The mugging financed a glorious three-day drunk that gave him oblivion. Feeling nothing was feeling good.

Jose woke lying in a high mountain canyon. A fierce thirst drove him to a nearby creek. After a drink, he flopped on his back, wrestling with a headache and a roiling gut. Shit, time to put an end to all this.

Wading into the frigid stream, he fell to his knees in a shallow pool to watch eddies playing at the edges before lying face down in the icy water. He let go and tried to think of nothing. Finally forced to take a breath, he came up choking and gagging. Coughing his lungs clear, he rolled over on his back. He'd heard drowning was a good way to go, but it didn't seem that way to him.

Snowy clouds dappling the blue sky morphed into a white wraith. Mary Sue! He closed his eyes. Didn't help. The mist cavorted, moving toward him and swirling away like a playful child. A second apparition pulsed in the fog. Willi! Little Willi. He reached for them, but they remained beyond his grasp. The fog churned, agitated by fury, and took on the image of an *Indah* youth. One with yellow hair and vacant blue eyes.

Jose experienced an emotional jolt. He rose, and the water flowing from him sloughed away the old Jose. He was a changed man. A man with a mission. As his jarhead buddies used to say, the mission was the thing. And his mission had a name. Chandler. He'd make the bastards pay for witching him.

What a crooked path his life had taken. A life of false trails, false gods, false men. They'd lured him from the true path… the Way. He'd been lost in a foreign world, but he was home now. Home with a sacred mission. His new secret name would be He-Who-Walks-the-Straight-Path. He snorted. His wife—who wasn't a wife no more—could still call him "Walks."

Jose trod the mountain forest with a firm gait, his belly empty but behaving, his headache gone. He located his pickup and drove to his uncle's house and cleaned up before heading for the little store in White Pine. He'd heard old man Lynx needed a load of firewood hauled from the mill on the Mescalero Reservation. Maybe he still needed it done. He did, and Jose negotiated hard for the job.

The weight was almost too great for his old Ford, but he made the trip with no mishap, except for a flat tire. As he finished mounting his bald spare and reloading the pickup, the lowing of cattle caught his ear. A line of curious cows stood at the fence chewing cuds and watching him like gossiping old women. The brand on the livestock gave him a start. He looked around. He'd come to a halt on NM35 north of the white house. Hell, this was J-Bar-C land. Must be the *ga'an* telling him it was time to take the first step in fulfilling his mission.

He walked over to the fence for a closer look at the animals. They were in good shape, but J-Bar-C stock always was. Nobody ever said Chandler wasn't a good rancher. Jose drew a slack strand of barbed wire like a bowstring and sighted the round, brown eye of a heifer just beyond the fence. The wire whipped through the air. The cow bawled in pain and ran mindlessly in a circle. Jose pelted the cattle with rocks until they retreated out of range. He considered chasing them to run off more weight, but settled for cutting the wire on both sides of the highway with shears from his toolbox. He trembled with excitement like he was in-country harassing the enemy in his Corps days.

****

That evening, Jose found Tomas sitting on their customary boulder back of Harry's. They only had enough for a pint of the cheap stuff, and halfway through it, Jose was feeling no relief. All he could think of was scaring the Chandler kid shitless the other night. Looked too much like his mama to be a man. Shoulda fixed the son-of-a-bitch so no woman would ever look at him again. Jose got up and tossed the bottle aside. Tomas grabbed for it but missed.

"Hey, Bro! You letting that rancher get under your skin like a tick. You pull out a tick, his head comes off, and you got trouble."

Jose's eyes narrowed to slits. "Come on."

The drive through the cool night air cleared Jose's head. As they turned down the long gravel drive to the J-Bar-C Ranch headquarters, he killed his headlamps. Halfway there, he wheeled north onto a service road. Tomas hopped out to open the gate.

Leaving the pickup in a draw, they walked to the trees bordering the big lawn. A light from the stable caught Jose's attention. With Tomas hugging his heels, he silently entered through a back door.

Tall Rider and one of the ranch hands worked on an ailing horse in a stall at the front of the building. As Jose watched, the breed took a kettle of boiling water from a portable stove and turned back to his work. The naked blue flame of the burner pulled an idea out of Jose's head. He put lips to Tomas' ear. "You put a fire to his ass. That's how you get a tick outta your skin."

He inched his way up the row of stalls. The ponies sniffed suspiciously as

124

he passed. One nervous gelding whinnied. Jose dropped to the ground and slithered forward. He reached the stove and silently toppled it on its side. As he backed away, the gas-fed flame licked at strands of straw and raced quietly toward a nearby pile of hay. Once there, the hungry flames swarmed the dry fodder like Marines assaulting a position.

Jose swallowed the urge to yell "Oorah" as he and Tomas slipped into friendly darkness.

Chapter 26

Shortly after Ro's eighteenth birthday, Jim called him into the office on a Saturday morning. Unaccustomed to premonitions, a chill played up and down Ro's spine as he anticipated Jim's question.

"What the hell's going on? Every outfit has bad luck now and then, but damnation, we're under siege. Something every blessed day for the past two weeks. Cut wire. Maimed cattle."

"Maybe those Roswell UFOs are back." Jim seemed nonplussed, so Ro got serious. "Remember the day it started? The day somebody sliced the fence on both sides of the highway not a mile from here. Shortly after that, the stable burned down."

Jim looked up. "The stable? But that was an accident."

"That stove was sitting flat on the ground as solid as this chair. Planted it myself. And I told you the horses acted spooked." He paused. "You know Jose Peyote's back?"

"That mess was a year and a half ago. Jose doesn't strike me as a patient man. If he was gonna make trouble, he'd have done it before now."

Ro studied his boots. How could he talk about witches and spells to somebody like Jim Chandler? He drew a breath and tried. "I hear he's had it rough since he left. And if some people believe they're under a man's thumb, they'll do anything to get out from under it."

Jim sighed. "Maybe we're pumping a dry well. Might not be Jose, but to be on the safe side, I'll alert everyone it may be more than just harassment."

****

After nightfall, Ro drove to Harry's Bar where rez talk had Jose spending a lot of time. He found his quarry sharing a boulder with Tomas at the back of the building.

Jose held out his hand. "Yo, Cousin. We a little thin right now. You stand us a six-pack?"

Ro handed over a bill, and a few minutes later accepted a bottle from the six pack he'd just paid for. After he forced a mouthful down his throat, Jose pounded him on the back.

"Atta boy. You ain't too good to have a drink with us. Not like your snotty white friend. Much money as that bastard's got, he wouldn't buy us a drink."

"Paul? When did you see him?"

"Other day. Sent him off with his tail between his legs. Have another'n?"

"Still working on this one." Ro upended the beer and pretended to take a slug of the yucky stuff. "What do you mean, he went off with his tail between his legs?"

"Didn't like the company around here." Jose downed a quarter of his bottle. "What's going on at the ranch? Heard the stable burned down and killed some stock."

Ro made light of the incident, claiming Mr. Chandler was already planning to build a new stable. They'd saved the horses, so it was no big deal. Would Jose swallow that whopper?

"What do you hear's *gonna* happen, Jose?" he asked.

"Hell, I ain't no witch like She-Who-Was, but that ranch is jinxed. Clear out before the man turns on you."

"Mr. Chandler's been good to me."

"Bought hisself a Injun brat. Brother, you paid him back long time ago. He uses you. Someday he'll send you running and fix it so you can't get a job nowhere."

"I don't plan on beating up his son."

"Paul cold-cocked me. Nobody does that." Jose drained his bottle. "He still in town?"

Ro gave Jose a white man's look—right in the eyes. "Back at school."

Shortly after that, he tossed his bottle and headed for the *gowa*. Tired though he was, he kindled a flame in the outside fire pit and sat down to think. Paul had seen Jose at Harry's Place, and *something* about that meeting got under Jose's skin. How deep did it go? If the man believed the Chandlers were witching him, it could be bad.

That made no sense. Jose had been out in the white world... clear across the ocean to fight a war. He was emancipated. Or was he? Tonight, Jose had refused to say his grandmother's name. Ro also observed the name-avoidance custom, but that was out of respect. Jose had used Ro's personal name. Not unusual, except Jose didn't like to be called Walks.

The night pressed down on Ro. He sat alone and exposed. Old fears rose. He listened for the flutter of feathered wings or that trickster coyote. After tracing a cross of ashes on his forehead, he laughed. Was anyone ever totally emancipated?

Ro sobered. The Chandlers were white, and the coming struggle involved a fellow tribesman. What did he owe Jose Peyote? What did he owe the *Tinneh*?

He entered the *gowa* and took to his blankets. Tomorrow, he'd gather his belongings and go live on the ranch... at least for the next few months. She-Who-Was had been a wise woman. She'd understand.

127

The little wickiup shuddered in the violent grip of a sudden whirlwind. His skin crawled. Dust devils didn't happen at night.

Chapter 27

A bank of rose-tipped clouds in the east heralded the arrival of dawn as Ro began his five-mile run. The soft aura strengthened, chasing shadows from crevasses and laundering pink clouds snowy white. A ray warned his back as he finished the course. He packed the Jeep and, with a plucking in his guts, coaxed the engine to life. As the vehicle inched forward the *thing*—whatever it was—rent loose.

He found Jim in his office and told him of last night's meeting with Jose. The rancher heard him out without interrupting and then shook his head.

"Not enough for the sheriff. At least, we know who, but damned if I understand why."

Ro stood tongue-tied. What was on his lips tasted like superstitious nonsense, but once again, he had to try. "He's fixated on you. You're the reason he can't get a job. You're why his children died and his wife left him. And if that's what Jose believes, then it's gospel to him."

"Bullshit!" Jim said. "But I'll let the sheriff know we believe Jose's the one responsible for the mischief. And we'll tell the boys to keep a sharp eye out."

Ro groaned inwardly. Mischief? That's all it was to Jim? He had no more words to spend on the matter. "I'm moving back. My things are in the Jeep."

"Take Paul's room."

He opted for the bedroom at the end of the hall. As Jim announced what they had in mind at breakfast, Ro watched Judith obliquely. She seemed okay with the arrangement; Teresa appeared pleased. Did she miss her big brother so much she'd accept him as a poor substitute?

****

Now eighteen, Ro no longer had to pay Big Tom ten dollars on the first of each month or make sure Mr. Frawley wasn't tromping on his heels. But the homework grind in this, his last year in high school, more than replaced those irritants. Nonetheless, he kept at it. While he labored over his lessons, everyone was talking about General Ike beating Governor Stevenson for the presidency and carrying on over Great Britain's new Queen Elizabeth II.

The Chandlers held their Christmas celebration two days early to drive to Albuquerque and deliver Paul's present, a brand-new Studebaker Land Cruiser convertible. Since Teresa was out of school for the holidays, they intended to stay until New Year's Day.

Paul's Christmas card mentioned a new friend named Bull Sheldon. Apparently, varsity football players didn't often run around with sophomores, but Paul intended to bring his new friend for a visit when the semester ended. All Ro grasped was that his blood brother was coming home this spring. If the days had dawdled before, now they crawled.

That old Russian dictator Stalin dying in March distracted the world for a moment, but after that, time caught up with Ro's graduation day. Paul wasn't home yet, but the Chandler family came to watch him walk across the stage at Estrella High to receive his diploma.

He managed to snag the promise of a date for the school dance that evening from Ruby before the Chandlers whisked him off to dinner and a small celebration. After they gifted him with a new gold watch and a set of luggage, Jim handed over a bank book with a breath-taking balance, his savings plus the college money. Ro grew as shy as a five-year-old meeting an uncle for the first time. He struggled with a totally inadequate thank you until Jim took him off the hook with a toast.

Ro escaped the house and found a place to be alone as soon as he could without being rude. Sitting in the loft of the stable to mull over the day's events, he searched for an owl perched among the rafters but found nothing, at least nothing he could see. What *was* there, he could only sense. He whispered a plea for understanding and fled to the bunkhouse where the crew surprised him with a leather belt engraved with his graduation date and a silver buckle embossed with his initials.

"That'll look right nice when you pick up your gal tonight," Pete said.

The remark caught Ro off base without his hide-behind-face, and the cowpoke picked up on his reaction. "By crackies, he's got hisself a date. 'Bout time. This boy's the most reluctantest bull calf I ever seen."

Joe laughed. "Hell, ain't no wonder. I recollect the shape he come home in the last time he went tomcatting."

"Tell you what, son," Pete said. "Might be a mite safer if you'n me was to go to town for a leetle visit with Joe's gal. She don't beat up on her men folks."

Ro slipped out before they turned their attention back to him. After cleaning up, he snaked his new belt through the loops of his Levis and snugged it around his waist. Looked good. He ducked into the den long enough to let the Chandlers know he was leaving and had just settled behind the steering wheel of the Jeep when Teresa approached.

"Going to see that girl you were talking to at your graduation? What's her name?"

"Ruby."

Teresa picked a loose thread from her sweater. "She's not your type, you know."

"Didn't know I had a type."

"Lotsa things you don't know."

He watched her saunter toward the porch, shrugged, and threw the transmission into gear. Ruby was waiting for him in front of her house.

He was no more comfortable in Estrella High's gymnasium than he was in its classrooms. A few couples shuffled around the floor to the beat of a hi-fi-set. Ro and Ruby drank a glass of punch and tried out a few tunes. He didn't like dancing, not even powwow dancing. His body found the rhythm, but his feet couldn't handle the steps.

They ended up sitting high in the bleachers holding hands and watching couples swaying to the music as Ruby pointed out reservation kids and told him who was joining the Army, who was going to trade school, and who was looking for a job. He'd grown up with those kids, played sports with them, took classes with them, but he hadn't formed bonds. He'd run alone, played alone. Were his roots to the *Tinneh* so shallow?

Ruby pulled him out of his introspection. "Any more trouble on the ranch?"

"Some. Not much." He shifted on the bleacher. "Let's go somewhere else."

They returned to the rez and drove aimlessly. At least, Ro thought so until they entered the glen at Standing Rock. No sign of his old wickiup remained, and the little house looked deserted. He killed the motor.

Ruby turned to him. "Isn't it time you came back? Mr. Chandler can hire a hundred people. He doesn't need you, but there's so much you can do here."

He shook his head. "The tribe's livestock association people know a hell of a lot more about cattle than I do. But if I can get myself through college, I can learn to do something they can't. Anyway, I don't wanna talk about it. Not tonight." He reached for her, pulling her close.

She shook him off. "No, let's not talk about it. You'd rather screw me in the dirt than talk about it!" Ruby caught his face in her hands. "I'm sorry. I didn't mean that. But…."

"It's all right. I understand." Actually, he didn't understand at all. Uncertain of himself, he kissed her. She was soft and warm to the touch. He made shy little movements with his hands.

She didn't protest; he grew bolder. When she responded, he pulled a blanket from behind the seat and spread it on the ground. Then he lifted her from the vehicle and gently placed her atop it. Falling to his knees, he covered a breast with each hand and laid his head against the gentle rise of her belly. Strangely unhurried, he remained motionless for a long moment, inhaling her scent.

Ro removed her clothing slowly, pausing to explore each new expanse of bared flesh, becoming so involved that he ejaculated in his trousers. Feeling no shame and engulfed in the most glorious experience of his life, he examined this strange creature, the source of it all.

Totally sensory, he massaged with his hands, tickled with his tongue, caressed with his lips, teased with his teeth, promised with his loins… seeking to return the magnificent favor she bestowed upon him. Aroused by his fingers, Ruby whimpered. How wonderful to be able to do that for her.

"Rider," she murmured, fumbling with his shirt buttons. The touch of her fingers on his bare chest was more gentle than a snowflake, more exciting than a stampede. The wind puckered his flesh. Her hands worked his buckle and tore at the brass buttons of his jeans, causing his stomach to flutter. She moved inside his clothing, rubbing her fingers in his spilled seed.

He stripped away his clothing and knelt between her legs, leaning forward to experience the magic of contact.

Moving against her rapidly, slowly, deeply, shallowly, he sought to discover what gave her the greatest pleasure. He existed only for this beautiful being surrendering herself to him. He thrust and ground and worked and teased and brought her to climax.

Only then did he concentrate on his own needs and acknowledge the incredible sensation in his groin, his stomach, his nipples. Her hand touched his face and drove him over the threshold. He convulsed. The orgasm went on and on, leaving him weak and shaking.

He collapsed atop her and uttered a single word, "Wow."

Dumb ass! He should have been able to quote poetry after such an experience.

Ruby stroked his damp hair. "If you came back home, we…." She faltered as he flinched.

He rose and recovered his clothing. Why did she have to spoil the most glorious experience of his life? Why did she have to control him, stifle him? Was this what women did to their men? Had she lain with him just to lure him back?

"I can't!" he snapped. Immediately contrite and ashamed, he mumbled, "It won't be for long. I promise. Just…." His voice died as she sobbed. He stood, awkwardly, uncomfortable in his semen-soaked denims and uncertain of what to do while Ruby pulled on her dress.

He grew suddenly weary. "Let's go."

****

Halfway to the ranch, Ro pulled over and leaned against the Jeep to contemplate the night. A night like no other. A magnificent moon hovered just

132

beyond his reach. Stars sparkled excessively. The night air draped an uncharacteristic warmth across his shoulders. The earth smelled rich, female.

He scuffed the dirt with the toe of a boot and filtered out their uncomfortable parting to consider his feelings about the evening. Proud. Man proud. That was it. He'd been a man tonight. Took his first woman. The rest didn't matter.

He gasped at a sudden thought and stood up straight. What was Ruby's clan? He took a deep breath and reasoned she would have considered that before submitting to him. Ruby wasn't about to commit incest, no matter how you calculated it, the white man's way or the Indah way.

With that, he returned to his thoughts. Just being a man with a woman wasn't it... well, not all of it, anyway. Gratitude? Yes, part of it. Definitely. Ruby's gift made all others seem like hand-outs. She'd given her body and offered her soul. Overwhelmed with gratitude, he stifled a sob. It hadn't been just a roll in the hay, it had meaning. This girl—no, this woman—had initiated him into manhood. That was important. Profound.

Like Paul had said, it was for doing, not telling. Not even for sharing. For doing and holding dear. His heart seemed to leave his body, and he prayed it reached Ruby Chinol safely.

Chapter 28

Ro skipped his run to finish work early. Even so, it was past noon before he got back to the house. Paul's Studebaker ragtop sat in the drive. He rushed to bed down Colorado before finding the family in the den. Paul spotted him and lunged to his feet.

"Man, it's good to see you!" He grasped Ro's hand and pulled him into the room. "Want you to meet someone."

Bull Sheldon stood six-two and weighed accordingly. The jock offered a ham-handed shake and turned back to an interrupted conversation with Jim.

Ro studied the huge youth. Brown hair, thin on top. Sallow skin. Flat, bulldog face. The guy would be sloppy fat a year after he quit working out with the team. Ro noticed Teresa watching his reaction. She wrinkled her nose. That pretty well summed up Bull for him too.

****

Ro didn't see much of his brother for the next couple of days. By the time he got in from work, Paul and Bull had usually gone somewhere. But Monday, Paul came into the stable as Ro unsaddled Colorado.

"Hope you're not too tired to hang."

Ro put aside his weariness. "Give me fifteen minutes."

Paul and Bull talked football in the front seat of the Lincoln while he sat in back, already sorry he'd come along. They circled the main drag and found everything dead. On their way back to the ranch, Bull spotted the washed-out neon atop Harry's Bar. At his urging, Paul parked, and the two college men got out. Ro sat where he was.

"What's the matter?" Bull asked. "Don't they serve sarsaparilla? Man, it's dry out here."

"Just one beer, okay?" Paul frowned when Ro pursed his lips toward the sign on the bar's door. "Sorry, I forgot."

"Don't tell me they gonna make trouble over IDs in this dump." When Paul pointed to the sign prohibiting dogs, minors, and Indians, Bull squinted at Ro. "You an Indian? Hell, I thought you was Mex. Okay, you hang here. We won't be long."

After Paul and Bull disappeared inside, Ro crawled out of the car and claimed a seat on one of the boulders behind the building. His mood didn't improve when they came out to join him later. He accepted the beer Paul handed him. Still didn't like the stuff. Tasted like horse piss, but Bull would think him a pussy if Ro didn't drink it.

His gut clenched when Jose Peyote and Tomas Wingfield came around the corner and beat on the back door. Harry appeared and accepted their money.

"Shit," Paul muttered beneath his breath.

"That the skin who bushwhacked you?" Bull asked. "Which one?"

After Paul fingered Jose, Bull finished off his beer and heaved the empty bottle in the general direction of the two men and swaggered to the rear entrance to beat on the door. "How about some service!" The bartender appeared and took his order.

Ro half-hoped Jose would leave, but the man lingered, his black eyes fixed on Bull for an instant before sliding to Paul.

"What you staring at, skin?" Bull demanded. "Don't like being stared at by a couple of drunk fairies."

"Don't make no difference to me what you don't like," Jose said.

"Be my pleasure to change your mind, Chief."

Jose looked up at Bull. "Bug off, white boy. I ain't done nothing to you."

The jock turned as if to walk away and brought his heel down on Jose's instep. The man grunted. His face darkened.

"You're big, but big ain't always enough."

Bull exhaled noisily and made his move. He was fast, but Jose danced to one side. Bull's beefy fist slammed into the wall. Jose landed two solid blows to the kidneys. Bull whirled and lunged again. Jose sidestepped, keeping out of reach and delivering blows almost at will. Bull absorbed them and kept coming back for more.

Then Jose stepped on a beer bottle. As he fought to recover his balance, Bull threw a roundhouse to his chin. Jose reeled backward and slammed into a boulder. His head bounced off the stone with a dull thud. Bull gave him no time to recover. He sent hard jabs to Jose's face and belly. Jose struggled, but he was hurt.

Tomas had watched the fight without moving. Now he darted for Bull's broad back. Paul caught him in the throat with the side of his hand, dropping him.

As Bull systematically pummeled Jose, Ro lunged forward and grabbed the big youth's arm. Bull sent a fist to Ro's mouth, sending him tumbling in the dirt.

"Bull!" Paul jumped between them. "Stop it!"

The hulking jock dropped his arms. "Sorry. Didn't know which Indian you was."

Paul pulled Ro to his feet and examined his split lip. "You okay?"

Bull shoved them toward the parking lot. "Nursemaid him later. Right now, we gotta split."

Hand to his bleeding lip, Ro nodded to Jose. "He needs a doctor."

"Uh-uh. Gotta haul ass," Bull warned. "I ain't gonna spend my vacation in the pokey."

His companions hustled a resisting Ro into the car and cut out of the place. Once on NM35, Paul glanced into the back seat. "You won't tell the folks, will you?"

"Not if he knows what's good for him," Bull said.

"Naw, but not because of him."

They were quiet the rest of the way home. After arriving at the ranch, each went to his own room. Ro stopped the bleeding from his split lip before rapping on Paul's door.

"Promise you'll be careful while you're home," he said when Paul answered his knock.

"No sweat. Jose learned his lesson tonight."

"Paul, Jose was whipping that bully until he slipped on a bottle. And Jose's not gonna let that go. Our trouble didn't start until you got into it with him at Harry's. You didn't tell me or your dad about it. We had to find out the hard way."

Paul reddened. "Okay, I'm warned. Uh... how you gonna explain that lip?"

Ro grinned, causing the wound to bleed again. "Colorado rode me into a low limb. Gave him the devil for it."

Ro took breakfast with the crew rather than risk questions about his fat lip at the big house. He could face the Chandlers individually, but as a group around a table? He wasn't sure.

Pete eyed his mouth. "Oh, shit. He done had another date. Musta been a leetle gal this time, that's all she done."

Wade laughed. "Somebody gotta teach this kid how to do it. It ain't supposed to hurt, Ro."

****

A few days later, Ro and Pete worked at a dipping station situated in a wide draw that made managing cattle easy but restricted vision and interfered with the reception of the radio system Jim used to keep in contact with the field. By two o'clock, Ro'd run out of patience waiting for Wade to bring the last bunch of cattle, so he mounted Colorado and rode up the hill at the back of the station to raise the cowboy on his radio unit.

Upon reaching the crest, he forgot all about Wade and his fifty head of cattle. Empty beer bottles littered the back of the hill. Someone had parked a horse at the base and climbed to the top. Several times, judging from the scattered trash.

Jose!

Ro grabbed the radio hanging from his pommel and called headquarters to learn Paul and Bull were heading Ro's way on horseback. He warned Jim that Jose might be on the ranch and—yelling for Pete—laid heels to Colorado, keeping to the high ground and praying he was worked up over nothing.

Two sets of fresh tracks crossed in front of him. Two sets. Two ponies. He broke into a sweat and checked his rear. Pete was still a distance behind, but Ro didn't wait. He pushed Colorado to his limit.

Far ahead and below him, two horsemen rode down a broad draw at a leisurely gait. One towered over the other. Paul and Bull. Ro scanned the high ground. Nothing suspicious. He had covered half the distance to the riders when sunlight glinted off something in the rocks above them. His heart hammered. His belly knotted. He stood in the stirrups, waving wildly and shouting at the top of his lungs.

Hauling Colorado up short, Ro clawed for his Winchester and got off three warning shots before two rifle reports came from the rocks. Fighting to control his spooked mount, he saw Bull Sheldon tumble backwards out of the saddle. Paul jerked sideways and rolled in the dust.

Ro raced down the hill and sawed frantically on the reins, flinging himself into the dirt as two more shots rang out. Bullets whined close by. He dropped his head and played possum.

Moments later, he peered from under the brim of his hat as two horsemen topped the rise ahead of him. Slowly, he raised his rifle and aimed at the nearer rider. He squeezed off a round. The bushwhacker went down, taking his mount with him.

The second man pulled up and fired from the saddle. The bullet fell short, kicking dirt into Ro's face. A stinging pain in his forehead distracted him momentarily. Another rifle barked as Pete joined the fray. By the time Ro cleared dirt from his eyes, the ambusher had turned tail and was almost over the ridge. Ro tossed off two quick shots and thought the fleeing man slumped over his saddle.

A red haze blurred his vision. A stone or a fragment of lead must have gashed his forehead. He swiped at his eyes as he ran to Paul. Pete rode for Bull.

The fleshy part of Paul's left arm near the shoulder oozed blood. Ro straddled him, immobilizing the injured limb. Jerking a kerchief from around his neck, he staunched the flow of blood with a tourniquet. Paul squirmed in pain.

Ro stood. "You'll be all right. They're gone."

"Bull?" Paul gasped, blue eyes blinking wildly. Shock or fear? Probably both.

Ro glanced at Pete and caught the shake of his head. "Looks like he's had it. I'm going for help. You lie still." He called for Pete to keep a sharp eye out.

Colorado, frightened by rifle fire, had taken refuge on the far side of a hill. The other two horses were halfway to the stable by now. Ro talked his way to the nervous chestnut's side and got a firm grip on the reins.

He raised Jim on the mobile to report what had happened, learning the rancher and Judith were already on the way. When the air was free again, Ro radioed for Wade to join them.

He checked Paul's tourniquet while Pete covered Bull with a poncho. It took both of them to get Paul aboard Colorado. The Chandler boy floated in and out of consciousness as Ro mounted behind him and walked the horse toward home.

The world went silent as they plodded along, but the roar of a motor soon broke the quiet. Jim braked the pickup and rushed to Paul's side, Judith right behind him.

"How bad is it?" she asked.

"His arm. Lost some blood."

"Are you all right?" Jim asked.

Ro removed his hat and stuck his finger through holes in both the brim and the crown. The heavy felt likely saved him from a worse injury. "Just a scratch. Two shooters. I got one."

After they helped Paul into the bed of the pickup, Jim climbed in beside his son. The rancher eyed Ro sternly. "Wait for me. I'll be back as soon as I get help for Paul."

Wade had joined Pete by the time Ro got to the ambush site. The tall cowboy motioned to the fallen bushwhacker. "Good shot, man. See if you can tell who it is."

Odd way to put it. Ro rode up the slope and discovered why. He took one look and gagged. An ugly hole yawned like a spare mouth where the bridge of the man's nose should have been. Some sort of matter obscured most of the face. Although logic told him it was Tomas, he couldn't be certain. He turned away and threw up. The men pretended not to notice.

"Pete, Wade!" he shouted louder than intended, "I'm not waiting for Jim. Let's go after the son of a bitch."

The bushwhacker's trail led straight toward the reservation, but soon, the horse's stride shortened. The fugitive had slowed to a walk. Wordlessly, they dogged the tracks until Wade pointed to a cloud of dust rising along their back trail. "Boss coming."

They reined in and waited. In a few minutes, a pickup shot over a rise, lurching dangerously before settling back on four wheels. The rancher slid to a halt. A man Ro recognized as Sheriff John Valera jumped out of the passenger's seat into a cloud of swirling dust.

"Pete, Wade, give us your mounts," Jim ordered. "Wade, take the truck back to the house. Judith and Teresa went with Paul in the ambulance. Somebody's gotta be there in case the hospital calls. Pete, you wait with the bodies for the medical examiner."

"How's Paul?" Ro asked as the rancher settled into Wade's saddle.

Jim shook his head. "Too soon to tell."

They set out on the trail again until the tracks led through a gaping hole cut in the reservation fence.

"Hold it," Valera said. "That's tribal land. My badge don't carry weight over there."

Jim pointed. "That's where the bushwhacker went, so that's where I'm going."

The lawman sighed acceptance. "Ro, you lead the way."

The hoofprints gradually drifted toward the mountains. A bit later, Ro dismounted. "Something's wrong with these tracks."

The sheriff knelt on the ground beside him. "What?"

"Don't think we're following the same horse."

Jim snorted. "Course we are. We've dogged his trail for hours. Let's keep after him."

A bit later, Ro reined in. "Well, that does it."

"Damnation!" Jim muttered.

The fleeing man's tracks merged into a wide, freshly traveled cattle trail.

"He'll either join the herdsmen and hope they'll cover for him, or he'll trail them and cut out when he gets to hard ground," the sheriff said. "We'll never find him."

Jim nudged his horse forward. "Can't quit now. And we don't have time to poke along."

They caught up with the herd shortly before dark. The drovers had already pitched camp. Ro greeted the headman, whom he knew slightly, and engaged in a spirited conversation for a few minutes before turning to the others.

"They haven't seen Jose or a lone rider all day."

"You ask about the tracks we were following?" Valera asked.

"One of his grandsons went wandering a way back. I'm betting Jose spotted the trail and merged his tracks into the kid's."

"How do we know he's telling the truth?" Jim asked.

"I believe him," Ro answered. "The old man's an honest fellow. These are good people."

"Just because they're Apaches don't mean you can't believe them," Valera added.

A sliver of pain stabbed Ro's chest. The bluff lawman had spoken the

139

rancher's thoughts.

"Let's go," Valera said. "Nothing more we can do here. We lost him."

Ro remounted and kept a few paces ahead of the two men. When they got back to the house well after dark, Wade met them at the door and told them Judith had called to say they were giving Paul a blood transfusion and keeping him at the hospital overnight. "Tried to raise you," the cowboy added, "but musta been outta radio range."

The sheriff sat with the others at the kitchen table while Wade poured hot coffee. He took a sip and leveled a finger at Jim. "You realize we got nothing to hold Jose Peyote on, don't you?"

"He and that Tomas What's-His-Name—"

"Wingfield," Ro supplied.

"Tomas Wingfield were practically joined at the hip."

"Hell, Jim, that ain't proof. Ro, here, killed a man this afternoon. That doesn't mean you was in on it. We'll start an investigation, but you leave it to us, you hear me?"

He leaned back in his chair and looked at Ro. "Tell me what's been going on."

Valera had him tell the story three times before the lawman sat back, finally satisfied.

"Well, the fight gives us a place to start. At a bar, you say? Oughta be plenty of witnesses.

Ro shrugged. "Out back of Harry's. So far's I know, nobody knows about the fight except for Jose, Paul, and me. Nobody left alive, that is."

"There'll be a separate hearing on this afternoon's shooting. It's the DA's call. Doubt the feds'll want in since it didn't happen on Indian land. Ro, I'll have to take your rifle with me." He started to rise, but Valera held up a hand. "Hold still. I know where it is. Lucky Pete was on your tail. He can back up your story. Keep me posted on how Paul's doing."

Jim saw the sheriff to the door before turning to Ro. "Dammit, don't make too much out of Valera's remark at that drover's camp. Maybe I *was* thinking something like that, but if they'd been white, I'd have been thinking the same thing. My boy'd been shot, and they were strangers. I don't apologize for what I was thinking, just that it hurt you."

"It's okay." More was coming.

"Why didn't you tell me about the fight at the bar?"

Ro's frustration broke free. "Because Paul's a grown man. Am I supposed to run and tell every time he's naughty?"

Jim rubbed a hand across his eyes. "Of course not. But you know Jose better than Paul."

Ro slammed a fist into his palm. "It was that damned bully! He started the

140

whole thing and nearly killed Jose. I tried to warn Paul that Jose'd get even. But he wouldn't listen. *You* wouldn't listen when I told you the other day. Nobody would listen, and it happened. And there's not a damned thing I can do about it."

Jim put a hand to Ro's shoulder. "You did try to warn me. You tried, but I didn't understand. Well, I do now." He walked to the door. "I'm going to the hospital. Don't even think about coming with me. You turn in. I have a feeling it's gonna be a rough day tomorrow."

After Jim left, Ro headed for the shower and let jets of hot water burn away his tension. He dried off, pulled on clean shorts, splashed iodine on his forehead, and fell into bed to worry about Paul until exhaustion put out his lights.

****

A lone horseman rode his dream. A warrior in harmony with the world, at peace with his brethren. Then a terrible roar shattered the calm. The warrior crashed to the ground and kicked away his life in the dirt.

Ro woke in the grip of a chill, yet sweat oozed from his pores and turned icy on his skin. He lurched into the bathroom to vomit and shiver until he could no longer hold himself erect. Crawling back to bed, he burrowed beneath the covers for warmth. Gradually, he stopped shaking and puzzled over the meaning of the dream.

The slain warrior was not the man he'd killed yesterday. The warrior was a symbol. A symbol of the *Tinneh,* which put a new sweat on him because if he slept again, he would see who had murdered beauty and tranquility and the natural order of things. And he knew it would be Román Otero—Roan Orphan, Tall Rider, grandson of She-Who-Had-Been-Cane-Woman. But for him, those two worlds would have never met, much less clashed.

141

Chapter 29

Eyes closed, Jose sat against a lodge pole pine outside his tent in a nameless canyon. A thrill ran the length of his body. He was a man now the way men were counted when the *Tinneh* lived free and unconquerable.

He may or may not have slept, but the reverie came in any case. Dark mists smothered the feeble moonlight. The tinkle of silver bells heralded the approach of the *ga'an*, Devil Dancers. They appeared out of the murk with the careless grace of stags, wearing great horned headdresses and clacking wooden wands. A host of warriors with fascinating death wounds and bloody axes marched through clouds of vapor, recounting heroic deeds and murderous crimes. But no ghost would harm him now. This thing, this killing was powerful medicine.

He and Tomas had prowled the J-Bar-C for days without a sign of the Chandler kid and that big buddy of his. Then they spotted the two, and he got his opportunity. Rider almost spoiled things with his traitorous alarm. Almost, but not quite. The fat boy dropping from his saddle like a big sack of oats almost gave Jose an orgasm. He saw Tomas go down, but when bullets came close enough to sing, he fled, leaning over the pony's neck to make a smaller target.

As the nag he rode flagged, Jose had slowed up and smartened up. Rider wouldn't come for him right away. He'd go to Paul first, but when he came, Jose's trail would be easy to follow. Then the gods took a hand. He came across the fresh trail of a lone rider. It was easy to merge his own tracks into the others and make straight for home, leaving his pursuers to follow an unsuspecting innocent.

Jose roused as a wolf howled from somewhere deeper in the mountains. Or was it Tomas calling? He grew colder still. Night things crawled through the brush. His earlier bravado forgotten, he cursed at his foolishness. He'd talked with ghosts. Called up the name and image of He-Who-Had-Been. Dangerous because that one hadn't been forgotten a whole day, much less four. He could easily be called back. Jose sniffed the damp air. It was a night for ghosts, dark and wet. An owl called; a whippoorwill answered.

The twenty yards to his tent were the longest he had ever traveled. Inside was little better, cold and clammy and dark. He struck a match to moss he'd laid earlier that day. As the frail flames caught, raindrops fell on the canvas over his head, hesitantly at first, then building to a steady thrumming like a powwow drum. The firepit ashes were still hot when he put them to his forehead and ears and laid a circle around the edges of his shelter. Breathing shallowly, he crowded the fire, seeking not only heat but also energy.

Jose wiped cold sweat from his neck. What was happening? He'd long ago given up fearing the night. He tried to imagine this was a Devil Dog tent in the middle of a jungle on an island in a foreign ocean. But this was no stifling Pacific rain; rather it was a chilling downpour in mountains that had hidden witches and ghosts for hundreds of years.

Life had moved in a great circle. His conversion had been so swift he was caught with only the faint protection of ashes. Tomorrow he would gather sage and pollen, but tonight he settled for fashioning a medicine bag of sorts. After that, he laid down more ashes and sought to think pure thoughts. He had wandered far; the way back would be treacherous. The Chandlers had to be dealt with first. And that White Apache who used to be Tall Rider. Yet, at the end of that demanding journey lay peace and harmony.

Chapter 30

The next morning, Jim drove Ro and Pete to the sheriff's office where they were put in separate rooms. Half an hour went by before a white man in a suit and tie entered and asked if Ro wanted a lawyer. He shook his head. The man made him say it out loud before asking if he'd shot Tomas Wingfield. Could the newly departed be lured into a jailhouse by calling his true name?

Over the next few hours, his interrogator's tone ranged from harsh to conciliatory. Ro never varied from the truth of what had happened. Was Pete in another room answering the same questions? Half the day went by before the *Indah* left the room. A few minutes later, Sheriff Valera came in to say Ro was free to go.

Shame lay like a second skin across his shoulders as he followed Jim and Pete out of the sheriff's office. Some of the Wingfield family—stone-faced and solemn—were among a small crowd gathered to witness Ro's mortification.

After the Lincoln got underway, Jim cleared his throat. "Son, I know that was tough on you, but that should be the end of it. Pete was able to corroborate what you said."

Unwilling to look up and face the world, he kept silent. Yeah, the end of it. The end of his going home.

As soon as they arrived at the ranch, Pete headed for the field, but Jim told Ro to stick close to the house.

"Jose's only after Paul and me, and I'm packing Paul off to his grandmother's until school starts. I can watch out for myself. But we better keep an eye on the women… just in case. That's your job. Don't let either of them stray from the house alone."

"Got it," Ro said. "What about Bu… uh, the football player? You know, his body."

"Talked to his family twice now. I'm shipping him back to Illinois."

Straightening things in the stable probably fell under Jim's definition of working around the house, so Ro headed there. At least, he worked physically, but his mind replayed the day's events. He'd handled himself badly. The lawyer had to ask him to speak up several times. A man speaking truth should talk strong. His shame would weaken with age, but his image of the law was irrevocably altered. He didn't like cold, calculating strangers determining his future. But hadn't the *Indah* been doing that forever?

And then there was the big thing. He had taken the life of one of the People just when his thoughts were turning back to the reservation. Now the *Tinneh* would see his white blood and deny him kinship. On top of that, Jim's request had slipped a chain on him, a chain forged of words but no less confining for lack of iron.

Dreams and night sweats returned. Ro told no one about them, not even Paul, although he drew comfort from his brother's presence. Even that boon was soon denied him. Once the doctor pronounced Paul fit for travel, he stood in the railway station—his left arm in a sling—bitching about his mother not letting him drive to Virginia. As they waited for the train, Paul draped his functioning right arm across Ro's shoulders.

"Well, kiddo, guess you'll have to wrangle the ragtop to UNM for me this fall, okay?"

He swallowed before he could answer. "Sure."

After Paul was safely away, Jim dumped paperwork on Ro, likely to keep his mind occupied while he was confined to the house. Within days, he was ready to gnaw leather.

****

One night his grandmother, disdaining owls and coyotes and other messengers, came in her own form to stand at the foot of his bed and stare him awake. Perspiring like he had just emerged from a sweathouse, Ro traded the darkness of the room for the umbra of the night. Clad only in briefs, he ran to flee something that could not be fled.

With a heaving chest, he spoke to a shade sensed but no longer seen. "I can't go back home now. Need time." He gulped air. Giant owls could have ripped him to bloody shreds for all he cared.

Later that morning, Teresa demanded to go for a ride. Since Jim was working in the office, Ro agreed, thanking her for freeing him as they mounted and rode east.

She sniffed. "You think that was for you? I was bored out of my mind."

Gradually the two of them fell into a daily routine. His dreams grew less intense, more occasional. Teresa proved a balm to his restless spirit, and he came to look forward to their jaunts. She was growing up and getting to be fun… for a fifteen-year-old girl.

Ro returned to working the pastures a week later, and Teresa gave her attention to other matters. Although he preferred the long hours and hard work, he missed their rides.

Often, when in the south pasture, Ro sought out high ground to look across to the reservation. On occasion, he climbed the fence and walked the land of his birth. He didn't understand why, but the earth felt different there.

What did Ruby think about what had happened? She was much on his mind lately. The memory of that night at Rising Rock still warmed him. Time to go see her.

What he was planning must have shown. Saturday afternoon, the crew started in on him.

"Oh, shit!" Wade said. "Haul out the iodine and bandages, Ro's going crowing tonight."

Pete chimed in. "Now, Ro, try to stop shy a breaking bones. Ain't no gal worth that kinda pain."

After dinner that evening, he headed down the highway in the Jeep. As he turned off NM35 onto the reservation, he fought the feeling that even the trees turned their backs on him. After two or three stops, he traced Ruby to a dance at the school gymnasium in White Pine. His hands shook as he parked. Sweat moistened his upper lip even though the night was cool.

A crowd jammed the school's gymnasium bleacher section to watch couples sway to the beat of a record player. Wingfield family members scattered among the throng made him uneasy. He had no appetite for more trouble. Ruby, dancing with a powerfully built young man, made him forget everything else.

"Who's that with Ruby?" he asked a fellow standing beside him.

"You ain't forgot Clarence Wolf, have you? Put some meat on his bones, didn't they? But I guess he won't be beating on you no more. Got too much Korean lead in him."

"Wonder if they made him a scout?" someone asked. "A goddamned Injun scout."

Old Clarence still dogged his trail. Ro left and returned to the J-Bar-C.

Chapter 31

Our Red Patrons Are Welcome. Dogs and Minors Still Not Allowed.
Jose walked past Harry's new sign, slapped half a dollar on the bar, and collected a beer. He didn't know many dates in history, but August 15, 1953 was the day good old General Ike—he was president now—made it legal to serve Indians in bars. Off the reservation, of course, so the whites could still get their drinking money. Jose found it odd to stand in the middle of a bunch of *Indahs* guzzling booze. Sorta like taking a leak in public.

Jose had quit watching for the sheriff on his tail, but he knew an investigation of the big white bully's killing was still going on. The fact they hadn't come for him meant they didn't have anything on him. Either Rider hadn't been close enough to identify Jose as the shooter, or else, he'd kept his mouth shut. Either way, Jose'd snookered the bastards good. But could he really count on that white Apache to keep silent? He'd have to think on that. Hard.

His old friend, Charles Beaver, showed up from wherever he'd disappeared to. He'd make a decent buddy in the place of He-Who-Had-Been. Only thing was, the big man finished his Army time in the brig. That rubbed on a Jarhead who'd served out his enlistment.

But the sight of the hulking guy—fully as big as that white bread Jose'd sent to hell—kicked off an idea in his head. Maybe Beaver being a jailhouse vet would come in handy.

One evening, as they met in front of Harry's, Jose'd barely finished saying howdy before the big man started bellyaching. Broke. No job. Jose steered him around behind the bar.

"I got enough for a pint, but then I'm busted. But they gonna pay the hands at the ranches come Friday." Beaver squinted but said nothing. Jose went on. "Lotsa drinking money in them payrolls. Been thinking on getting my hands on some of it. But I need a partner."

The big man paused only a moment before nodding.

****

Thursday afternoon, Jose headed into Terreon to be seen at Harry's and make sure old man Chandler was attending his monthly lodge meeting. As soon as Jose saw the black Lincoln parked at the hall, he sped as fast as the old truck would go to yell Consuela and her brother Wilson Smallhorse out of her mother's house. They listened and agreed to meet him at his camp later... for a price. Jose appropriated two ponies from a communal herd and went to meet Beaver.

"Bareback?" the big man complained.

"Didn't have time to swipe no saddle. Got gloves and masks. Only what I got's better'n masks." Jose pulled two cotton sheets from a paper grocery bag. Beaver grunted approval.

They cut the lock on the gate in the south pasture that white Apache used to go back and forth between the ranch and the reservation. Lights burned in both the ranch house and the bunkhouse. No one moved about outside.

After hiding the horses behind the stable, they slipped into gloves and sheets with eyeholes and secured them at the neck by twine. The kitchen door was locked, but Beaver had it open in two minutes flat. They entered the house silently.

"Anyone want something to drink?" That was Chandler's wife.

"I'll get it, Mother. Coffee okay?" The girl sounded older.

"I'll help." Tall Rider. All accounted for.

They backed through a door and allowed the young couple to pass before easing into the den. The Chandler woman fiddled with a television set, her back to them. An arm over her windpipe choked off her cry. As soon as she stopped struggling, he motioned Beaver to the side of the door and loosened the pressure slightly. He wanted a scream loud enough to carry no farther than the kitchen. She gave him one.

Footsteps raced down the hall, and Rider flew through the doorway. Beaver bounced him off the deck. When Rider tried to rise, the big man smashed him in the face, putting him back on the carpet.

"You scream, he'll break yo mama's neck!" Beaver said to Teresa, who stood frozen in the hallway. He grabbed her arm and pulled her inside.

Jose eased his hold, and Judith choked on fresh air. When Beaver told her what they wanted, the woman went stubborn until he threatened Rider with Jose's Marine KA-BAR knife.

Abandoning the still unconscious Rider, they followed Chandler's wife into the dark office. Beaver kept a tight grip on Teresa as he closed the blinds over the window. Jose snapped on the overhead light and pushed Judith toward the desk.

The woman clawed at the big painting of a warrior until it swung aside to reveal a wall safe. She fumbled with the knob. The tumblers clicked, and the door opened.

Beaver shoved the two women into a closet and rasped a warning. "Any trouble, we kill the kid in there." He closed the door, twisted the key, and moved over to the safe where Jose scooped the contents into a grocery bag.

They froze at the sound of a vehicle on the drive, but it passed the house and came to a stop somewhere near the bunkhouse.

Intent on making sure he got all the money from the safe, Jose almost missed Rider lunging for the letter opener on the desk, but Beaver stepped forward and sent the kid crashing against the far wall. Seizing the opportunity to eliminate a possible witness against him, Jose took the KA-BAR from his partner and raised it. Beaver caught his arm.

"Uh-uh. I ain't getting mixed up in no killing."

Jose masked his rage and walked away. As they recovered the horses, he tried to talk Beaver into splitting up. The big man would have none of it until they were well into the mountains. By then the opportunity to return to the house was lost.

****

Jose gave a false laugh as they watched the two sheets burn beside a mountain stream on the reservation. "You rich now, amigo."

"Walks, you ain't that dumb. We got squat. Ain't more'n fifteen hundred here, and seven-fifty don't make a man rich." Beaver crammed his share into his pocket. "You went there to settle a score, and that means there's bad blood 'tween you'n that rancher. You had me do all the talking, so I'm putting distance 'tween you'n me before morning. And hear me, Brother, you get caught and turn me in, I'll kill you slow and painful, don't matter how long it takes."

Jose slapped Beaver on the back. "You got the right idea. Ain't many men in these parts your size, and that's all they got to go on."

Once Beaver took off, Jose backtracked to erase their trail for a distance before tying the ponies' reins to his truck bed and leading them back to the herd. Satisfied no one had seen him, he headed for camp. When Jose arrived, there was no sign of his wife or her brother. A worried frown puckered his face. The bastards were supposed to be waiting. Two minutes shy of Jose losing his cool, Consuela and her brother stepped into the clearing.

Chapter 32

Judith strained to hear through the closet door. Earlier sounds of violence had raised her fear for Román. Then everything went quiet. She fumbled for the light chain and clicked on a weak bulb. All she saw were Jim's outdoor clothing and fishing gear.

Teresa lunged against the unyielding door and rattled the knob. "Mom, Ro needs help!"

No one reacted from the office, so Judith assumed the robbers were gone. Jim's tackle box yielded a pair of needle-nosed pliers. It wasn't much, but it was all she had. She pushed Teresa out of the way and punched the door. Her first jab left a deep gouge in the wood. She drew a breath and started a steady pounding.

When she flagged, Teresa grabbed the tool and went at it with a vengeance. By spelling one another, they worried a hole in the panel large enough for Judith to reach the key. As they stumbled out into the room, Teresa screamed and rushed to Román, who lay slumped against the wall, head forward on his chest. Judith's fingers found a pulse.

"He's alive. Dial zero and tell the operator we need the sheriff and medical assistance. I'll get help from the bunkhouse."

Teresa grabbed her arm. "Don't go out there. Use the radio."

Judith raised Pete before taking the phone from Teresa to leave an urgent message for Jim at his lodge.

Pete and Wade hit the kitchen door within one minute, pistols in hand. The two cowboys listened to her story as they eased Román flat on the floor.

Pete took charge. "Wade, stay with Miz Chandler and Miss Teresa till the boss gets here." He turned to Judith. "I'll saddle up and go take a look. I just come in from town and didn't meet nobody on the road, so they mighta been horseback. Maybe I can pick up a trail. Worth a try, anyways."

"There are two of them, Pete. And one of them's big. Wouldn't it be better—"

"Excuse me, ma'am, but the quicker I get to tracking, the more likely we'll catch 'em."

"Take a radio with you."

After the bantam cowboy headed for the stable, Judith turned her attention to Román. His complexion seemed terribly dark. Teresa knelt beside him, clutching his hand and weeping softly. She clasped her daughter's shoulders.

"Did you get through to the emergency operator?"

Teresa nodded. "They're calling Dr. Barger and the Sheriff. Let's move Ro to a bed."

"No, ma'am," Wade said. "Ain't a good idea. Might not even shoulda laid him flat till the doc said it was okay. If he's got something broke, it's liable to tear up his insides."

"Cover him with the afghan from the couch," Judith said. "I'm going to make fresh coffee. We're going to need it before this night's over."

The shakes caught up with Judith as soon as she was out of sight of the others. Her knees gave way. She leaned against the kitchen counter to keep from falling. The ringing phone gave her a start. She picked up the wall receiver and heard her husband's voice.

"Thank God! Come home, Jim. Two men robbed...." She sobbed into the instrument, drew a deep breath, and tried again. "Two men robbed us. Forced me to open the safe. Román's hurt. The emergency operator's trying to reach the doctor and the sheriff, but... but I need you."

Judith stood with the dead phone in her hand, wishing she could wait for her husband, but she had to get back to Teresa. She put on the coffee and returned to the office.

****

Dr. Barger, a pudgy, middle-aged man who exuded confidence and calmed frayed nerves, arrived first. He turned to Judith after a lengthy examination of Román. "He'll be all right. Don't believe he's got any broken bones. Concussion's the thing we gotta worry about."

Cars squealed in the driveway as the doctor and Wade carried Román to a daybed in the sunroom adjacent to the den. Jim burst through the door followed by Sheriff Valera.

"Teresa?" Jim asked.

"She's fine. We're fine. The doctor's with Román now."

Judith's self-control returned with the presence of her husband. She calmly described the events of the night as she led them into the office.

"Any idea who it was?" Sheriff Valera asked.

"Jose! That's who," Jim said.

All Judith had seen were bed sheets, but she told them one of the men had been huge—much bigger than Wade. The other was Román's size.

"John," Jim said. "I had a hundred dollars in marked twenties in the safe."

"Give me the serial numbers, and I'll notify the bank first thing in the morning. Raise Pete on the radio and see if we can give him a hand."

A tear-stained Teresa appeared in the doorway. "Ro's awake, Daddy."

Judith trailed Jim into the sunroom and winced at the boy's battered face.

151

"You okay?" Jim asked. Román nodded. "Could you tell who it was?"

Román licked his lips. "One of them... big. Only one... from rez that big... Charlie Beaver." He swallowed audibly, his breath, shallow gasps. "Other... coulda been Jose."

Jim touched the boy's shoulder. "I'm just grateful you'll be all right."

Román sighed and closed his eyes.

Judith tarried after the others left, but she heard the sheriff caution her husband the robbers might not be from the reservation. "Rest now," she said to the injured youth. "You'll feel stronger in the morning." She wasn't certain whether or not Roman heard her. "If you hadn't been here, no telling what they'd have done to Teresa and me."

He flinched at her words.

She closed the door behind her and leaned against it. The whole event played before her like a reel of moving picture film. She saw everything clearly, catching details she had missed as she lived them. The film froze, etching one vivid image upon her consciousness: Teresa kneeling over Román as he lay unconscious on the floor. The look on the girl's face had been unmistakable. Judith closed her eyes and shivered so hard the door rattled in its frame.

Chapter 33

Pete radioed he'd trailed two sets of hoofprints to the reservation gate and found the lock cut. Jim cussed before turning practical.

"The sheriff and I'll take it from here. You'n Wade look after the women and Ro."

White Pine was locked up tight; not even the police station was open. Jim and the sheriff banged on residential doors until they found someone willing to point them in the direction of Jose Peyote's place. After an hour of wandering the mountains, they spotted a campfire deep in an isolated canyon. The sheriff killed the motor and doused the lights.

Valera picked up a heavy flashlight before getting out of the cruiser. "Let's walk from here." As they approached three shadowy figures huddled around a fire before a pitched canvas tent, the sheriff muttered. "Damn. They're waiting for us."

Jose's eyes reflected the campfire as he rose and stood with his hands on his hips. A woman and another man gave them looks of impersonal suspicion.

Jose walked toward them, not even trying to hide the sneer in his voice. "If it ain't Mr. Chandler and his pet lawdog. Don't guess you're here official, Sheriff."

"I can roust the tribal police or the FBI, if you want. Where you been all evening?"

"Ain't none of your business, but I was right here with my wife and her brother."

Jim glanced at the woman. Not yet out of her twenties, a haggard look hardened otherwise pleasant features. Her brother identified himself as Wilson Smallhorse.

"That right, Mrs. Peyote? He been here all evening?" Valera asked. The woman stared into the fire and said nothing until the sheriff repeated his question. She replied with a curt nod.

"You, Smallhorse, stand up," Valera said.

The man rose. About forty, he was stout but not as big as the man Judith had described.

Valera gave him a long look before nodding toward the tent. "Peyote, since you're being so reasonable about this, you won't mind if we take a look around, will you?"

"You got no right...." Jose shut up as Jim stepped forward. The man set his legs, making Jim realize a physical confrontation was what he wanted.

Valera stepped between them. "You come with me while I check out your place. Don't want you squawking I stole something off you."

"Shit, you as bad as a white man, you know that?"

The sheriff led the way into the tent. They were inside only a few minutes. Valera shook his head as he emerged. "Peyote, don't go taking a trip anytime soon."

Jim and the sheriff walked back to the cruiser without speaking. Once Valera had his vehicle's nose pointed toward White Pine, Jim sighed aloud. "I'm tired of that man making us look like incompetent fools."

"If he's got that marked money, it'll show up sooner or later. Then we'll get our shot."

****

Jim managed to grab a couple hours' rest before the demands of the day had him struggling off the couch where he'd catnapped. He and Judith sat at the table and ate breakfast without enthusiasm. Teresa stayed in the sunroom to keep Ro awake since the doctor didn't want him sleeping just yet. Pete, looking as beat as Jim, stopped in to let the boss know he and Wade could wait until Monday to be paid. Jim thanked them, but said he was going to the bank later that afternoon. They'd have their money today.

Before leaving for town, he stopped in the sunroom to check on Ro. "Feeling better?"

"Some. I'll be up and around this afternoon."

"You might have a concussion, so don't rush it." He briefed Ro on events and asked if he'd remembered anything else. Ro hadn't. "Son, are you ready to swear in court Jose was one of the robbers last night?"

Ro grimaced. "No."

"Better get a move on. Gotta see a banker about money." He paused. "You know you're gonna be a week late getting up to school, don't you? Judith will call Paul and explain."

Jim headed for the Lincoln but decided to take the Jeep when he saw Ro had removed the canvas top, leaving the vehicle open to the air. A breeze on his face might help keep him awake.

Damn, he missed Paul. A man took his family for granted when they were all home, but let one go away, and it left a big hole. He smiled. He couldn't see Teresa going away. Growing up, yes. Away, no. And he was unable to picture Ro leaving… despite that lawyer thing.

Once across Deep Water Arroyo culvert—a misnomer since the wash was desert dry except during runoff—Jim geared the jeep down to cut across the desert as the highway began a long curve to the southeast. Driving this particular stretch was like sitting a bucking bronc or chasing a wild heifer into the brush. He enjoyed it.

Coming to a halt, Jim reached down to pull a pale blue blossom from its stem. How like Judith... beautiful and delicate, yet strong and resilient. He laughed. Lost more'n a week's payroll last night, and here he was picking flowers.

He threw the jeep into low, nosing into a wash. At the bottom, he fed gas and bounded up the far side. Almost too late, he saw the last rain had collapsed Deep Water's wall directly in front of him. Jim spun the wheel and shot forward, then he stood on the brakes as a bend in the arroyo came up fast. The Jeep slued sideways and stopped at the brink of the dry gully.

"Close!" While Jim stared into the deep ditch, the Jeep moved. He scrambled to his feet as the soft embankment gave way. The vehicle lurched sideways, throwing him off-balance. He grabbed for the steering wheel, but missed and fell, landing on his back on Deep Water's sandy bottom, breath knocked from his lungs.

The vehicle tumbled down the side of the crumbling arroyo like a child's toy. He kicked himself out of the way as the vehicle dropped on four wheels in the spot where he had lain moments before. The Jeep bounced, gyrated onto its side, and settled back to earth, pinning his legs. For a moment he felt nothing. Then pain ripped an agonized cry from him before he fainted.

Chapter 34

Ro's bruised face burned, and he ached all over. Those were annoyances. His pounding head was what really rattled him. Teresa peeked through the door.

"Want some more company?" Her smile brightened the room. "Feeling better?"

"Any better, I'd be out working."

"Liar. If you're in pain, the doctor left some medicine."

"Makes me sleepy, and you claim I'm not supposed to sleep."

"Mom called Paul about the robbery and all." Teresa shivered and hugged her arms as if she were cold. Her shoulders shook.

"Teresa? What's the matter?" He was half out of bed before remembering he was in his underwear. He covered back up.

"Oh, shut up! I'm just... commiserating."

"Christ, is it catching?"

He flinched as she slapped his shoulder. Contrite, she placed a hand to his cheek, and the throbbing in his head abated.

"I thought they'd killed you last night. Couldn't have stood it! I'd have died too."

He felt his cheeks flush. "Didn't know you cared."

She pulled away. "Didn't know I cared? You big lummox! You don't know anything. You don't know I'm alive. Or that I've been in love with you since I was eight years old."

His chin dropped. "You dunno what you're saying."

Her voice held a bite. "I know what. Just not why."

His vision went out of whack. "Teresa, I... I—"

"Don't say anything. I've made a fool of myself."

"How?"

"What else do you call saying that to someone who loves another girl?"

She was jumping around too much for him. "Another girl?" The skin on his arms flicked like Colorado's when a horsefly bugged him. "Ruby? Love her? I... I dunno."

"You don't know? Have you made love to her?" Her eyes went wide, and she flung herself on him. He gasped in pain. "Don't answer that. I don't wanna know... ever."

His arms went around her. His head was splitting. She crushed his bruised ribs, but the pulse in her temple against his neck made him forget all that. He cupped her chin and sought her lips. It was different... almost like kissing for the first time. He felt immature, unlearned.

"Teresa," he pulled her head to his shoulder. "I—"

"Don't! Don't say it unless you mean it." She sat up. "And you won't mean it."

"Can I at least tell you how good it is to know you care?" He gulped. "It's like being out in the cold and having the sun come up and smile on me. Makes me warm and cozy. And other things don't matter so much."

"For me, it's like touching a rainbow."

They kissed again. Although his mangled lips burned, the contact stirred his blood. "Teresa," he mumbled, "what if your folks come in?"

She sighed. "It would look pretty awful. But we're half-safe. Dad's not back from town."

Ro glanced at his watch and frowned. "Gone for over two hours now. Shoulda been back by now."

She looked out the window. "Lincoln's in the drive. Maybe he's home. Let me check."

Ro stared at the empty doorway, mulling over what had happened. Teresa—Paul's little sister—affecting him like that. It wasn't right. Wasn't decent. Why not? What was wrong with it? She wasn't *his* sister. Well, almost. He'd have to think about this.

Teresa came through the door. "Daddy isn't back yet. He took the Jeep."

Moments later, Judith came into the sunroom, her face drawn. "I called the bank. Jim didn't make his appointment."

Ro sat up in bed. "Call the sheriff and tell him to look for Jim in town. I'll begin at this end. Get Pete and Wade on the radio and have them come in."

"You can't get up," Teresa said.

"I've got to. "Now get out and let me put some clothes on."

Ro was weaker than he thought. Simply pulling on his trousers set his head to roaring. His fingers wouldn't cooperate, so he left his shirt hanging open.

Judith hung up the phone as he lurched into the hallway. "The sheriff will start looking."

As they headed for the car, Teresa joined them. "I raised Pete on the radio. They'll come in right away. I'm going with you, Ro."

He winced as his belly rolled. "One of you has to stay here. Jim or the sheriff might call."

"Mother, I'm going. You stay." Teresa slid behind the wheel of the Lincoln. Ro crawled in beside her. She sprayed gravel getting down the drive.

Feeling every bump in the road, he gritted his teeth and endured it until they crossed Deep Water and hit the long curve just beyond the southern boundary of the ranch.

"Slow down. Your dad likes to short-cut across the desert when he's in the Jeep."

Teresa braked. "There! There are his tracks."

"All right, now go around to the other side of the curve where the arroyo crosses the road again. Let's find where he came back on the highway."

She stomped on the accelerator. They completed the long curve and came to the culvert.

"He didn't come out," she whispered.

"Turn around and go back to where he left the road."

She pulled a U-turn and halted on the other side of the curve. Ro almost went blind struggling out of the car. Teresa sounded the horn. Nothing.

He staggered along the Jeep's tracks until he saw what he had feared. Shouting for Teresa, he slid down the wall of the arroyo, falling to his knees beside the overturned Jeep. Jim lay pale and motionless, his face muscles slack. Ro touched his shoulder.

The rancher groaned and stirred. "Wasn't sure... find me."

Teresa slid down the hill and collapsed in the dirt. "Daddy! Oh, Daddy!"

"It's okay, baby," Jim mumbled.

Hearing fright in the man's voice, Ro pulled Teresa to her feet and pushed her to the other side of the overturned vehicle. "Get a grip on yourself. He's in bad enough shape without you scaring the hell out of him."

"I'm sor... sorry. I'm all right now." She brushed hair from her face and wiped away tears with a dusty arm.

"Shoulda put a radio unit in the Lincoln," Ro muttered. "Toss me the jack from the car, then drive to the house for help. I gotta get the jeep off him."

Ro leaned against the side of the gully and fought to keep from passing out. The sound of the Lincoln racing away brought him back. The car jack lay in the sand ten feet away. He hadn't even heard it hit the ground. Rousing, he picked it up and staggered to the Jeep for its jack.

The rancher revived as Ro explained he was going to raise the vehicle, pep talking himself more than Jim. He took a deep breath as a spell of vertigo swept him.

He had trouble situating the two jacks. They had a tendency to twist in the soft sand when he put pressure on them, but by switching from one to the other, he managed to move the vehicle slightly. Jim bellowed in agony. He ignored the man's cry and kept on struggling. The mass of steel slowly rose until the rancher's legs were free. Ro paused to catch his breath and outlast another dizzy spell.

"It's slipping!" Jim cried.

The left jack twisted, dropping that end of the Jeep slightly. Ro grunted as he tried to steady the swaying vehicle. "Crawl out! Crawl out! I can't hold on!"

Jim levered himself backward with his hands. "God in Heaven, it hurts!" Inch by inch, using only the power of his arms, he dragged himself from beneath the jeep. The left jack collapsed, throwing Ro to the ground. The falling vehicle slapped the soles of Jim's boots, but he was free. The effort had been too much for him. He fainted again.

Head thundering, Ro crawled to the man's side and made a tourniquet of his belt to staunch Jim's bleeding right leg. That done, he flopped down in the dirt beside his boss. When a car squealed to a halt on the highway, Ro figured it was all right to pass out.

Chapter 35

Judith studied a swollen-eyed Teresa and an ill-looking Román sitting in the hospital waiting room. She rose as a green-clad man came down the hall. Her life depended on what this stranger, this specialist who salvaged crushed bodies, was about to say. He was so young.

"We can save the legs, but it's doubtful he'll ever walk again."

"Oh, no!" Her hand flew to her mouth. "Does he know?"

The surgeon shook his head. "We need more tests before pronouncing that kind of sentence on a man. Mrs. Chandler, you can see him for a minute." He pointed to Ro. "Then I want you to take this young man home. He should be in bed. Preferably one of ours."

Judith followed the doctor down a hall reeking of chemicals to Jim's room. She paused to wipe her eyes and push her hair into some kind of order before entering. Her husband lay motionless, his eyes closed, his breathing heavy. She moved quietly to his side.

Jim clasped her hand as she sat on the edge of the bed. "Made a mess of it, didn't I?" he mumbled, no timbre to his voice.

"The doctor only gave me a minute. Teresa and Román send their love. They can visit tomorrow." She studied his pallid features.

"Judith, promise you won't let them take my legs."

"Nobody's going to take your legs. But you've got to be prepared for a long, hard battle."

His mouth trembled. The hand attached to a dripline fluttered. "The ranch?"

"I ran it while you were in the Army, didn't I? Our hands know exactly how you like things done. Besides, you'll still be here. I simply have to—"

"Be my legs." he finished.

The despair in his voice arrowed her heart. She stiffened her spine. "All right, that's exactly what I meant. I'll be your legs for a month or two or three or however long it takes. Now stop feeling sorry for yourself and concentrate on getting out of that bed. I'll take care of the rest. Is it a deal?"

"Did I just get a tongue lashing?"

The doctor appeared in the doorway. "Better let him rest."

She brushed his cheek with a kiss. "I have to go now, but I'll be back tomorrow."

****

On the way home, Judith sat in the back seat of the Lincoln staring out the window, seeing nothing. Realizing how close she'd come to losing her husband of twenty-one years brought silent tears. He was her life. Everything reminded her of him. The land, the cattle, the house…the young couple in the front seat.

When Teresa brought the Lincoln to a halt in the driveway, Judith sat a moment to dry her eyes and gather her strength. Common, mundane, life-sustaining tasks waited to be done. No one had eaten since breakfast, so she forced a light meal on them.

As they finished, Pete and Wade, hats in hand, knocked on the back door. Judith brought them inside to share the situation and hand over personal checks in lieu of the usual cash payroll. Once the men left, she ordered Ro to bed. Instead, he took a chair in the den.

"I'm not going to college next semester," he said when Judith and Teresa were seated.

"Ridiculous," Teresa said. "Everything's arranged. You've planned this for years."

"If I'm here on the ranch, Paul will stay in school. If I'm not, he'll come home. Besides, the trouble's not over yet."

Judith hesitated. Jim would rest easier knowing Román was around. In truth, she would, as well. She couldn't shake the belief loathsome things might have happened if he hadn't been there last night. Even though he'd been helpless, his presence had inhibited those men.

Still, there was another consideration. Her eyes cut to her daughter, who watched the boy closely. How deep did Teresa's feelings run? Getting Román out of the house and a hundred miles distant might prove politic.

"Just for one semester," he argued.

"Why don't we sleep on it and talk tomorrow?" Judith suggested. "How's the headache?"

"About gone."

He was lying, of course, and Judith suspected Ro knew he'd already won the battle.

****

The next month was a nightmare. Jim underwent two operations, and Judith practically lived at the hospital. Paul announced he was coming home for a semester but relented when Román made clear he was staying on the ranch until Jim got better.

Judith turned her husband's homecoming into a festive event. Ensconced in a bed in the little sunroom beside the den, Jim's sunken cheeks gradually

161

filled out and smudges disappeared from around his eyes. Her own, Judith covered with makeup as he drained her day by day. She knew he fought more than mangled legs. He also battled the conviction he was only half a man.

She gave daily thanks for Román. He recovered from his beating quickly and assumed management of the spread. Pete and Wade, older and more experienced, never questioned his role. Román sought the men's advice, accepting and rejecting suggestions as he saw fit. A tall, taciturn pillar of strength, he seemed much older than his eighteen years. He never left the family alone. When he had to be in the field or in town, he assigned one of the other men a chore somewhere in the vicinity of the house. At night, he labored over bookwork in the office, a job Judith knew he hated.

After Jim graduated to a wheelchair and took over the paperwork, Judith's day brightened. But her husband's progress proved a double-edged blessing, as she discovered when she walked into the office one day and caught him scowling at a ledger.

He slammed the book shut and tossed it on the desk. "Before the accident, I was running the show, thinking I was doing a pretty fair job. So what happens? A teenager got the yearling weight up, ran the gathering, shipped the cattle, and got top dollar. The boy's a born rancher. You manage the house and family like you always have. I'm a liability, not an asset."

Judith's eyes narrowed. "How *dare* you say that. Everything we have, you've given us. If you hadn't done such a fine job raising those children, do you think they'd be so capable?"

He rolled his wheelchair around the desk. "Just feeling sorry for myself again."

She slipped to the floor and rested her head in his lap. He stroked her hair. "I love you, you know that, don't you? The day we married I thought you were the prettiest woman on earth. Would you believe you're even more beautiful now?"

"No, but tell me anyway. By the way, I love you too."

"You had a wild kind of beauty then. Like a fine colt that knows she's something special. Perfect in its time and place, but the years have made you something truly wonderful. In spite of what I said, I wouldn't trade places with any man I know. God's been good to us."

They sat as they were, content with the silence until she spoke. "Paul's coming home for Christmas this year. He's going to tell you he's planning on managing the ranch this summer."

"Ro can do a better job."

Judith sat up straight. "You can't tell him that."

"Of course not. Ro will help him, and everything will work out fine." He lifted her chin so that she looked into his eyes. "I've been making some plans, myself."

"You have? And how long have you been doing that?"

"Ever since you unloaded on me five minutes ago. I'm gonna put in a covered swimming pool, pipe in some heat, and start exercising my legs. I don't want them atrophying."

"That's a wonderful idea! I can swim with you. It'll be good for both of us."

Judith laid her head back in his lap, smiled, and hugged his legs. Jim had reached a watershed. He'd start working at it now. Working to save his legs.

Chapter 36

Sheriff John Valera studied the man seated across from him in the interview room. Valera, a stocky man slightly below average height with a short, bristly, gray-flecked moustache, was a coyote—a man with both Anglo and Spanish blood. An honest man living off his salary and the little truck farm his wife and sons ran, he was proud of his twelve-year record as sheriff. Capable of a wink when that accomplished more than creating a record—especially for the young people of Chacon County—Valera dealt fairly with all three major ethnic groups under his jurisdiction.

The deliberate flaunting of the law was repugnant to him, and Jim Chandler's comment a few months back about Jose Peyote making monkeys of them had grated hard on his sense of justice. The J-Bar-C robbery had taken place in August, and he'd been butting his head against a wall ever since. That was why the man sitting across from him was of so much interest.

Wilson Smallhorse had bought a used pickup from a car dealer yesterday afternoon, paying five hundred dollars cash. Not unusual. Many banks and loan companies wouldn't extend credit to reservation Indians, so they saved or pooled their money until there was enough to buy a vehicle. *This* cash transaction was unusual because forty dollars of marked money from the J-Bar-C robbery showed up in the car lot's bank deposit.

After Franklin's Used Cars traced the money back to the Smallhorse transaction, a county deputy caught the man off the reservation and hauled him to the sheriff's office. Valera had forgotten the name, so his eyes bugged when he recognized Consuela Peyote's brother, the man who'd claimed to be with Jose at his camp during the J-Bar-C robbery. Smallhorse decided not to take a rap that belonged to his brother-in-law and admitted he and his sister were paid to provide Peyote with an alibi.

The Sheriff had the whole story but couldn't figure how to lay it squarely on Jose Peyote's doorstep. This was an iffy case, the word of one person—two if he could scare Consuela into talking—against another. There was the marked money, of course, but even the rawest public defender would point out a man often tried to cast his own guilt onto someone else. Whether a jury would buy Valera's case was open to question.

According to his confession, Smallhorse had filched the stolen money from his brother-in-law's hiding place, confirming the man's greed was stronger than his intelligence. Five hundred dollars lay on the table, about a third of what had been taken in the Chandler robbery. Allowing for the split with his accomplice and fifty dollars each to Smallhorse and Consuela, that meant Peyote hadn't spent much of his share. Likely just drinking money. Smart.

Valera rubbed his chin. Chances were, Peyote still believed the stolen money was safely hidden. As soon as he learned of his brother-in-law's arrest, the man would know what was up.

The sheriff stretched to relieve his aching back while he considered his options. He could go with what he had and risk the District Attorney refusing to prosecute. Or he could release Smallhorse and hope he and his brother-in-law got into a showdown involving the law. But it was more likely the frightened man would take off without even stopping to say goodbye.

Valera recalled the rash of muggings a while back, and reminded himself they ceased when Peyote went to California. Then there was that Sheldon boy's killing. None of those past sins would ever be taken before judge and jury. But there *was* one thing he could do to nail the son-of-a-bitch.

Abruptly, he ordered Smallhorse locked in his cell and put half the stolen money in his evidence safe. He called the Federal Bureau of Investigation in El Paso before leaving the office. Passing up the official vehicles, he got into his own unmarked pickup and headed north.

****

Late that same afternoon, Sheriff John Valera accompanied an FBI agent onto the reservation where they recovered two hundred-fifty dollars from Jose Peyote's tent. One twenty-dollar bill was identified as marked money taken in the J-Bar-C robbery. Valera thought—hoped—Peyote would put up a fight, but the man allowed himself to be arrested.

The rest of the world might recall Wednesday, March 9, 1954 as the day Edward R. Murrow criticized Senator Joseph McCarthy on the television show *See It Now*, but Valera would remember it as the day he sat in court and heard the judge sentence Jose Peyote to five years in the state penitentiary.

Despite his highly developed sense of ethics, Valera didn't think twice about how he'd brought it off.

Chapter 37

The van entered a gate in the ten-foot chain-link fence topped with razor wire and came to a halt at the sally port of the New Mexico State Penitentiary in Santa Fe. Two deputies ushered three men through a series of high-security metal doors into a room where they removed shackles and restraining chains from the prisoners and seated them on a bench.

Jose Peyote watched a heavy-set man—well on his way to being fat—jaw with one of the deputies who'd delivered them. Fatso seemed to be in charge of the prison side of things. The other two prisoners shifted impatiently while the hacks joked about what a crappy place the pen was. Jose sat without moving. He was in no hurry. He wasn't going anywhere.

Jose allowed his eyes to roam gray, concrete walls and black, iron bars. Lots of bars. He'd spent a night or two in jail, so he'd seen bars before. These were different. Permanent, not temporary.

Eventually, the deputies left, and the dumpy prison guard—backed by two other officers—turned to the prisoners. "Stand up when your name's called. Inmate Patote!"

Jose sat where he was.

"Inmate Patote!" the guard repeated in a loud voice. Jose still didn't move. The man stalked into the area where the prisoners sat and lifted a photograph, comparing it to Jose. "How come you didn't answer when I called your name, boy?"

"Didn't hear nobody call my name."

The prison hack leaned over, his face so close his breath almost made Jose recoil. "Nobody likes a smart-ass con. And 'specially nobody likes a smart-ass Injun con. Whenever me or any other official of this penal institution calls out your name or anything even close, you stand up and let out a hoot and a holler. So if I says Inmate Patote or Inmate Patootie or Inmate Papoose, you jump up and kiss my ass, you hear? Inmate Papoose!"

Jose rose slowly enough to be noticeable and fast enough so the man couldn't complain. "I'm Jose Peyote."

It was gonna be a long five years.

Chapter 38

Four monsters—one from each cardinal direction—came for Ro. The flesh-eating Wild Ones. He hid. They found him. They raised the stink of fear on him, and they could smell fear. He crossed hard rock where he left no trail and waded Wandering Water where he left no spoor. They followed anyway, hazing him like a stray calf back toward Rising Rock.

Ro bolted upright in bed and drew a ragged breath. This was the fourth nightmare since Jose Peyote had gone to prison. Forgotten two years now, She-Who-Had-Been still had the power to reach out and touch his life. No more sleep tonight, so he wiped crud from his eyes, threw back the covers, and swung his legs over the side of the mattress to slip out of the house for his run earlier than usual.

The chill of the false dawn was no colder than his dream. A mile into the run, he decided to capitulate, to move back to the reservation—less out of fear of ghosts than for the need of a good night's sleep. Time to test the nature of the *Tinneh's* embrace.

****

The crew finished receiving and settling a load of new steers late in the afternoon. He and Paul—home briefly for spring break—cleaned up and joined the family at the supper table. When Ro made his announcement about moving, Jim accepted the decision. Judith kept her own counsel. Paul merely frowned, but Teresa spoke up, fire in her eyes and ice in her voice.

"Ridiculous. Such a long, needless ride. It eats up hours out of your day."

He tried to treat an important matter lightly. "Just need to check out the old homestead. I'll take a bed in the bunkhouse for when I work late or don't feel like going home."

Jim rolled his wheelchair back from the table. "Keep your own room. But drive the Jeep back and forth. No sense wearing out Colorado."

"Thanks." He liked driving the Jeep. The hardy little vehicle suffered damage in the accident, but Jim's mechanic had made the necessary repairs.

Teresa wouldn't let go. "Why are you moving now? You'll be leaving for college by the end of the summer. Or are you planning on wasting two more semesters?"

Ro studied the chandelier over the table, fascinated by the way the crystal planes shattered light into a prism. "Guess so, 'cause I'm not going this fall.

I'm needed here."

"That's why you're moving off the place? You're needed *here*."

"Don't mix the two things up, Teresa. One's got nothing to do with the other. I just need to go home for a while."

"Okay, but what about college?" she asked.

"That's another matter," Jim agreed. "Son, all that Jose trouble is behind us. And that armistice over in Korea might break down anytime."

"They're still drafting guys," Paul said. "The big SSS might just come and haul your... uh, you off. And guess where you'll end up? Korea, truce or no truce. If someone has to stay, it oughta be me."

"Don't I have a say in this?" Jim asked. "There's no need for either of you to sacrifice. Judith and I can handle everything. I'm getting stronger by the minute. I'll be out of this chair any day now."

"Good," Ro said. "I can enroll next semester."

Jim studied him for a long moment before answering. "All right, but send in your application for the winter semester pronto. When the time comes, I want you registered and packed, and I'm going to deliver you myself."

"Yes, sir." Now the matter was settled, Ro wanted out. "Think I'll go to town." What would everyone say if he invited Teresa to go with him? He bulldogged that thought and asked Paul, instead.

His brother declined, saying it was his turn to do paperwork this evening.

****

Ro drove to town feeling like old Brutus on the prowl for heifers. After fruitlessly cruising downtown, he stopped at the malt shop and asked for a strawberry shake before taking a seat in a booth to trace spider web designs on the Formica tabletop with his finger.

"Hello, Cousin."

He jumped to his feet. "Ruby! Sit down."

She motioned to a noisy foursome in a corner booth. "I'm with some of the girls, but all right, just for a minute." She slipped into the seat opposite him.

Ro ordered a shake for her. She preferred chocolate. "Nice to see you."

"I'm not hard to see," she came back at him. "Just drop by the trading post anytime."

His finger returned to working the table's web design. "Been thinking about it, but something always gets in the way. How you been?" Her eyes intrigued him.

"Working hard. Not much else to do. And you? Heard about all the trouble. You know, the robbery and Mr. Chandler's accident and Jose and everything. Did they hurt you bad?"

168

"Banged me up a little."

"How's Mr. Chandler?"

"Getting better. But it's tough on him. He's a hard-riding guy."

"Kind of tough on Jose too. I don't know much about those things, but everyone says five years is an awful lot for the first time."

"The fact they punched my lights out added something to it," he said. "Look, I know Jose's *Tinneh*, and it's them against us and all that. But he did some really bad things. If Jose was white, he'd get his kicks stomping on Indians and Mexicans."

Ro gave an exasperated sigh. "Jose used to be a good guy, but he went off the rails somewhere. He could have stopped dealing trouble anytime, and it wouldn't have cost him a thing. Instead, he kept on making the situation worse. He killed that football player, Ruby. I saw him, but he was too far away to swear to it." He paused. "By the way, I'm moving back to the rez. I said I was staying until the trouble was over. It's over."

"What did they say when you quit?"

"Quit? I didn't quit." He licked dry lips. "I'll come back home to live, but I'll still work on the ranch. Are you seeing Clarence?" Where did that come from?

"Uh-huh. But he's out of town delivering some stock for the Cattlemen's Association."

"Then how about going to the movie with me? Or are you jacketed?"

"We've been going places together, but he hasn't asked me not to see anyone else."

"Does he know—you know—about us?"

Ruby lowered her eyes and shook her head.

Ro had never heard of the movie the theater was showing, but he bought tickets anyway. In the semi-darkness of the theater, he took her hand while images flickered across the screen. When the house lights came on, they waited until the rush was over before leaving. He draped Ruby's sweater around her shoulders as they reached the lobby.

"Well, hello."

He looked up, flustered by Teresa's steady gaze. She looked great in a pink skirt and blouse. Ro grappled for something to say. "Been to the movie?"

"Just going. If you hadn't been in such a hurry, I'd have bummed a ride."

"Oh, sorry." He remembered his manners and introduced the two.

Teresa nodded at the introduction. "Well, enjoy yourselves."

Ruby smiled sweetly. "We will."

"Just going home," Ro blurted. He mustered a weak grin and turned to find Ruby already headed out the door. He could almost see frost dripping from her shoulders on the short walk to the Jeep. He asked a casual question to get things back to normal. "Like the show?"

"Which one?"

Ro gave up and kept to his own thoughts as he drove. When they turned off NM35 onto the road to White Pine, Ruby asked him to stop. Remembering the last time they were alone, he stomped on the brake.

"Isn't that Chandler boy home?"

"Just for spring break. But he'll be back soon for the summer."

"Have you thought over what we talked about?"

They hadn't talked about doing it, so she must mean the other thing. His voice likely reflected his disappointment. "I told you I was moving back."

"Clarence says the tribe's cattle association is looking for men to work with the herd. You've got lots of experience working for that white man. Come back home, marry, have a family, and run for tribal office someday."

His neck heated up. "Sounds like you've got my life all planned out."

"Take me home."

****

The next morning, Ro met Teresa in the hallway as they went downstairs for breakfast. "Like the movie?"

"So-so." She flashed him a look and tripped down the stairs.

Why the hell had he gone to town last night? He shook his head and scowled into his coffee mug. Teresa ignored him, and Ruby was mad at him. What had he done wrong? He headed to work where he was shorter with the crew than usual.

"Uh oh," Pete said. "Woman trouble."

"He treats them like he treats us, ain't no wonder," Wade groused.

Ro lightened up.

The evening meal was no more comfortable than breakfast. Paul talked him into a chess game where he proved to be easy pickings. His mind, anywhere but on the game. Teresa knitted as she watched the family's new RCA color television set. The picture flickered and occasionally dissolved into unexpected snowstorms, but the program apparently fascinated her.

****

After his run the following morning, Ro packed his things in the Jeep and drove away with a sour feeling in the pit of his stomach. On the reservation side of the gate he utilized to go back and forth, he picked a glade near a small, running stream to fashion a larger, more permanent wickiup than his last one. That done, he set up a sturdy cot, a camp table and chairs, and a footlocker. Then he strung lights, hooking them into a portable gasoline generator. Was this progress… or going soft?

170

He took a pick and shovel to a copse of trees well away from his water source. His *gowa* would have an honest-to-goodness privy. Long before he finished digging, he heard someone crashing through the trees.

Tom Bearclaw appeared at the edge of the pit. "Hello, nephew. Heard you was back. Snuck up on you pretty good, didn't I?"

"Like a shadow, Big Tom."

The man patted his stomach. "I might be getting a mite heftier, but I still cross the meadow like a mountain cat. Don't nobody know when I come and go."

Ro smiled from the bottom of the pit. "Nobody crosses the meadow like you do."

"Gold or shit?"

"Crapper."

"You getting to be one high-class Indian. We ever settle up on that uncle thing?"

"Pretty near a year back," Ro said.

"Thought so, but just checking. You don't need no uncle again, do you? That was the sweetest deal I ever made. I bargained you hard but fair."

Ro dug around in his pocket. "I've got a twenty for a blanket to use as a rug for my wickiup. Anything you come in under is yours."

The man leaned over his stomach to reach the bill. "Oughta be back in a coupla hours."

"You wanna help me with this, I got another ten."

Big Tom backed away. "Nope, gotta go get my tradin' done."

Once Ro enclosed the new toilet, he tackled his water system, setting aluminum pipe in the spring so the flow of the stream brought fresh water virtually to his door. He finished with a sense of accomplishment. The camp was cozy and remote and pleasing to his nature.

He cleaned up and dressed in fresh clothing before Big Tom returned with an acceptable blanket to serve as a rug. The fat man sat down to talk a spell before extorting a pound of coffee by claiming there'd been nothing left over after buying the blanket.

Big Tom's coming along was a stroke of luck, and the fact he'd stayed to talk an hour or so was a good sign. Tom had been shunned for years, but he'd wormed his way back into the community. Maybe there was hope for Ro as well.

Along about twilight, he ate a meal of jerky and fruit. After switching off the light, he lay back on his cot to enjoy the cool calm of the night. His previous, ill-defined angst gone, he felt at peace. Just before dropping off to sleep, he let out a chuckle. How was he going to tell the Chandlers his new home was at a place called Snakehead Spring?

171

Time laid back its ears. Paul returned to classes, but it seemed only days before he was home for summer vacation. They worked together almost constantly and found time to do things after work. They hunted and fished, but he went into town with his blood brother only a few times. Perhaps he was selfish, but he didn't like sharing their time with others.

****

Mid-August, Paul headed back to the University. Ro watched the convertible out of sight and hurried to the stable to saddle Colorado. In a few minutes, he sensed someone behind him. He turned. Teresa stood quietly in the doorway. Her red-rimmed eyes wandered his face. "Why can't we get used to him leaving?"

"Do sisters really miss brothers that much?"

"This one does. And don't even pretend you don't miss him."

Ro led the big red outside. "He's my brother too. I better get to work."

She decided to accompany him as he headed south to see if they were overgrazing. They rode without words beneath the summer sun until Teresa suddenly spoke. "We're lucky. We live in the greatest place in the world. A place where I want to live and die!"

She touched boots to her mare's flanks and raced ahead of him, her raven hair crowned by a black Stetson haloed by a pure white cloud in the blue sky. He sped after her and brought his mount alongside as she pulled Princess to a halt. Her breasts rose and fell with the excitement of the ride. His eyes crawled over her.

"Ro?" Her voice was uncertain.

The ponies shifted, and his leg brushed hers. On impulse, he leaned toward Teresa, hesitating a moment before kissing her.

She pulled away. "Why did you do that? Why now? Why right now?"

"Let's walk." They dismounted and strode side by side while he considered his answer. "A while back, up on the butte, you said you loved the desert. When you said it again just now, I saw you in a different way. Not... not like a—"

"Little sister? I scared you when I said those things last year." She tossed her head. "It hurt when you didn't do anything about it. But now I understand. I was just some silly goose of a girl with a crush on the hired hand."

He scooped up a stone and flung it away. "I didn't think that."

"No? And it's taken you a whole year to discover me all by yourself. Talk about dense."

He slipped an arm around her, but she spun away. "Stop that!" he cried. "Stop flitting around like a little bird. That's going to be my secret name for you. Flitting Bird. Now you're christened. You're Flitting Bird forever."

172

"What's your secret name?"

"Tall Rider." An odd feeling swept him at revealing something so intimate to an *Indah*.

She examined him with dark brown eyes. "It fits."

"Thanks." He moved toward her.

She stopped him with a hand on his chest. "What about Ruby? You were with her the other night. How do you feel about her?"

"The other night? That was the beginning of summer. She's a friend."

"Is that your 'aw, shucks' way of saying you love her?"

The answer came easily. "I thought I did… once."

"When you made love to her?"

"You said you didn't wanna know."

"I don't… do. But you'll hurt me if you say yes. And I know you have. I just know it."

He found a flat rock and sat. Colorado nuzzled his shoulder, begging for a goodie. Ro rooted in his pocket and found a small carrot for the gelding. "Why does it matter so much?"

"Because that's the most intimate, loving thing a man and a woman can do together. It has to mean something. Otherwise, we're no different from Colorado or Princess here."

"Sure feels funny, talking about it with a girl."

She laughed. "You'd rather discuss it with Paul?"

"No! I mean—"

"You're afraid of being in love."

"I don't know if I've ever been in love. Some people say it's a curse."

Her eyes went flat. "It's no curse, Román Otero. And someday you'll find that out." She swung into the saddle and raced toward the big house. How had he pissed her off this time?

He stared after her until she was out of sight. Then, as his grandmother had taught him, he gathered good thoughts and sent them after Flitting Bird, praying they would reach her safely.

Chapter 39

Upon arriving at Snakehead the next evening, Ro knew something was wrong. He listened a minute before sliding out of the Jeep and approaching the *gowa* by foot. He'd had visitors. Bald tire tracks showed a vehicle had come in from Big Split Rock, rolled through the outdoor fire pit, and crashed into the brush shelter. The wickiup listed but hadn't collapsed.

Satisfied the intruders had gone out the same way they came in, he inspected the damage. The piping had been jerked out of the spring and the toilet overturned. Everything inside the *gowa* had been tossed, but nothing seemed to be missing except his generator and two jerry cans of gasoline. It was October—a few days shy of his nineteenth birthday—but too early for Halloween pranks.

****

Ro left the ranch the next afternoon pulling a horse trailer behind the Jeep. Old man Fish, the shopkeeper in White Pine who'd sold him soda pop when he was a kid, waited on him again. Ro piled a carton of Lucky Strikes, a few plugs of tobacco, a handful of Juicy Fruit gum packets, and a case of strawberry pop into the Jeep before negotiating for a likely looking gelding from the livestock barn. Once the pony was loaded in the stock trailer, he headed for Clearwater Canyon.

The logical explanation for vandalism at his camp was some Wingfields on a rampage over He-Who-Had-Been-Tomas. Ro's gut clenched at the thought of driving into the camp of the man he'd killed, but he needed to find out how serious the problem was.

The place looked about as he remembered, except for a new cement block house standing alongside two venerable log cabins. The Wingfields would have heard his motor for at least the last quarter mile, consequently some of the family stood in a cluster near the largest cabin. Ro parked his vehicle and got out.

An older man detached himself from the small group. They shook hands and muttered wary greetings. August Wingfield acted as spokesman, although the grandmother was the real head of the family. August, a formidable man with a lined face and long, iron gray hair bound by a cloth headband in the old manner, led Ro to a table in the shade of a tall pine where they took seats in homemade outdoor chairs. After waiting silently for coffee mugs to arrive, they drank the strong, black, unsweetened brew in the same manner. Ro handed over a pack of Lucky Strikes.

August began the conversation once his cigarette's tip glowed. "Good thing you come in a four-wheel. Road's getting bad."

"You oughta get the Agency to blade it." Uh-oh. Said like a white man.

Wingfield made a face. "Keep promising. But ain't seen no action outta them shitheads."

Ro's voice took on the rhythm and patois of the reservation. "I drug center even in the Jeep. And the stock trailer, that was something else. The council better get at it before winter sets in, or a tall horse'll git lost in them ruts."

"Oughta be done once in the spring and once in the fall, but it sees a blade once ever two, three years," August said.

Ro had no reservation gossip, so he had to make polite talk out of things he observed, all the time struggling to keep from jumping right into the reason he was here. Exposure to the white man's way put a strain on his reservation manners.

"Camp looks good." He indicated a supply of firewood. "Expecting a hard winter?"

"Gonna come early and go late. Fur's already heavy on the dogs."

Ro flicked a hand toward a small, tilled field. "See you still raise some crops."

"Potatoes, few beans. We Wingfields ain't really dirt scratchers. We're traders."

"She-Who-Was always said to go see August Wingfield if I wanted a fair trade."

"That so?" The man looked uneasy at the mention of Ro's grandmother, but his clumsy remark sped things along. "Heard you moved up Big Split Rock way."

"A bit past that. At Snakehead," Ro clarified. "Been gone a long time. Time to come back."

"Camping close to the gate, huh? That mean you still working for that white outfit?"

"Still punching cows."

Wingfield chuckled and allowed a small silence to grow.

Time to state his business. Ro picked up the talk. "Only thing is, I've had some trouble at my *gowa*. Somebody busted up a few things."

"Sure it wasn't no wild animal?"

"Don't figure a wild animal would haul off a generator. Some folks rode in on four bald tires, and one of them wore boots with a crack right at the toe of the left one. This is little trouble, but I don't want it to grow into big trouble. Can't quite figure it. Always got along with everybody. Me'n Clarence Wolf

175

squared off a couple of times, but that was a long time back." He paused to drag out a plug of tobacco. "Have some?"

August muttered his thanks and clipped off a corner with a pocketknife. Ro tore off a cut to be polite. He set off a rush among the kids by saying there was chewing gum and soda pop in the back seat of the Jeep.

"Far's I know," Ro said, "I got no enemies unless there's some hard feelings over that trouble a while back. Figured you'd be the one to know."

August took his time replying. "There's some that hold it agin you. Me, I figger when a man's where he ain't oughta be, doing what he ain't oughta do, then he takes his own chances. Some a the younger bucks don't see it that way."

Ro leaned forward. "Mr. Wingfield, I didn't know what was going on. Somebody started shooting at me. I'd never been shot at before. I coulda hightailed it outta there and maybe got shot in the back. Or I could protect myself. I'm as cautious as the next man, and right then returning lead seemed the safest thing. If I'd known who was up there…. Well, I gotta own my words. I don't know what I'd of done. But the fact is, I didn't know."

Ro licked dry lips and continued. "Sir, I don't want no feuds or no kinda trouble, so it seemed like the best thing was to come say it right out loud like a man. If some don't wanna let it alone, then let's get it on. But that's not my way." He settled back in the chair and tried to take the edge off his words. "Besides, I got me a gelding to trade."

The whole camp went silent—kids and dogs included—while August Wingfield considered Ro's words. After an ungodly long pause, the man spoke. "Always use a good horse."

Within an hour, the pony was sold, the cigarettes distributed to various Wingfields, and Ro headed back down the mountain only a little poorer from his underwater swap. He hadn't traded too sharp, wanting Wingfield to make a good deal without being able to figure him for a fool. Would his ploy work? Only time would tell.

As he approached the trading post outside of White Pine, Ro glanced at his watch. Five-fifteen. Might as well wash the tobacco taste out of his mouth. He selected a strawberry pop for the job. The big round-faced man who'd sold him his own turquoise ring almost nine years ago was still behind the counter. So was Ruby, who was getting ready to leave. Ro paid for his pop and offered her a lift home.

As he started the Jeep, Ro asked if she minded riding out to Rising Rock. She didn't object, so he drove to the pine grove. Nothing remained to show his home had ever stood in the little glade. The old couple's house looked sad at being vacant. He eyeballed the place.

"Thinking about moving in?" Ruby asked.

"It's not in bad shape. Do you know if the old folks died there?" His question took him by surprise. Why did that matter? Old habits die hard, that's why.

"They both crossed over in the PHS clinic. This could be nice if it was fixed up some." Her voice softened. "I could help you." She met his eyes in a steady gaze—like a white woman.

He forced the door to the cabin and led her inside. Very deliberately, so his intentions couldn't be mistaken, he arranged the beat-up couch cushions on the floor. There was an urgency—a desperation—to their lovemaking this time.

****

Ro, tired and confused, star-watched while sitting in front of his wickiup. Once, when he'd achieved orgasm with Ruby in that little house earlier that evening, he'd imagined Bird beneath him. Phantom lovemaking freaked Ro out. Did other guys do that?

The next day, Ro wasn't himself. Even he recognized that. Too confused to face Ruby, he avoided her. Teresa was more complicated.

Flitting Bird was Jim's daughter, Paul's sister. Jim was his spirit father, Paul his brother by blood rite. So what did that make Teresa? He had grown up with her, known her as a bratty kid, a gangly youngster, and an awkward teenager. How could he think of her *that* way?

He left the solitude of his wickiup every morning to go to work and returned to loneliness each evening. If Bird came too close when he was on the ranch, he bolted. Ro was so addled his missing generator and two empty jerry cans mysteriously reappearing in front of the *gowa* barely registered.

By the time Paul came home for the holidays in mid-December, Ro was coping better. He'd risked a couple of "hellos" with Ruby at the trading post and noticed she was sharp and irritable, When he asked about it, she shut him down.

****

The Chandlers insisted he stay at the ranch for the holidays, expecting him to participate in the celebrations. Paul's presence made it easier for Ro, so he agreed.

The J-Bar-C hands, who usually ate Judith's cooking in the bunkhouse, joined the family in the dining room for the Christmas feast. Jim officiated from his wheelchair at the head of the table, carving a ham and obviously enjoying the table talk.

The wranglers—normally nonstop yakkers—didn't say much during the meal, but after Jim brought out cigars, things eased up. As usual, Pete did Ro

177

in.

"You give up on the ladies? Reason I ask is you ain't been beat up lately."

Paul wanted in on the joke, so Pete and Wade fed him—and everyone else at the table—details, even though they were details with two-year-old whiskers.

Paul whacked him on the back. "Why you old dog."

"Yes," Teresa said, "you old dog. By the way, did Ro tell you my new name?"

His heart dropped into his stomach. That was a private thing.

"What's that, sweetheart?" Jim asked.

"He says my Indian name is Flitting Bird."

"It fits," Paul said. "You're always flitting around."

Pete squinted across the table. "Think the boy hit onta something. A purty little bird."

Teresa put a modest hand to her breast. "Why thank you, sir."

Paul ended things by challenging him to a game of chess. Ro cleaned his clock.

****

By the time 1955 was christened with a New Year's Eve champagne toast and good wishes all around, Ro realized he'd had a good time at the party. He even enjoyed the firm, closed mouth kiss Bird gave him at midnight, but he couldn't help wondering how Ruby was celebrating the New Year. With Clarence, most likely.

Over the next few days, Ruby was on his mind so much Ro figured she'd witched him. Wednesday, he knocked off early enough to reach the trading post by closing time. The round-faced white man who owned the place was the only person in the store.

"You're Cane-Woman's grandson, ain't you?" Had the *Indah* called up her shade? "You looking for Ruby, she ain't here. Her and Clarence was in a car accident on New Year's Eve."

After learning she was at the clinic, Ro made a beeline for the place, his heart thudding wildly. The receptionist directed him to a side entrance where he found a glum and bandaged Clarence waiting for her to be discharged. Her father sat in a nearby car.

"What happened, man?" Ro asked.

"Steering went out coming off Snowflake Pass," Clarence said. "Frigging tie rods."

"Ruby gonna be all right?"

The man clipped his words. "That's what they say. Banged her up inside some. Me I got a broke arm."

178

A nurse pushed Ruby down a ramp in a wheelchair with her mother walking at her side. Ro knelt beside the chair, but Ruby wouldn't look at him. The shine was gone from her eyes.

"Can I come see you?"

She pulled her blouse close around her neck. "Not now."

"But—"

"I said no."

She got out of the wheelchair and slid into the back seat of her father's car. His chest ached as the vehicle pulled away, leaving him standing on the sidewalk.

****

During unseasonably warm February days, Teresa rode out to visit the crew on the job. She was as casual with Ro as she was with the other hands. But she touched him often, laying a hand on his arm, brushing dust from his brow, even asking for help mounting her pony. He almost laughed as he gave her a leg up. She'd been climbing aboard a horse without assistance since she was a little girl in bloomers.

Slowly, Ro grew easier with his life. The trip back home at night became a time for reflection, not an ordeal. But sometimes—often at work—he'd get lost in his thoughts, and his mind would slip away to a secret place. Pete noted out loud that his attacks of stupid seemed to come when that purty little Flittin' Bird was in the vicinity.

Spring prom rolled around, and Teresa made a big deal out of dressing up—with diamonds in her ears, no less—and going to a dance with some good-looking white guy named Johnny. The guy arrived to pick Teresa up in a sporty Corvette with no top. How would Teresa's careful coiffure hold up to the wind.? Recognizing it as a spiteful thought, he tried to spit it out of his brain. He wasn't very successful.

After the couple left, Jim and Judith wondered aloud why more boys weren't hanging around their beautiful daughter. Ro excused himself.

The Jeep headed into Terreon without much help from him. As he trolled the main drag, he spotted Ruby coming out of a drug store and called her over.

"You're looking better. Hope that means you've recovered."

She nodded. "Clarence is waiting in the car. Can't talk right now."

His stomach soured as she walked away.

The quiet clump of pines at Rising Rock beckoned. He parked on the wagon track and walked through the trees, halting when his eyes strayed to the little house where he and Ruby had made love. He built a small fire and stretched out on the ground, covering himself with a denim windbreaker. Presently a solitary star fell from the heavens.

"Ah, Grandmother. It's been a long time." He paused, listening for a message in the wind. "Roan Orphan is Tall Rider now. All grown up… and lonely. Tell him who he is again."

A prairie wolf howled somewhere in the distance. Fool coyote recognized a brother yapping at the moon. Twinkling stars reminded him of diamonds in Teresa's earlobes.

Bird. His answer was written right there in the heavens. She'd said she loved him once. A schoolgirl crush or more than that? In that magic moment, he understood: wherever she was… that was where he wanted to be.

Ro listened to the night sounds: the breeze playing in the trees, a rustling in the brush, the faint barking of dogs. A vehicle on a distant road. The sharp scent of pines assailed his nostrils, but the gentler aroma of grass soothed his soul. He became little Roan Orphan again, drowsing under the watchful eyes of his grandmother. Peace and sleep stole to his side as twins.

Ro woke with a start. Shivering, he crawled to his feet and squinted at his watch in the moonlight. Two o'clock. There'd be a better chance of speaking with Bird privately if he spent the rest of the night at the ranch. He examined his thinking as he drove and could find no fault with it. There was no doubt who claimed his mind and spirit.

The house was dark except for a light in the hallway. He entered by the kitchen and slipped off his boots to tiptoe to his room. A glimpse of himself in the upstairs hall mirror showed his face and clothes powdered with dust. Twigs in his tousled hair.

A gasp pulled his attention down the hall. Teresa stood, eyes wide, a hand pressed against her mouth. Ro started to speak, but she closed her bedroom door. He rapped softly. No answer.

Chapter 40

Ro dropped into a restless stupor sometime before dawn. The insistent buzz of the alarm roused him too late for his run, so he staggered down to breakfast. Teresa's icy good morning cleared away the cobwebs fast. He ate bacon and eggs, embarrassed by her long, disjointed account of last night's prom. Teresa was usually the center of attention, but not like this. He studied her from beneath lowered lashes and understood she was as miserable as he was. He sent his heart to her, but if she received it, she didn't let on.

Jim came to his rescue by asking him to check out the condition of the high ranges. The rancher believed prices were going to be good this year and wanted to go heavy on stock. Ro hung back after breakfast, hoping for a word alone with Teresa, but she retreated to her room. He shook his head and went for the Jeep.

After an hour on the muddy ranch road, Ro reached the place he called Valle Escondido, Hidden Valley. Surrounded by a range of high hills at the edge of the Capuchas, the basin lay cloistered from the rest of the world. Deer and elk lived there. He'd seen cougar sign. Bears took refuge higher in the hills. And Bear was a spirit animal to the People, a protector. They often called him "Uncle."

Ro parked and walked a distance, assessing conditions as he went. Mother Earth was still thawing, but soon lush strands of grama would rise to dance with the wind. Streams, swollen by snowmelt, would refresh the distant Rio Chacon with pure mountain water. Maybe he'd build a summer camp on the east side of the valley near one of the streams.

Pulling his collar closer against the crisp air, he tramped on numbed toes back to the Jeep and sent the vehicle bouncing along the faint track. As he fell rapidly toward the desert, the sun warmed the atmosphere. His mind and heart hummed a duet.

Far ahead, a splendid horse raced up the hill in great, rolling strides. Princess. He admired the beast a moment before turning his attention to the figure huddled over the whipping mane. The horse stumbled, recovered, and flew onward. A quirt flashed, urging the beast to full stride. What the hell was Teresa doing?

Horse and rider reached the road and came directly toward him. He cursed and jammed on the brakes. His rear end slid sideways in the muck. The mare flashed past, circled, and shot ahead of him again, disappearing over a rise. He floored the gas pedal. The Jeep gained traction and crested a small hill. He hit the brakes again. Teresa stood in the middle of the road, Princess at her shoulder, blowing noisily. He managed to halt the vehicle three feet from her.

"Are you all right?" she asked.

"Am… am *I*?" he sputtered.

"Well, I saw you lose control back there and—"

He leapt from the seat with a bellow and was on her. A flush of pleasure engulfed him at the quick fear in her eyes. He shook her shoulders. "What's the matter with you? First you won't talk to me. Then you damn near kill us both."

She brushed his hands away. "You don't know, of course. You're just a total innocent."

He started for the Jeep. "Make sense, will you?"

"Did you enjoy fucking her?"

He froze. "What the hell are you talking about?"

"We left the prom last night to get Johnny some cigarettes, and I saw you with Ruby."

He turned and moved toward her. "I ran into her on the street and said hello, that's all."

"When you finally came home you didn't bother to clean up. You were… disgusting!"

He stopped as though slapped. "Disgusting? Yeah, guess I was. Just another disgusting Indian sniffing around the white folks."

"Stop it! I never think of you that way. Except, when I do it's… exciting. It's what makes you… you." She turned away, looking unhappy. He stepped behind her and pulled her into his arms. She resisted feebly before collapsing against him. She cried as he stroked her hair.

Ro leaned against the Jeep and held her close. "It wasn't like you thought. I hung around the house after you left, but your mom and dad were talking about the prom and that jerk… uh, Johnny. And, well, I couldn't take it anymore."

"You were jealous?"

"I coulda strangled the guy. Anyway, I drove to town and saw Ruby coming out of the drug store. We said hello, and she went on her way. I drove around and ended up back at the grove where I grew up, built a fire, and plopped down in the grass to do some thinking."

"About what?"

"About you and me and what little I have to offer."

She twisted around and laid her hand across his mouth. "I won't have you running yourself down like that."

He shrugged. "Gotta face facts."

"Then face them the way they are, not like you imagine them when you're feeling sorry for yourself. You do that, you know."

"That's all there was to it. Fell asleep, and when I woke up, I came back to the ranch so I could talk to you early this morning. But it didn't work out that way."

"What did you want to talk about?"

"To tell you that when you told me how you felt, it scared me. It scared me because you were Paul's sister and Jim's daughter… and pretty much my sister too. And then that day when I kissed you on our ride, I saw you in a different way. It confused me."

She snickered. "That's why you ran every time I came near?"

"Was I so obvious?"

"I'm surprised the cattle weren't gossiping about it. Why were you confused?"

He held her close and thought hard for a moment. "If I answer your question, I'll have to tell you something you might not want to hear."

She clutched his arm, her face hidden from him. "Tell me anyway. I need to understand."

He sighed. "I'd made love to Ruby." He felt her move and hugged her tighter. "Not last night, but earlier. Anyway, when I did it the last time—"

"The *last* time!"

"Man, I'm not doing this very good. Anyway, something strange happened."

"What was it? Or is it something else I don't want to know?"

"You do because it's the answer to your question. The last time… the last time…."

"Go on. The hard part's over with."

"Seems pretty hard to me." He gulped. "The last time I thought I was loving you. And it was the best ever!"

"Me? And just how many times did you do it to her?"

"That night?"

"*That* night? How many nights were there?"

His cheeks burned. "Uh, three times."

"Three times or three nights?"

"Well, two times that night," he blurted.

She jerked out of his arms and stomped to her pony, causing Princess to shy. She whirled. "Three times? Twice that night? And how many other Rubys have there been?"

"None." He cast around for some way to salvage the situation. "Doesn't it mean anything that the best was when I imagined it was you?"

She glared at him for a moment or two before bursting out laughing. "You

183

stand there looking like a hunky man and sounding like a guilty little boy. You're a clod, but at least you're not an insensitive one. I didn't have any call on you. You were… are… free to do what you want."

"I don't wanna be free. I've never felt this way. If I'm not careful, I'm gonna be lost."

"I think you just came as close to saying you love me as you're capable of. And I won't say it back because I'd scare you straight back to the reservation." Her face softened. "But at least we know we have feelings between us."

"After what I just went through, sure hope so. I know *I've* got feelings."

"Lummox! I already told you I've been in love with you for ages. When you rode in on that skinny old mare and pulled your lower lip at me, it was all over."

"Bird," he almost lost his voice. "I won't see Ruby. I won't see anybody but you."

"And I won't go with anyone but you."

"Maybe that's not a good idea. Your folks keep wondering why you don't go out much."

"Because you never ask me. And I don't want to go out with anyone else."

"Let's clear that up for them."

Teresa clutched his forearms with both hands. "Ro, please don't misunderstand what I'm about to say, but I don't think we should tell them yet. I'm not sure they're ready for it."

He felt the air go out of him. "Is that the only reason?"

She punched his shoulder. "Román Otero, if I've learned one thing from you, it's to own my words. When are you going to get over feeling inferior?"

"I *don't* feel inferior. But some people look at me that way."

She hugged him around the chest. "Then I pity them. I'd say I love you, but I'd have to chase you down over in the next county. But seriously, do you agree? About the folks, I mean."

He gave a wry frown, "Don't know if I can hide the way I feel. Especially from Jim."

"Come on, everybody knows Indians are stoic."

"Stoic maybe, but not stone." His cheeks tingled. Aware that part of his anatomy belied his words, he pulled away slightly.

She molded herself to him. "It's not fair. Ruby knows what you look like, and all I can do is feel you through your clothes. Can I take a peek?"

He let out a breath. "You do, I won't be responsible for what happens."

She pretended to pout and mounted Princess. "Fine. But you're right. I can't cut off the boys at school." She studied him. "If this ends up the way it's headed, you gotta promise me to do better on our wedding night."

His jaw dropped. "Better? You mean better than twice?"

"You got it, buster!" She wheeled Princess and rode away laughing.

"Not a problem," he called after her. "At least, I don't think so," he muttered to himself.

Time was not a constant. It ran in spurts. Work hours counted out every second. When Ro was with Bird, it raced as fast as his pulse. On rare occasions, they sneaked away to a movie or for a ride in the Jeep, but usually they stayed on the ranch. He often took advantage of the Chandler's swimming pool after work with Teresa joining him more often than not. Ro spent more nights at the big house but didn't totally abandon his camp at Snakehead. Teresa dated others as infrequently as she dared.

The school year ended, and she still held him to his pledge of silence. Being less than forthright with Jim prickled, but if that's what Bird wanted….

****

The Jeep's headlamps exposed the *gowa's* primitive nature. He'd tried to talk Bird out of coming, but she wanted to see where he lived. He frowned, unsure why he was reluctant to share that part of his life. Yet, he could hardly refuse a reasonable request to visit his home. He leveled his gaze. He was getting good at the white man's stare.

"Sure you want to be alone up here with me at night?"

"Don't be silly. I know I can trust you."

He killed the engine, got out, and fired the generator to turn on lights before inviting her inside. "Nice place to live, isn't it?"

"You chose it over a pretty comfortable house, so there must be something to it." She looked around. "Were you happy living like this as a child?"

"Only thing I knew."

"What was she like?"

An unexplained shiver ran down his back. "Strange. But when I was little, I thought other people were the strange ones. They were afraid of her. Called her a witch." His voice faltered. "She was good to me though. Sometimes she went hungry so I could eat."

"*Was* she a witch?"

"That's a question I can't answer. But the whole reservation thought so."

"Build a fire… please." After he had a small blaze going, she asked him to turn out the lights. He watched by the glow of the flames as she nodded. "Yes, I think you were happy."

He laughed. "A lot you know. Ten minutes in a wickiup on a nice spring night, and you've decided that's the way to live. Sit down."

"Did you have chairs then?" When he shook his head, she sank to the rug.

He dropped to the blanket beside her, and they stared into the fire. "Ro," she broke the stillness, "don't get spooked, but I love you."

"I don't spook that easily."

"You did last year. I love you more than anyone in the world. Think about you in the daytime and dream about you at night." She snickered. "Some of the dreams aren't so nice. Well, they're *nice*, but not nice. Do you love me?"

"Of course, I do."

"Then say it."

"I've said it a thousand times, you just didn't hear me."

"I want to hear it, but only if you truly own your words."

"I love you, Bird. With all my heart and mind and spirit."

"Don't ever stop saying it. Tell me every day. Every time you see me. When you can't see me, just whisper it, and I'll know you're saying it."

He sobered. "Whenever you see a star twinkle, that's me saying I love you."

She reached up and clasped his neck, pulling him atop her as she lay back on the blanket. He made as though to rise, but she hugged him closer and spread her legs, making a natural place for his hips. "I love you, Tall Rider." Her eyes glowed like a live coal from the firepit.

He crushed his lips to hers. Her breasts pressed against his chest. He took a ragged breath and buried his head in her neck. She moved, pushing against him.

He staggered to his feet, breath coming in gulps. "Christ! Don't tell me how much you trust me and then do something like that."

She scrambled up and threw her arms around his shoulders. They rocked back and forth. The fire spat sparks, momentarily lightening the gloom. Eerie shadows cavorted over the walls. A thin spiral of acrid vapor wafted through the smoke hole in the roof.

Slowly he steadied himself. "Al—almost lost control."

"My fault. I wanted you to do it."

"Marry me, Bird," he rasped.

"I will! I will. Oh, yes, I will. But we can't until I'm eighteen. We can wait ten months, can't we? But I'll marry you in spirit. This can be our wedding night."

"God, I love you." He pulled her to him and then thrust her away. "But we'll do it right. Then they'll have to respect us and be proud of us." He smiled.

"What are you grinning about?"

Ro glanced around the wickiup. "How wrong my grandmother was when she said I'd never be happy with you."

The last flickering flame in the firepit abruptly died, leaving a pulsing red ember.

Chapter 41

October... the glittering, beaded headband on the year's greatest season. Indian Summer. The first hard frost was behind them, and the temperature was now in the seventies. Flitting Bird's absence marred Ro's twentieth birthday, but after she'd received her high school diploma at the end of summer school, he pressured her into attending college because that was what her folks expected. She chose New Mexico State, the school closest to home.

Until then, he'd been negligent about going to Snakehead, preferring to stay close to Bird. Now he returned nightly to his camp, except when she came home on weekends.

****

Big Tom Bearclaw dropped by the *gowa* late one Sunday afternoon. The fat man's appetite for gossip had kept pace with his demand for food, and it troubled him not at all that his host had no tidbits to offer in return.

"Been too long, nephew. You don't know nothing about your people no more. Don't you worry, Tom knows what goes on, and he'll put you wise to things."

With half an ear and about as much interest, Ro listened politely to an hour of news about the denizens of the Edge of Mountain Reservation. Finally, one item snared his attention.

"Ruby lost a baby? How do you know?" He bit his tongue. Everyone knew everything on the rez. He was probably the last to find out.

Big Tom chose not to embarrass him. "Everbody figgers it was Clarence's, but his moccasins don't make no noise. Thought they'd get married, but they ain't."

Ro's stomach rolled. "Baby?"

"Lost it in that car wreck last New Year's." Tom cocked his head and squinted at him. "She was always sniffing around your tipi, weren't she? She get your blood up? Make your dog-bone stand up and bark?"

Time to change the subject before he became one of Tom's tidbits. "Sorry to hear that. Always liked Ruby. Anybody hear how Jose Peyote's doing in the pen?"

"Clarence was up to Albuquerque a few weeks ago and run into a Ogalala just outta the joint. Said some of them white cons up there raped Jose's ass." The big man shook his head, which jiggled his belly. "Figures. Jose looks good enough to be a girl. Course, I ain't gonna say that to his face. This Sioux claimed Jose killed one of them. Said he done it smart, so nobody can pin it on him."

Bad news. Jose would come back spitting poison. He'd been locked up about a year and a half, which meant he still had three and a half to go.

****

Ro settled into a routine and rode it until winter. On the morning of the first snowfall, Jim asked him to go for a ride. Huge wet flakes drifted like goose down to cover the desert with a white blanket that muffled sound and muted light. Despite the snow, or perhaps because of it, the weather wasn't excessively cold, so they decided against buttoning canvas on the jeep. Both men donned gloves, sheepskins, and Stetsons before Jim adroitly shifted from wheelchair to passenger's seat. Ro drove.

He glanced up at the gray sky, down geared the Jeep, and started up an incline. "It'll give out come morning."

"Along about midnight," Jim predicted. "Damned early for snow. Glad we stocked up heavy on feed. Looked at the prices lately? Gone crazy."

As a silence grew, Jim gave him sidelong glances. The man was working up to something. Finally, the rancher motioned to a yellow pine standing guard beside the road and asked him to pull over. Ro nosed in close to take what shelter he could.

Jim heaved a deep sigh. "This is a funny place to talk, but I like it out here. Rain, shine, snow, or whatever it's better than being cooped up in a stuffy house."

Ro chuckled. "When I was a kid, that's the one thing that really stumped me. I couldn't fit you to that house."

"It's Judith's mostly." Jim cleared his throat. "Son, ever since my accident I've leaned on you hard and haven't been too good at saying thanks. If you hadn't stayed, Paul would've dropped out of the university, and I want him to finish his education more than anything." He paused. "You both could have gone to school, but it sure has been easier on me this way."

Ro swiped snow from the steering wheel. "Wasn't nothing."

"It was everything. You sacrificed time, and when you're my age, you'll understand how precious time is. But now there's something I'd like to do. In a sense, it's nothing because I've waited too long. You'll be twenty-one in less than a year and a man in your own right. But I want to let you and the world know how I feel… how we feel. Son, I'd like to adopt you."

A constricted throat robbed Ro of his voice.

Jim twisted in the seat to look at him. "Don't you like the idea?"

"Can't tell you how much I like it." Something crawling around in his gut

188

reached up to choke his voice. He made another stab. "When I was little and heard Paul call you Dad, I used to whisper it to myself. You've always been my father whether you knew it or not."

"And I've always regarded you as a son. It's foolish to have waited so long."

Flitting Bird. He needed to talk to Bird. But he couldn't just string Jim along. "Judith's all right with this?"

"Hell, she took me to task for waiting so long." Jim's smile faltered as Ro sat like a piece of rock. "What is it, son?"

"I... we... Teresa and I are in love. We want to get married." Jim's mouth dropped open. Ro rushed on. "If you adopt me, I don't know what that means legally."

"You and Teresa? My little girl and you? Why didn't you say something?"

His mouth went dry. Oh, crap! How was Jim taking it? "She... uh, we decided to wait until she turned eighteen." He felt like a man caught in another fellow's tipi. "We were afraid you'd say we were too young."

A huge grin cracked the rancher's windburned face. "You and my little girl. You and Teresa. That's wonderful."

Ro exhaled, and the world moved again. "I wasn't sure you'd like the idea."

"Hell, didn't I just try to adopt you?"

"It's not exactly the same thing."

"Guess it's not at that. Come on, son. Let's go home." Jim's hearty slap on Ro's back sent powdered snow flying. "Let's break the news to Judith."

His stomach did flip-flops. "Maybe we oughta wait until Bird comes home. I mean, she might like to be the one to tell her mother. You know, get her approval."

"Of course, she'll approve. Judith's fond of you."

Feeling woozy, Ro ground the starter and pulled onto the almost invisible road. Things were moving too fast. Screw it, their secret was out now. His heart soared. *Finally*, they could stop sneaking around and let the whole world know. God, he wished Bird were here. He'd phone her tonight.

After they parked in front of the garage, Ro had trouble with the wheelchair in the snow, but as soon as they were on the veranda, Jim told him to go give Judith the news.

She was in the kitchen looking domestic in a white apron. "Back already?"

"Yes, ma'am." He felt like he was on the reservation where etiquette demanded small talk before addressing big things.

She smiled. "I can see he got around to telling you."

"Yeah. I can hardly believe it, but...." This was harder than he'd expected. Instinctively, he knew it was her mother who worried Bird. "I guess I oughta

189

tell you...." His voice gave out.

"That you and Teresa think you're in love?"

He blinked. "You know?"

"You weren't very subtle about it. The way you looked at one another. Found time to be alone together. You never go back to the reservation when she's home."

"But Jim didn't know."

"He's her father. I'm her mother."

"Jim said you pushed the adoption idea."

"If you're wondering if that means I disapprove of your relationship, that's exactly what it means."

"But I love her! More than anything. And she loves me. We want to marry."

"She's too young. Let her try her wings and taste life. She's seen so little, done so little. You have no right to tie her down now. Give her time. Is that asking too much?" Judith drew a breath. "Of course, waiting carries a risk. After she matures, she may decide she doesn't love you. But isn't it better to find out before you're too involved?"

He struggled for words. "I've been doing my job for a long time. Doesn't that show some maturity? I want to make a life with her. Have children and raise them with her. Put down roots. Be a family."

Judith brushed her brow with the back of a hand. "Perhaps the idea of family and roots are more important than *who*. And the adoption gives you that. Makes you part of our family. Even more than you already are. Teresa's pretty and available. You're comfortable with her. That's why you believe you're in love."

Ro flinched and took a step backward, feeling so heavy his legs would hardly hold him. "That isn't true! I love Bird... *Teresa*. Not the idea of being in love. Judith, you know me. I'm not a romantic. I know who and what I want. And I know I'll be good for her."

"You're steady and reliable and perhaps mature enough to know what you want, but she's younger emotionally as well as in years. She needs more time, more experience."

"She is the most level-headed girl I know."

"Exactly the point. Girl. Teresa is a girl. Give her a chance to grow into a woman. To do anything less would be to admit you're afraid she'll meet someone else."

He moistened dry lips. "If I'm afraid, why did I talk her into going to college this semester? She wanted to stay here with me."

"Then give her time. Pop songs to the contrary, what feels like love isn't necessarily the real thing. You've always been a realist. You avoided running off to the university with Paul because you know what he plans isn't right for you. And you've done it without hurting him."

She had worked things around neatly, using his own nature against him. And she saw the lawyer thing clearer than anyone else. "Jim thinks it's okay."

"All he sees are two people he loves attracted to one another. When he thinks it through, he'll see I'm right. So will you, if you're fair about it."

"Is that really why you're against it? If Teresa came home with a blond, blue-eyed college man in tow, you'd be tickled pink. You don't like the idea of me being Apache."

Jim rolled into the room and came to a halt.

A flush crossed Judith's face. "I'm disappointed in you. Is that your insecurity showing? Or are you deliberately playing on your race? We've had you in our home as part of our family for years." She put a hand to her temple. "No, I owe you honesty. I don't want to hurt you, but you're pushing me to the wall. You're a good man, Román. You'll make someone with the same interests and background a wonderful, dependable husband. But what can you offer Teresa? You are not the man for her."

He staggered as if struck by a physical force. Suddenly tired, his voice went flat. "Because I'm Indian."

He bolted and brushed past Jim.

"Wait, son! Let's talk…."

Ro fled into feathery white snow dropping straight from the sky and made for the stable to saddle Colorado. He flung himself aboard the gelding and kicked the horse into a run. Jim called from the back porch, but Ro closed his eyes and let the horse have his head. There was no air between the flakes. He was suffocating. What did it matter? The world had already ended.

Colorado, conditioned by previous journeys, headed straight for Snakehead Spring. Ro absently opened the gate and walked the rest of the way to his camp. He had presence of mind enough to make sure Colorado was comfortable in his shed before entering the wickiup.

The remainder of the night, Ro huddled beside a fire in the wickiup toting up his losses. It wasn't just Bird. He'd also lost a father, a brother, and a job he loved. Hollow as a reed, he felt a feathery pulse at his wrist. For a moment, he understood Jose Peyote better. But he didn't want revenge. He wanted to die. Even so, his rifle remained in the scabbard, his knife in its sheath.

****

Ro ran through snow-clogged mountains in a clear, crystalline dawn without slipping to his death on icy trails, despite deliberate carelessness. Unable to eat, he tore through his belongings in a frantic search for cigarettes. He found none. No surprise. He rarely used the things.

The trip to White Pine for tobacco was more trouble than it was worth. While in the store, he heard talk of a rogue mountain lion making problems for the tribe's cattle association. Clutching a pack of Lucky Strikes, Ro walked on numb, stick legs to his horse. Lighting a tobacco stick, he took two drags, gagged, and threw the pack away. Not until he turned toward the trading post, did he understand where he'd been heading all along.

Ruby gasped when he walked through the door. He caught a look at his sweat-stained clothes and uncombed hair in a glass display case. Damn, he hadn't cleaned up after his run. He spun on his heel, but she caught up with him and grabbed his leg as he swung into the saddle.

"Go to my place," she said. "Door's not locked. Clean up, and get some rest. I'll come when I get off for lunch."

He entered her small house like one of the walking dead and fell into a chair near the front window. That's where Ruby found him when she came home. She bullied him into the bathroom where he roused enough to strip and climb into the tub. After he was clean, he wrapped himself in a blanket while Ruby washed his filthy clothing. Then she talked him into eating soup and tortillas while dragging the story out of him. He knew his talk of Teresa struck Ruby like a physical blow, but once started, he couldn't put a rein on his tongue. After Ruby returned to work, he lay down on her bed and fell into a fitful sleep.

A black dream filled with owls and coyotes and Judith Chandler woke him in the middle of the afternoon. Confused by his nakedness, he stumbled around until remembering where he was. Remnants of the dream chased him out of the house into the cold where his still-damp clothing chilled him to the bone. He found the reservation bootlegger and returned to Ruby's, to sit in her front room while drinking vile, home-brewed moonshine.

The whiskey didn't help. Judith's shade—as vivid awake as it had been in the dream—chased him around the house, chiding him for trying to be someone he wasn't, hating him for who he was. Bird—no, Bird was dead— *Teresa* stood behind her mother, repeating every word.

His anger, his fear, his guilt erupted. He shattered the whiskey bottle against a mirror above the sofa. Seizing the broken neck, he slashed the cushions before falling to his knees and going numb. He woke from his stupor when Ruby came through the door and let out a cry.

Red-faced, Ro scrambled to his feet and staggered over to pick up shards of glass. "Sorry. Pay you for the damage."

They shared a bed that night, but all he remembered was being too sick to do anything but hang onto the mattress. In the morning, he lurched outside to throw up. With nothing left in his stomach, he pressed a handful of snow to his hot forehead and went back inside. The smell of alcohol seeping through his pores made him ill again.

After Ruby left for work, Ro rode into White Pine for something to settle his stomach. He was guzzling a bottle of pink stuff when he ran into August Wingfield. Trying to listen through his misery, he came to understand the man was speaking of the puma he'd heard about yesterday.

"Hear you ain't working for that white outfit no more," August said. "That so, you oughta sign up to hunt the panther. Shooting something'd likely do you some good right now. Association's paying a decent bounty."

Ro held out a trembling hand. "Couldn't hit a cougar if he walked up and stuck his nose in my barrel."

"Hangover, huh? Go have a slug of what bit you, and you'll get over it. Anyhow, the hunting party ain't leaving till Friday. You want, I'll put in a word for you."

"Sure. Why not?"

Ro paid August five dollars to drive him to the bank in Terreon where he bought a cashier's check and drew out some cash. He pocketed the money and mailed the check to Jim Chandler.

Even sicker by the time they got back to White Pine, Ro reclaimed Colorado and started for Snakehead. First hot and then cold, he got so dizzy he changed directions and headed for Big Tom's place. The fat man took one look, threw him into the sweathouse, and wouldn't let him out until judging him about done. After that, Tom put him to bed in a small hut at the edge of the camp. As Ro's physical ailments eased, his emotional ills grew. In the dead of night, he'd wake with tears on his face thinking of Teresa. One more flaw in his character.

Friday morning, August drove into camp to inform Ro he was officially a part of the hunt. The party was setting out from the association's cattle barn at one o'clock that afternoon. Ro paid Big Tom for his help, saddled up, and rode by the trading post. After pressing money into Ruby's hand to replace her mirror and couch, he told her he was okay now.

Upon arriving at the cattle barn, he learned he was going into the mountains on a hunt with Clarence Wolf and Buck Wingfield, Tomas's younger brother.

Chapter 42

Terreon's narrow, snow-packed streets forced the bus driver to slow below the speed limit. As they approached the depot near the plaza, Teresa speculated which car would pick her up. The Lincoln meant Ro and one of her parents. The Jeep signaled Ro was alone.

The Lincoln. She fought disappointment as she collected her small overnight bag and stepped from the bus. A faint uneasiness fluttered in her breast. Ro usually drove, even though the car was fitted with hand controls, but tonight her father was the car's only occupant. He leaned over to accept her kiss on the cheek after she slipped into the passenger's seat.

"Where's Ro?"

He avoided her eyes. "Honey, I don't quite know how to tell you this."

She cried as he related what had happened, but she was dry-eyed by the time the car turned down the drive to the ranch house. "He's been gone a week. Why didn't you call me?"

"I wanted time to try and put it right. Why didn't you tell me about you two?"

"Isn't it obvious? I was afraid of something like this."

He patted her hand affectionately. "If you'd confided in me, maybe I could have helped."

"Oh, Dad, I wish I had, but I was afraid you'd send him away."

"How do you know you really love him?" he asked. "Do you even know what love is?"

"At first, it's wanting someone so badly you cry. Being possessive and jealous of anyone demanding his time. Even your father and brother. It's suffering when he's out of sight. Imagining accidents. Other women. Then it changes. You still want him as badly, just not so selfishly. You get comfortable sharing him. And the feeling it's right for both of you gets stronger. It's aching when he touches you. Knowing he's not perfect, but he's perfect for you. Being able to disagree, argue, fight, and know it doesn't make any difference. I'm ready to wash his socks, his underwear, *him*. It's building things together, a family, a home, a life."

"Oh, baby, that sounds right to me."

"Do you know where he is?" she asked.

"Camp's still at the same place. One of us checks on him damned near every day, but the place is always deserted. He hears us coming and hides out.

Tomorrow, you go bring him back, and I'll start to work on your mother. No promises, but I'll do what I can." He parked in front of the garage and turned to face her. "Honey, don't be too hard on your mother. She did what she thought was best." He cleared his throat. "Talk to her before going to look for him."

Judith stood on the porch looking older than she remembered. "Teresa-"

"How could you, Mother?"

"I did it for your own good."

"That old saw?" She strode into the house to change clothes.

Her mother followed. "Teresa, I want to talk to you."

She whirled. "Why? So you can give me details on how you drove away the man I love? I already know what you're going to say. We're too young. How many times has that lame excuse been used?"

Judith colored. "Just one minute, young lady. I'm still your mother, and I demand a little respect. You will at least have the courtesy to hear what I have to say."

Teresa was suddenly a little girl caught being naughty.

Judith softened her tone. "What do you know of love? Have you ever been in love before? Believe me, it's difficult to tell what's real." She stepped closer and spoke gently. "Forever is a long time, and that's what it is when you marry a man. I have a responsibility to you no one else in this world can assume. When you were a little girl, I had to deny you things you wanted. You were angry then too. I'm merely doing what I've always done. You know I'm fond of Román, but he isn't the one for you."

With a start, Teresa realized her mother had been getting to her. "If you're so fond of him, why don't you call him Ro like everyone else? Why isn't he the one for me?"

"You wouldn't be challenged. You'd lose interest. You're a bright, active girl. You should meet and fall in love with an intelligent, dynamic young man."

"Ro *is* intelligent. Dynamic? He excites me almost more than I can stand."

"Of course, he does… physically. He's a handsome man."

"It's more than physical. Everything he does is interesting and challenging. I love *him*. I want to spend my life with him, be the mother of his children. I've been in love with Román Otero since I was a kid. He *is* the one for me, and I'm going to find him and tell him so."

"I can't stop you, but in a little over three months, you'll be eighteen. Promise me you'll not run off and elope. At least tell us before you marry. And, Teresa, don't make a mistake."

"For your information, Mother, I've already offered myself to him. I got him so hot and bothered he actually ached. But he's smarter than I am. He wants to wait until we're married."

Judith flinched, making Teresa regret her cruelty. She planted a quick kiss on her mother's brow and fled to her room.

****

Twilight. That eerie time of day when a driver needs headlamps, but they do absolutely no good. Upon reaching Big Split Rock Gully, Teresa killed the motor and abandoned the Lincoln. If Ro was avoiding company, he would hear the car coming. She walked the rest of the way in gathering gloom. Snowdrifts made the going tougher. Ahead of her lay the quiet copse of trees sheltering his camp. No sign of Colorado.

She entered the hut and played the flashlight she carried around the dark interior. His belongings littered the place. Not in his usual neat way but scattered carelessly. Cold fire pit. Disappointed, she made her way back to the car. Where could he be? She knew so little of his life on the reservation. The one name she knew raised a chill on her back. Ruby.

Unable to consider that probability, she turned to mulling over where he could have gone in town. Nowhere. He didn't drink—unless this had driven him to it. He had no life outside of the ranch and this camp. She watched fruitlessly for Colorado as she drove through White Pine on the way back to the house where she spent the night tossing and turning.

Early the next morning, she rode Princess to the gate at Snakehead Spring. When the camp was still deserted, Teresa returned home and found her father in his office.

"No sign of him... or Colorado." She flopped into a chair. "I won't go back to school until I know he's all right."

"And prove your mother's point? If Ro doesn't want to be found, he has half a million acres to hide out in. I have a call in to Bud McElhaney, the fellow who owns the trading post outside of White Pine. They don't talk much to outsiders over there, but Bud probably knows the Apache better than any other white man. We'll find him, Teresa, but it's gonna take time. Go back to school, and let me have till Christmas break to come up with results."

"And if you can't?"

"We'll talk about it then. I'll do my best. Take one of the pickups to school. That way, you can come back in a hurry if you need to."

Encouraged, Teresa made another useless visit to Snakehead Spring the next day in what had been Ro's Jeep. On the way back to NM35, she noticed the ramshackle trading post. What had her father called the man who owned it? McElhaney? That was it. She pulled into the parking area and went inside. As soon as the door closed behind Teresa, her breath caught in her throat. Ruby stared at her from behind a glass showcase.

Teresa recovered her composure and walked to the counter. "Hello,

196

Ruby." She received a mute nod in reply. "Is the owner in?"

"Mr. McElhaney's out of town. I'm in charge while he's away. What do you want?"

"I'll wait until he's back, thank you. When will that be?"

"Monday." A long pause. "Leave Román alone. You've hurt him enough."

"Hurt him? I love him."

Ruby sneered. "He's your plaything, that's all. Do you tell your rich girlfriends about your Indian lover? Or maybe it's the other way 'round. Maybe he's playing with you, telling everybody about his pale little girlfriend."

"You're talking trash, but I guess that comes natural to you." Teresa bit her tongue. Fighting with Ruby wasn't the way to find out what she knew. "My business is with Ro."

"He's Román, not *Ro*. You think you can make him fit in your world by calling him Ro? He is who he is. You'll kill him if you don't leave him alone."

"I know who he is, a man who loves me. But I'll tell you what *will* kill him. Cutting him off from the ranch where he's worked and lived half his life. That means I can offer life. What can you offer?"

"Only a woman of his own blood who loves him. A life on the land where he was born. That big ranch isn't yours to give. Your mama already took that away. All you can offer is pain."

"I'm not going to let him go. I'm going to find Rider, and I'll keep coming back until he tells me not to."

Ruby's eyes narrowed—possibly at Teresa's use of Ro's familiar. "He's out of your reach now. He didn't save himself for you. He did it to me. Do you hear? He fucked me!"

Teresa spoke through her pain. "Nice choice of words. I notice you didn't say he made love to you. You're right, he fucked you."

Ruby slammed a fist on the counter. "I carried his child."

Teresa staggered as if punched. But Ruby's odd phrasing raised her suspicions. "Where's the baby now?"

"I… I lost it."

She heard the deep chord of sadness in the woman's voice and knew it was true. "If you're trying to shock me, forget it. I'm a rancher's daughter. I know all about sex. I didn't expect a virgin in a man. And thank you for letting him practice on you. Oh, I see it now. He's so good in bed, you're trying to hold on. But I know one thing. He hasn't touched you since he told me he loved me. Unless you got to him while he was hurt. If so, that doesn't mean a thing, except it was you who took advantage of him, not me."

Ruby dropped her gaze. "Go away, white girl! I hate you! *He* hates you!"

Chapter 43

Teresa went through the routine of attending classes while her mind rehearsed what she would say when she finally faced Ro. She called home regularly, but her father had no news other than he'd received a check in the mail returning Ro's school fund.

She cut class on Friday and started home. As she reached the turnoff to White Pine, Teresa whipped the pickup to the right and bounced down the muddy road to the trading post. A big, bluff man with hoarfrost for hair introduced himself as Bud McElhaney and told her Cane-Woman's grandson and some others had gone to hunt a rogue mountain lion. "Been out a week or so. Dunno if they're back yet," he finished.

Teresa drove to Ro's camp. The wickiup was empty. From the looks of the hut, he hadn't returned. She picked up his scattered belongings and placed them neatly around the wickiup. When darkness fell, she gave up and drove home.

****

The next morning, ignoring her parents' objections, Teresa packed food, warm clothing, and a sleeping bag aboard Princess. She'd stay at the wickiup until she had to go back to school at Las Cruces.

Even before she entered the hut at nightfall Saturday, Teresa knew Ro hadn't been back. She fed Princess some of Colorado's oats and made sure the mare was comfortable in the shelter Ro had built in the big red's corral. After the horse was snug, she wrestled with the generator until the lights worked. That done, she built a fire and forced down a light meal. Around midnight she fell asleep on his cot.

At first light, Teresa used the privy and washed up in Snakehead Spring. She found the trail he used on his morning runs and trod the entire six miles, imagining his spirit walked beside her.

Teresa remained until Sunday evening before going home to get ready to leave for the university. By the time she departed the ranch, she and her mother had reached a tacit truce. They could share a room without lowering the temperature, but the relationship wasn't what it once had been. Would it ever be?

Teresa herded the pickup down the drive and turned south on NM35. She should have gone north, but she wanted—needed—to check on Ro one more time. After passing through White Pine, she turned north out of Swallowtail Meadow and east into Big Split Rock Gully. Teresa was startled when her headlights picked up Colorado's ears flicking in her direction.

Now the moment was near, she grew frightened. Was Ruby with him? Teresa turned off the motor and killed the lights. She sat in the cold silence to gather her strength. Finally, she got out of the truck and entered the wickiup.

The glow of a small fire broke the darkness. Ro had ignored his cot and stretched out on the rug. His discarded boots stood against a wall, but otherwise he was fully clothed. A blanket, thrown aside in his sleep, lay wadded against his side. He looked tired and thinner. As Teresa covered him again, he twitched and muttered something in his own tongue but didn't waken.

A hand against her mouth, Teresa sobbed in relief before snuggling her back against him. In a moment, Ro turned into her, spoon fashion. His breathing told her he still slept. For the first time in over a week, she fell into a dreamless slumber.

Teresa woke sometime in the middle of the night when he pulled her to him. His face in her hair, he mumbled, but it was dream talk… sleep talk. Hips pressing against her buttocks, a hand cupping her breast, set her afire. She knew the instant he came awake, sensed his confusion, and gloried in the sound of his voice.

"Teresa?"

She pushed against him. "No, it's Flitting Bird."

His voice held a harsh rasp. "Flitting Bird is dead. What are you doing here?"

She turned and lay full length against him. "You wouldn't come to me, so I had to come to you. Ro, you just disappeared. Why didn't you call?"

He sat up. "Because your mother's right. You don't belong with me."

She buried her face in his neck. "Don't say that."

He pushed her away—not harshly, not gently. "I'm raunchy. Been out in the field all week."

"Good!" she said, snuggling again. He smelled of sweat and leather and tobacco and gunpowder and musk, an exciting amalgam.

"Stop it! Judith is right. After we married, you'd get tired of me. All I know are cows. After the kids started coming, you'd want to go to town and belong to this club and that club, and I'd be miserable there. I'm just a cowboy, Teresa."

"And I'm just a cowboy's daughter."

"You're more than that."

"And so are you. You've proven that ten times over."

"How? By conning Paul into believing I'm gonna be a lawyer when I never

199

wanted to? By getting too big for my britches and thinking I'm somebody I'm not? Your mother and She-Who-Was-My-Grandmother have something in common. They see things clearer than we do. They're both telling me the same thing."

"Then they're both wrong. Answer one question, and tell me the truth. Do you love me?"

He dropped his eyes. "Enough to let you go... no matter how much it hurts."

"Then don't tell me it won't work. I've disobeyed my mother and lied to my teachers just to find you. And I'd do it again. I'll never let you go. I'll keep hounding you until you either come back or tell me to get the hell out of your life."

"Ahmm, you said a dirty word," he teased, as if she were still a manipulative brat.

"So tell on me! But right now, there's a man north of here who needs you almost as much as I do. Dad's going crazy worrying about you."

"All right, I'll call him. But I can't go back to the ranch. I'm going to take a job working with the tribe's cattle association."

"You can't desert him just because things got uncomfortable."

"Tell that to your mother."

"I'm not talking about my mother. I'm talking about the man who was your father for half your life. You're running away from him, and that's wrong. Not just for him—not even for me. It's wrong for you." His face darkened, so she pressed. "At least, call him and let him know you're all right."

"Said I would. Or doesn't my word count for anything anymore?"

"Course, it counts. But I'm going to test it." She took him by surprise by reaching around his neck and pulling him atop her. She spread her legs and he fell through. She felt him harden, and a thrill ran up her spine. She ground her lips against his, searching his half-opened mouth with her tongue.

Ro pulled away suddenly, a wild look in his eyes. He passed a hand over his face and moistened his lips. It was the sexiest thing she'd ever seen. "Can't do this. I'd be taking revenge on your mother and feel rotten because of your dad. And you'd just be paying Ruby back."

He caught her wrist a second before she slapped his cheek. Her voice was tight. "Ruby has nothing to do with this. Neither do my parents. This is between you and me, Román Otero."

He turned away, frightening her. "Ro, I love you, and I know you love me. I'm going to leave here today knowing exactly what's in store for me when our time comes."

She pushed him onto his back and moved her hands over his face. The stubble surprised her. He was always clean shaven. She roamed his neck and chest as if blind. She unbuttoned his shirt and loosened his Levi's. He lay mute and unmoving until she knew everything.

Chapter 44

Ro leaned over Colorado's saddle horn fighting the feeling he was a skinny, scared ten-year-old astride a stringy paint. A pompadour of billowy white clouds crowned the Chacons, just as on that long ago day. If he turned back, would She-Who-Was be waiting to see the reward the *Indah* rancher had given him? He twisted the turquoise ring on his right hand and spoke softly to Colorado. The gelding pranced before breaking into an easy trot, clearly pleased to be going home. If only Ro felt that way.

When he'd called Jim, as promised, the rancher had talked about the ranch and the crew and asked about the lion hunt.

"We got him," Ro said.

"Be straight with me. You got him, right?"

Some of the ice in Ro's brain thawed. "Yeah, I shot him."

After that, conversation became easier, but he rebelled when Jim insisted on a visit, claiming to be busy with his new job at the tribal cattle association. He was too ashamed to admit he was simply a drover, hazing cattle from here to there—and already in trouble because he'd suggested changes to the round belly running the place. But he finally agreed to come over Saturday to pick up his belongings.

As Ro dismounted and ground-hitched Colorado, Jim wheeled onto the small porch outside his office and held out his hand, a big smile splitting his face.

"You're looking good. Thinner, but good. Son, are you okay? We've been worried sick about you. All of us."

Ro accepted the handshake. "Bent out of shape at first, but I'm okay now."

Jim surprised him by turning back to the door. "It's all right, we'll be alone. Teresa's due in from Cruces any time now, but I guess it'll be all right with you if she barges in."

Jim rolled over to his swivel chair at the desk and deftly switched seats. "Got tired of that damned thing. Feels good to get back in the old chair. At least the legs aren't wasting away. Swimming keeps them halfway alive. I'm able to kick with them a little. Judith's been working with me." He straightened pens on the desk. "She wants you back as much as any of us."

Ro couldn't call the man he had idolized for a decade a liar, so he kept his mouth shut.

"I know that's hard for you to understand, but it's true. She looks on you as family. Son, you should have trusted me. I think I've earned that."

His mood plunged. "Wasn't my decision alone."

"Yes, I know. Teresa swore you to silence. Well, that's water under the bridge."

Ro dropped into a chair in front of the desk. "Never meant to tear your family apart."

"There's a rift between Teresa and her mother, but it'll heal. This family's too strong for any one of us to pull apart. And I include you in that. You've been family for half your life. If you think Judith hasn't put every one of us in our place over the years, you have a short memory. She's straightened me out a few times, I can tell you. And she's not often wrong."

Ro's muscles tensed. "So you think she's right?"

Jim dry-washed his face. "Frankly, this is one of those rare times when she's dead wrong. I know how my baby feels about you. She wants you for the man you are, and you're the only one who can put an end to it. If you tell her to go away, she'll go. So what's next?"

"When Teresa's eighteen, we'll get married."

"Not much of a plan."

Ro swallowed his anger. From a white man's point of view, he guessed it wasn't.

Jim went on. "The way I see it, you can take her away from us, which is sort of what you're suggesting. Or the two of you can build a life right here where you belong. The choice is yours." The rancher paused. "Ro, I need a foreman. If you're set on not coming back, I gotta go find one. I don't wanna do that, so here's my proposition."

Ro could continue to live at Snakehead or move into the bunkhouse or build a house nearby, but he'd take the job of managing the ranch. He could use some of his savings to buy a few head of cattle and run them in the south pasture. He'd register and build his own brand.

"And," Jim added, "one's not conditioned on the other. Do either one or both."

His interest level rose. Of course, he could do the same thing with the tribe's cattle association, but he liked the J-Bar-C's way of doing things better. "Might work. I'll think on it."

They glanced out the window as a pickup pulled into the drive. A minute later, Teresa bounced into the room. "Hope you're finished talking because it's my turn now. Ro, Princess needs exercise."

"It's winter out there."

"When has that ever stopped us?"

****

203

They sheltered in a draw at the base of Harrigan's Butte. Ro gathered driftwood for a fire before sitting against the cold, stone face of Sleeping Turtle with Teresa nestled in his arms.

"Did you settle anything?" she asked at length. "Are you coming back?"

"It was good seeing him again. But no, I'm not coming back."

He expected her to start in on him. She didn't. "What did you talk about?"

"The cougar hunt, my job, you. Lots of things." Ro paused. "He made a suggestion."

She sat up and faced him. "What?"

"He thought I should buy a few head of cattle and run them on the south pasture. Register my own brand."

"That's a great idea. Buying cattle's easy, it's the land and water that are hard."

"Sometimes I forget you're a rancher's daughter."

"I never forget it. What do you think of his idea?"

"Might be all right if he charges me a fair grazing fee. Fair to both of us."

"So tell him that." She lay back against him. "Your own brand. The R-O." She bounced up again. "Your grandmother had something to do with the eagle. How about the Eagle Brand?"

"How about the R-Eagle-O?" Ro countered. "And he wants me to manage the ranch. But I don't have to do that to run my own brand."

They talked until approaching twilight and a cold wind drove them back to the house. Wade had already left for town, but Pete was there to shake his hand and grin at him.

"Good to see you. I put the things you left behind in the stable like the boss said. We was a hoping you'd be bringing your belongings, not carting 'em off. Wade said to tell you he had pressing business in town."

Ro laughed. "I can imagine what kinda business."

Teresa said goodbye on the lawn with a deep kiss, giving Pete something to tell Wade. A sudden itch tickled the back of Ro's neck. Was Judith watching from a window?

He walked to the stable through snow turned blue by moonlight to collect Colorado and load his belongings. As he finished packing his saddlebags, his neck tingled again. He turned to find Judith standing behind him. She was beautiful in a pale, aristocratic way. Teresa would never be like that. Her beauty was dark and earthy.

Judith held out a folded shirt. "Here's one we missed. Were you going to leave without saying hello?"

"Didn't know you wanted me to."

"You're making it difficult for me to keep my respect for you. Of course, I expect common courtesy when you visit our home."

Once again, he swallowed his anger. Maybe the Apache mother-in-law avoidance custom wasn't a bad idea. "Sorry. Wasn't sure you had any respect for me."

"You know better than that." He had the impression she was looking through him. Then as though waking from a trance, the green eyes focused on him. "Román, I know I hurt you. And for that, I'm truly sorry. There was undoubtedly a better way of making my point, but you must understand it was a point I had to make. So I ask your forgiveness for my clumsiness, but that doesn't mean I wasn't sincere or what I was saying wasn't valid."

Judith brushed her brow with the back of a wrist. "Try to think past the excitement of a wedding and a wedding night and setting up a new home with one another. Look six months... a year into the future. What will your life be like? Teresa's a social animal. She'll likely be interested in things going on in town. Would a woman's club or a Chamber of Commerce function be of interest to you? All I'm asking is to look honestly at your interests and her interests and how they would mesh as you grow older."

Ro's heart slowed, and he thought he was growing dizzy. "We... we're interested in the same things. The ranch. Family." His voice sounded hollow in his own ears.

"Is that enough?" She smoothed her skirt in an absent gesture. "At any rate, in March, Teresa will turn eighteen, and I've asked her for a promise. Now I want yours. Promise you'll tell us before you run off and get married."

"That's a promise I can make."

"Thank you. Now I want to ask something else of you. I want the two of you to refrain... well, to behave yourselves the way you know her father and I would want you to."

He flushed, remembering last Sunday night. "Behaved so far. Mean to keep it that way."

"Thank you again. And now since we're likely to be seeing one another from time to time, we might as well call a truce. If we can't be friends, at least we can be civil."

He forced the bitter words between his lips. "Truce it is."

"And just so we're absolutely clear, Jim does need your help."

****

As troubling as his relationship with the Chandlers was, his reservation life had turned just as bad. He'd voiced his opinions on a couple of things to Bernardo Sam, the stocky, stolid man who had headed the association for two decades. Sam made it clear no kid was going to tell him how to run his business. Ro figured he'd be a drover for a long, long time.

One day, Buck Wingfield, who also worked for the association, corralled him. "Hear Sam's been riding your ass. He's a good man, cuz."

"He is. But if he would just listen—"

"Maybe you oughta do the listening. You getting a rep, bro. Cool it."

He shriveled on the inside. "Been acting like a white man, I guess."

"That's the word I hear. Say, how about a brew after work?"

Ro hesitated. It was Friday, and Bird was coming home for the weekend. "Thanks, but I got something on already. Maybe another time."

"Yeah, sure."

Another mistake. Buck had been moving cautiously toward friendship ever since the cougar hunt, and this was the first time he'd asked Ro to join him and his pals.

****

Ro spent Monday mucking out barns and went home tired and filthy. By Wednesday, it was clear Bernardo Sam was determined to make him quit. The crap details continued, but that wasn't the worst of it. He began overhearing scraps of conversations. How come he never went out drinking like a regular guy? Didn't he like to get drunk? Fight a little? How come nobody ever saw him with a woman? That last one was pure crap—they all thought old man Chandler had canned him for screwing his daughter. But it cut, anyway. And that got him to thinking.

As soon as he got to work the next morning, he hunted up Buck and invited himself along for the next night out with the boys. That wasn't until Friday. Bad, because Bird was driving home for the weekend. He went for it, anyway.

Buck nodded. "Just gonna have a few at the T." The Teepee was an Indian bar about a mile north of Harry's.

Ro endured the usual crap details all day and then stopped at the trading post to call Bird at school to let her know he couldn't see her until Saturday.

After work on Friday, Ro made a beeline for the *gowa* to clean up and meet Buck and a couple of others at the schoolyard around seven. When he got there, he found he was too duded up for the company. Too late now. He piled into the bed of Buck's pickup beside Clarence.

"H'lo, Rider. You going catting or drinking?"

"These are my drinking clothes."

"Sure like to see your catting duds."

Ro and Clarence pulled hats down over their ears and hunkered down against the winter wind. Clarence could have ridden up front with Buck and his cousin, but he shared the bitter cold with Ro out of politeness. A good sign. When they got out of the truck and stomped circulation back into their feet, Ro hung back with Buck as they entered the T.

"Might need some backup tonight."

206

The man eyed him a moment before nodding.

They paid the dollar cover charge and walked in for a look-around. The place was jumping. As Buck headed for a vacant table, dodging dancing couples along the way, Youngman Sam, Bernardo's nephew and chief hatchet man, beckoned them over. "Time you guys showed up. Party's already started. Hey, new guy buys first round!"

As the night wore on, Ro tried to watch his alcohol intake, but he could feel the effects. Fed up laughing at the worst jokes he'd ever heard, he nonetheless delayed making his move until the crowd at the table thinned.

"Hey, Youngman. How come I never see you with a woman? Something going on?"

The noise level at the table dropped to zilch. Youngman got up. "What you saying?"

Ro stood three inches taller than the other man but weighed thirty pounds less. "I'm saying you can talk trash, but you can't take it."

Youngman sneered. "I fuck women. What do you fuck?"

"Right now… you."

"Outside," Buck said. "Fair fight. One-on-one."

Youngman hitched up his trousers and swaggered outside. "Don't need no help with this white bastard."

Ro and half the establishment followed.

On the way out the door, Buck elbowed Ro. "Sure you know what you're doing?"

"Know a better way to end it? Win or lose, I took him on."

"Shit, that's your plan?"

Ro grinned. "Pretty much. Keep his friends off my back, okay?"

Youngman stood in the parking lot with his cronies solidly behind him. To Ro's surprise, Clarence joined Buck in backing him up.

He planted his feet. "Youngman, you claim I don't belong here because I'm white. I'm as much *Tinneh* as you are. Maybe more. You're mostly Pueblo, if I remember right." Ro drew a breath. "But right now, I'm gonna show you I'm as much a man as you are."

"You gonna talk me to death, or we gonna fight?"

"Anytime you're ready."

Without warning, Youngman launched himself, but Ro avoided the charge and sent a sharp right jab into the man's armpit. Youngman whirled and caught Ro on the side of the head with a backhand. He staggered but managed to stay out of reach. Whatever else, he had to keep away from those thick arms.

Ro was a schoolyard fighter, not a boxer. But he'd watched some bouts on the grainy black and white television at the J-Bar-C bunkhouse, and he copied what he'd seen. He danced in and out, always moving, always circling to the

207

left. He was faster and had a longer reach than Youngman, but the other man was a moving brick house. Ro got in three shots to his opponent's one, but they didn't seem as effective as Youngman's. A couple of times, Ro heard bells. He relied on one thing: He ran six miles a day. Youngman didn't. All that dancing and shuffling took six times the energy. If his opponent ran even one mile a day, Ro was a dead man.

He took another roundhouse to the head and heard chimes again. Blindly lashing out, he flattened a thick nose with his knuckles. A follow-up caught the man in the eye. Youngman came back for more.

They exchanged jabs across half the parking lot, dodging parked cars and people. The circle of spectators moved right along with them. Ro's arms grew heavy, his legs leaden. The gambit had failed. He was gonna go down. Then he caught Youngman under the armpit again. This time, the man grunted and froze. Ro staggered in and gave him a jab to his eye and followed up with one to the jaw with everything he had left. Youngman grunted again, dropped both arms, and tottered but didn't go down.

Milling spectators yelled for him to finish Youngman off, but Ro'd made his point. As he paused, someone shoved him from behind and sent him reeling into his foe's arms. Youngman grasped him in a bear hug but didn't have the strength to hold on. Ro got in another jab to the armpit, which did the trick. As his opponent's knees dumped him on the asphalt, Ro risked a look behind him and saw Clarence and Buck struggling with Youngman's buddies.

That was all he saw before something bounced off his skull. He dropped in his tracks.

Chapter 45

Ro pried an eye open to see who was pounding on his head. Nobody. But light from a naked bulb pierced his retina and lanced his brain. Simply sitting up was a struggle. He stared at a row of black bars. Jail? Rushing to the commode, his retching drew a uniformed officer who took a look before disappearing. A moment later, John Valera strode into the area.

"You decide to wake up? You look like crap."

"Way I feel." That took all Ro's energy. "What happened?"

"You know how it is, Ro. Get drunk and fight, you land in jail."

Everything came back in a rush. He rubbed a bump on the back of his head and winced.

"The doc figures somebody threw a bottle," the sheriff said. "What went on?"

"Another fellow and me had a disagreement."

The sheriff threw his head to the left. "That one over there?"

"Yeah. It was me," Youngman Sam said from the adjoining cell.

"Get it settled?"

"Dunno," Ro said. "Did we, Youngman?"

"Far's I'm concerned."

The sheriff nodded. "I called Jim. He'll be here shortly."

"Aw, man, why'd you do that? He's got nothing to do with this."

"He's the only contact I had for you. You're not getting out of here till somebody picks you up. Let you know when he gets here."

Youngman sat up on his bunk after the sheriff disappeared, and Ro did a double take. Two black eyes and a lumpy nose.

"What you staring at?" the burly man asked. "You don't look so hot yourself. Where'd you learn that armpit shit?"

"Only place I could get to when you threw a punch."

"Gotta remember that next time," Youngman said.

"Gonna be a next time?"

The burly man tried to laugh. It didn't work. "Always be a next time. Maybe not for you'n me, but somebody." He rubbed his right eye gingerly. "Ro... that your white name?"

"You know white folks. Always turn your name into something. Like Richard is Dick, and Robert is Bob. Román is Ro."

"You okay, Rider. I was wrong about you. Ain't gonna have no more trouble from me."

"Mighty white of you."

Youngman snickered. "Yeah. You bet… white."

Pete bounced into the cell area and stopped short. "Aw, shit, Ro! Am I gonna have to tell Teresa yer fooling around with gals again?"

"Don't make me laugh. Hurts too much."

Valera appeared with a ring of keys and opened Ro's cell. "Just kept you overnight till you sobered up. No charges filed. Go on, get outta here."

Ro pointed with his chin to the next cell. "What about him?"

"Same thing. Soon as his people pick him up, he's free to go."

"We'll take him with us."

A few minutes later, Youngman climbed into the front seat of the Lincoln beside Pete. Jim and Ro rode in the back. After Youngman got out in White Pine and Ro gave directions to Split Rock, Jim turned to him. "Wanna tell me what happened?"

"Getting some flack on the job." His tongue was working better, but his head was still screwy. "Decided to put a stop to it. A night in jail's what it cost."

"Is it over now?"

Ro touched a sore ear. "Think so. Thanks for coming to get me. Uh, does…?"

"No, she stayed over and did some schoolwork. She'll pull in sometime this afternoon. But one look at that face, and you'll have a lot of explaining to do."

"Maybe you better tell her you got me outta jail."

"What does the other fellow look like?"

"You gave him a ride home."

"Hell, boy, you done all right," Pete said from the front seat.

After Ro arrived at the wickiup, he stripped, warmed as much water as he had pots to hold, and sat scrunched in a tiny tub to soak. Despite the uncomfortable position, he must have dozed. A slamming door woke him. He got out of the cold tub and struggled to stuff himself into clean jeans and a pullover before Teresa barged inside. And it was Teresa. It sure as hell wasn't Flitting Bird. He could almost see steam rising off her.

"So something came up, did it? You couldn't meet me last night because you had to go get drunk and fight? You look awful."

"You're pretty when you're mad."

She took a swing. He dodged but grunted. "Oh, Ro! I'm sorry."

He held her in his arms and told her what had been happening on the reservation. "It's over now. Guy I had it out with was in jail with me, and we got it settled." He pulled her as close as his sore ribs allowed. "I'm probably

210

to blame. I'm not handling things too good."

"Me neither. I'm not going back next semester."

He begged her to reconsider. Her mother would blame him for the rest of her life for Teresa not getting an education. She countered with the demand he go to school with her.

"Can't. I'm taking your dad up on his offer. I'll start buying cattle in May, and after that there won't be time. Besides, don't have enough money for both."

"Dad hasn't cashed your school money check. And the crew can tend the cattle until summer break. We'll get married and find an apartment off campus."

"Uh-uh. I'll do it my way or not at all. Worked it all out. I can buy twenty-five head. Figured what it'll cost to maintain them. The whole works." He laughed. "They'll be eating better than I am, but I can handle it okay." He chucked her under the chin. "Let's get engaged and pick a date. I guess I oughta ask you formal like. Bird... Teresa, will you marry me?"

"Yes, yes, yes, yes!"

"When?" he asked, feeling drunk again.

"Now, tomorrow, the next day, anytime!"

"We'll have to put it off a little longer than that. We promised to tell your folks first, and I mean to keep that promise."

"Oh, all right. It'll be my birthday present to both of us. Before March the fifth is over, we'll make mad, passionate, *legal* love to one another. More than twice," she added.

He brushed her lips with his, only partially setting his bruises afire. "That's an engagement kiss. But don't say anything to your folks. I oughta be the one to tell Jim, and my bruises need to heal first." He bussed her again. "But we can go look at rings next weekend."

The following Saturday, they picked out a ring. It wasn't as large a stone as he wanted, but even so, it looked great on her finger. Ro put it on layaway, meaning the clerk stowed the ring in a little black box and hid it somewhere in the back of the store until it was paid for.

****

While his relationship with the crew at the cooperative improved, Ro couldn't manage to hit it off with Bernardo Sam. The man's dislike was so obvious Ro puzzled long and hard over the cause, finally deciding Bernardo wanted to leave his position to Youngman when he retired. Ro was a threat to that plan. That was acceptable. It wasn't personal.

He registered his brand, ordered the irons, and went about opening his accounting system the way Jim had taught him. He dragged out an old grazing agreement at work and created one between the J-Bar-C and the R-Eagle-O for Jim to approve. He was congratulating himself on turning his life around when the roof fell in one Friday afternoon.

"What do you mean I'm laid off?"

Bernardo flushed. "Just that. Slow time of year. You the newest, so you get laid off first."

Ro's temper got away from him. "Bullshit! We're coming up on spring. That's the busiest time of year. You just don't like someone who has an idea of his own."

"When things pick up, we'll be hiring again."

While Ro was right about spring being busy, the fact was, February wasn't spring. He contacted a couple of ranches in the area, but he knew in his heart nothing was available. Sooner or later Jim Chandler would hear about him looking for a job if he kept calling on locals, and he didn't want that to happen. Damn! He'd had a steady job since he was ten years old, and then some paranoid bastard fired him. He'd have to figure his budget a lot tighter.

Bird had stayed at school that weekend to prepare for tests, so Sunday morning, he decided to drive into Terreon to get a newspaper. Maybe the want ads would turn him on to something. He put on a heavy coat against a blustery day and rattled through White Pine in the ancient Chevy pickup he'd bought with his share of the bounty from the lion hunt.

Spotting Buck's truck parked among several others at the trading post, he stopped to see what the crowd was all about. Buck and Clarence intercepted him.

"Man, you better get outta here," Buck said.

"Why? What happened?"

"You don't know?" Buck looked over Ro's shoulder. "Bernardo… uh, I mean He-Who-Was-Our-Boss went away last night. Car wreck. Took another one with him."

"Youngman?" Ro asked.

Clarence winced at the name but nodded. "Went off the road coming back from the T. You really didn't know?"

"How would I? Been at my place all day yesterday and today. Anybody know what happened?"

Buck and Clarence studied their boots while a chilly wind raised dust around them. Clarence finally spoke. "Benjamin Gareta was in the car." Gareta was one of the workers at the association. "He claimed a big owl swooped down on the windshield. The old…uh, He-Who-Was panicked and went off the road."

A sinking feeling claimed Ro's guts. "Damn! Now everybody figures I'm responsible."

A commotion drew their attention to the small crowd. A gray-haired old woman stalked forward, pointed at Ro, and called out in a thin, reedy voice, "Witch! She raised a witch."

Clarence pushed him into his pickup. "Get outta here."

His shoulders slumped. "I'll go home. If they want me, that's where I'll be. Fellas, I'm telling the truth. I didn't do anything."

"Know you didn't," Buck said. "Shit, think I'd be standing here talking to a witch?"

The *gowa*, usually so comforting, felt bleak and forlorn. Two days later—dressed in his best jeans and shirt—he shocked the reservation by attending the joint funerals of Bernardo and Youngman Sam.

****

Ro sat in the dark wickiup and seriously considered getting drunk. Seemed like a whale of an idea... except he didn't like the taste of alcohol or the hangover that inevitably followed. And when he came out of it, his problems would still be there, staring him in the face.

He wasn't a good drinker. Hell, he wasn't good at anything. Punching cows and—shit, that was it. Punching cows. Ro shifted position on the blanket. The Chandlers were his whole life. When that went sour, he was nothing, A walking zero.

In the two days since the funerals, he'd suffered a little vandalism. Nothing serious. His beat-up old Chevy got egged. An icepick in one tire. Kids getting a thrill out of daring the devil.

Flitting Bird was the only bright spot in his life. He lived for the weekends she came home. The rest of the time he simply existed. But how could he think of marrying her now? He didn't have a job. They couldn't live on the reservation. Bringing a white woman here wasn't an option after what had happened. Besides, it wasn't right to drag her into it.

At first light, Ro dressed in layered clothing and went for his run, his mind as clear as the crisp new day. He wouldn't permit ignorance and superstition to rob him of life. If all he knew was cattle, then he'd raise cattle. He had his brand, his deal with the J-Bar-C, and almost enough money to see it through. That oughta prove he was good enough for Bird. Not next month. Not by the time her birthday rolled around. But he was on his way.

The run was a good one; the cold air invigorated him. He returned to the *gowa*, bathed for the first time in three days, shaved an almost non-existent beard, and got into fresh clothes. Whatever this new day brought, he would face it clean and healthy.

Buck showed up later with a cut on the palm of his left hand that wouldn't heal properly. His friend didn't come out and say it, but Ro got the idea. Did

213

the guy really think he was a healer? Ro poured horse liniment on the injury—and once Buck stopped dancing—slapped a bandage on it.

Buck had hardly left before Ro heard the solid thunk of a door. Not the bang of a pickup, a sedan. He watched from the doorway as Judith left the Lincoln at Split Rock to walk to Snakehead. Discomfited at the distaste she raised in him, he stepped outside to meet her. She appeared so upset his heart almost stopped. "Teresa?"

"It's Jim. He fell this morning switching from wheelchair to desk chair. Broke his hip."

"Come in," he said as the cold wind whipped her long coat around her legs.

"I've got to get back to the hospital, but I need a favor. Paul chartered a plane. It's due in Alamogordo in an hour. Can you pick him up?"

He resisted the urge to point out Pete or Wade could do that. "Truck needs a boost."

"Drive me to the hospital and take the Lincoln. Jim wants to see you before you go."

"Does Bird… Teresa know?"

"She's driving in from State."

Ro had the distinct impression Judith was close to crying several times on the drive to Terreon, but she didn't. She was one strong woman. If nothing else, he liked that about her.

When they arrived at the hospital, Jim was obviously hurting.

"He wouldn't take any medication until he talked to you," Judith explained.

The rancher looked at him through pain-filled eyes. "Made a mess of it. Damned chair rolled right out from under me. Ro, gotta call on you again." He grimaced. "Judith, tell them I'm ready now." He spoke haltingly as she left the room. "Son, Paul's gonna want to stay home. He's only got one more year, and I want him to graduate. Can you get time off from your job and come back… at least for a while?"

"No problem. Be there tomorrow morning."

"Same deal," Jim said. "You're foreman and on salary. Damnation this thing hurts. Don't let Paul quit. He'll fight you, but don't let him quit."

The doctor arrived with a hypodermic that knocked Jim out almost immediately.

"Do my best," Ro told the unconscious man. He turned to Judith. "You okay with this?"

"I support it completely. Always have."

Ro pursed his lips and planned aloud. "I'll move into the bunkhouse until the weather turns. Then go back to Snakehead at night… if it lasts that long.

He's liable to be back in the saddle before then."

"Not so sure of that," Judith cautioned. "The doctor won't know the condition of his bones until after the operation."

****

The young man who deplaned from the Cessna wasn't the carefree skirt chaser Ro saw last summer. The toll law school was taking lay plainly stamped on Paul's features. He wrapped Ro in a bear hug. "Good to lay eyes on you, bro! You seen Dad?"

Ro pounded his back and mumbled greetings. "For about one minute at the hospital. Come on. Fill you in on the way."

The drive to Terreon gave them time to catch up on news. Ro remained wary until Paul seemed okay with the thing between Teresa and him. A few miles down the road, he tackled the subject that worried Jim. "I'm coming back to the ranch, Paul."

"Be good working with you again. This time we won't even pretend I'm the boss."

"That makes no sense. You're too close to your goal. And while I'd like to see if you remember anything at all about cows, it's not gonna happen. Jim made me foreman, and I'll fire your ass the first day you show up."

Paul laughed. "I believe you would too. Have you thought about going to school?"

"I'm a cowman, Paul. Registered my own brand and gonna run a few head on a grazing lease from the J-Bar-C. That and managing the ranch are all I want."

"Gotcha. What can I do to help?"

"Tell your folks right up front you're going back to school. Gotta get that law degree so when I get in trouble you can get me out. Judging from recent history, that might be harder than you think." He rushed on before Paul could ask questions. "That, and be my friend, Paul. Be my brother."

"Always, Ro. Always. And to ease your mind, I'll go back to class soon's I know Dad's okay. That way, if you screw up, you can't blame me."

Jim was in recovery by the time they arrived. Teresa stood at Ro's side as the surgeon told them Jim's bones were healthier than anyone had a right to expect. Even the muscles looked decent, thanks to his pool therapy. Nonetheless, Jim was in for a lengthy recovery.

Chapter 46

Ro cleaned cobwebs from what had been Chuck Griggs' private room in the bunkhouse and moved in, feeling as if he'd never been away. Before long, he and Judith worked their way past treating one another like strangers.

After Jim came home to a bed in the sunroom off the den, Ro took to driving the Jeep to the wickiup for the night. Ranching was a 'round-the-clock business, but he and Bird managed to snatch time together on weekends.

One Saturday afternoon, Buck parked his '54 Ford pickup at the wickiup and got out. "Yo, Rider! Got any brews?"

"Not a drop. But I can fill you up with soda pop."

Buck made a wry face but accepted a strawberry. After settling on the blanket—nobody bothered with the chairs—they spent thirty minutes on small talk before Buck said Benjamin Gareta had admitted making up the story about the owl. Booze, not magic, did the Sam men in.

Buck wrinkled his nose at his empty pop bottle. "Now how about going for a real drink?"

"Like to, but there's a pretty white gal who'll lift my scalp if I'm not here to greet her."

The other man grinned. "Hear she's got your moccasins tied on a short string. But when you're ready, let me know. Hell, I'll even let you buy the drinks."

Buck was hardly gone before Clarence stopped by and turned down the offer of pop with a grimace. He'd heard about Gareta's confession, but his goal was different. Clarence only spent fifteen minutes getting around to telling Ro that he and Ruby got married last week.

"I know she lost your baby in that wreck," Clarence finished in a neutral voice.

Ro frowned. "That was before you two got together. I'm glad for you, man. You got a real fine woman there. And she's getting a good man. You two'll be good for one another."

****

The day Ro went to the cattle sale in Terreon raised his excitement level more than expected. He purchased J-Bar-C stock before buying twenty handsome steers for himself. Being laid off had cost him five head, but he'd still do all right when he sold his animals in the fall. Of course, it all depended on the weather, the grass, and beef prices. Sorta like playing poker with Mother Nature when she held all the wild cards.

New Mexico had been a hot iron state all the way back to the Spaniards. His new brand—a stylized thunderbird separating the initials R and O—was properly registered with the New Mexico Livestock Board, and the first time he applied the iron to cowhide was like getting high without the hangover.

When he and Flitting Bird went riding in the south pasture one day, they dismounted to walk arm and arm through lush strands of grass. At almost six feet in his boots, he stood half a head taller than she. Teresa looked up at him and made a suggestion.

"Honey, let's get the ring out of layaway and tell the folks we're engaged." Her smile died when he frowned. "What's wrong?"

He gathered her in his arms. "Now don't get mad, but getting laid off put me behind. Not sure I'll be in shape to get married on your birthday."

"Ro, you're working for better wages, and you'll sell your cattle in the fall. Why wait?"

"Is this the way it's gonna be? I make up my mind, and you talk me out of it?"

"Only when you want to be talked out of it," she came back at him.

Her throaty laugh touched him in the groin. "Guess I've got enough to get the ring out," he said.

"Okay, we'll make our big announcement next weekend. Uhm, making wedding plans gets me horny."

"Bird!"

"I can talk dirtier than that. Wanna hear?"

****

When they entered the house the next Saturday, Bird wore a modest ring that sparkled in the sunlit kitchen like one of its bigger cousins. Judith noticed it right away and led them to where Jim lay propped on a lounger, reading the newspaper.

"Sir, I… we…." Ro swallowed. "Uh, I asked Teresa to marry me, and we got this ring."

"You're engaged!"

Jim's smile bolstered Ro's courage. He avoided looking at Judith. After all, she was gonna be his mother-in-law, and old habits don't just wash away in the first cloudburst.

After congratulations all around, Jim spoke up. "Where you gonna live? Course, you're welcome here, but I have an idea you'll want a place of your own."

"Haven't really talked about it."

217

"Of course not, get married first and worry about where to live later." Jim patted his daughter's hand. "Your mother and I have talked it over, and we thought maybe you'd like to build a home here on the ranch. There's a nice grove of trees just off the highway in the south pasture where your cattle are."

Ro turned wary. "Thanks, but I can't afford a house."

"Thinking about it as a wedding gift." Jim held up a hand as Ro started to object, proving he had the measure of his man. "We'll pour the foundations and provide the materials. You can do the framing. We'll hire the electrician and plumber, but you can do the rest yourself. The crew want in on it too... as their present. Pete was a roofer and Wade, a cabinetmaker in their younger days. What do you say?"

Ro visualized the peaceful grove Jim had mentioned and nodded. "If you'll let me buy ten acres on time, it's a deal."

"Judith," the rancher said. She pulled out a set of rolled up plans and handed them over. "Can't say this is a surprise," Jim went on, "so we took the liberty of having some plans drawn."

"Please don't take this wrong," Judith said. "But doesn't it make more sense to wait until Teresa finishes her semester before you marry? If you start on the house right away, you'll have it well on the way by the time May rolls around."

Ro met her eyes and found no guile. He looked at Bird. She nodded.

****

Ro didn't have a free minute for the next three months. After he gave the Chandlers their full measure of time, he worked on the house, towing his generator from the wickiup so he could work nights. The crew often labored alongside him. When Bird was home on weekends, she pitched in, as well. They missed getting the job done by semester's end but completed construction by early June.

Sand-colored to make it a natural part of the countryside, the flat-roofed adobe sported round, wooden vigas protruding through the stucco. Out back, they built a proper corral and stable for Colorado and Princess. Beyond that, Ro constructed a sweathouse where he could purify himself. They opted for a cheaper carport instead of a garage. Unused items the Chandlers had in storage made furnishing the place more affordable. After that, everything was ready.

****

On Wednesday, June 13, 1956, Teresa Nadine Chandler married Román Otero in a simple ceremony at a local chapel with guests confined to family and crew of the J-Bar-C.

A required course kept Paul at UNM, so he was unable to attend the wedding. Ro and Teresa considered changing the date, but neither wanted to wait until the summer session ended. Jim Chandler, wheelchair and all, served as best man.

Since Ro had no family, he invited Clarence and Buck. Both showed up for the ceremony, but ducked out shortly thereafter. Each left a gift: an incredibly soft, white buckskin throw pillow and a Pueblo, double-lipped wedding vase. Ro swallowed hard. He knew how dearly each had cost its donor.

Ro managed one surprise. When they came out of the chapel, a used but immaculate white, '53 DeSoto convertible sat gleaming in the afternoon sun. "Bet you thought we'd have to go home in my old pickup."

"Oh, Ro! You shouldn't have. I'm gonna bawl!" Teresa buried her head in his shoulder.

"Hey, not on my rented tux!"

They drove slowly, trying out the car and exploring their new roles. The Lincoln was already in the drive by the time they got to the big house.

Jim held out his arms as they entered the den. "Come here, baby. Let me tell you how happy you've made me."

Teresa collapsed on his lap, her ballerina-length dress a dazzling cloud.

"Román"—Judith's contralto startled him—"welcome to the family." She gave him a hug, making him vaguely uncomfortable.

After the crew arrived, the reception went downhill a bit, restrained only by Judith's moderating presence. As soon as they were able, the young couple made ready to leave.

Goodbyes and good wishes ate up another fifteen minutes before they were finally on the way to their own home. When they turned into the short drive to the stuccoed adobe, lights from the ranch house were visible in the distance. Teresa paused to gaze at them as they stepped out of the car.

She sighed. "It was home for such a long time." Ro opened the front door and effortlessly lifted her over the threshold. She giggled. "Didn't know you were so romantic."

"Not. You're too poky." He put her down, and they kissed.

"I love our new home," she murmured, "but can we go to the wickiup? Just for tonight?"

He had trouble getting words past his constricted throat. She couldn't possibly know how significant that was to him. "Thank you, Bird."

Wordlessly, they changed clothes and saddled the horses. They were still silent when he dismounted to open the gate at the reservation fence. The generator was at the new house, so all they had for light was the fire Ro laid in the pit.

He tossed pillows on the blanket, and they watched one another strip, hesitant yet eager. They lay without touching for a moment while he admired the spray of fine, ebony hair clouding Bird's pillow. Her long, sable lashes. His lips touched hers, kindling a long-denied flame. Her hand cooled his feverish brow.

Ro caressed his wife, inhaling her fragrance: the Wind Song he'd given her for her birthday masking an erotic Mother Earth musk. He knew little of women but suspected this was a bouquet unique to her.

He took his time, allowing her to grow accustomed to his probing. With infinite patience, he refrained from aggressive moves, exciting her with his lips and hands. When he applied gentle pressure to her legs, she locked them around his waist.

"Oh, God! I love you!" he murmured.

After a long while, Ro fell to his elbows, keenly aware of the frantic thudding of his heart. He traced her lips with a finger. "Well," he panted, "was that what you expected?"

"Need another sample before I can answer that."

Ro laughed and came to a sitting position. He showed the same patient consideration and unhurried assurance as before. Afterward, both of them dropped into a deep slumber.

Ro woke with a start in the semi-darkness of the *gowa*. An owl? Or a dream? He listened anxiously but heard nothing. Disconcerted—perhaps a little frightened—his eyes fixed on Bird nestled at his side. He watched for a few minutes before reaching for her. The night was long and beautiful.

Chapter 47

Teresa talked Ro into postponing a honeymoon until they could afford one later. Both had come from an environment where money was of little concern—although for totally different reasons—to a sudden awareness their cash reserves were painfully meager.

Bird—Teresa was almost exclusively Bird now—hoped Ro was as happy as she was. He must be. That invisible wall he hid behind was beginning to crumble. She had insights into her new husband she'd been denied before. Things she doubted he shared even with Paul.

When he scanned the pines and oaks surrounding the house, he searched for an owl or other signs of impending disaster... or his grandmother. He had loved the old woman yet lived in fear of her. Teresa went giddy knowing she could drive away those niggling concerns simply by reminding him that she would have wanted what was best for him... even a white woman. That always brought a quick frown that morphed into a smile.

Inevitably, that would elicit a comment that maybe he ought to raise some bull calves to donate to the tribe. She always rested easier after such remarks because she knew he struggled to remain connected with his people. Without reasoning it out, she understood if he ever became totally disaffected from the *Tinnneh*, he wouldn't be the same man.

On the Fourth of July, they went to dinner at the big house where Jim surprised them by walking into the den on a pair of crutches.

"Daddy!" Teresa bounded to his side and kissed his cheek. He wobbled unsteadily.

"Careful! Haven't learned how to smooch on sticks yet."

Before they left, Teresa suspected that was the most comfortable Ro had been in her parents' house since he fled in the middle of a snowstorm a year and a half ago.

****

On the Sunday Paul was expected home, Ro kept wandering to the window and looking toward the big house, even though it was too distant to really see anything.

"Will you sit down or go rope a steer or something," she said. "Why're you so nervous?"

"Why're you so grouchy?"

"Dunno. Feel kinda… icky."

"You need a doctor?" When she shook her head, he offered to make lemonade.

She turned up her nose. "Ugh."

Later, as dusk crept over the landscape, Teresa went to draw the drapes and saw the lights of a car on the long drive to the big house. "Paul's home. I'll fix us something to eat and then we'll go over." She started for the kitchen, but he stopped her with a hand on her arm.

"I'd like my dinner in the bedroom." He caressed the curve of her jaw.

"Honestly, you're the horniest man alive!" He backed away as she began to sob. She buried her face in his neck. "I'm…I'm sorry."

"What'd I do? Are you tired of me already?"

She tapped his cheek with her palm. "Don't be an ass! I love being married to you. It's just… it's just… Oh, hell! I don't know what it's just!"

He blinked and hugged her close. "I love you so much."

"You won't. Not after a while."

"Always! When we're eighty and hobbling around on canes, I'll be chasing you through the bedroom playing grab-ass."

She giggled. "You're sweet. Must be why I married you. But come sit down, you're getting a proper meal tonight." She served tuna salad, one of his favorites, and held his free hand as they ate in relative silence. Afterward, they worked side by side cleaning dishes until the doorbell drew Ro away. She heard Paul's voice coming from the hallway.

"Married two months, and you're already domesticated. Sis!" Paul swallowed her in a hug when she joined them.

She untangled herself. "Sit, and I'll bring coffee."

Instead, Paul got a tour of the house which ended as she delivered the steaming mugs.

"Where'd you go on your honeymoon?" her brother asked. "The folks didn't say."

She smiled as Ro answered. "Our honeymoon's walking around out there eating grass, drinking water, making methane, and dropping cow pies."

Paul laughed. "Wow! Talk about romantic." He sobered. "Smart move." He looked at each of them, "Both of you."

****

Teresa lay studying a slumbering Ro by moonlight flooding the bedroom. Dark hair crushed over his brow gave him a little-boy look. She traced his lean features with a forefinger… long, proud nose; thin, slightly parted lips; firm chin. The faint stubble of his sparse beard tickled her finger, sending a tremor straight to her heart.

222

This had been the most wonderful night of her life. Teresa had thought him the perfect lover, but tonight he had outdone himself. She should have realized how important Paul's approval had been to him, how he unconsciously held back until his blood brother gave the final, crucial blessing to their union.

She'd have to work hard to handle her stallion now he was unbridled. She resolved to anticipate his thoughts and fears in the future. He was hers, and she would keep him that way forever. She touched her forehead contentedly to his.

****

Teresa had hoped to sleep late the next morning, but Ro was up at first light, as usual. From the bed, she watched him dress for his run. She didn't want him to leave. Sudden tears took her by surprise. She stuffed the sheet into her mouth to muffle her sobs.

Fighting a queasy stomach, she had eggs and sausage on the stove by the time he returned from his run. He showered quickly and sat with her at the table. Usually, she liked to watch him eat. Today, he had taken only a few bites before she turned away. He didn't notice.

After he went to work, Teresa cleaned the dishes before lying on the couch. She was always tired nowadays. Idly leafing through a New Mexico State bulletin, she picked out classes she would have taken next semester. Time got away from her, and he was home before she started the evening meal. The surprised look on his face set her to bawling again.

"That's all right," he said. "I'll throw something together."

"You've been working all day. I'll fix a steak. Won't take long."

The meal done, he got up from the table and led her by hand to the couch. Pulling her down beside him, he gave her his awkward white man's stare. "You're bored with me."

"Course not. Whatever gave you that idea?"

"Can't pretend everything's all right. You haven't been my Flitting Bird lately."

She leaned against him. "Ro, what would you name your son... if you had one?"

"My son?" His eyes narrowed. He clutched her hand like an eager child told he can have a play-pretty. "Honey, you sure?"

"Think so. When I missed last month, I thought that was because of... well, you know, our love life. But I'm due again, and nothing's happened. Guess that's why I've been so bitchy and so nauseated and so... so—"

"Beautiful," he said, making her cry again. "Shouldn't I have said that?"

She slipped into his lap. "Yes. All the time. But you didn't answer me."

"Names! How can you think of names at a time like this? Plenty of time for that. And how do you know it's a boy?" Without waiting for an answer, he began to figure. "You think it happened on our wedding night? What was the moon then?"

"The moon? What's that got to do with it?"

"Dark of moon, a boy. Light of moon, a girl. Dark. It was dark. Just a sliver. A boy," he decided.

"Can we name him after his father?"

"No, James. Wanna name him James Paul. Little Jim."

She blinked away tears. "That's nice."

He slipped an arm around her. "What does he look like right now?"

"Right now? A frog, I imagine." A shudder played through him. "No, like a prince," she amended. "The bewitched one who was a frog until the princess kissed him."

His reaction frightened her. His eyes turned dark. "Don't say that! He's not witched."

"Honey, it's just a fairy tale. My favorite. It points up a truism."

Calmer now, he asked, "What?"

"A man's not a man until a good woman gets her lips on him."

"What about the princess who slept until the prince kissed her?" he asked.

"That's the other side of the coin. Takes a man to bring a woman to fruition."

"Pretty good arrangement, huh?" He nibbled her ear.

"Ro, will you still love me when I get fat and ugly?"

"You're not gonna get fat and ugly. You'll be beautiful carrying our son."

"I will. I'll get fat. I'll waddle like a duck!"

"Ducks are some of my favorite people."

Chapter 48

Eyes followed Jose Peyote's every move as he strutted across the exercise yard. Despite the chilly March day, he'd stripped off his shirt to give them one last show before putting the prison walls behind him. After three years, they were letting him go.

He laughed on the inside. They always watched him. Hacks and cons alike. He'd driven the pansies crazy, flirting and then hurting if they made a move. Whistles and catcalls followed him to the fence and back to the building.

Long hours on weights had purged his mind and body of every ounce of flab. He was something rare in this house of hardened, callous men—a pretty boy who refused to be anybody's bitch. The terrible retribution he'd exacted for his rape wrapped him in an invisible shield. Physically, he was in better shape than his Corps days. Except for his "Chandler arm." The right arm the rancher had clubbed with a rifle barrel.

Invisible to the eye, the weakness was nonetheless a constant threat. At times, he strained the arm almost beyond capacity on the weight bench, probably contributing to its weakened state. If the bastards ever sensed he was vulnerable, they'd flock like vultures to a rotting carcass.

The inmate clerk in the clothing room issued him two sets of civilian clothes an hour later. "This the day, Chief?"

"Yeah, I'm putting this clusterfuck behind me." Might as well be civil. The guy had occasionally slipped him extra socks and shorts.

****

Jose was supposed to stay on the bus all the way to Terreon, but he got off in Albuquerque for no good reason. Maybe because they'd told him not to. His boots no sooner hit the pavement than he started hunting for an Indian bar. A Navajo on the street told him the Last Spruce was way the hell out on the main drag... East Central, they called it. A long hike later, another skin and his girl picked him up opposite the University of New Mexico and drove him to the bar.

Jose walked into the Spruce and learned nothing had changed. Didn't matter if he had a nickel or a hundred in his pocket, somebody bought him drinks. He focused on a Chippewa chick who didn't mind payin' for beer.

She was a little chubby for his tastes, but three years was a long drought, so he went for it. She provided bed and comfort that night and bought him a bus ticket the next morning.

Jose spent his second night of freedom on a broken-down sofa at his uncle's place outside of White Pine. The following morning, he got a battery boost for the old Ford pickup he'd stored there and drove into Terreon to bullshit his way through a meeting with some Mexican in the probation office. The guy didn't even bother to mention Jose was two days late reporting in.

When the man outlined the program, stressing that Jose needed to find a job, it was all he could do to keep from smiling. He had a job. A full time job. Making the Chandlers pay.

Chapter 49

Ro stared at the calf's carcass. Throat cut. Nothing harvested, just left as carrion. His blood boiling at such waste, he examined boot prints in the dirt. Worn, but nothing distinctive. Finding where the killer took to saddle, Ro trailed hoofprints through a hole in the wire into the next pasture. The tracks lengthened. He found where the intruder had stampeded some stock. One heifer was down with a broken leg. Others stood with heaving sides and lolling tongues. The son-of-a-bitch couldn't be far away.

He made for high ground but saw no one. After alerting Pete by radio to salvage beef from the downed animals, Ro tracked the horseman south. As he spurred Colorado into a steady lope, the unseasonably cold March air stung his face. The horse strained to get his head. Ro cautiously reined him back.

The tracks grew fresher and led straight through a hole in the reservation fence. Ro kept going until the trail reached a stream. Figuring it would take too long to find where the fleeing horseman came out of the water, he settled for doing a crude job of mending the fence.

Satisfied he'd done all he could with what he had, he backtracked to where Pete and Wade loaded freshly butchered beef onto a trailer. Jim sat nearby in a pickup he'd rigged with hand controls.

The rancher pulled on a cigarette as Ro filled him in. "What you make of it?"

Ro shook his head. "Not sure. A rustler would've taken animals, not killed them. And he wouldn't take time to run ten pounds off stock. Looks like the same crap all over again. Word is Jose's out of the pen and back on the reservation."

A chill played down Ro's spine that had nothing to do with brisk weather. He didn't need trouble now. All he wanted was to go home to Bird every night and make plans for their son. She was getting close to her time.

"I'm gonna go talk to him tonight. Alone," he added, anticipating Jim's offer to send the crew with him.

****

Ro had difficulty getting away from Bird that evening. She'd become jealous of his time and went clingy or petulant if he was late or had to go out after work. When he explained he needed to go into town, she wanted to go with him.

"We never go anywhere anymore."

"Went to a movie Saturday and ate out Sunday," he reminded her.

"Oh, Ro, I feel so bloated and yucky and ugly."

He drew her into his arms. "Bird, you've never been more beautiful. You glow. And you're more important now. I'm not saying it right, but if one life means so much, then *two* have to mean lots more. You're living two lives all at the same time."

"How come I went to college, and you're so smart?"

"Just know how I feel. And I feel you're special."

"Special, right. Especially slow and clumsy and fat," she complained.

"You've seen an elk. Sometimes, it's slow, but it's graceful and—"

"An elk! I look like an elk? Why not a moose? Say it, I look like a damned moose."

Ro couldn't help himself, and his laughter made her angrier. "You white women. How are we supposed to make you understand us? You've got a whole different set of references."

Bird moved close and touched him. "Okay, Injun, make me understand."

He looked at her uncertainly. "You sure it's all right? Too much loving, and you'll have twins. Heap big bad luck. Gotta leave one on an ant hill."

"Oh!" she squealed. "You can't leave my baby to die on an ant hill!"

"Hush. Our baby's gonna be perfect, and nobody's gonna die. Promise." He carried her into the bedroom and lay beside her, ministering to her until she cooed and moaned in response. He stayed until she slept, which made him late starting for town.

****

Figuring the best place to look for Jose was Harry's, Ro drove to the bar and found the man sitting on a stool looking as if he had never been away. Ro took a moment to study him. Prison had been good for Jose, at least physically. Jose spotted him in the mirror behind the bar and lifted his bottle in salute.

Ro took a stool beside him. "When did you get back?"

"Few days ago."

"Was it rough?" Ro sensed rather than saw the change come over the man.

"Nothing I couldn't handle."

They collected a couple of fresh bottles and moved outside to the boulders at back. "Like it better out here, even if it's cold," Jose said. "Only go inside because it pisses them off."

Ro claimed a spot on a rock. "Got me a place in the pine grove at Snakehead Spring, but I don't go there much. You can move in if you want. Good water, pretty spot."

"Cut the bullshit," Jose said.

"All right, let's get down to it. There was bad blood with right and wrong on both sides. But both sides paid, so it's even."

"Even? How you figure? I got no job. No wife, no kids, no nothing. Spent three years... *three* fucking years in the state pen on a phony rap. Old man Chandler got three years richer, and Paul... well, the kid, he got three more years of going to his big school and three more years of pussy and three more years laughing up his sleeve at me locked up in Santa Fe."

Jose drew a ragged breath and wiped spittle from the corners of his mouth. "And Tall Rider? He got a white man's job, white wife, white daddy-in-law. Shit, even his car's white."

Ro's response was automatic. "I'm as much Apache as you are. Kept on living on the reservation. Hell, just told you about my place at Snakehead."

Jose leered. "You just trying to keep that witch from walking through your dreams. Powerful old bitch. Forgot all these years, and she still raises bumps on your backside."

This wasn't going right. Might as well bring it to a head. "Jose, stay off the J-Bar-C."

"Go wherever I want, Rider. Don't get 'tween me and them."

Ro tossed aside his beer and stood. "Then we better get at it. Let's see what three years of getting your ass fucked up in Santa Fe did to you."

Jose didn't say a word, he just charged. Ro danced aside and landed a blow to Jose's kidney. The man whirled and rocked him with a left to the chest. Ro shook off a right to the head, stepped back, and recovered his balance.

Suddenly, a bright light startled both of them. "What's going on here?"

Jose dropped his arms and put a smile on his face. "Horsing around, Officer. My cousin here bet he could throw me. Looks like he lost."

Sheriff Valera stalked forward, a hand on his holster. "That right, Ro?"

"Yes, sir. Just screwing around."

"Well, cut it out, else I might figure something different. Ro, can I see you a minute?"

By the time the sheriff finally pulled out of the parking lot, he'd accomplished what was probably his intention. Jose was nowhere in sight. Ro climbed into the DeSoto and started for home, his thoughts writhing and coiling like a pit of rattlesnakes. But one thing was clear. Trouble lay ahead. And the bone-headed way he'd handled things tonight had cost him the ability to mediate. Not after that dumb taunt about rape.

Jose was fast and fit and a better street fighter, but he wasn't unbeatable. The left jab to the chest had hurt like hell, but Jose's shot to Ro's head with his right should have left him flat on his back. Instead, he shook off the blow. Didn't make sense.

Chapter 50

Jose sat in the dark on the porch of his uncle's cabin and wished for many things. Peyote buttons. A rifle. A bottle. A woman. Did his seed infect his partners with hate? Maybe if he screwed enough women, he'd get it all out of his system. Except hate was what kept him alive.

Maybe he had everything backwards. All these years he'd thought the Chandlers led Rider around on a chain. But Tall Rider carried the blood of the biggest witch in the last hundred years. Was he using that power to control the whites? Hell, he'd snatched the ranch right out from under the Chandlers. He ran it, not the old man. Not Paul. Rider lived in a fine house and screwed the rancher's daughter.

Jose rounded on something else. Rider got fired from his job at the association, and the man who done it was gone. Rider fought with that one's nephew, and *he* died in the same wreck. Son-of-a-bitch! Was that where the power was coming from?

The moon hadn't yet risen. This was when *they* prowled. An owl hooting in the distance raised Jose's hackles. She was still around, but she couldn't stop him. He had a sacred mission.

Ignoring his balky old Ford pickup, he walked down the wagon track to the pasture. His boots were magical. Each step gave him strength and reaffirmed his purpose. Making a bridle out of a piece of rope, he walked a horse out of earshot of the cabin before mounting bareback and riding north in the silent night. Not even owls and whippoorwills dared get in his way.

He left the pony in a draw and stole to the ranch headquarters. The big house was dark, but lights came from the bunkhouse. He laughed aloud. Was he drunk? Why was he here? Hell, he didn't know. Maybe because this was where the Chandlers were.

Jose eased into the barn when he heard the bunkhouse door open. Footsteps. Men talking. Coming his way. He moved deeper into the stable as the voices grew louder, stumbling into a pile of hay and burrowing deep inside before the men flipped on the lights.

What were they doing? Why didn't they go away? But they didn't, and lulled by the warm comfort of his hiding place, Jose drifted off to sleep until a sudden noise woke him. Damn. Were the men still there? He inched his way from the depths of the stack, the rustling of hay loud in his ears. Daylight! He'd slept away the night in the Chandlers' stable.

Before he wiggled from beneath the hay, the noise came again. The crack of leather against leather. The stable door yawned. No one in sight. Then the Chandler woman—Rider's woman—strolled into view, slapping a short quirt against her riding boot. Christ, she was big as a buffalo cow. Near her time. Still, she was pretty.

Teresa walked into the stable. "How are you this morning?"

Still hidden by hay, Jose tensed, but a gentle snicker told him she was petting a horse. Why didn't she go? He had to get out of there. Someone would find his pony. *Go on! Get out.* But she kept patting the horse and talking baby talk. Jose stirred restlessly.

"Someone there? Ro, that you? Stop playing games."

He heard her approaching and—on impulse—stood.

The woman halted, her eyes widening. He got a rush from the sudden fear in her eyes. She clutched her stomach protectively and backed away. "Jose! What are you doing here?"

"Stuck up in Santa Fe when you and Román got married, so I come to say good luck."

"You delivered your message, so go."

Her cold tone set him on edge. "That ain't friendly."

She turned for the door. "We'll see what my father has to say about this."

Jose came to his senses and pulled her deeper into the stable. He tried to cover her mouth, but she tore free. Good. He liked a fighter. Aroused, he went for her. The quirt lashed out, stinging his cheek, bringing blood.

His vision turned dark. He struck her with an open hand. The force of the blow snapped her head back. The quirt flew from her hand. She was going to get it now! Better than Rider ever done it to her.

Teresa moved away, mouth opening to scream. He rushed her. She staggered and lost her balance, stumbling backward into the pony's stall. The frightened animal reared. She fell beneath him. She cried out as one hoof caught her in the head. Then she lay still.

Jose stared at the motionless form. She was alive, but her breath came in short gasps. Blood poured from a gash in her forehead. He glanced around. No one had seen him. No one but her. She'd claim he attacked her, and they'd send him back to Santa Fe.

He hesitated only a moment before waving his arms to spook the nervous colt again.

Chapter 51

Ro leaned back in the saddle, one hand propped on Colorado's rump, and watched the Jeep flying across the desert. He usually had a radio, but one unit was malfunctioning, and he'd loaned his to Pete. He straightened up. Bird! Was the baby coming? Anticipation—laced with fear—played down his spine as he rode out to intercept the vehicle.

Wade skidded to a halt and yelled through swirling dust. "Teresa! Accident! Big house."

Ro booted Colorado into a dead run. The big animal ate up the distance in long strides, taking arroyos and gullies in reckless leaps and thundering across the broad lawn, digging divots in the soft turf. Ro flung himself from the saddle and stumbled up the steps.

A pale, drawn Judith opened the door. "Sunroom."

As he raced down the hall, a great owl flew at him, talons reaching for his eyes. Ro halted like he'd run into a wall. A blink of the eye, and it was gone. Moaning, he ran for the sunroom.

Bird lay unconscious on the bed breathing shalowly, covered to the waist by a thin blanket. Two bloody gashes on her forehead brought a cry to his lips. He knelt and clutched her hand, his gaze shifting to her bloated stomach. The child? No matter. Just let her be all right.

Jim's voice at his side sounded hollow. "Ambulance on the way."

Ro had partial control of himself again. "What happened?"

"She was out for a walk. Must've had a dizzy spell in the stable and spooked the colt."

****

Ro didn't recall the race to the hospital. As he sat in the waiting room, the only thing real to him was a strong, astringent smell that left a bitter taste on his tongue. Why didn't they come tell him she was all right? He sat motionless… and died by degrees.

He didn't see the green-shrouded man until he stood before him, Ro rose and met the steady gaze.

"I'm sorry, Mr. Otero. We lost her."

Judith's cries hit him harder than the doctor's words. Judith never cried, so it must be true. Ro sank back onto the chair, his breath coming slowly. He blinked away tears. He wouldn't cry, not in this foreign place. He was an empty shell. Then what hurt so much?

The doctor broke the silence. "Before she went, she gave birth to a fine boy."

He heard Judith gasp as if that were something to grab onto. He knew better.

The medic babbled on. "He's strong and healthy. He'll make you a fine man someday."

Someday. But Bird wouldn't be there.

"Thank God!' Judith sobbed.

"Would you like to see your wife?" the doctor asked.

"You go on," Jim said hoarsely. "We'll be along in a minute."

Ro trailed the physician's green shroud down an endless corridor on boots that walked without his help. Perhaps if they never got there, she wouldn't be gone. Then the medic halted and opened a door. Ro forced himself inside.

Bird lay on a clean bed, a white bandage covering her forehead. Relieved, he moved to her side. The doctor was wrong. She was sleeping. He'd been talking about someone else.

"Bird. Teresa?" She didn't stir. He put out his hand... and knew. He dropped onto the chair at the side of the bed and moaned as the screeches of four giant owls filled his head. A torrent of tears hissed like scalding steam as they fell upon the raging inferno that was his heart.

Out of the corner of his eye he saw Judith, her purse clutched to her breast, enter the room. Jim rolled his chair bedside and timidly touched his daughter's hand.

The sound of his own voice startled Ro. "Promised her everything would be all right. Nobody'd die. I didn't have the power to make that promise. So the colt and the baby killed her to punish me. Shoulda took me."

Judith put a hand—damp from her tears—on his arm. "Román... Ro, we have to go now."

"Can't leave her alone." Why wasn't he terrified of her corpse? Cadavers were bad.

"Let her father have a minute with her. We'll come back later."

He glanced at the rancher. He'd never seen the man he loved like a father so helpless... so broken. Ro got to his feet and leaned over to whisper words of love in her ear. Once so powerful, now meaningless gibberish.

"This way." Judith pulled him into the corridor. He followed as she led him to a window where a nurse wheeled up an incubator. "Look, there's your son. Isn't he beautiful? He's named James Paul Otero, just as you and Teresa wanted."

He flinched at the sound of her name, then glanced at the baby. The infant wasn't even human yet. Ro stared a moment before wandering aimlessly down the hall.

****

No one had an appetite, but Judith bullied them into nibbling on something to keep up their strength. Paul arrived around seven. The sight of the tall, handsome young man returned Ro's heart to his chest. He came out of his seat, and they hugged, desperately clinging to one another in search of mutual strength. The moment passed. Ro sank back into despair.

Judith made coffee, and then everyone pulled chairs around Ro in the den and started talking. Why? Words didn't matter now. They were carrying on as if nothing had happened. But something had happened. The world... his world had ended.

She-Who-Had-Been-His-Heart was barely gone, yet all they could talk about was the infant. The baby who'd killed its mother. She hadn't had strength enough for both of them, so she gave her life for him. Ro shuddered. He'd killed his own mother like that.

****

He retreated inside himself where nothing could touch him. No one was allowed there, least of all the infant who stole his life. He suffered through the long funeral services, eyes fixed on a gleaming, gray casket as he cultivated sadness like an old companion. Ruby and Clarence came to lend silent support. Buck showed up for the graveside burial, the back of his pickup all but filled by Big Tom Bearclaw. His friends led Ro away so the attendants could close the grave. He left every ounce of love he possessed in that pit. There wasn't any left.

From habit, he stood in the driveway and waved goodbye when Paul returned to school. Not even that had meaning. Judith fixed a nursery in Teresa's old bedroom, which was all right with Ro. The wizened, dark-headed child provoked no feelings. Not even hate.

Ro rebelled when Jim wanted him to move into the big house again. He preferred to haunt the home where they had lived so briefly—so happily—sitting at the table where they ate, lying in the bed where they slept and made love and came to know one another. He should have abandoned the place. Burned it to the ground, or at least broken windows and torn off doors.

Often, a memory would rise up and suck the breath out of him, leaving him gasping for air. At times, he knew she was there with him. He got up in the middle of the night and wandered the rooms... searching. Did he have ghost sickness? Did it matter?

One night, he abandoned the adobe and drove his old truck to Snakehead because he was dreaming again, visions so real he could almost touch them.

Bird came with him to the *gowa*, but another vied for his mind and spirit. Two dead women fought over him. As his grandmother became ascendent, he grew weak from the lack of sleep and fled the wickiup.

He drove in a daze to the edge of Wandering Water and splashed to a sandy islet in the middle of the river. Heedless of hot spring sun and cold night wind, he remained on the barren sandbar using every trick he knew to protect against *ashee*: flowing water, sage, ashes, and his black, bone-handled knife. Slowly the madness that owned his brain burned itself out.

Ro woke one morning to realize he was filthy and shrunken from lack of food. He sat puzzling over where he was. At length, he drank from the river and constructed a sweathouse from branches and twigs along the shore. Hours in the purifying steam leached poisons from his system. Only then did he bathe in the clear, swollen waters of the rio.

Ro showed up for work early one morning without warning to punish his body and numb his mind, refusing to quit until his strength was gone. Then he returned to the lonely adobe and memories of his wife or to Snakehead to be closer to those of his childhood.

After three months, he relaxed a little. The crew was a godsend when he finally allowed their earthy, unstated affection and respect to penetrate his shell. One day, he startled Jim by agreeing to come to the big house for dinner. After that, he dropped by often, sometimes to eat or simply to visit and play chess. Never once did he set foot in the nursery. Judith brought the baby around at every opportunity, but each time he was tempted to touch the child, he remembered that except for that infant, *she* would have lived.

His life improved as Indian summer arrived. He ignored his twenty-second birthday. It had no meaning. Even so, work became a reasonable occupation, not a means of self-flagellation. He got a thrill out of selling his R-Eagle-O cattle… until he realized she wasn't there to share his joy.

****

Ro checked his watch against the sun. Today, it would be good to clean up and go to the big house for dinner. He'd promised Jim a game of chess. He was heading for a bath at his own place when he noticed a car in the Chandler's driveway. Long, black cars frightened him ever since he'd followed the long, black hearse on She-Who-Had-Been-His-Heart's final trip.

Suddenly, unaccountably, his skin prickled. Setting Colorado into a fast gallop, he raced to the big house. His guts twisted into a knot as he spotted the distinctive green medallion on the license plate. A doctor's car. The baby!

Abandoning Colorado at the stable, Ro stumbled up the porch steps. Judith talked with someone he couldn't see in the living room as he raced up the stairs without pausing. The child lay in his crib, fretting and whimpering softly.

235

"God," he whispered, "don't let anything happen to him! Please!" His spontaneous words lifted something oppressive from his shoulders. For the first time he really looked at the baby. While others saw him, he saw the boy's mother. Her nose, her eyes, her frown. He almost sobbed as the dry husk that was his body filled with veins and arteries and organs and nerves. He lifted the child awkwardly against his shoulder just as Judith stepped into the room. She faltered and clutched at the doorframe for support.

"Will he be all right?"

She smiled. "It's only colic."

"The doctor came all the way out here for colic?"

"Came to see Jim and checked the baby while he was here."

Silent tears streamed down his cheeks, yet he felt no shame. "Good. She would have wanted him to live."

Judith swiped her eyes. "More than anything." She stumbled forward, clasping them in an embrace. "Welcome home, Ro. Good to have you back."

He took Little Jim to the nursery Bird had prepared for the child at the adobe. Ro cared for the boy at night and turned him over to Judith during the day. They shared the baby, his laughter, his pains, his love. For the first time since Bird went away, Ro smiled and even laughed a little.

****

Early one Saturday morning in November, Ro, with Little Jim tucked in the crook of his left arm, rode Colorado to the tiny cabin home of Water Willow on the reservation. The old woman seemed to have aged twenty years in the four since he'd last seen her. She shuffled to the front porch and hailed him with a toothless grin and a high-pitched cackle.

"My old eyes think they see Tall Rider right here on my doorstep. Must be the magic buttons coming back on me after all this time." She stepped closer and peered at the bundle in his arms. "What's that? A baby? Where'd you steal it? And don't go telling me it's yours."

Ro nudged Colorado closer to the porch, "This is my son, Spotted Deer."

She took the infant from his arms. A bony hand stroked the child's smooth cheek tenderly. "You give him a good name. Deer give us good meat and fine hides. Fast and smart. Takes a good hunter to kill him. Deer's a careful critter. What a fine name this child'll make for hisself when his time comes." She glanced at Ro. "Good you give him a birthname."

"Needs to be put to cradle. You were the only one She-Who-Was-Cane-Woman called a friend, and I hope you'll be good enough to do it for him."

The old woman could scarcely conceal her pleasure. "You got everything?"

"Yes'um. But he was born in a white man's hospital, so I don't have any life cord."

"Make do with what we got. Bring it all inside."

As Ro rummaged in his saddlebags, he heard a wagon approaching and knew without looking Big Tom Bearclaw was coming. Ro hadn't told anyone of his plans, but he'd bought a cradle at the trading post. The moccasin telegraph at its best. He knew the man would have a cradleboard with transverse pieces made from sotol as befitted a boy-child. Sure enough, when Tom pulled his team to a halt—mules this time—he confirmed Ro's suspicions.

"Thought I might find you here. The old woman gonna do it? Good." Tom labored down from his perch and wheezed to the side of the wagon. "Ah, here it is." He brought out a newly made cradleboard lined with sheep's fleece and laced with rawhide thongs.

Ro made appropriate noises. "Be proud to buy this for my son."

"Ain't for sale," Tom snapped. "Present for the son of my nephew."

"Thank you, Uncle."

Ro delivered the four gifts required before Water Willow could perform the cradle rite. A comb for her hair made from abalone shell. A fine sheep's skin, a pair of soft, beaded moccasins, and a beautiful, hand-woven blanket. The Apache weren't blanket Indians, but a warm cover was always welcome in the cold time. Then he honored his son with a tiny necklace of silver and turquoise and a small, beaded sack containing certain selected items... a medicine bag.

Water Willow, known to the whites as Lena Boggs, lifted the child to the heavens with the discreet assistance of Big Tom.

"Oh, Giver-of-Life, look down on us unworthy ones," she intoned. "We bring you a new son. Thank you for his life. Watch after him and guide his steps." Four times, she held the infant aloft and chanted a prayer. Then she placed him in his cradleboard, drawing the laces tight. Unaccustomed to such restraint, the baby squirmed and fussed.

The old woman covered his mouth and pinched the tiny nose just as any grandmother would have done a hundred years earlier when the welfare of the entire band depended upon the silence of even its least member. The child's cry became a muffled struggle for breath. Ro controlled his impulse to snatch the withered hand away. Just when he could restrain himself no longer, she released her grip.

The baby grabbed one deep breath and let out a roar. Ro forced himself to remain still as she repeated the lesson again and again until the infant remained more or less quiet when she removed her hand. Satisfied, she daubed his forehead with sacred pollen and continued to pray. Finished, she turned to face them. "Spotted Deer's a good child. Learns fast."

Ro accepted the baby. "Thank you. I feel good now he's been put to cradle. My son and I would like you to accept this." He pushed 50 one-dollar bills into her gnarled old hands. Far too much, but it would help her through the coming winter.

She politely hid the money in her skirts without looking at it. "Thank you, Tall Rider. You be a good father. Be firm and teach him the Old Way. And stay away from the bottle. Liquor ain't no good for nothing."

Ro and Tom backed out of the cabin and vacated the clearing as she continued to enumerate the evils of the world according to her lights. "Too much tobacco ain't no good. Don't let Spotted Deer have none until he's been on his first hunt. Teach him to hunt. Our young people don't know how to hunt no more." She was still talking when they rode out of hearing.

"Whew! She made me thirsty," Big Tom said. "How 'bout you, nephew?"

"Be good to celebrate my son with a drink."

Barely out of sight of Water Willow's cabin they dismounted and sought the shelter of a mountain pine. With the baby— still in his cradle—lying between them, Ro drank sparingly while Big Tom killed a bottle of liquor he just happened to have with him. This time, when Ro offered payment, the fat man cheerfully accepted.

The next morning, Ro stood alongside Jim and Judith in the local church while their holy man sprinkled water over his son in yet another ceremony. Ro saw no conflict. After all, who was Ussen if not the One-Great-God-Who-Was-Three? Ro smiled on the inside of his mouth. That would make him the One-Great-God-Who-Was-Four. That was much better.

238

Chapter 52

Paul returned home for Christmas vacation uncertain of the situation he'd face. He arrived to find his mother coping and his father handling his sorrow and growing stronger daily. Ro was the surprise. Paul had expected a basket case, but his brother seemed normal, perhaps more morose, more remote. Except with the infant. Ro was completely wrapped up in the baby.

Perceiving the child as the center of the family's universe, Paul wormed his way into the infant's life. Each time someone talked about Little Jim, he countered with Little Paul. Within days, the child became Jim-Paul, which Paul turned into JP.

Paul had his own emotions to contend with. The homecoming had been incomplete. He missed his sister more than he believed possible. Even so, he soon felt the need to get away briefly. Ro begged off going into town with him. The guy would play chess, deal cards, talk, wrestle, share a brew at the kitchen table, get into a spitting contest, *anything* so long as he could do it at home with his son.

Paul ventured into Terreon alone, and soon realized his old friends had left or were married and had families. A single visit exhausted all they had to share.

One night, while making his way home, he turned into the parking lot of Harry's Bar. The joint must recycle the same putrid air. It smelled exactly like the last time he'd been there. Brew in hand, he selected a table and sat down.

Halfway through his beer, someone walked up to speak to the bartender. Paul grunted under his breath as he recognized Jose Peyote. If the guy had suffered up at the pen, it wasn't apparent. After some animated talk, something changed hands, and the bartender handed Jose a beer. The man froze with the bottle halfway to his mouth when he spied Paul in the mirror.

The smile spreading over Jose's lips never reached his eyes as he stalked over to the table. "Been wondering where you was." He flipped a chair around and sat astride it, hands folded over the back, beer bottle gripped loosely in his left.

Except for the glaze of the man's eyes, Paul wouldn't have known Jose was drunk. Maybe it was his law training, but Paul suddenly wanted to know what made the other man tick.

"You're back from the pen, I see. Was it worth it?"

"Worth what? Didn't do nothing. Your daddy's pet sheriff set me up."

Paul leaned forward on his elbows. This was what being a lawyer was all about, interviewing people and getting to the truth. "Course not. You wouldn't hurt a fly."

"A pesky fly, maybe." The fake smile came out again. "Heard what happened to your sister. Real sorry about that."

"Yeah, sorry you didn't do it."

The world stood still for a millisecond. That meaningless retort got a reaction. Nothing more than a single instant during which Jose's eyes flickered. His hand flew halfway to his cheek, but he halted the reaction. The air grew thick as a wave of suspicion swept Paul. "Or did you?"

"Kinda talk's that? The river run dry, you blame it on Jose?" The man was tense and tight. A peculiar mark on his left jaw fairly glowed.

Paul's skin prickled like a hunter catching scent of prey. "Tell me something, Jose. Why blame my family for all your problems?"

The hate in the man's voice made Paul recoil. "Two years I work on that ranch. Best hand you had. So I drink some. I do my work. Do it good. Think the old man even like me a little. Now, ex-con. Got no job, no money, no family. I got nothing."

Paul was unable to take his eyes off the livid mark on the man's jaw. "Why's that?"

Jose sucked breath through clinched teeth. "Why? A punk kid slugged me when I was drunk. Don't take that from nobody. I'm a man, not a dog. Rough up the fucker when he comes back from a fancy shindig dressed up like a pretty girl. So his old man takes a rifle to me. Fix it so I can't get no job." The blemish on Jose's cheek seemed to pulse.

"Few holes in that story. You killed my friend and are responsible for getting me shot. You deserve to be locked up for thirty years not three."

Jose sneered. "Shit, man, why leave out crippling up your daddy?"

The hollow mockery in Jose's voice got to Paul. He leaned over the table. "Maybe it was a mistake to omit that. And my sister too. But I'll put those omissions right. The sheriff will see that bill's paid. Not a threat, Jose. It's a promise. And here's another one. I ever see you on the ranch, I'll kill you. Put a bullet through your brain like any other rattlesnake."

"Listen to the big lawyer talk. That what you learn up there in that school? Blow a big wind?" Jose got up and swaggered away.

Pretending a calm he didn't feel, Paul walked out of the bar. He'd lost his temper, and ceded that round to Jose. Next time would be different.

The December night air whipping through the open window of the Studebaker chilled Paul's temper and allowed him to think more rationally. He'd learned something. Nothing tangible. A hunch. *Jose knew something about Teresa's accident.* Perhaps his father's, as well.

The light was still on in the office when he got home. He rapped on the outside door and entered. Jim was finishing up paperwork and asked how Paul was enjoying his holiday.

He dropped into a chair and stuck his long legs in front of him. "Not bad, considering the circumstances. Not much going on in the evenings."

"What are your plans after you graduate in what... one more semester?"

Paul nodded and spent a few minutes talking about passing the state bar exam and taking a job with a Santa Fe or Albuquerque law firm to gain experience before opening his own practice in Terreon. Then he edged into what he wanted to explore.

"Hard to believe it's been four years since your accident. On the same day as the robbery, wasn't it?"

Jim dug at the bowl of his pipe to loosen tobacco. "Next day."

After his father described the incident in detail, Paul was satisfied Jose hadn't been involved and switched subjects. "What time of day did Teresa's accident happen?"

"Morning. We found her about nine or so. Drove herself up from the little house early and went to say hello to a colt. Been outside for twenty or thirty minutes. Why the questions?"

Paul shrugged. "Thinking about the hand fate's dealt us the last few years. Ro's doing better than expected. I had the impression he was off his rocker."

Jim dry-washed his face. "He disappeared after the funeral. The boys found him on a sandbar in the Rio Chacon. No trees, no shade, nothing but a damned bare island. Stayed there for days."

Paul nodded. "Four days, I'll bet. Four's some sort of special number to them. He was out on a sandbar all that time?"

"Mystified me too, but Bud McIlhanney at the trading post said the Apache believe ghosts can't cross water."

"Oh, God! He was haunted."

"I came down and parked behind some cottonwoods and watched him," Jim said. "He just sat there. The boys left food on the riverbank, but if he saw it, he didn't pay any attention. Staying away from him's the hardest thing I ever did, but I knew if I tried, he'd run for the deep mountains where it would take another Apache to find him. He had to fight the battle his own way. And he was strong enough to win. Showed up one day scrubbed clean, skinny as an overused rope, and started working his tail off. Been at it ever since."

"Thanks. I've got the picture now."

****

Early the next morning, while his mother got ready to visit Teresa's grave, Paul checked out the stable, although he had no idea what he was looking for. He was about to give up when something lying in the hay caught his eye. He

241

picked up a quirt. Teresa's quirt. One he'd given her for her birthday two years ago. Was she carrying it that day? Paul examined a stain on the very tip before returning to the house and putting the whip in his room.

Later, when he and his mother got out of the car at the cemetery, Judith arranged a bouquet of hothouse flowers in an urn on her daughter's headstone. Stepping back to his side, she clutched his arm.

"I don't believe Ro ever visits."

"He wouldn't," Paul said. "It's got something to do with his culture. Even Ro's got some of the Old Way in him. He never went back to his grandmother's grave after he buried her. He put her in the ground himself, you know."

"*He* buried her? Oh, Paul, he was little more than a child."

"All by himself someplace in a canyon where nobody'll ever find her. It was years before he told me." Paul put an arm around his mother. "You were wrong about them, you know."

"Yes, they loved one another. Like your father and me. It was a good marriage."

"You're one hell of a woman."

She smiled wanly. "And it's only taken you twenty-four years to learn it."

They left shortly after that. He waited until he handed his mother into the Studebaker's passenger seat before bringing up his sister's accident. "Was Teresa going riding that day… you know, the day of the accident?"

Judith stared out the car's side window as he pulled away from the curb. "She couldn't ride any longer. Would've had the baby soon."

"What was she wearing?"

"A maternity outfit, light blue. Why?"

Paul raised his shoulder. "No one's told me much about it, and I kinda feel left out."

She touched his arm. "Sorry. We were all so grief-stricken we didn't do a very good job of sharing with you. She was in corduroy maternity trousers and her high riding boots. I don't know how she got into them. Ro must have helped her."

"Did she carry anything? You know, like a purse."

"Just a quirt she picked up in her room. She'd left it behind and was going to take it home with her. So far as I remember, that's all she had."

Paul's blood turned to ice. He heard his mother from afar. Please, God, don't let her look at him. She'd know if she did.

But Judith kept staring out the window. "Good Lord, I dread this first Christmas!"

He gripped her hand. "Mom, we'll make it. Won't be easy, but we'll make it."

Paul avoided Ro for the rest of the day. He didn't trust himself. His buddy read him too well. After dinner, he retreated to his room and took a long shower before heading for town.

With the quirt on the seat beside him, Paul went over his strategy on his way into Terreon. If he handled this right, Jose Peyote would be out of their hair once and for all. If not? Well, he was leaving for school soon, and no one else would be involved.

He drove straight to Harry's, but Jose wasn't there. Halfway through a watered-down whiskey, the Apache arrived, headed straight for Paul's table, and dropped into a chair. Like two curs, they were hostile but unable to stay apart.

"Good," Paul said. "Wanted to continue our talk." Jose's eyes narrowed. "Did you mess with my father's Jeep so he'd have an accident?"

The man stared at Paul's left earlobe. "What if I say I did?"

"I'd beat you within an inch of your life before hauling you to the sheriff."

"Hell, for a promise like that, I oughta say yes."

"Don't bother. That was a test. Something to measure your next answer by, because you *did* kill my sister, and I can prove it. Found your bottle in our stable."

The man reminded Paul of a coiled serpent preparing to strike. "Didn't have no…." Jose rubbed his nose. "Didn't find no bottle of mine."

Paul trembled. He knew now. *Don't rush.* Play your hand. "That's right. No bottle, but there are fingerprints." Jose's face was a mask. Nothing registered on his features. Paul laid the quirt on the table. "And then there's this."

"Ain't mine. Never had no quirt."

Bitter vetch collected at the base of Paul's throat. He was close. Careful now. "This was my sister's. Just wanted to match it to something." He raised the end of the whip to the man's cheek and smiled when Jose flinched. "To this new scar of yours."

Jose touched the mark on his jaw. "You a crazy bastard."

"A man you've never heard of, a doctor named Edmond Locard, is gonna convict you of murder. Or at least the work he pioneered will. He called it 'trace evidence.' An expert can tell me if this quirt made that scar. A microscope will pick up your blood and skin tissue on the leather. The last time my sister had this, the *only* time she could've made that mark on your cheek is the morning she died. This little scrap of leather's gonna lock you up for the rest of your miserable life."

Jose put his face inches from Paul's. His lips turned black. "Fuck you, white man!"

Then he was gone, leaving Paul semi-elated. He hadn't known guilt had an odor. But he'd gotten a whiff of it a moment ago. Jose was scared, and that was good.

Chapter 53

Jose stood in the cold darkness behind Harry's and fingered the mark on his jawline. Could Chandler do what he said? Frustrated, he picked up an empty beer bottle and hurled it at the back of the building. A tall airman with sergeant's stripes breezed around the corner just as it shattered into slivers.

"Hey, man! Watch what you're doing, greaser. Oughta kick your ass."

A smile touched Jose's lips—a real smile. His shoulder caught the man in the solar plexus. The airman reeled backward and tripped on the back step of the building. He went down. Jose's boot caught him on the chin. He threw a hard left, but the man managed to get his head out of the way, and Jose's fist slammed into a concrete block. Hurt and half out of his mind, he stomped on the flyboy's nose, and it was all over. He took the unconscious man's money, bought a pint of whiskey, and sat in a crappy little park with more sand than grass to work on the bottle.

****

The midmorning sun found Jose's eyes. He struggled to consciousness with a queasy stomach and thunderous headache. Suffering through a bout of heaves so bad he couldn't get up without the help of his hands, he put weight on his left fist. A sharp pain shot halfway up his arm. What the hell! Busted knuckles. Shit, the fight with the flyboy.

He focused on more important matters. How serious was that quirt? Up in the joint, he'd heard about one hair putting some con up for life. New stuff they called forensics or something.

Jose broke into a sweat that had nothing to do with the winter sun. The Chandler girl must be a witch to reach out from the grave and lay cold fingers on him. That brother of hers was too stupid to know he carried a corpse on his back.

The hike back to his truck at Harry's raised a thirst. The bar wasn't open yet, so he pounded on the back door. Harry peeked out and gave him hell before slamming it in Jose's face.

He saw red. Intending to give Harry what he gave that flyboy, he twisted the knob, and—to his surprise—the door swung open. The barman had disappeared, but the sight of bottles of every kind of booze he could think of lined the wall, chasing thoughts of Harry right out of his head.

Grabbing the closest carton, Jose ran for his truck. As soon as he was out of sight, he checked to see what he had. He didn't like vodka much, but these six quarts would bring a heap of floating steps and a lot of drifting mind.

The banks of Wandering Water made a comfortable place to drink until dark, but the vodka wasn't working. His problems wouldn't go away. They rattled around in his head. He had to take care of Paul Chandler. For that, he needed a gun. His uncle had lost his to a pawnbroker. His breath caught in his throat. Tall Rider had a 30-30.

He drove to his uncle's to spend the night. The next morning, he gave the old man a quart of vodka for the use of a pony.

Chapter 54

Ro reined in Colorado and looked at Paul. "You talked to Jose since you got home?"

His blood brother pulled up beside him and made a face. "Night before last. Turned nasty, so I threatened to take what I know to the sheriff."

Ro cocked an eyebrow. "What do you know?"

"He let it slip he might have had something to do with the accident." Ro's head jerked up, and Paul stuttered. "D-Dad's accident. I know he didn't, but I wanted to start off with that and work around to killing Bull Sheldon."

Ro's heart pumped. Paul was treading dangerous ground. "Why didn't you tell me this before?"

"Wanted another crack at him before I said anything. He almost admitted it. When I said I was going to Sheriff Valera, he puffed up and walked out the door."

Ro leveled the best white man's stare he could muster. "You're playing with dynamite. Have you told Jim?"

Paul shook his head. "If Jose tries anything, he'll go for me. I'll be careful until I go back to the U. Don't say anything, okay?"

"Paul, you don't realize what you're up against."

"You're wrong." Paul rubbed his shoulder. "I'm carrying a bullet scar, remember? Which way you headed?"

"South pasture. You?"

"Spring Creek." Paul slapped his saddlebag. "Damn, forgot to pick up a radio."

"Take mine. You need it more'n I do."

Ro handed over the unit and watched Paul ride away. This was a slack time on the ranch. Cattle had been gathered and delivered. There was enough ground cover for carryovers. The weather was holding. Cold enough so they had to break ice on stock tanks and not much else, except put out a little salt, toss some feed, and mend and repair. Always mend and repair. The sun still had a bite, but with the coming new year, weather would change for the worse. More importantly, Paul would go where he was safe.

Aware his brother hadn't told him everything, Ro decided to pay Big Tom a visit and see what gossip he could pick up, so he headed home for a couple of bottles of booze left over from the wedding reception. Upon arrival, he ground-hitched Colorado in the yard and went inside.

As soon as he set foot through the front door, Ro knew something was wrong. Then he saw it. When his wife had gone away, Ro overcame his upbringing enough to keep two personal mementos... two photographs. Both were gone, missing from their frames. Ashes in the fireplace were probably all that remained of them. His skin crawled.

After quickly checking and finding no additional damage, Ro raced outside and located fresh hoofprints. Following at a gallop, he finally spotted a rider near the border of the reservation. Ro brought Colorado to a halt, dragged his rifle from the scabbard, and threw a wild shot in the direction of the intruder. Colorado bolted at the noise, and Ro had trouble getting control, but the distant horse stumbled and fell. The rider rolled free and broke for a piece of high ground capped by some rocks and a line of junipers.

Throwing caution aside, Ro set off after the man, rifle still in hand. He raced past the fallen horse and ran Colorado up into the rocks, determined not to give his quarry an opportunity to escape. He saw the trap at the last minute. A large branch, pulled almost double, sprang forward to sweep him from the saddle. His forehead struck a rock as he tumbled, and everything went black.

Stones rattled nearby. Ro sat up, eyesight blurred, and was surprised to find he'd held onto his rifle. Blood trickled into his eyes. He pulled the weapon up defensively.

"Come on, Jose! Let's end it! Right here! Right now!"

The wind was his answer.

Muffled sounds came from the other side of the hill. A whinny. Hoof beats. A half-shouted oath. Colorado! Jose was trying to get to Colorado. Ro climbed to his feet. Swaying unsteadily, he lurched forward. The horse screamed in pain. Ro crested the rise and swiped at his eyes, willing them to see. The intruder had slipped away into the brush, leaving the big red to hop in circles, dragging his rear legs. Blood coursed down the sleek hide. Ro cried aloud. The horse hadn't let Jose mount, so the man had hamstrung him.

Half blind from a bleeding head wound, Ro tried to examine the confused animal. Colorado snorted and danced in pain. Ro removed his saddle and bridle before putting the suffering beast out of his misery. Still unable to focus well, Ro threw the saddle over his shoulder, and started the long hike back to the big house. Hours later, he stowed the rifle, saddle, and tack gear in the stable before entering the kitchen.

"What in the world happened to you?" Judith exclaimed.

Ro removed his hat and gingerly explored his forehead. "Collided with a rock. Won't look so bad after I wash up. Paul come in yet?"

"In his room."

His brother whistled when Ro went upstairs. "What hit you?"

"Jose." He related what had happened. "I hung onto my rifle, or he'd have come for me."

"Damn, Ro." Paul dampened a cloth in his bathroom. "Like they say, this is gonna hurt you more'n me."

He cursed as Paul tended his wound. "Why would he break into my place? He didn't take anything. Was he looking for something special, or maybe he did what he came to do."

"He didn't come to burn two photographs he didn't know existed," Paul reasoned.

"Everything I own was there except my horse, my saddle, and my rifle. And if he was after my rifle, you'd better keep an extra sharp eye out." Ro's head drooped. "Those pictures… they were all I had left of her that was… you know, personal."

"You've got her mare. Guess you'll be riding Princess from now on. But don't worry about photos. Mom has a copy of every picture ever made of her. As for Jose, I'm gonna find that bastard and kill him!"

"Now *you're* talking crazy Let's go to Jim. He'll know what to do."

Paul dropped down on the side of his bed. "No, don't. You're right though, can't let Jose bend me his direction. But this business started because of me, and by God, I'm gonna be the one to end it. I'm about ready to go to the law about"—Paul hesitated—"you know, Bull. Just need a couple more things, and I'm going to Harry's tonight to get them. I'll bring dad up to date tomorrow."

"Jim needs to know what's going on," Ro insisted.

"This is my battle, and I'll finish it my way. You gonna hold off?" When Ro nodded, Paul expelled air. "Thanks. How you gonna explain about Colorado? I know, he stepped in a hole and broke his leg. That's how you got your head split open. Let me tell them." Paul tried for a grin. "Lawyers are good at telling stories. Let's go eat. Mom waited dinner on you."

Paul spun his tale at the table, and everyone expressed genuine sympathy at the loss of the big red. After the meal, Ro watched Paul's car out of sight on the highway before looking for Judith to plead a headache and asking her to keep JP for the night.

Ro drove the Jeep home to pick up a couple of bottles before heading for the reservation. He hadn't argued with Paul because he was sure Jose wouldn't be anywhere near Harry's. Ro believed he understood the significance of the burned pictures, yet he wanted confirmation. The hour was late, but Big Tom wasn't married to the white man's clock.

The man came out of his cabin at the first beep of the horn and peered through the gloom, breaking into a broad smile when he recognized Ro. "Nephew. What you doing here so late?"

"Got a bottle and decided not to be selfish. Came to share it with my uncle. If I woke him up, I can go drink it by myself."

The fat man skipped the last few steps. "No, no! Wasn't asleep. What's in the bottle?"

"Have two. One's bourbon. Other's gin." He knew the man had a fondness for both. The Jeep took a decided list to the right when Tom squeezed his girth into the seat.

"Uh, oughta drive down the road a piece. Kids're asleep. Don't wanna wake them."

Despite his impatience, Ro forced himself to observe the amenities. They sipped in silence until Big Tom began his news report on reservation events. Ro suffered through all of it without learning a thing about Jose Peyote.

"Uncle," he said during a lull in the conversation, "somebody broke into my house this afternoon and burned two pictures of She-Who-Had-been-My-Wife."

"Why would you have a picture of someone who's forgot?" The big man sighed aloud. "Must be your white blood. To answer what's worrying your head, some might figure them pictures was witches' tools."

He forgot himself and posed a blunt question. "Have you heard anything?"

Tom didn't seem offended. "Well, there's one here who figgers he's witched. Things coming down on him pretty bad since he come back from up north, and he's feeling worried. Everybody's watching him close."

Tom had said nothing and everything. After holding out his hand and finding it steady—Tom had done most of the drinking—Ro donated the second bottle, and headed back to his house, where he loaded the rifle with fresh cartridges and saddled Princess.

Chapter 55

Light from the cabin window spilled across Jose's shoulders as he sat on his uncle's porch, thinking furiously. Things were bad. Two powerful forces raced toward him. The Chandlers, like all white men, used money and the law to get what they wanted. They'd send him back to Santa Fe.

But witching was the real danger. Whites could kill his body; witches could kill his soul. That old woman was reaching out from her mountain grave, and Tall Rider worked her will. Wasn't no way Rider coulda known he'd be at that house on the J-Bar-C. The man oughta been out working, but there he was, right on Jose's tail.

When he'd entered the breed's house to steal a rifle, the photos confirmed there was a second witch. A dead white woman. Sooner or later, she'd tell Rider how and why she died. He'd delayed it by burning the pictures, but she'd find a way.

When no one had come for him this afternoon, Jose knew Chandler hadn't gone to the sheriff yet. Paul was probably sniffing around Harry's right now looking for him. But when the kid *did* come with the sheriff in tow, they'd arrive in noisy cars, giving him warning. He'd go high into the mountains and cross into Mexico. That had been the way of the *Tinneh* for hundreds of years. Rile up the Americans and escape to Mexico. Piss off the Mexicans and slip back across the border.

Not jumping the breed this afternoon had been a mistake. But Jose'd been groggy from the fall when his horse went down. And while Rider was hurt and lugging a saddle, he'd also been toting a loaded rifle. Jose nodded. He'd finally cut through the smoke and reached the fire. Rider would come like an Apache, not a white man. So, the breed had to die.

Rider would be worried after what had happened, so he'd be where he could watch over the Chandlers. If riled enough, he'd be guarding them from outside the house. Jose smiled. Rider would come meet him… man-to-man. The *Ga'an* would see to that.

He walked into the cabin in search of a weapon. An ancient bow and a quiver of arrows lay on a shelf, but they were of no interest. His eye fell on two short lances hanging on the wall. His uncle often claimed a medicine man had made them using the proper ceremonies and singing the right songs. Jose balanced one in his hand. Sturdy. He jabbed the air. This was a weapon his ancestors had carried to punish their enemies.

Power flowed from the holy wood into his arm… his right arm. History coursed through his veins. Now he knew what to do. Taking both spears, he walked through the darkness to steal the last of his uncle's horses.

Chapter 56

Ro chose a flat, sandstone rock at the edge of a natural amphitheater lying midway between the big house and his adobe. After hiding Princess in a clump of bushes, he lay atop the boulder, facing southwest. By turning his head, he had a decent view of the Chandler's house. He was betting Jose was somewhere on the ranch, watching and waiting. Paul, safe enough at Harry's, would be vulnerable when he came home. Ro's bones told him it would be tonight. Jose would come tonight.

Suffering from the loss of the beautiful horse he'd ridden since he was ten years old, Ro glanced at the icy, shimmering heavens. Countless winking stars reminded him of She-Who-Was. But maybe the stars weren't symbols of love tonight. Maybe they were laughing at him for lying in the darkness, suffering a cold wind. He snugged the sheepskin's collar around his neck. This was foolish. He oughta go to Jim.

A faint glow haloed the far distance and morphed into a pair of headlights. Paul coming from town. Ro abandoned his perch and rode Princess back to the big house.

"What're you doing here so late?" Paul asked when Ro rode up.

"Just now heading home. What happened?"

"Son-of-a-bitch didn't show. Bartender said he hadn't been in all day. He's flaked out somewhere drunk. But a deal's a deal. I'll tell Dad in the morning."

"Paul...." Ro swallowed his words. He'd do this alone. "I'll hold you to that promise. Goodnight."

Once Paul was safely inside, Ro returned to the shelf of rock to resume his patient vigil. After another couple of hours of staring through the winter night, the very shadows jumped and moved like elusive phantoms. He closed his eyes and rubbed them gently.

He may have dozed, but the hoot of an owl raised chill bumps on his arms and caused him to sweep the horizon. A horse and rider materialized before his eyes. How long had Jose sat motionless astride his pony at the edge of the semi-circle of small boulders? Ro's nerves went on edge. The owl wasn't a good sign.

Ro slowly lifted his rifle. The man made a perfect target in the cold moonlight. He cocked the weapon. His finger tightened on the trigger, but he lowered the barrel and eased the hammer down. He couldn't kill in cold blood. Jose had bet his life on that.

The horseman sat like a statue, waiting for him. For *him,* not Paul. He stood in full view of the other man. Jose remained motionless as Ro mounted Princess and reined in across the little amphitheater to eye his opponent.

"You're trespassing," he called. "I could kill you right now and no one would do a thing about it." Jose said nothing. His pony pawed the ground nervously. Ro pressed. "Forget the white eyes, and they'll forget you."

"Won't never let me alone. I live under a curse. A witch's curse."

"That's bull, Jose. They don't know about things like that."

"*You* do."

"Me? I'm a cowman, not a medicine man. You're talking foolishness. All you have to do is get out of here and mind your own business. You're making a mountain out of a sandpile."

Jose tossed his head. "Go hide in your white man's house and don't get in my way."

Ro sighed aloud. "Not until this is done."

"The *Ga'an* told me I'd have to kill you."

"The Mountain Gods won't save you if I pull this trigger."

"Won't. They won't let you. Won't let anyone stop me."

Ro lifted the rifle. "Go home and there won't be blood between us."

"Not with the white man's weapon, Tall Rider." Jose held up a lance in each hand. "Not like white eyes. Like warriors." He buried the point of one lance in the sand. "I'm a man, a *Tinneh.* I don't gotta hide behind guns and bullets. What are you? A man? Or have the whites turned you into a woman?"

The rays of an invisible sun blushed the cloud tops a delicate rose. "Jose, I'm not here to argue my manhood. Got too many people relying on me. Have to do this my way."

Ro raised his rifle and fired three quick shots into the air. Jose lowered his lance and charged before Ro brought his startled mount under control.

****

Paul started awake. Heart pumping, he got up and glanced out the window. Dawn. At least, the darkness was graying a bit. The hands would be stirring soon, perhaps already were. Crap, there was absolutely no reason to get up so early this time of year.

His breath caught in his throat. Why had Ro met him outside the house at two o'clock in the morning? Was his brother baby-sitting him? He dialed Ro's number from the hall phone. No answer. He threw on clothes and went downstairs. Voices drew him to the kitchen door.

"Goddammit, them was gunshots," Pete said.

Paul stepped outside. "Heard 'em too. Think Ro needs help. Saddle up." He raced to his father's room. The rancher was already awake and dressed.

"Did I hear gunfire?"

"Dad, I gotta tell you something." He quickly brought his father up to date.

"Why in God's name didn't you tell me!" Jim roared.

"Jose knows he'll go back to prison if he tries anything. I'm not sure—"

"Well, Ro's sure! He's out there trying to pull your ass out of the fire. Roust the boys. Saddle Chigger for me."

Paul's eyebrows climbed. "Sure you can ride?"

Jim set his mouth. "I'll ride. Damned right, I'll ride. He struggled with his crutches for a moment, then threw them away in a fit of frustration, taking jerky, half-controlled steps on his own.

****

Jose's lance struck the butt of Ro's rifle and slammed it against his ribs. The gun went spinning into space. Princess bolted, almost throwing him. He brought her under control and made for the spear Jose had left upright in the ground. As his fingers closed around the haft, he heard the rush of hoofbeats behind him and bent low over his pommel. Something brushed his exposed back. Jose had counted coup. Next time he would kill.

They faced one another across the expanse of desert. Jose's mount advanced; Ro spurred his pony. He caught the tip of his foe's lance with his own, forcing it away harmlessly. They passed in the semi-darkness.

At opposite ends of the amphitheater they whirled and raced toward the center. Another pass without advantage to either. The horses wheeled and rushed again. As Jose neared, he lunged over the pony's neck, his weight behind his weapon. Ro lurched sideways, almost bringing his animal down. He grabbed for the saddle horn and regained his balance.

Jose spun and thundered back to press his advantage, but Ro was ready. As Jose lunged again, Ro's spear ran down the length of his enemy's shaft. The shock against his arm told him he'd struck home. With an effort, he held onto the lance while sawing the reins to turn Princess. Jose was still horseback, but a dark spot marked his shoulder.

They paused, glaring at one another through the gloom. Maybe Jose was ready to quit. But the man gave a cry and flailed his mount into a run. Ro spoke to the mare. She pulled her long legs beneath her and sprang forward.

Suddenly, Jose crossed in front of Ro. With a savage yell, he launched his lance in a swift, underhanded throw. Ro twisted in the saddle, seeking to avoid the deadly missile. The spear tore flesh from his side. Thrown off balance by his weight, Princess stumbled. Ro crashed to the ground, stunned from the fall.

Jose, crouched over his mount's neck, thundered down on him, a long knife in hand. Ro evaded the blade and grabbed at the man's shirt, but he lost his hold and ate dirt.

255

That was enough to bring Jose to earth. The knife clattered off into the rocks. Ro was on him before Jose regained his feet. The man wiggled free and slammed a boot into Ro's chest.

Jose slithered away and whirled to face him. Temporarily winded, Ro staggered forward. He had to press the man, take advantage of that shoulder wound. Then Jose came at him with bare knuckles. He slammed his left fist into Ro's cheek, but it seemed as if he'd pulled the punch. They grappled, parted, and flailed away at one another. There wasn't much strength behind Jose's blows. He began to give ground. Ro got inside his guard, rocking him with solid punches to the mouth and heart.

Jose fell backward and planted a boot in Ro's gut, sending him to the ground in a fetal position. Gasping for air, Ro rolled out of the way of a rock intended to crush his skull. Jose's arm shot out... probably for another stone, but he encountered the rifle. Ro leapt for the weapon. Jose brought it around. They froze.

Jose panted. "Think maybe you... shoulda gone home."

Ro waited, the rifle aimed squarely at his head. The bore seemed huge.

"Gonna kill you. 'Fore I do... gotta tell you. Killed your woman. Knocked her under a horse. But you know that."

For a moment Ro thought the bullet had already struck. Something hit his heart like a hammer blow. "Teresa? Bird? How would I know?"

"She was a fucking witch. She told you."

Ro moaned. The sound was hardly human. "She wouldn't even know what you're talking about. She was good. She was—"

"A witch! She was a witch. She told you I did it. Like she told her brother."

"Paul knows?"

"He knows." Jose grunted in pain. "After... kill you. Gonna kill all the rest."

"Not the boy, Jose. Please, not the boy! He's *Tinneh.*"

Jose's laugh ended up a cough. "Gonna kill them all. Old man, Paul, the woman. Brat."

This was it. His life was over. He would join Bird. Ro would have welcomed death—*if it weren't for the boy*. He waited for Jose to cock the rifle. He did so in a quick, easy motion. Ro sprang forward, throwing Jose off balance. The rifle went off. The muzzle flash seared Ro's arm. The shot went wide.

Jose staggered out of reach. Unable to halt his momentum, Ro fell to his hands and knees. His fingers closed over a lance. He heard the oiled click of the bolt as Jose cocked the gun again.

Ro leapt forward, brushing the rifle aside. The spear bit. Blood spurted halfway down the shaft. Jose's mouth flew open. The rifle slipped from his nerveless fingers as he tumbled over backward and danced a spastic jig in the dirt.

It was over. Tension drained from Ro, leaving him weak and exhausted and bleeding.

"Oh, Teresa! Bird," he sobbed. Strength gone, he dropped to his knees in the sand beside the body of a man he had once admired.

Epilogue

A great owl dropped from a solitary pine on silent wings to strike the flank of a coyote lurking in the feeble light. The beast whirled and snarled before trotting off to the west.

The monstrous raptor swooped again, its passage ruffling the hair of an exhausted, bleeding young man before wheeling north to glide over four horsemen riding at speed toward the silent amphitheater.

A bank of low clouds moved rapidly across the Chacons, obscuring the new sunrise. A stiff breeze chilled the winter air and whipped a restless cloud of sand across the desert.

About the Author

Born and raised in a small town in Southern Oklahoma, Don Morgan contracted childhood tuberculosis, and as a result, grew up in libraries rather than on sports fields. Indulging a fascination for Native American cultures, he wrote essays and short stories as a child. These soon turned into short stories.

After graduating from TCU with a degree in History and Government, he joined the Army, and marched over the mountains of Southern Germany, learning he was capable of what every other young man of his age was doing. But the die was cast.

While pursuing a business career he ended up in New Mexico, which soon became his favorite place in the world. Creative, he tried oil painting, but soon returned to writing. A lapsed Southwest Writer's Workshop member, he gave back to the community by teaching a weekly writing class in an Albuquerque community center for nine years. Don is widowed and the father of two adult sons.

About the Publisher

Creative Texts is a boutique independent publishing house devoted to high quality content that readers enjoy. We publish best-selling authors such as Jerry D. Young, N.C. Reed, Sean Liscom, Donald Travis Morgan, Laurence Dahners, and many more. Our audiobook performers are among the best in the business including Hollywood legends like Barry Corbin and top talent like Christopher Lane, Alyssa Bresnaham, Erin Moon and Graham Hallstead.

Whether its post-apocalyptic or dystopian fiction, biography, history, true crime science fiction, thrillers, or even classic westerns, our goal is to produce highly rated customer preferred content. If there is anything we can do to enhance your reader experience, please contact us directly at info@creativetexts.com. As always, we do appreciate your reviews on your book seller's website.

Finally, if you would like to find more great books like this one, please search for us by name in your favorite search engine or on your bookseller's website to see books by all Creative Texts authors. Thank you for reading.

www.ingramcontent.com/pod-product-compliance
Lightning Source LLC
Chambersburg PA
CBHW072348020726
47506CB00004B/1058